THE METAMORPHOSIS

FRANZ KAFKA

THE METAMORPHOSIS

Translated and edited by
Stanley Corngold

MODERN LIBRARY
NEW YORK

2013 Modern Library Paperback Edition

Published in the United States by Modern Library, an imprint of The Random House Publishing Group, a division of Random House LLC, a Penguin Random House Company, New York.

The translation of *The Metamorphosis* that is reprinted here was originally published in 1972 by Schocken Books, an imprint of The Knopf Doubleday Publishing Group, a division of Random House LLC. "Franz Kafka: A Chronology" and "Kafka's *The Metamorphosis:* Metamorphosis of the Metaphor" by Stanley Corngold and the translations of "Wedding Preparations in the Country" and "Letters and Diaries" by Stanley Corngold were originally published in *The Metamorphosis: A Norton Critical Edition* by W. W. Norton, New York, in 1996.

Library of Congress Cataloging-in-Publication Data
Kafka, Franz, 1883–1924.
[Verwandlung. English]
The metamorphosis/Franz Kafka; translated and edited by Stanley
Corngold— Modern Library paperback edition.
pages cm—(Modern library classics)
ISBN 978-0-8129-8514-6
eBook ISBN 978-0-8129-8519-1
I. Corngold, Stanley, translator. II. Title.
PT2621.A26V426133 2014
833'.912—dc23 2013021937

Printed in the United States of America

www.modernlibrary.com

2 4 6 8 9 7 5 3 1

Preface

Franz Kafka's novella *The Metamorphosis* is perfect, even as it incessantly provokes criticism. Its perfection was noted by the Nobel Prize–winning author Elias Canetti, who wrote: "In *The Metamorphosis* Kafka reached the height of his mastery: he wrote something which he could never surpass, because there is nothing which *The Metamorphosis* could be surpassed by—one of the few great, perfect poetic works of this century." But what is distinctive about such *literary* perfection is that it does not leave the reader's mind settled, satisfied, at peace with itself. Its perfection is not aesthetic. Instead, it never stops irritating the reader to produce a kind of brother or sister work in the mind that will be simpler, plainer, and altogether better behaved, intellectually speaking, than the story itself. For this story, if Kafka's own criticism can be trusted, is not only *about* a monster; it comes into the world trailing clouds of monstrosity. "What *is* literature?" Kafka declared. "Where does it come from? What use is it? What questionable things! Add to this questionableness the further questionableness of what you say, and what you get is a monstrosity." The monstrous aspect of the story is clear, no doubt—it assaults us with its image at the outset—but where, then, is its perfection?

It must be, first, in the perfection of the hopelessness that settles on Gregor Samsa and his family in the face of a nightmare they have never before seen or heard of. And it must also lie in the supreme irony with which this hopelessness is depicted, as if from the standpoint of an unnamed god who has arranged it all for his amusement.

The Metamorphosis raises such questions, certainly, but it also states facts as hard, concrete, and undeniable as the armor-like shell in which Gregor Samsa is born again one rainy morning. This disparity between the underlying structure of impossibility and the wealth of atrociously detailed facts makes for the uncanny disturbance at the center of the story. Everything is in place in the family to deny the arrival of this monster in its midst. All the explanations are at hand, especially in the average, everyday awareness of Gregor himself, who thinks at various times that his metamorphosis is only a fantasy, a bad cold, a hindrance or—as his mother puts it—a momentary absence of the real Gregor, who will surely "come back to us again." But the vermin's body refuses to be any of these things. It is what it materially is and does not let itself be denied so long as Gregor is alive: it is its wildly waving legs, its snapping jaws, its obscene craving for decaying vegetables and dark crevices, and, yes, for fiddle playing, too. It harbors the little red apple flung by Gregor's father deep into his back and left to rot and kill his son, but it also sparks the acrobatic bliss that Gregor feels, hanging and falling from the ceiling, when he finally lets his body do what it wants. "A little horrible," Kafka called his story, writing to his fiancée Felice Bauer, perhaps understating the case, and then, the next day, perhaps overstating it, "exceptionally repulsive." But while Kafka's judgment here repeats the verdict of the Samsa family, the judgment of literary history has been very different. Readers have been drawn again and again to this monstrosity by the desire to get it under control—to interpret it in place of understanding it, for no one yet has so fully understood it that it might "go away."

The fascination continues. Literally millions have read this story, so to begin to read it now is to enter with a thrill into a community of those who have struggled to master something that has struck them—as the critic Theodor Adorno says—with the force of an onrushing locomotive. Kafka collapses aesthetic distance between text and reader: "Interpret me!" the story declares. "Interpret me! . . . Or be overwhelmed." This is as it should be. "A book," Kafka wrote, "must be the axe for the frozen sea in us," stressing the redemptive opportunity the shock might finally provide. It is to be hoped that the present translation of *The Metamorphosis*, which tries to follow Kafka's actual idiom more closely than previous translations, produces something of this effect.

The translation is based on the authoritative text of *Die Verwandlung* prepared by Dr. Hans-Gerd Koch at the Research Center for German Exile Literature at the University of Wuppertal, in Germany. Dr. Koch, along with several colleagues, directed the publication of the so-called Manuscript Version of Kafka's complete works; and he kindly made the text of *The Metamorphosis* available to me before it appeared in print.

The critical essays offered in this volume are of two kinds—the first are immediately compelling by the force of the author's reputation: they will illuminate both Kafka's work and the author's. In general, they deal with Kafka's life and art. Other essays, written by university scholars, intend to bring to light specific features of Kafka's story that may have escaped notice at a first reading. If they cannot hope to—or want to—"pluck out the heart of the mystery," they do mean to get our minds around it, in a phrase that might be a good enough description of what it means to "understand." These essays also illustrate some of the main currents of criticism now practiced in the university, which aim to keep in balance details of Kafka's text and elements (literary, historical, and psychoanalytic) of his cultural identity. All these background and critical materials are designed to stimulate and guide the reader to his or her own creative encounter with *The Metamorphosis* while suggesting the richness of the modern attempt to grasp the *Schriftstellersein*, the "being-literature," to which Kafka sacrificed his personal life.

Thanks are due to Sam Nicholson, my exemplary editor; Vincent La Scala, my ever vigilant production editor; and especially Sam's brilliant assistant, Madison Pauly, for their courteous and perceptive help in bringing this book to light.

Contents

Introduction

Stanley Corngold

Franz Kafka was born on July 3, 1883, into a German-speaking Jewish family in Prague, the capital of the Czech Lands of the Austro-Hungarian Empire. He died, at the age of forty, with the dubious luck of one who died too soon to experience the Nazi terror. His favorite sister, Ottla; his second fiancée, Julie Wohryzek; and his lover, Milena Jesenská, a brilliant Czech writer, were all murdered in concentration camps. Kafka never married—though he fell in love easily, and was easily loved—despite having been engaged three times, twice to the same woman, Felice Bauer. Felice survived the terror and left an extraordinary, voluminous collection of Kafka's letters, which are testimony to her courtship by one of the century's strangest cavaliers, as eloquent in his charm as he was insistent on his unsuitability. Kafka broke off his second engagement to Felice after he contracted tuberculosis, which, in the end, consumed his larynx and caused him excruciating pain, so that he could barely speak and literally starved to death.

Kafka pursued many different paths to fulfill a life lived under intense self-scrutiny and, especially in the later years, considerable moral precision. His many friends testify to his unfailing courtesy, good humor, readiness to help—and exquisite phrasing. In response to his bullying father's complaint that his behavior was "crazy, meshuggah, not normal," Kafka replied, "Not being normal is not the worst thing. What's normal, for example, is world war."[1]

Kafka's moral qualities only added to the attractiveness of his person: he was a handsome man, some six feet tall, athletic, and at 135 pounds able to wear beautiful clothes to advantage. He was much valued for these qualities, as well as for his lawyerly brilliance, especially at the Workmen's Accident Insurance Institute for the Kingdom of Bohemia, in Prague, where he rose to the position of senior legal secretary shortly before his death; and yet all the substantial good he did there could never amount to his justification. He read voraciously in nine languages, thought intensely, cared passionately for the welfare of Jewish refugees, and even pursued gardening seriously, but the path he followed—and, to judge from his posthumous fame, found—was, despite several interruptions, the way of writing. Only a few of his stories were published in his lifetime, and the novels for which he is most famous—*Amerika: The Missing Person*, *The Trial*, and *The Castle*—appeared after his death. But from the "enormous world I have in my head," from his traffic "with spirits to darkness bound," he has enriched and haunted our imagination with such imperishable figures as Gregor Samsa, a feckless traveling salesman who wakes up one morning to find himself changed into a verminous beetle; Joseph K., a high-ranking bank official, accused of a nameless crime for which he is stabbed to death in a quarry; a prisoner in a remote penal colony, strapped down on a writing machine designed to cut his sentence into his flesh; a pretend land surveyor, who, lost in the snow, desperately seeks entrance to a castle; and countless others.

Kafka's appeal to the public mind has steadily expanded. His audience of readers is vast and worldwide in scope: his works have finally been translated properly into Czech and Russian and other Eastern European languages. Kafka scholars in America receive emails from Kafka scholars in China, asking for an exchange of ideas. For palpable proof of his appeal, you have only to visit the Franz Kafka Bookshop in the Old Town Square of Prague (also called "the Goltz"), just yards away from the Kinsky Palace, where Kafka went to high school and his father had his business in ladies' finery. Here you will see visitors from all over the world poring over the copious new editions and translations of Kafka's work. And to this audience of readers add an audience of theatergoers and connoisseurs of new music, as witness the ongoing performances of Philip Glass's chamber opera *In the Penal Colony* and György Kurtág's song cycle *Kafka Fragments* for soprano and violin—works that in their own way constitute incisive readings of Kafka. Kafka's audience is by no means limited to high-culture devotees. Casual spectators of the media circus will hear his name; expert readers of current legal discourse will see his name appear in the most serious contexts, where it—or the adjective *Kafkaesque*—is regularly invoked by learned judge or counsel to excoriate unjust procedure. Many prominent cases figure in the pages of Westlaw, the online resource for case law, in which the sufferings of the accused appear to have leaped from the pages of *The Trial* and may be acknowledged as such. There have been trials in American courts conducted in a language that the accused literally could not understand, and others in which the condemned was not present in court when his sentence was read. In one such case, counsel alludes plainly to the penultimate paragraph of *The Trial:* "Where was the judge he'd never seen?" (*T,* 31). In a situation that is poignantly relevant, in *O'Brien v. Henderson,*

> the *pro se* petitioner claimed that the Board of Parole had violated his due process rights by revoking his parole without the proper explanation that was constitutionally required. The District Court granted his habeas corpus and mandamus petitions. Commenting on the unusual volume and vagueness of the petitioner's pleadings, Circuit Judge Edenfield noted that not even the most skilled of counsel, finding himself in the Kafkaesque situation of being deprived of his liberty by a tribunal which will adduce no reasons for its decision, can complain concisely and clearly of his objections to such a decision. . . . [Such a situation] leaves the prisoner no recourse but to approach the court with an attempted rebuttal of all real, feared, or imagined justifications for his confinement.[2] (368 F. Supp. 10)

Kafka is extraordinary not only for the volume of citation he has inspired; he is extraordinary for having attracted virtually endless interpretation. The power of his work to compel interpretation seems inexhaustible. In the words of the critic Theodor Adorno, whom we have encountered in the preface, "To read a story of Kafka's appears to *require* from the reader that he or she interpret it" (emphasis added). This challenge has tended to produce answers involving vast quantities of information; in this sense, Kafka criticism cannot fail to be instructive. This small, seemingly introspective body of work turns out to have responded seismographically to a wide range of intellectual, cultural, political, and social real-world forces.[3] Hence, interpretations that might be characterized as theological, economic, biographical, existential, gender-political, psychoanalytic, neo-Gnostic, Marxian, etc., have all proved rewarding in their own way.

Did Kafka at any point intuit his reception? The stereotypical answer is: Of course not. He was just "a little clerk," the author of works whose central figures are colorless nobodies, a writer unknown in his own time, a failure in life and art. None of this is true. The first thing to say about Kafka is that he was a genius, and he would be the last person to dispute this fact. (Readers who are uncomfortable with the category of "genius" may prefer Mark Harman's ascribing to Kafka "the intuitive certainty of a somnambulist" [*C,* xv]). In regard, however, to extraordinary powers, there would seem to be no two ways about it, nothing irrationally exuberant about this claim. In a book titled *Paganism, Christianity, Judaism,* Max Brod (Kafka's friend, editor, and fervent booster) called Kafka a *Diesseitswunder*—a miracle occurring down here, on this side of the heavens—adding that the existence of Kafka as a miracle, *and a Jew,* argued for the superiority of Judaism as a religion. Kafka read this book, saw this claim, and replied to Brod, stating that none of the evidence that Brod had adduced argued for the superiority of Judaism, but—notice!—he did not rebut the description of himself as a down-here miracle. In fact, such claims were not entirely a novelty to him.

In 1911, even before he had published a line of any significance, Kafka wrote in his diary:

> The special nature of my inspiration—in which I, the happiest and unhappiest of men, now go to sleep at two in the morning [perhaps [this inspiration] will remain—if only I can bear the thought of it, for it exceeds all that came before] [~~and—without a doubt—I am now the midpoint of the intellectual & spiritual life of Prague~~]—this inspiration is this, that I can do everything, not only with respect to a par-

> ticular piece of work. If I write down a sentence at random, for example. "He looked out the window," it is already perfect.[4] (*KSS,* 195; *D*1, 45)

Lucky readers may have seen this diary page on display in Oxford's Bodleian Library—Kafka's claim to be *im Geistigen der Mittelpunkt von Prag*—and it is inked through again and again. Kafka saw what he had written and blushed. In black ink.

But not for long—or forever. A glorious passage in the middle of Kafka's oeuvre reads:

> You lead the masses, big, tall field marshal, lead the desperate ones through the mountain passes, which are under snow, discernable to no one else. And who gives you the strength? He who gives you the clarity of your gaze.[5] (*D*2, 220)

"Clarity of your gaze" (*die Klarheit des Blickes*) is a phrase that recurs throughout Kafka's confessional writings. It is the central virtue and, along with patience, the great bulwark against the thousand mortifications of daily life to which Kafka was subject: as a Jew in an anti-Semitic climate; as a conscientious official sensitive to the outrage of what was, by and large, a disenfranchised working class; as a German speaker and therefore the target of Czech animosity, especially in the years of the disintegration of the Austro-Hungarian Empire; and, worst of all, as a grown man somehow self-condemned to live most of his life with his parents and his sisters in a crowded apartment, under the sway of an angry father.

If it were possible to rationalize Kafka's genius, it might be said to consist, first of all, in the force of his literary imagination, his power to metamorphose the remains of the day. In Prague he lived alongside a river, the Vltava—or Moldau—and he would have seen or read of people who drowned, whether by accident or otherwise. "In the course of the 1870s," Benno Wagner writes,

> statistics, accumulated with increasing precision, identified the Habsburg Monarchy—in comparison with the rest of Europe and according to the then current trend—as a "breeding ground of suicide."[6] Especially in Bohemia, this trend to an abnormal increase in suicides persisted into the 1880s as well, where Prague once again emerges as the statistical capital. (*GM*, 44)

But few would have been able to transform such an event into the aphorism, as Kafka does, "The man in ecstasy and the man drowning—both throw up their arms. The first does it to signify harmony, the second to signify strife with the elements" (*DF,* 77).

We cannot discuss Kafka's genius without acknowledging the scope and depth of his erudition. We noted that he read in nine languages; his letters and diaries report that he discussed with Prague friends at least the following dialogues of Plato *in Greek: Apology*, *Charmides*, *Crito*, *Euthydemus*, *Euthyphro*, *Ion*, *Lysis*, *Phaedo*, *Phaedrus*, *Protagoras*, *Symposium*, *The Republic.* Indeed, the current working hypothesis of Kafka scholars is that no book published in Kafka's day and age can be excluded as a figure in or under the carpet of his prose. We do not know for certain of any such book that Kafka did *not* read; the explicit absence or bare mention of the names of great contemporary literary figures in Kafka's oeuvre does not prove that they went unread. At no point does the name Nietzsche appear in any of Kafka's published works or in the documents that have survived him, and yet proof of Kafka's acquaintance with Nietzsche is incontestable. Kafka studied him, a fact that can be deduced from patterns of imagery and persiflage plainly evident in his early work "Description of a Struggle"; they point to an intimate knowledge of *Thus Spoke Zarathustra.* It cannot be an accident that the haunting figure of the Hunter Gracchus, in the prose-fragment of this title, fell to his death while in pursuit of a chamois. One need only consult "The Other Dancing Song," from *Zarathustra,* to find the (astonishing) sentence: "I am the hunter; would you be my hound or my chamois . . ." (*PN,* 337).

Kafka mentions Thomas Mann only twice—once in his travel diaries and once in a letter—but in the latter Mann is "one whose writings I hunger for." The surmise arises that *The Metamorphosis,* with its famous imagery of hungering, might allude to a scandalous short story by Mann. At the close of *The Metamorphosis,* Kafka describes Gregor's way of experiencing music as his *use* of music. On hearing his sister's violin playing, Gregor heads directly for her shapely neck, which he intends to kiss while remaining on aggressive alert for intrusive strangers, as she plays her violin entirely for him. At this point we can detect a wild parody of the final scene of Mann's story "The Blood of the Walsungs," which tells of the incestuous lovemaking between a brother and sister after they have been enthralled by the music of Wagner's opera *The Valkyrie.*[7]

As a final remark on Kafka's genius, we will simply advertise to readers who have not yet learned German that reading Kafka in the original ought to be a great incentive: much of the power of his work arises from the elegance and refinement of his writing. His prose in German is unlike that of any of his contemporaries. Even when he complains of arrested inspiration, the lament is beautiful.

All these components of Kafka's genius must be understood as expressions of creativity under great duress. While other minds caught up in the swiftly expanding industrial modernity of Bohemia, called "the Manchester of Central Europe," produced so much coal, so to speak, in Kafka that pressure produced diamonds that (not to coin a phrase) "burn always with this hard, gem-like flame."[8] It is important to grasp the sense of hardship and oppression that beset him when he wrote, and which testifies to extraordinary inner resources. Recall, too, that he was ill with tuberculosis, especially during the last decade of his short life, an ailment much aggravated in 1918 by the Spanish flu—the pandemic that killed some fifty million people worldwide. Without that additional trauma, he might well have been cured of his tuberculosis.[9]

Furthermore, there was Kafka's professional life: he was gainfully employed. From the beginning, he wrote his stories and novels—his copious letters and diary entries—at night, after having slept only a little and after having put in six consecutive hours of concentrated work at his extremely demanding day job as a high-ranking lawyer and bureaucrat. But this pressure is, again, a very mixed affair. On the one hand, his work in the office was grueling, even "hellish";[10] on the other hand, his office experience nourished his fiction, a fact that has not been sufficiently appreciated. Kafka's considerable responsibilities also constituted a field for creativity in the law. Indeed, during the years of the First World War, he was the virtual CEO of the Workmen's Accident Insurance Institute, a post he was able to occupy because, although initially accepted for military service, he was later deferred on the grounds of his indispensability to the firm.[11] Our knowledge of the demanding nature of Kafka's day job matters enormously for our sense of how he came to his night's work. Kafka's prose poetry arises not after a day spent finger-tapping at an anonymous office desk but, typically, after writing or dictating intricate briefs of genuine social importance. Many lives and livelihoods depended on Kafka's success in introducing such safety measures as cylindrical lathe shafts, which were less inclined to chop off workers' fingers, and prohibiting brandy drinking and pipe smoking in the immediate vicinity of dynamite sheds in quarries.[12]

The office writings play an important role in Kafka's fiction. They move spectrally through his fiction; this is an adverb that should be taken quite literally, since, in a letter to his lover, Milena Jesenská, Kafka describes the office as not a machine in which workers like himself might be "a little cog" or "a big wheel." Rather, "to me," he wrote, "the office is a human being—watching me with innocent eyes wherever I am, a living person to whom I have become attached in some way unknown to me." The office, in his words, "is not dumb, it is phantasmal" (*BM*, 169).[13] These phantasms might also refer, as Paul North has noted, to "the sociological, political, and legal concepts regularly left out of Kafka criticism—including empirical psychology, theories of mass behavior, developments in industrial machinery, accident statistics, social insurance laws, and actual court battles."[14] Kafka's experience in the office—and on site—undergoes the transformations of his "dream-like inner life" but still emerges as recognizable for what it once was.

Consider a few examples, beginning with farms and quarries: they are two of the workplaces that preoccupied Kafka. One aspect of insuring farms seems to have had a lasting impact on him. For a number of pragmatic reasons, the Institute proposed the solution of offering small farmers flat insurance rates, simply related to acreage and the kind and number of machines in use.

In his report for 1908, Kafka wrote that a prerequisite for flat-rate insurance is "to establish the particulars pertaining to the extent of the fields and pastures as well as of the net income" of the individual farms. But in a note of protest sent to the Ministry of the Interior in 1911, he declared that this project was foundering on the issue of competent land surveying. Many small farmers had complained about the resulting flat-rate calculations, arguing that, owing to the mountainous nature of their land, the surveys were invalid. Lacking reliable data, Kafka's note concludes, the Institute would have to operate in "complete darkness" until new legislation for comprehensive insurance was passed.[15]

A number of Kafka's oblique diary entries bearing on his fictional work arise from this situation. He writes of "a connoisseur, an expert, someone who knows his *field*, knowledge, to be sure, that cannot be imparted but that fortunately no one seems to stand in need of" (*D*1, 395). Here he is thinking, surely, of his inner life and the writings that come out of it. But what he had to deal with in early days were pseudo-experts who did *not* know their fields—did not have the knowledge, to be sure, that can be imparted and that, unfortunately, *everyone* seems to stand in need of.

The situation of incompetent land surveying throws light on the hero of *The Castle*, who is also a pretend surveyor. Kafka scholars, very few of whom have bothered to familiarize themselves with Kafka's tribulations with flat-acreage taxation, have had to take a long way round to get to the truth of the hero's situation and pretensions. The German word for this functionary is *Landvermesser,* someone who "measures the land." Some critics have preferred to break the word down into its components: *Land* (land, country) and *Vermesser* (measurer) but, by dint of the prefix *Ver*-, also *mis*-measurer, with the result that we have in the character K. a country-bumpkin mis-measurer, a dense misapprehender of things—a figure consistent with Kafka's interest in Hasidic fables, which speak of the *"Mann vom Lande,"* the countryman who comes to hear the rabbi's elliptical wisdom but does not *get* it or, as in Kafka's great parable "Before the Law" (*T,* 215–17), who comes seeking entrance to the law and who does not get *in.* But there is a certain chutzpah in that effort to gain entry, a notion tipped off by the ghostly presence, in the word for surveyor (*Landvermesser*), of the German word *Vermessenheit* (hubris, insolence, overweening ambition), so what we now have—in lieu of a land surveyor—is a country-bumpkin, hugely impudent mis-measurer of things.

Now, this reading, which like almost any reading of Kafka of a certain ingeniousness is bound to be at least a bit right, can still be brought down to earth, as it were, by a knowledge of Kafka's early experience of pretend farmland surveyors.

In the case of the quarries, we have one more instance of a vivid and suggestive congruence between Kafka's workaday world and his literary dreamworld, owing to the clarity of the legal scholar Jack Greenberg's gaze. "One visit to a quarry site," Greenberg has written,

> may have imprinted itself on Kafka's memory and found its way into *The Trial.* The 1914 report on quarry safety described a quarry in which there was "a loose stone block 1 m^3" and accompanied the text with a photograph. That year, Kafka began writing *The Trial,* which ends in a chilling execution scene in a quarry. . . . As the executioners lead K to his execution, the author relates that "the other man searched for some suitable spot in the quarry. When he had found it, he waved, and the other gentleman led K over to it. It was near the quarry wall, where a loose block of stone was lying." It is not difficult to surmise that the loose 1 m^3 block of stone of the quarry report prompted Kafka's imagination of the

> loose block of stone of *The Trial.* At that spot, they executed K with a knife to the heart. He died "like a dog." (*OW,* 357–58)

This is a find that gives us a great deal of morbid pleasure but also gives us work to do when we try to grasp the meaning of the spin that Kafka has put on the stone. In the quarry report, the stone presented a mortal danger to workers: it lay on the path of their wagons. It would be easy to stumble over it and crash onto steep rock. It is a kind of danger immanent to the life of the worker. Now, Kafka's hero in *The Trial* is a high-ranking bank bureaucrat who, by all appearances, has given little thought to the working conditions of the underclass—or, for that matter, to anything other than his normal pleasures and progress upward through society. Is Kafka expiating pangs of social conscience when he has this average bourgeois—who, in certain respects not unlike his author, is inattentive to the pain of others—stabbed to death, *Inferno*-like, on that very stone?

Let us turn, now, more particularly, to another scene of punishment, to *The Metamorphosis*, which Kafka wrote, in a troubled state, between November 17 and December 7, 1912.

Body Language in *The Metamorphosis*

In Kafka's "breakthrough" story, "The Judgment," written immediately before *The Metamorphosis,* a young man quarrels with his father, who, angered by their conversation, sentences his son to death by drowning. His son obeys and, in a kind of bliss, leaps over the railing and into the river that, "nothing short of infinite," runs alongside their house, crying out, "Dear parents, I really always loved you."

In "A Report to an Academy," a story from the middle of Kafka's writing career (1916), an ape submits a report to a learned academy, describing his ascent into the human condition, which includes his memory of having emptied many a good bottle of red wine with the head of the firm that had him shot and caged.

In Kafka's very great, very last story, "Josephine, the Singer or the Mouse People," a mouse sings onstage, with all the glamour and all the grimaces of a diva, enthralling the mouse people and girding their loins for war, although, on reflection, singing is actually unknown to the mouse people. So what sort of singing is this? It is enough, for with her passing on, "she will enjoy the heightened redemption of being forgotten, like all her brethren."

Consider, now, *The Metamorphosis:* A traveling salesman wakes up as a monstrous verminous insect and, having been briefly cared for by his family, is condemned to death by his sister after becoming much too excited by her fiddle playing. This hapless monster survives among the images that Kafka conjures—images that might be called "surreal" or, on his authority, "dream-like," because they are exceedingly vivid, like nightmares or hallucinations, and thus contrary to fact. They do not actually envisage anything we might experience in daylight (leaving aside the Satanic light of the media circus).

In a celebrated remark made in 1945, the English poet W. H. Auden declared, "Had one to name the author who comes nearest to bearing the same kind of relation to our age as Dante, Shakespeare, and Goethe bore to theirs, Kafka is the first one would think of."[16] Kafka, Auden says, stands in the same relation to the past hundred years as Dante, Shakespeare, and Goethe stood to their centuries—he is our representative, the poet who gives us shape and form. But how can Kafka, who creates images that do not literally reflect anything in our experience, be our representative to all future times and places? This is the riddle that Kafka puts before his readers.

One way to think about his tremendous relevance is to consider an aspect of the images and situations he invents or which slumber in his image archive: they contain endless opportunities for story development. These images are his rich beginnings—dense, compact, pregnant with possibility. "When Gregor Samsa woke up one morning from unsettling dreams, he found himself changed in his bed into a monstrous vermin" (3). This appalling picture is enough to set one's mind racing with questions; once bitten by the bug, it cannot stop. How could such a thing have happened? What does it feel like to be a vermin—a creature held to be obnoxious by everyone, oneself included? Why has Gregor Samsa been so degraded and despised? What will become of him? What can he ever make of it? Kafka noted often and well the denseness of the images that attacked him from within. At times they burst out of him—as he wrote of his story "The Judgment"—in "a complete opening out of the body and the soul." He noted

> the fearful strain and joy, how the story developed before me, as if I were advancing over water. Several times during this night I heaved my own weight on my back. How everything can be said, how for everything, for the strangest fancies, there waits a great fire in which they perish and rise up again. (*D*1, 275–76)

Consider that! A story is a great fire in which images perish, and rise up again. Images that leap out, even from dreams or somnambulistic states, can be immersed in the destructive element—the process, *writing,* that Walter Benjamin called "the combustion of the dream." In the course of the story, they unfold according to an "unknown, perhaps unknowable, but felt" law, and there they survive.[17]

In diary entries written in 1911, the year before he composed *The Metamorphosis,* Kafka spoke of having "experienced states [in 'the field of literature'] . . . in which I completely dwelt in every idea, but also filled every idea, and in which I not only felt myself at my boundary, but at the boundary of the human in general" (*D*1, 58). These are "times of exaltation, times more feared than longed for, much as I long for . . . them; but then the fullness is so great that I have to give up" (*D*1, 152). These times are the surreal times of dreams or dreamlike states, explicit in the diary entry in which he wrote of "the power of my dreams, shining forth. . . . It is a matter of more mysterious powers which are of an ultimate significance to me" (*D*1, 76).

But not long after composing these sublime diary entries, Kafka wrote *The Metamorphosis,* "the charming pages" of which pleased him well enough but finally horrified him, especially on account of its "damaged" ending. It's important that Kafka criticized the ending of the story but never its *beginning*—that first rush of images—which supports his claim that he was "not dissatisfied" with his inspiration until a business trip prevented him from realizing its fullest implications (74).

Now, in allowing his stories to develop in *just one way,* has Kafka wasted the power of his dream, drained it of creative possibilities? "The tremendous world I have inside my head," he wrote. "But how [to] free myself and free it without being torn to pieces. And a thousand times rather be torn to pieces than retain it in me or bury it. That is why I am here, that is quite clear to me" (*D*1, 288).

Consider, then, in this perspective, *The Metamorphosis* and the way in which the story unfolds. After the initial shock, the traveling salesman Gregor Samsa struggles to regain his equilibrium. The family, failing to call for either a locksmith or a doctor, open their door to the office manager. Grete Samsa assumes the care of her unfortunate brother, but then, growing bored, becomes bratty and impatient. His father, who abhors Gregor, takes his revenge, bombarding him with small, hard apples. Gregor crawls back into his room and meekly, tenderly, dies, whereupon the family celebrate their liberation by going on a picnic.

Every single such plot element actually realized implies the death of other possibilities. And this narrowing down of narrative choices does not occur simply or innocently. Gregor's speech sputters; his eyesight grows dim; we hear of his deprivation with dismay: it will crush the life chances of this almost-human being. We read on with the fading hope, perhaps, that Gregor might be rescued, liberated; we sympathize with his "eager[ness] to see how today's fantasy would gradually fade away," and yet we must suffer his depletion all along—and hence the whole story's depletion—for this is Gregor's story only, narrated from a standpoint virtually congruent with Gregor's own. His world of misery is the Samsas' only world.

At the same time, this dwindling away of Gregor's life chances does not exclude a richness that we readers can realize. It is like a consolation for the lost variety of plot possibilities: the richness of interpretations we can bring to bear on the one story line that we have. This is Kafka's genius: from his openings he conjures the one story line that will invite interpretation through all the discourses of his time and of times to come. For Gershom Scholem, an eminent reader of his work, nothing compares with the attraction of working out an incisive interpretation of a text. But here the word "attraction" is too casual, certainly in the view of the philosopher Theodor Adorno, as we have noted. The reader's attempt at an incisive interpretation is not optional. Kafka's sentences come at us with the force of an onrushing locomotive: "Each sentence of Kafka's says 'interpret me.' Through the power with which Kafka commands interpretation, he collapses aesthetic distance. He demands a desperate effort from the allegedly 'disinterested' spectator of an earlier time, overwhelms you, suggesting that far more than your intellectual equilibrium depends on whether you truly understand; life and death are at stake."[18]

Explanatory religious concepts (Christian, Jewish, mystic, other) might come to help. The Irish poet William Butler Yeats, Kafka's contemporary, wrote a story called "The Crucifixion of the Outcast," a phrase that casts a suggestive light on Gregor. Consider his cruciform posture at the end of Part I, when he's being tormented, with his father's willing cooperation:

> Gregor forced himself—come what may—into the doorway. One side of his body rose up, he lay lopsided in the opening, one of his flanks was scraped raw, ugly blotches marred the white door, soon he got stuck and could not have budged any more by himself, his little legs on one side dangled tremblingly in midair, those on the other were painfully crushed against the floor—when from behind his father gave him a hard shove, which was truly his salvation, and bleeding profusely, he flew far into the room. The door was slammed shut with the cane, then at last everything was quiet. (21–22)

That is Gregor's crucifixion, as it were. Consider, too, his manner of dying: "He remained in this state of empty and peaceful reflection until the tower clock struck three in the morning. He still saw that outside the window everything was beginning to grow light. Then, without his consent, his head sank down to the floor, and from his nostrils streamed his last weak breath" (59). This image will call up the Gospel of John (19:30): "When Jesus therefore had received the vinegar, he said, It is finished: and he bowed his head, and gave up the ghost." The three o'clock may have been suggested by the Gospel of Matthew (27:40), where the scoffing multitude says, "Thou that destroyest the temple, and buildest it in three days, save thyself," or by the last three hours of the agony: "Now from the sixth hour there was darkness over all the land unto the ninth hour" (Matthew 27:45).[19]

One scholar—Kurt Weinberg, who comes from the Jewish tradition—interprets Gregor's early failure to catch the five o'clock train as an allegory of spiritual failure, for Kafka has coded into the five o'clock train (recall the Five Books of Moses) the train of redemption, the train of the sacramental time that brings the Jewish Messiah: Gregor is thus literally the *stiff-necked* unbeliever.[20] For the aforementioned Gershom Scholem, it is the very gloomy dereliction of the scene, the radical absence of divine justice, that, by an effort of the conceptual will called "dialectical theology," affirms the necessary existence of a higher order that promises redemption.

Then there is the Eastern mystic reader, who connects Gregor Samsa's transubstantiation to an esoteric tradition called, in Sanskrit, *saṃsāra,* "[which] refers to the cycle of reincarnation or rebirth in Hinduism, Buddhism, Jainism, Sikhism and . . . related religions."[21] Since the German for the title *The Metamorphosis* is *Die Verwandlung,* a word that can mean "transfiguration," we see that the gates to every sort of religious reading are open—leaving only the question of whether that gate leads to an apprehension of what Kafka called "the gleam of the imperishable fire"—the light of the law that fashions this story (*DF,* 87).

Such is the discourse of religion. Following closely, and not far behind, is the discourse of economics, which the story takes no pains to hide and which has produced an abundance of critical essays all more or less titled "Marx and Metamorphosis." Gregor's parents are indebted to his employer—debts that Gregor feels obliged to repay. The German word for these debts is *Schulden,* but this word in German also refers to one's "guilt." Can we speculate that Gregor's horrible appearance is the external expression of the guilt he bears, a symptomatic expression of the unclean relation to the debts he has assumed, to something falsely messianic in his nature?

There is a second, striking metamorphosis of the economy of money and music in this story. In Gregor's pre-metamorphic years, we learn two important facts about his money and his musical culture. On the one hand, owing to his parents' debts (his decision to pay off the debts accumulated by his ancestors!), Gregor needs to earn money—a lot of money! How everyone rejoiced when "his successes on the job were transformed, by means of commissions, into hard cash that could be plunked down on the table at home in front of his delighted and astonished family" (30). But, being made of more sensitive metal, Gregor is interested in something finer that money can buy: a ticket of admission to the conservatory of music for his sister. So, at the end of the rainbow, there's something more than an escape from poverty and social disgrace for his family; Gregor harbors a notion of cultural improvement—and, hence, of the implicit social advancement of his family—at the same time that his enjoyment of the concrete thing that music is, is only vicarious: for "it was his secret plan that she, who, unlike him, loved music and could play the violin movingly, should be sent next year to the Conservatory" (30).

The exact definition of this cultural attitude, which seeks to acquire social distinction by publicly trafficking in the institutions of art, is philistinism. As long as Gregor is at work earning money, he is this philistine. But something interesting happens to him after his metamorphosis, which, in the economic sense, means becoming unemployable. Gregor becomes enthralled by the music of his sister's violin, so enthralled, as it turns out, that he will risk—and lose—his life for it. "Was he an animal, that music could move him so?" the narrator asks (54).

Now, at this point we will conjure up a rival to the economist reader—the sentimentalist reader, who interprets Gregor's question as a mere rhetorical question, meaning, "Oh, of course he cannot be an animal. Look how fine his responses are!" Gregor's newfound love of music, the sentimentalist reader thinks, signals his ascent to a higher plane of aesthetic enjoyment. He is on his way to acquiring the dignity of a higher kind, in the sense of Schopenhauer and Nietzsche. But our economist reader disagrees and will not interpret Gregor's question as a mere rhetorical one. He considers the question to be a real question and supplies an informed answer. "Was Gregor an animal?" Of course, he's an animal. He is unemployable! He stands outside the society of market exchange, what Kafka calls the world of "property and its relations" (*DF,* 40).

As a consequence of the music Gregor hears, he never ceases to be at least animal-*like:* fiddle playing strikes a licentious chord in him. As we recall, he has his sister's naked neck in his sights, which he means to kiss after making certain, by hissing and spitting at intruders, that from now on she will play her music for him alone. Our economist's point is that we may understand the metamorphosis as inverting his relation to capital: with money, as a man, he is a music philistine; without money, "a vermin," he is a music lover of sorts—or, more accurately, the debased lover of a musician.

Kafka's stories may be thought of as having windows, windows that are at once lucent and opaque, which take in the light of interpretive minds and also give back that light at an angle of refraction, since no single interpretation can penetrate to its glimmering law. In *The Interpretation of Dreams,* Freud conceived of the dream as "a window, through which to cast a glance into the interior of the mind."[22] Each dreamlike image in Kafka's stories is such an opening through which to glimpse its "mind." Yet no such window is entirely transparent; no gaze is sufficiently focused not to glance off its glassy surface. And because each of Kafka's stories has many windows, a glance at one will communicate with another. The windows catch one another's light: perspectives scintillate.[23]

Let us proceed to peer into a few more windows in *The Metamorphosis.* The one I now have in mind is a dirty window. Readers alert to the gutter ideologies of Kafka's time will not fail to recognize the racist, biopolitical dimension of Gregor's metamorphosis: Austro-Hungarian cranks and crackpots were eager to attack their Jewish neighbors by vilifying them with low comparisons; and the dictionary of anti-Semitic insults included qualities that are found, by analogy, in Gregor's appearance and in his behavior. It is unpleasant to repeat such epithets: he is a "parasite," he "scuttles" about on his business, he is unmusical, he is licentious, etc. But soon the comparison breaks off, and its truth value is compromised, because Gregor also enjoys an acrobatic lightness of being and dies with the desire to please his family—almost. Kafka also takes pains to write that "Gregor's conviction that he would have to disappear was, if possible, even firmer than his sister's" (59), which makes her the agent of his disappearance and leaves him as something less than saintly leper—though a good deal more than abject scum.

Are there other interpretations? Indeed there are. There is

the medicinal: Gregor's predicament is a replica of Kafka's intuitive forecast of his own tuberculosis, which could lay him low. "Of course," we recall, Gregor saw "that he would not be able to keep up even this running for long, for whenever his father took one step, Gregor had to execute countless movements. He was already beginning to feel winded, just as in the old days he had not had very reliable lungs" (42).

There is the biographical interpretation. Gregor is the family invalid: he punishes the family with his odium by assuming a cripple's or pariah's existence. True, he is himself punished by his sick body and by his dependency, but he achieves, thereby, the covert, doubly aggressive expressiveness of the tyrannical invalid and the family idiot.

Another biographical interpretation summons up the plight of the artist, the writer, who, in Kafka's family, is a changeling, a negative miracle, an outsider. For a moment we have plain evidence of Kafka's taste for such semiprivate games. Gregor thinks, "Well, in a pinch [he] could do without the chest, but the desk had to stay" (38). Here Samsa becomes an alias of Kafka, a notion given support in an (unfortunately) unreliable book by a young friend of Kafka's, Gustav Janouch. He claims to recall one of their conversations, which now borders on the cryptogrammatic:

> "The hero of the story is called Samsa," I [Janouch] said. "It sounds like a cryptogram for Kafka. Five letters in each word. The S in the word Samsa has the same position as the K in the word Kafka. The A . . ."
>
> Kafka interrupted me.
>
> "It is not a cryptogram. Samsa is not merely Kafka, and nothing else. *The Metamorphosis* is not a confession, although it is—in a certain sense—an indiscretion."

"I know nothing about that."

"Is it perhaps delicate and discreet to talk about the bedbugs [*Wanzen*] in one's own family?"[24]

There is the etymological interpretation, to which I'm partial: Gregor is the embodiment of a distorted metaphor (as I shall explain). But this *etymological* interpretation should not be confused with the *entomological* interpretation, which will briefly occupy us. Vladimir Nabokov, who greatly admired the story, considered it, as did Elias Canetti, a literary work that nothing could surpass—one of the few great, perfect poetic works of the twentieth century. At the same time Nabokov believed that Gregor's melancholy and his feelings of alienation might be cured with a little scientific enlightenment. He could have been spared all his desolation. Nabokov wrote, if only he had recognized that he is "a domed beetle, a scarab beetle with wing-sheaths." His promise of happiness lies in his flying out the window and joining all "the other happy dung beetles rolling the dung balls on rural paths."[25]

But there is a good objection to this interpretation. Interestingly, the phrase "dung beetle" does appear in *The Metamorphosis,* quite as if Kafka had been forewarned about Nabokov's reading of his hero's predicament. "Come over here for a minute, you old dung beetle!" says the "gigantic bony cleaning woman" who presides over Gregor's end (46). But then, significantly, we read: "To forms of address like these Gregor would not respond but remained immobile where he was, as if the door had not been opened" (49). He is not a dung beetle; he is "a monstrous vermin"—a proper English epithet that has an exact precedent in the language of a pamphlet written in 1581 by an English Protestant, Walter Haddon, against the Portuguese bishop

Jerome Osorio de Fonseca in a theological dispute about papal authority: "O monstruous vermine: did I ever speake or think any such matter?"[26] Gregor is a "monstruous vermine" and not an insect of a specifiable kind. He is an *ungeheures Ungeziefer,* and it may not be irrelevant that the modifying word *ungeheuer,* which Kafka chose, goes back to a Middle High German word (Latin: *infamiliaris*) meaning a creature having no place at the hearth, one that is outside all human family; and that the word for vermin, *Ungeziefer,* goes back to a Middle High German word meaning a creature unacceptable as sacrifice to the gods and, hence, outside the world order altogether. (Kafka studied Middle High German at Charles University, in Prague, before majoring in law.) At this point, we might recall our economic interpretation, where the post-metamorphic—and hence unemployable—Gregor had become unsuited as a sacrifice to the gods of capitalism.

There appears to be no end to these discussions, which have taken the place of theological dispute, in many instances retaining the same angry language. But the language of this discussion can also be of the whimsical sort; and so we have the novelist Philip Roth imagining Kafka, despite his death in 1924, fleeing the Central European concentration camp of the 1930s and surfacing in Newark, New Jersey, as a Hebrew teacher and romancer of an Aunt Rhoda (113). "In poetry," the novelist J. M. Coetzee writes, "the metaphoric spark is always one jump ahead of the decoding function . . . another unforeseen reading is always possible."[27]

With respect, then, to our original question as to the power of Kafka's opening images, we now know that these images are surreal (brilliantly incisive, but contrary to fact) but, more than that, they are *super*real. Once they have originated a plot, they invite a seemingly endless variety of perspectives, types of explanation, which draw on all the conceptual resources of Kafka's time—and all times to come.

Kafka demands interpretation, and his work lives and breathes only as it excites this demand. But *how* does it do this with its one unique story line? This is the question that still needs to be addressed.

Hermeneutic Excitement

Kafka's stories produce their hermeneutic excitement, I believe, by exerting what William Butler Yeats called, in almost the same hour of Kafka's writing his story, "the fascination of what's difficult." But if, in Yeats's poem, the speaker is exhausted by his fascination—"The fascination of what's difficult / Has dried the sap out of my veins, and rent / Spontaneous joy and natural content / Out of my heart"—the fascination of what's difficult enlivens Kafka's reader.

This is so because Kafka is only half in love with difficulty; he is also in love with clarity, with "difficult" images exquisitely delineated and seen. "Just go forward, hungry beast," he wrote late in life, as if recalling his story of Gregor Samsa. "The way leads to nourishing food, breathable air, a free life, even if it is all behind life." This late diary then makes a turn upward, as if Kafka were no longer reflecting on his monstrous creation but on Kafka the creator at the end of his writing career, which at times had not failed to strike him as marvelous: he who had been, as we have heard, the "big, tall field marshal" leading "the desperate ones through the mountain passes, which are under snow, discernable to no one else," on the strength of the *clarity* of his gaze (*D2*, 220). "The mountain passes, which are under snow": not a bad image for the path of understanding through the constellated images of Kafka's dreamlike art.

The creator, the author, has "the clarity of the gaze"—and so, in literary formalist terms, his way is not to load one symbolic detail after another onto his original image, a tactic widely practiced by other Prague writers (Max Brod, Franz Werfel), whose art is overloaded, cluttered, too rich. Expert readers might recall the hero's undergoing one vision after another in *Reitergeschichte* (cavalry story), by Hofmannsthal, Kafka's contemporary. It is as if, by our imagining a parallel, Gregor's transformation into a monstrous sort of vermin were only one, the first, of an ongoing series of visions, and as if the setting for his transformation had changed, in Part II, for example, into a palace in an enchanted forest, along the lines of, say, Maeterlinck's *Pelléas et Mélisande.* Kafka maintains a classic unity of scene and character, even in his altered state.

But what then separates Kafka's manner of presentation from a *realism* that is also hermeneutically exciting? We might reflect for a moment on the masterpieces of two writers whom Kafka greatly admired: Dostoyevsky and Flaubert. After all, the Underground Man, in Dostoyevsky's story of that name, is hermeneutically exciting. He excites interpretation, even in being quite recognizable as a realistic social product—the product of an unfulfilling, merely imported 1860s German romantic idealism and a dispiriting 1880s Russian socialism. The Underground Man is a bureaucrat by virtue of the meanness of his administration. We *recognize* him by the shiny worn trousers he wears, his colicky liver, his spitefulness, though it is extreme. And his behavior, too, excites a variety of interpretations, each of which he sets running in his own story. Why has he become a horror? Well, as a boy he was despised; furthermore, he lives in St. Petersburg, that most "intentional" (read: "artificial") of cities; add to this his need to confess, and also to avenge himself. His purpose in demeaning the oppressed prostitute Liza, he says, is also intentional, pedagogic: he means to heighten her self-awareness through her debasement.

But, in a way, all these alleged motives come together as one: he is a dizzy, spinning consciousness without roots in (what the critic György Lukács calls) an "integrated" civilization. This multiplicity of apparent causes is really only a single cause: the Underground Man is a machine for spinning alibis for his failure to do what Kafka understands as the right thing, to *act* in accordance with the knowledge of good and evil. *The Man from Underground* fits perfectly Kafka's incisive description of culture as *an evasive accumulation of knowledge,* which perverts the commandment to *do* the right thing while assembling the images, simulacra, and logical phantasms that Kafka calls *Motivationen* (alibis, justifications) (*GW,* 299).

The engine in Dostoyevsky's story, having been set in motion, must run in the one way it does. "I am a sick man.... I am a spiteful man." I do not think that readers can attribute to the author the option of multiple plot possibilities. The same one-track, bone-crushing determinism is at work in Flaubert's *Madame Bovary,* starting with the first facts of the case—Emma Bovary's passion for the romantic legends inked into the plate that *meat knives* have chipped away. From this point on, the novel must really run all one way: to ever-greater disillusionment, to ever-greater suffering, and to the heroine's death, in one form or another, before her time.

In its own canny way, by including in *The Metamorphosis* an implicit, realistic reading of its action, which it then ridicules, Kafka distinguishes himself from his realist predecessors. *The Metamorphosis* holds up to ridicule from the start the efforts of the stricken Gregor Samsa to interpret his predicament in a conventional way: "That the change in his voice was nothing more than the first sign of a bad cold, an occupational ailment of the traveling salesman, he had no doubt in the least" (7). And so Gregor continues to reason, as at the outset: "How about going back to sleep for a few minutes and forgetting all this nonsense" (4). At this point, we can intuit a necessary condition of realistic writing. Such situations tend to dictate only one explanation, and it is of a plausible, ready-made kind. That is what happens when Gregor Samsa assumes that the drastic changes in his body—a hard-shelled back and a great many "squirmy" legs—are due to his stressful job: "This getting up so early . . . makes anyone a complete idiot. Human beings have to have their sleep" (4).

Now, if indeed Kafka had pursued this story line—the story of a traveling salesman who had caught a bug—by showing him sitting with his legs in a hot bath and his mother and his sister bringing him an ice bag for his forehead and a thermometer for his mouth—it is unlikely that we, as interpreters, would feel called upon to exercise the full range of our interpretive skills, would feel obliged to delve into all the conceptual systems at our disposal in order to get a grip on what was happening to this triste employee of a fabric manufacturer in turn-of-the-century Imperial Austria.

There's an intriguing detail here in the way Kafka presents Gregor's effort to think realistically. When Gregor struggles to grasp his metamorphosis as the result of a cold, this German—or, better, Austrian Imperial—text uses the word *Verkühlung*. Yes, this means a cold, but the word is local and colloquial. The German of the German Empire would require the word *Erkältung*; and so it is as if the bad realist character of this explanation were signaled by the local vulgarity of its diction. But, no, it was no *Verkühlung*—no cold. And from this point on, the *universal* allegorical character of the story unfolds, concrete proof of which can be found in the story proper, when Gregor, at the end of Part I, hears the furious voice of his father behind him, and it "did not sound like that of only a single father" (21). Kafka has an amazing, if difficult, aphorism to describe his getting free of the language of realism. "For everything outside the world of sensation," he wrote (and the fictive mutant Gregor is such a being),

> language can be used only in the manner of a hint or allusion (*andeutungsweise*) but never even approximately in the manner of a comparison or simile (*vergleichsweise*), since corresponding as it [language] does to the world of the senses, it [language] is concerned only with property and its relations. (*DF,* 40)

I understand this thought to mean that when the language of fiction undertakes to represent people and situations as they are ordinarily experienced in the world, it degrades itself to the language of property law, which is concerned with establishing the rights of ownership and the rights of use. It then segments and delineates the world as definite parcels of property; people, scenes, acts, and judgments within the story relate to one another as parcels of property and, more important, relate to *themselves* as property. Kafka had a profound perception of the word *Sein* in the German language—which means, as he points out, at once "Being" and also "His, Belonging to him." To be is to belong to . . . another. It is hard to detect the tonality with which Kafka represents this idea: it might be with both wonder and anguish.

But things outside the frame of ordinary sensuous experience—fictions, phantasms, monsters—do not belong to themselves; they are not at one with their natures as these natures seem to be given. A realistic reading of the story—that is, its translation into familiar, recognizable categories of experience—would make property law the arbiter of relations within the story. Under the sway of such normal relations, there could be no metamorphosis in the relation of the thing to itself. But then this is exactly what has happened to Gregor. He finds himself changed—become radically *not* himself—even as he attempts to act and think in conformity with his given nature.

This is not a truth that Gregor can accept. He attempts to compare his new being to his old in such a way that the distinctiveness of his new being is simply absorbed into his old. The meaning of his monstrous shape is reduced to the meaning he has always had for himself.

This is why some readers—canny readers, but those who are unwittingly seduced by Gregor's way of seeing—are inclined to argue that, fundamentally, Gregor has not changed: he was always a sort of creepy-crawly, scuttling creature kowtowing to his boss, always a sterile parasite on his family, for it could be said that he has imposed on them the idea that he is indispensable to their survival. Such an interpretation evades the challenge of reflecting on this *disturbance* to the world of property relations, in which, as a rule, things belong to themselves and nothing can break apart the fixity of this bond. It is again in this context that we can understand the cryptic sentence that Kafka wrote in his diaries in 1910: "For he and his property are not one, but two, and whoever destroys the connection destroys him at the same time."[28] The metamorphosis of Gregor Samsa is such an event. It occurs in the language of fiction that Kafka calls "allusive"; it quite logically puts him outside the world of ordinary speech, of ordinary language, which is based on the premise that entities are owners of themselves. It is precisely the allusiveness of this story of metamorphosis that calls forth, and will continue to call forth, a virtual infinity of interpretations. The language of ordinary sensuous speech is the language of property law. Kafka experienced himself otherwise. "What have I in common with Jews?" he wrote. "I have hardly anything in common with myself" (*D*1, 11).

The best poets, Marianne Moore wrote, "can be / 'literalists of the imagination' . . . and can present for inspection, 'imaginary gardens with real toads in them.'" You might think that here Kafka does Marianne Moore one better, with his real gardens with imaginary vermin in them. But on closer inspection her remark is truer to his case: the monster is real, and the familial world is, in a sense, illusory.

I will conclude by proposing the most apt figure for the kind of being that Gregor has become: a figure of speech that I'll call the "metamorphosed" metaphor (158ff). Astute readers will observe that Gregor's relation to his bug shape is more than just a relation of similarity; it is more than Gregor is *like* a bug. They conclude: Gregor wakes up and *is* a bug. That is it—he is the soul of the literalized metaphor, the soul of literalization. The argument proceeds: Gregor's relation to his new form is the relation of a thing to its metaphor—"This man *is* a louse." We have a deep incorporation by the one sort of being (traveling salesman) of certain properties of another being (a louse), properties that underline characteristics of the man, who might be said to be spineless and . . . to crawl . . . and to scurry about. Here, astute readers say, we are dealing with an identity: Gregor is, through and through, this louse, this vermin.

Aha! But is he? Of course not. He is an uncanny mix of the features of the one thing and of the other, a mix never before seen on land or sea, a morally sensitive creature but also a lustful louse—an acrobatic but also a scuttling roach. All the qualities of both man and insect are commingled. We don't know whether we have an insect that has miraculously acquired the sensibility of a man or a man who has miraculously acquired the body of a beetle. We have something less than identity but more—or worse—than a relation of sharing based on the normal metaphor. It is as if a metaphor went on expanding in the most unruly way, as if having determined to call, say, Richard I Richard the Lionheart of England, we were to attach to him all the properties of the lion and give him, along with a very thick, muscular heart, a tufted tail and drooling jaws. Kafka has taken the structure of metaphor, by which we speak and think, and transformed it. The verminous insect Gregor Samsa is less a mutant entomological event than he is a mutant etymological event, having more the structure of a metaphor gone mad than that of an eighty-pound dung beetle—who, at one juncture, we read, "could not repress a smile at this thought [of calling his parents for help]" (9). This is surely the strangest smile in world literature, but perhaps it is a knowing smile. What Gregor may be saying is: I am not a metaphor. I am not anything you have ever held me to be. I am neither man nor beast. You have never seen the likes of me. I am, dear reader, your most frightful possibility.

A Chronology of Franz Kafka's Life

1883 Born in Prague on July 3, son of Hermann Kafka, a fairly affluent tradesman, and his wife, Julie (née Löwy). Hermann Kafka's father was a butcher; among Julie Löwy's forebears were several learned rabbis.

1885–1887 Birth and death of his brother Georg.

1887–1888 Birth and death of his brother Heinrich.

1889, 1890, 1892 Birth of his three sisters—Gabriele (Elli), Valerie (Valli), and Ottilie (Ottla), his favorite. All three were murdered by the Nazis.

1889–1893 Attends elementary school (German Boys' School) at the Fleischmarkt in Prague.

1893–1901 Attends the Old Town Gymnasium, together with

mostly middle-class Jewish boys. First attested reading of Nietzsche in the summer of 1900.

1901–1906 Studies law at the German University in Prague, along with occasional courses in German literature.

1902 Vacation with Uncle Siegfried Löwy, a country doctor. Meets Max Brod, his lifelong friend and future editor, and participates in discussions on empirical psychology at the Café Louvre in a reading group known as the Louvre Circle.

1904–1905 Writes "Description of a Struggle."

1905 Vacation in Zuckmantel and first love affair. Meets regularly with friends who share his literary and intellectual interests, including Oskar Baum, Max Brod, and Felix Weltsch.

1906 Works in a Prague law office before graduating with a doctor's degree in law. Begins a year's internship in Prague, first at the penal court and then at the civil court.

1907 Writes "Wedding Preparations in the Country," part of a novel. Begins his first regular job at the Assicurazioni Generali, an Italian insurance company.

1908 Moves to the partly state-run Workmen's Accident Insurance Institute for the Kingdom of Bohemia, in Prague, where he will rise to a position of considerable authority (*Obersekretär*) until he is pensioned in 1922. His first publication, eight short pieces under the title "Meditation," appears in the journal *Hyperion.*

1909 Spends vacation with Max Brod in Riva, on Lake Garda in Austrian Italy. Publishes "Airplanes in Brescia" in the daily newspaper *Bohemia*, the first description of airplanes in a German newspaper. Additional publication of two pieces from "Description of a Struggle."

1910 Begins keeping a diary. Sees a performance by a traveling Yiddish theater. Trips to Paris and Berlin.

1911 Repeatedly attends performances of another Yiddish theater troupe from Eastern Europe (Yitzak Löwy and his players). Studies Hasidic tales and parables. Becomes interested in alternative medicine: vegetarianism, sunbathing, natural healing. Writes earliest drafts of the (unfinished) novel *The Missing Person* (aka *Amerika*).

1912 Gives a public address in Prague "On the Yiddish Language." On the evening of August 13, with Max Brod, puts together his first published book, *Meditation* (1912), and meets his future fiancée Felice Bauer, with whom he will correspond for five years. Writes "The Judgment" in a single night, September 22–23. This is followed, in September and October, by "The Stoker" and by an early version of *The Missing Person.* From November 17 to December 7, he writes *The Metamorphosis,* reading parts of the unfinished story aloud to friends on November 24. In December, he gives a public reading of "The Judgment." *Meditation* is published by Rowohlt.

1913 Reads the whole of *The Metamorphosis* aloud at Max Brod's. Meetings with Felice in Berlin. Publication of "The Stoker" (the first chapter of *The Missing Person*). Publication of "The Judgment." Kafka visits Eleventh Zionist Congress in Vienna.

1914 In June, formal engagement to Felice Bauer in Berlin, followed, in July, by its being broken off. World War I breaks out as Kafka begins writing *The Trial.* In October, work on *The Trial* having come to a standstill, he writes "In the Penal Colony" as well as the last chapter of *The Missing Person.*

1915 Wins the Fontane Prize for literary achievement for "The Stoker." Reunion with Felice Bauer. In Prague, lives for the first time in an apartment of his own. *The Metamorphosis* is published in *Die weissen Blätter* and then in book form.

1916 Spends time with Felice in Marienbad. Gives a public reading of "In the Penal Colony." Writes several of the stories later collected in *A Country Doctor: Little Stories.*

1917 Lives in rooms in Alchemists' Lane, in Prague, then in the Schönberg Palace. Continues work on *A Country Doctor* and writes other stories. Second engagement to Felice Bauer shattered by the diagnosis of his tuberculosis in September. Takes leave from his office and joins his sister Ottla in Zürau. Writes a series of aphorisms. In December, the engagement is dissolved.

1918–1919 Studies Kierkegaard. Meets with Julie Wohryzek. "In the Penal Colony" and *A Country Doctor* are published. Becomes engaged to Julie Wohryzek. Writes a never-mailed "Letter to His Father."

1920 Conversations with Kafka allegedly recorded by Gustav Janouch. Correspondence with the Czech literary personality

Milena Jesenská. End of the engagement to Julie Wohryzek. Resumes literary work after a hiatus of more than three years.

1922 Beginnings of *The Castle.* Writes "A Starvation Artist" and "Investigations of a Dog." Last conversations with Milena. Lives with his sister Ottla in Planá, in the Czech provinces, where he continues work on *The Castle.*

1923 Meets Dora Diamant, his last consort, and goes to live with her in Berlin-Steglitz. Inflation and cold. Writes "The Burrow." At Kafka's behest, Dora allegedly burns several of his manuscripts. The collection *A Starvation Artist* goes to press.

1924 Very ill with tuberculosis of the larynx, Kafka writes "Josephine the Singer" while attempting to recover in his parents' apartment in Prague. Visits various hospitals and sanatoriums and finally settles on the Kierling Sanatorium near Vienna, where he is accompanied by Dora Diamant and his doctor, Robert Klopstock. On June 3, at the age of forty, Kafka dies; on June 11, he is buried in the New Jewish Cemetery in Prague. Milena writes in an obituary, "His stories reflect the irony and prophetic vision of a man condemned to see the world with such blinding clarity that he found it unbearable and went to his death." *A Starvation Artist* is published posthumously.

1925 Posthumous publication of *The Trial.*

1926 Posthumous publication of *The Castle.*

1927 Posthumous publication of *The Missing Person.*

THE METAMORPHOSIS

I

When Gregor Samsa[1] woke up one morning from unsettling dreams, he found himself changed in his bed into a monstrous vermin.[2] He was lying on his back as hard as armor plate, and when he lifted his head a little, he saw his vaulted brown belly, sectioned by arch-shaped ribs, to whose dome the cover, about to slide off completely, could barely cling. His many legs, pitifully thin compared with the size of the rest of him, were waving helplessly before his eyes.

"What's happened to me?" he thought. It was no dream. His room, a regular human room,[3] only a little on the small side, lay quiet between the four familiar walls. Over the table, on which an unpacked line of fabric samples was all spread out—Samsa was a traveling salesman—hung the picture which he had recently cut out of a glossy magazine and lodged in a pretty gilt frame. It showed a lady done up in a fur hat and a fur boa,[4] sitting upright and raising up against the viewer a heavy fur muff in which her whole forearm had disappeared.

Gregor's eyes then turned to the window, and the overcast weather—he could hear raindrops hitting against the metal window ledge—completely depressed him. "How about going back to sleep for a few minutes and forgetting all this nonsense," he thought, but that was completely impracticable, since he was used to sleeping on his right side and in his present state could not get into that position. No matter how hard he threw himself onto his right side, he always rocked onto his back again. He must have tried it a hundred times, closing his eyes so as not to have to see his squirming legs, and stopped only when he began to feel a slight, dull pain in his side, which he had never felt before.

"Oh God," he thought, "what a grueling job I've picked! Day in, day out—on the road. The upset of doing business is much worse than the actual business in the home office, and, besides, I've got the torture of traveling, worrying about changing trains, eating miserable food at all hours, constantly seeing new faces, no relationships that last or get more intimate. To the devil with it all!" He felt a slight itching up on top of his belly; shoved himself slowly on his back closer to the bedpost, so as to be able to lift his head better; found the itchy spot, studded with small white dots which he had no idea what to make of; and wanted to touch the spot with one of his legs but immediately pulled it back, for the contact sent a cold shiver through him.

He slid back again into his original position. "This getting up so early," he thought, "makes anyone a complete idiot. Human beings have to have their sleep. Other traveling salesmen live like harem women. For instance, when I go back to the hotel before lunch to write up the business I've done, these gentlemen are just having breakfast. That's all I'd have to try with my boss; I'd be fired on the spot. Anyway, who knows if that wouldn't be a very good thing for me. If I didn't hold back for my parents' sake, I would have quit long ago, I would have marched up to the boss and spoken my piece from the bottom of my heart. He would have fallen off the desk! It is funny, too, the way he sits on the desk and talks down from the heights to the employees, especially when they have to come right up close on account of the boss's being hard of hearing. Well, I haven't given up hope completely; once I've gotten the money together to pay off my parents' debt to him—that will probably take another five or six years—I'm going to do it without fail. Then I'm going to make the big break. But for the time being I'd better get up, since my train leaves at five."

And he looked over at the alarm clock, which was ticking on the chest of drawers. "God Almighty!"[5] he thought. It was six-thirty, the hands were quietly moving forward, it was actually past the half-hour, it was already nearly a quarter to. Could it be that the alarm hadn't gone off? You could see from the bed that it was set correctly for four o'clock; it certainly had gone off, too. Yes, but was it possible to sleep quietly through a ringing that made the furniture shake? Well, he certainly hadn't slept quietly, but probably all the more soundly for that. But what should he do now? The next train left at seven o'clock; to make it, he would have to hurry like a madman, and the line of samples wasn't packed yet, and he himself didn't feel especially fresh and ready to march around. And even if he did make the train, he could not avoid getting it from the boss, because the messenger boy had been waiting at the five-o'clock train and would have long ago reported his not showing up. He was a tool[6] of the boss, without brains or backbone. What if he were to say he was sick? But that would be extremely embarrassing and suspicious because during his five years with the firm Gregor had not been sick even once. The boss would be sure to come with the health-insurance doctor, blame his parents for their lazy son, and cut off all excuses by quoting the health-insurance doctor, for whom the world consisted of people who were completely healthy but afraid to work. And, besides, in this case would he be so very wrong? In fact, Gregor felt fine, with the exception of his drowsiness, which was really unnecessary after sleeping so late, and he even had a ravenous appetite.

Just as he was thinking all this over at top speed, without being able to decide to get out of bed—the alarm clock had just struck a quarter to seven—he heard a cautious knocking at the door next to the head of his bed. "Gregor," someone called—it was his mother—"it's a quarter to seven. Didn't you want to catch the train?" What a soft voice! Gregor was shocked to hear his own voice answering, unmistakably his own voice, true, but in which, as if from below, an insistent distressed chirping intruded, which left the clarity of his words intact only for a moment really, before so badly garbling them as they carried that no one could be sure if he had heard right. Gregor had wanted to answer in detail and to explain everything, but, given the circumstances, confined himself to saying, "Yes, yes, thanks, Mother, I'm just getting up." The wooden door must have prevented the change in Gregor's voice from being noticed outside, because his mother was satisfied with this explanation and shuffled off. But their little exchange had made the rest of the family aware that, contrary to expectations, Gregor was still in the house, and already his father was knocking on one of the side doors, feebly but with his fist.[7] "Gregor, Gregor," he called, "what's going on?" And after a little while he called again in a deeper, warning voice, "Gregor! Gregor!" At the other side door, however, his sister moaned gently, "Gregor? Is something the matter with you? Do you want anything?" Toward both sides Gregor answered: "I'm all ready," and made an effort, by meticulous pronunciation and by inserting long pauses between individual words, to eliminate everything from his voice that might betray him. His father went back to his breakfast, but his sister whispered, "Gregor, open up,

I'm pleading with you." But Gregor had absolutely no intention of opening the door and complimented himself instead on the precaution he had adopted from his business trips, of locking all the doors during the night even at home.

First of all he wanted to get up quietly, without any excitement; get dressed; and, the main thing, have breakfast, and only then think about what to do next, for he saw clearly that in bed he would never think things through to a rational conclusion. He remembered how even in the past he had often felt some kind of slight pain, possibly caused by lying in an uncomfortable position, which, when he got up, turned out to be purely imaginary, and he was eager to see how today's fantasy would gradually fade away. That the change in his voice was nothing more than the first sign of a bad cold, an occupational ailment of the traveling salesman, he had no doubt in the least.

It was very easy to throw off the cover; all he had to do was puff himself up a little, and it fell off by itself. But after this, things got difficult, especially since he was so unusually broad. He would have needed hands and arms to lift himself up, but instead of that he had only his numerous little legs, which were in every different kind of perpetual motion and which, besides, he could not control. If he wanted to bend one, the first thing that happened was that it stretched itself out; and if he finally succeeded in getting this leg to do what he wanted, all the others in the meantime, as if set free, began to work in the most intensely painful agitation. "Just don't stay in bed being useless," Gregor said to himself.

First he tried to get out of bed with the lower part of his body, but this lower part—which by the way he had not seen yet and which he could not form a clear picture of—proved too difficult to budge; it was taking so long; and when finally, almost out of his mind, he lunged forward with all his force, without caring, he had picked the wrong direction and slammed himself violently against the lower bedpost, and the searing pain he felt taught him that exactly the lower part of his body was, for the moment anyway, the most sensitive.

He therefore tried to get the upper part of his body out of bed first and warily turned his head toward the edge of the bed. This worked easily, and in spite of its width and weight, the mass of his body finally followed, slowly, the movement of his head. But when at last he stuck his head over the edge of the bed into the air, he got too scared to continue any further, since if he finally let himself fall in this position, it would be a miracle if he didn't injure his head. And just now he had better not for the life of him lose consciousness; he would rather stay in bed.

But when, once again, after the same exertion, he lay in his original position, sighing, and again watched his little legs struggling, if possible more fiercely, with each other and saw no way of bringing peace and order into this mindless motion, he again told himself that it was impossible for him to stay in bed and that the most rational thing was to make any sacrifice for even the smallest hope of freeing himself from the bed. But at the same time he did not forget to remind himself occasionally that thinking things over calmly—indeed, as calmly as possible—was much better than jumping to desperate decisions. At such moments he fixed his eyes as sharply as possible on the window, but unfortunately there was little confidence and cheer to be gotten from the view of the morning fog, which shrouded even the other side of the narrow street. "Seven o'clock already," he said to himself as the alarm clock struck again, "seven o'clock already and still such a fog." And for a little while he lay quietly, breathing shallowly, as if expecting, perhaps, from the complete silence the return of things to the way they really and naturally were.

But then he said to himself, "Before it strikes a quarter past seven, I must be completely out of bed without fail. Anyway, by that time someone from the firm will be here to find out where I am, since the office opens before seven." And now he started rocking the complete length of his body out of the bed with a smooth rhythm. If he let himself topple out of bed in this way, his head, which on falling he planned to lift up sharply, would presumably remain unharmed. His back seemed to be hard; nothing was likely to happen to it when it fell onto the rug. His biggest misgiving came from his concern about the loud crash that was bound to occur and would probably create, if not terror, at least anxiety behind all the doors. But that would have to be risked.

When Gregor's body already projected halfway out of bed—the new method was more of a game than a struggle, he only had to keep on rocking and jerking himself along—he thought how simple everything would be if he could get some help. Two strong persons—he thought of his father and the maid—would have been completely sufficient; they would only have had to shove their arms under his arched back, in this way scoop him off the bed, bend down with their burden, and then just be careful and patient while he managed to swing himself down onto the floor, where his little legs would hopefully acquire some purpose. Well, leaving out the fact that the doors were locked, should he really call for help? In spite of all his miseries, he could not repress a smile at this thought.

He was already so far along that when he rocked more strongly he could hardly keep his balance, and very soon he would have to commit himself, because in five minutes it would be a quarter past seven—when the doorbell rang. "It's someone from the firm," he said to himself and almost froze, while his little legs only danced more quickly. For a moment everything remained quiet. "They're not going to answer," Gregor said to himself, captivated by some senseless hope. But then, of course, the maid went to the door as usual with her firm stride and opened up. Gregor only had to hear the visitor's first word of greeting to know who it was—the office manager himself. Why was only Gregor condemned to work for a firm where at the slightest omission they immediately suspected the worst? Were all employees louts without exception, wasn't there a single loyal, dedicated worker among them who, when he had not fully utilized a few hours of the morning for the firm, was driven half-mad by pangs of conscience and was actually unable to get out of bed? Really, wouldn't it have been enough to send one of the apprentices to find out—if this prying were absolutely necessary—did the manager himself have to come, and did the whole innocent family have to be shown in this way that the investigation of this suspicious affair could be entrusted only to the intellect of the manager? And more as a result of the excitement produced in Gregor by these thoughts than as a result of any real decision, he swung himself out of bed with all his might. There was a loud thump, but it was not a real crash. The fall was broken a little by the rug, and Gregor's back was more elastic than he had thought, which explained the not very noticeable muffled sound. Only he had not held his head carefully enough and hit it; he turned it and rubbed it on the rug in anger and pain.

"Something fell in there," said the manager in the room on the left. Gregor tried to imagine whether something like what had happened to him today could one day happen even to the manager; you really had to grant the possibility. But, as if in rude reply to this question, the manager took a few decisive steps in the next room and made his patent leather boots creak. From the room on the right his sister whispered, to inform Gregor, "Gregor, the manager is here." "I know," Gregor said to himself; but he did not dare raise his voice enough for his sister to hear.

"Gregor," his father now said from the room on the left, "the manager has come and wants to be informed why you didn't catch the early train. We don't know what we should say to him. Besides, he wants to speak to you personally. So please open the door. He will certainly be so kind as to excuse the disorder of the room." "Good morning, Mr. Samsa," the manager called in a friendly voice. "There's something the matter with him," his mother said to the manager while his father was still at the door, talking. "Believe me, sir, there's something the matter with him. Otherwise how would Gregor have missed a train? That boy has nothing on his mind but the business. It's almost begun to rile me that he never goes out nights. He's been back in the city for eight days now, but every night he's been home. He sits there with us at the table, quietly reading the paper or studying train schedules. It's already a distraction for him when he's busy working with his fretsaw.[8] For instance, in the span of two or three evenings he carved a little frame. You'll be amazed how pretty it is; it's hanging inside his room. You'll see it right away when Gregor opens the door. You know, I'm glad that you've come, sir. We would never have gotten Gregor to open the door by ourselves; he's so stubborn. And there's certainly something wrong with him, even though he said this morning there wasn't." "I'm coming right away," said Gregor slowly and deliberately, not moving in order not to miss a word of the conversation. "I haven't any other explanation myself," said the manager. "I hope it's nothing serious. On the other hand, I must say that we businessmen—fortunately or unfortunately, whichever you prefer—very often simply have to overcome a slight indisposition for business reasons." "So can the manager come in now?" asked his father, impatient, and knocked on the door again. "No," said Gregor. In the room on the left there was an embarrassing silence; in the room on the right his sister began to sob.

Why didn't his sister go in to the others? She had probably just got out of bed and not even started to get dressed. Then what was she crying about? Because he didn't get up and didn't let the manager in, because he was in danger of losing his job, and because then the boss would start hounding his parents about the old debts? For the time being, certainly, her worries were unnecessary. Gregor was still here and hadn't the slightest intention of letting the family down. True, at the moment he was lying on the rug, and no one knowing his condition could seriously have expected him to let the manager in. But just because of this slight discourtesy, for which an appropriate excuse would easily be found later on, Gregor could not simply be dismissed. And to Gregor it seemed much more sensible to leave him alone now than to bother him with crying and persuasion. But it was just the uncertainty that was tormenting the others and excused their behavior.

"Mr. Samsa," the manager now called, raising his voice, "what's the matter? You barricade yourself in your room, answer only 'yes' and 'no,' cause your parents serious, unnecessary worry, and you neglect—I mention this only in passing—your duties to the firm in a really shocking manner. I am speaking here in the name of your parents and of your employer and ask you in all seriousness for an immediate, clear explanation. I'm amazed, amazed. I thought I knew you to be a quiet, reasonable person, and now you suddenly seem to want to start strutting about, flaunting strange whims. The head of the firm did suggest to me this morning a possible explanation for your tardiness—it concerned the cash payments recently entrusted to you—but really, I practically gave my word of honor that this explanation could not be right. But now, seeing your incomprehensible obstinacy, I am about to lose even the slightest desire to stick up for you in any way at all. And your job is not the most secure. Originally I intended to tell you all this in private, but since you make me waste my time here for nothing, I don't see why your parents shouldn't hear too. Your performance of late has been very unsatisfactory; I know it is not the best season for doing business, we all recognize that; but a season for not doing any business, there is no such thing, Mr. Samsa, such a thing cannot be tolerated."

"But, sir," cried Gregor, beside himself, in his excitement forgetting everything else, "I'm just opening up, in a minute. A slight indisposition, a dizzy spell, prevented me from getting up. I'm still in bed. But I already feel fine again. I'm just getting out of bed. Just be patient for a minute! I'm not as well as I thought yet. But really I'm fine. How something like this could just take a person by surprise! Only last night I was fine, my parents can tell you, or wait, last night I already had a slight premonition. They must have been able to tell by looking at me. Why didn't I report it to the office! But you always think that you'll get over a sickness without staying home. Sir! Spare my parents! There's no basis for any of the accusations that you're making against me now; no one has ever said a word to me about them. Perhaps you haven't seen the last orders I sent in. Anyway, I'm still going on the road with the eight o'clock train; these few hours of rest have done me good. Don't let me keep you, sir. I'll be at the office myself right away, and be so kind as to tell them this, and give my respects to the head of the firm."

And while Gregor hastily blurted all this out, hardly knowing what he was saying, he had easily approached the chest of drawers, probably as a result of the practice he had already gotten in bed, and now he tried to raise himself up against it. He actually intended to open the door, actually present himself and speak to the manager; he was eager to find out what the others, who were now so anxious to see him, would say at the sight of him. If they were shocked, then Gregor had no further responsibility and could be calm. But if they took everything calmly, then he, too, had no reason to get excited and could, if he hurried, actually be at the station by eight o'clock. At first he slid off the polished chest of drawers a few times, but at last, giving himself a final push, he stood upright; he no longer paid any attention to the pains in his abdomen, no matter how much they were burning. Now he let himself fall against the back of a nearby chair, clinging to its slats with his little legs. But by doing this he had gotten control of himself and fell silent, since he could now listen to what the manager was saying.

"Did you understand a word?" the manager was asking his parents. "He isn't trying to make fools of us, is he?" "My God," cried his mother, already in tears, "maybe he's seriously ill, and here we are, torturing him. Grete! Grete!" she then cried. "Mother?" called his sister from the other side. They communicated by way of Gregor's room. "Go to the doctor's immediately. Gregor is sick. Hurry, get the doctor. Did you just hear Gregor talking?" "That was the voice of an animal," said the manager, in a tone conspicuously soft compared with the mother's yelling. "Anna!" "Anna!"[9] the father called through the foyer into the kitchen, clapping his hands, "get a locksmith right away!" And already the two girls were running with rustling skirts through the foyer—how could his sister have gotten dressed so quickly?—and tearing open the door to the apartment. The door could not be heard slamming; they had probably left it open, as is the custom in homes where a great misfortune has occurred.[10]

But Gregor had become much calmer. It was true that they no longer understood his words, though they had seemed clear enough to him, clearer than before, probably because his ear had grown accustomed to them. But still, the others now believed that there was something the matter with him and were ready to help him. The assurance and confidence with which the first measures had been taken did him good. He felt integrated into human society once again and hoped for marvelous, amazing feats from both the doctor and the locksmith, without really distinguishing sharply between them. In order to make his voice as clear as possible for the crucial discussions that were approaching, he cleared his throat a little—taking pains, of course, to do so in a very muffled manner, since this noise, too, might sound different from human coughing, a thing he no longer trusted himself to decide. In the next room, meanwhile, everything had become completely still. Perhaps his parents were sitting at the table with the manager, whispering; perhaps they were all leaning against the door and listening.

Gregor slowly lugged himself toward the door, pushing the chair in front of him, then let go of it, threw himself against the door, held himself upright against it—the pads on the bottom of his little legs exuded a little sticky substance—and for a moment rested there from the exertion. But then he got started turning the key in the lock with his mouth. Unfortunately it seemed that he had no real teeth—what was he supposed to grip the key with?—but in compensation his jaws, of course, were very strong; with their help he actually got the key moving and paid no attention to the fact that he was undoubtedly hurting himself in some way, for a brown liquid came out of his mouth, flowed over the key, and dripped onto the floor. "Listen," said the manager in the next room, "he's turning the key." This was great encouragement to Gregor; but everyone should have cheered him on, his father and mother too. "Go, Gregor," they should have called, "keep going, at that lock, harder, harder!" And in the delusion that they were all following his efforts with suspense, he clamped his jaws madly on the key with all the strength he could muster. Depending on the progress of the key, he danced around the lock; holding himself upright only by his mouth, he clung to the key, as the situation demanded, or pressed it down again with the whole weight of his body. The clearer click of the lock as it finally snapped back positively woke Gregor up. With a sigh of relief he said to himself, "So I didn't need the locksmith after all," and laid his head down on the handle in order to open wide [one wing of the double doors].[11]

Since he had to use this method of opening the door, it was really opened very wide while he himself was still invisible. He first had to edge slowly around the one wing of the door, and do so very carefully if he was not to fall flat on his back just before entering. He was still busy with this difficult maneuver and had no time to pay attention to anything else when he heard the manager burst out with a loud "Oh!"—it sounded like a rush of wind—and now he could see him, standing closest to the door, his hand pressed over his open mouth, slowly backing away, as if repulsed by an invisible, unrelenting force. His mother—in spite of the manager's presence she stood with her hair still unbraided from the night, sticking out in all directions—first looked at his father with her hands clasped, then took two steps toward Gregor, and sank down in the midst of her skirts spreading out around her, her face completely hidden on her breast. With a hostile expression his father clenched his fist, as if to drive Gregor back into his room, then looked uncertainly around the living room, shielded his eyes with his hands, and sobbed with heaves of his powerful chest.

Now Gregor did not enter the room after all but leaned against the inside of the firmly bolted wing of the door, so that only half his body was visible and his head above it, cocked to one side and peeping out at the others. In the meantime it had grown much lighter; across the street one could see clearly a section of the endless, grayish-black building opposite—it was a hospital—with its regular windows starkly piercing the façade; the rain was still coming down, but only in large, separately visible drops that were also pelting the ground literally one at a time. The breakfast dishes were laid out lavishly on the table, since for his father breakfast was the most important meal of the day, which he would prolong for hours while reading various newspapers. On the wall directly opposite hung a photograph of Gregor from his army days, in a lieutenant's uniform, his hand on his sword, a carefree smile on his lips, demanding respect for his bearing and his rank. The door to the foyer was open, and since the front door was open too, it was possible to see out onto the landing and the top of the stairs going down.

"Well," said Gregor—and he was thoroughly aware of being the only one who had kept calm—"I'll get dressed right away, pack up my samples, and go. Will you, will you please let me go? Now, sir, you see, I'm not stubborn and I'm willing to work; traveling is a hardship, but without it I couldn't live. Where are you going, sir? To the office? Yes? Will you give an honest report of everything? A man might find for a moment that he was unable to work, but that's exactly the right time to remember his past accomplishments and to consider that later on, when the obstacle has been removed, he's bound to work all the harder and more efficiently. I'm under so many obligations to the head of the firm, as you know very well. Besides, I also have my parents and my sister to worry about. I'm in a tight spot, but I'll also work my way out again. Don't make things harder for me than they already are. Stick up for me in the office, please. Traveling salesmen aren't well liked there, I know. People think they make a fortune leading the gay life. No one has any particular reason to rectify this prejudice. But you, sir, you have a better perspective on things than the rest of the office, an even better perspective, just between the two of us, than the head of the firm himself, who in his capacity as owner easily lets his judgment be swayed against an employee. And you also know very well that the traveling salesman, who is out of the office practically the whole year round, can so easily become the victim of gossip, contingencies, and unfounded accusations, against which he's completely unable to defend himself, since in most cases he knows nothing at all about them except when he returns exhausted from a trip, and back home gets to suffer on his own person the grim consequences, which can no longer be traced back to their causes. Sir, don't go away without a word to tell me you think I'm at least partly right!"

But at Gregor's first words the manager had already turned away and with curled lips looked back at Gregor only over his twitching shoulder. And during Gregor's speech he did not stand still for a minute but, without letting Gregor out of his sight, backed toward the door, yet very gradually, as if there were some secret prohibition against leaving the room. He was already in the foyer, and from the sudden movement with which he took his last step from the living room, one might have thought he had just burned the sole of his foot. In the foyer, however, he stretched his right hand far out toward the staircase, as if nothing less than an unearthly deliverance were awaiting him there.

Gregor realized that he must on no account let the manager go away in this mood if his position in the firm were not to be jeopardized in the extreme. His parents did not understand this too well; in the course of the years they had formed the conviction that Gregor was set for life in this firm; and furthermore, they were so preoccupied with their immediate troubles that they had lost all consideration for the future. But Gregor had this forethought. The manager must be detained, calmed down, convinced, and finally won over; Gregor's and the family's future depended on it! If only his sister had been there! She was perceptive; she had already begun to cry when Gregor was still lying calmly on his back. And certainly the manager, this ladies' man, would have listened to her; she would have shut the front door and in the foyer talked him out of his scare. But his sister was not there; Gregor had to handle the situation himself. And without stopping to realize that he had no idea what his new faculties of movement were, and without stopping to realize either that his speech had possibly—indeed, probably—not been understood again, he let go of the wing of the door; he shoved himself through the opening, intending to go to the manager, who was already on the landing, ridiculously holding onto the banisters with both hands; but groping for support, Gregor immediately fell down with a little cry onto his numerous little legs. This had hardly happened when for the first time that morning he had a feeling of physical well-being; his little legs were on firm ground; they obeyed him completely, as he noted to his joy; they even strained to carry him away wherever he wanted to go; and he already believed that final recovery from all his sufferings was imminent. But at that very moment, as he lay on the floor rocking with repressed motion, not far from his mother and just opposite her, she, who had seemed so completely self-absorbed, all at once jumped up, her arms stretched wide, her fingers spread, crying, "Help, for God's sake, help!" held her head bent as if to see Gregor better, but inconsistently darted madly backward instead; had forgotten that the table laden with the breakfast dishes stood behind her; sat down on it hastily, as if her thoughts were elsewhere, when she reached it; and did not seem to notice at all that near her the big coffeepot had been knocked over and coffee was pouring in a steady stream onto the rug.

"Mother, Mother," said Gregor softly and looked up at her.

For a minute the manager had completely slipped his mind; on the other hand at the sight of the spilling coffee he could not resist snapping his jaws several times in the air. At this his mother screamed once more, fled from the table, and fell into the arms of his father, who came rushing up to her. But Gregor had no time now for his parents; the manager was already on the stairs; with his chin on the banister, he was taking a last look back. Gregor was off to a running start, to be as sure as possible of catching up with him; the manager must have suspected something like this, for he leaped down several steps and disappeared; but still he shouted "Agh," and the sound carried through the whole staircase. Unfortunately the manager's flight now seemed to confuse his father completely, who had been relatively calm until now, for instead of running after the manager himself, or at least not hindering Gregor in his pursuit, he seized in his right hand the manager's cane, which had been left behind on a chair with his hat and overcoat, picked up in his left hand a heavy newspaper from the table, and stamping his feet, started brandishing the cane and the newspaper to drive Gregor back into his room. No plea of Gregor's helped, no plea was even understood; however humbly he might turn his head, his father merely stamped his feet more forcefully. Across the room his mother had thrown open a window in spite of the cool weather, and leaning out, she buried her face, far outside the window, in her hands. Between the alley and the staircase a strong draft was created, the window curtains blew in, the newspapers on the table rustled, single sheets fluttered across the floor. Pitilessly his father came on, hissing like a wild man. Now Gregor had not had any practice at all walking in reverse; it was really very slow going. If Gregor had only been allowed to turn around, he could have gotten into his room right away, but he was afraid to make his father impatient by this time-consuming gyration, and at any minute the cane in his father's hand threatened to come down on his back or his head with a deadly blow. Finally, however, Gregor had no choice, for he noticed with horror that in reverse he could not even keep going in one direction; and so, incessantly throwing uneasy side-glances at his father, he began to turn around as quickly as possible, in reality turning only very slowly. Perhaps his father realized his good intentions, for he did not interfere with him; instead, he even now and then directed the maneuver from afar with the tip of his cane. If only his father did not keep making this intolerable hissing sound! It made Gregor lose his head completely. He had almost finished the turn when—his mind continually on this hissing—he made a mistake and even started turning back around to his original position. But when he had at last successfully managed to get his head in front of the opened door, it turned out that his body was too broad to get through as it was. Of course in his father's present state of mind it did not even remotely occur to him to open the other wing of the door in order to give Gregor enough room to pass through. He had only the fixed idea that Gregor must return to his room as quickly as possible. He would never have allowed the complicated preliminaries Gregor needed to go through in order to stand up on one end and perhaps in this way fit through the door. Instead he drove Gregor on, as if there were no obstacle, with exceptional loudness; the voice behind Gregor did not sound like that of only a single father; now this was really no joke anymore, and Gregor forced himself—come what may—into the doorway. One side of his body rose up, he lay lopsided in the opening, one of his flanks was scraped raw, ugly blotches marred the white door, soon he got stuck and could not have budged any more by himself, his little legs on one side dangled tremblingly in midair, those on the other were painfully crushed against the floor—when from behind his father gave him a hard shove, which was truly his salvation, and bleeding profusely, he flew far into his room. The door was slammed shut with the cane, then at last everything was quiet.

II

It was already dusk when Gregor awoke from his deep, comalike sleep. Even if he had not been disturbed, he would certainly not have woken up much later, for he felt that he had rested and slept long enough, but it seemed to him that a hurried step and a cautious shutting of the door leading to the foyer had awakened him. The light of the electric street-lamps lay in pallid streaks on the ceiling and on the upper parts of the furniture, but underneath, where Gregor was, it was dark. Groping clumsily with his antennae, which he was only now beginning to appreciate, he slowly dragged himself toward the door to see what had been happening there. His left side felt like one single long, unpleasantly tautening scar, and he actually had to limp on his two rows of legs. Besides, one little leg had been seriously injured in the course of the morning's events—it was almost a miracle that only one had been injured—and dragged along lifelessly.

Only after he got to the door did he notice what had really attracted him—the smell of something to eat. For there stood a bowl filled with fresh milk, in which small slices of white bread were floating. He could almost have laughed for joy, since he was even hungrier than he had been in the morning, and he immediately dipped his head into the milk, almost to over his eyes. But he soon drew it back again in disappointment, not only because he had difficulty eating on account of the soreness in his left side—and he could eat only if his whole panting body cooperated—but because he didn't like the milk at all, although it used to be his favorite drink, and that was certainly why his sister had put it in the room; in fact, he turned away from the bowl almost with repulsion and crawled back to the middle of the room.

In the living room, as Gregor saw through the crack in the door, the gas had been lit, but while at this hour of the day his father was in the habit of reading the afternoon newspaper in a loud voice to his mother and sometimes to his sister too, now there wasn't a sound. Well, perhaps this custom of reading aloud, which his sister was always telling him and writing him about, had recently been discontinued altogether. But in all the other rooms too it was just as still, although the apartment certainly was not empty. "What a quiet life the family has been leading," Gregor said to himself, and while he stared rigidly in front of him into the darkness, he felt very proud that he had been able to provide such a life in so nice an apartment for his parents and his sister. But what now if all the peace, the comfort, the contentment were to come to a horrible end? In order not to get involved in such thoughts, Gregor decided to keep moving, and he crawled up and down the room.

During the long evening, first one of the side doors and then the other was opened a small crack and quickly shut again; someone had probably had the urge to come in and then had had second thoughts. Gregor now settled into position right by the living-room door, determined somehow to get the hesitating visitor to come in, or at least to find out who it might be; but the door was not opened again, and Gregor waited in vain. In the morning, when the doors had been locked, everyone had wanted to come in; now that he had opened one of the doors and the others had evidently been opened during the day, no one came in, and now the keys were even inserted on the outside.

It was late at night when the light finally went out in the living room, and now it was easy for Gregor to tell that his parents and his sister had stayed up so long, since, as he could distinctly hear, all three were now retiring on tiptoe. Certainly no one would come in to Gregor until the morning; and so he had ample time to consider undisturbed how best to rearrange his life. But the empty high-ceilinged room in which he was forced to lie flat on the floor made him nervous, without his being able to tell why—since it was, after all, the room in which he had lived for the past five years—and turning half unconsciously and not without a slight feeling of shame, he scuttled under the couch where, although his back was a little crushed and he could not raise his head any more, he immediately felt very comfortable and was only sorry that his body was too wide to go completely under the couch.

There he stayed the whole night, which he spent partly in a sleepy trance, from which hunger pangs kept waking him with a start, partly in worries and vague hopes, all of which, however, led to the conclusion that for the time being he would have to lie low and, by being patient and showing his family every possible consideration, help them bear the inconvenience which he simply had to cause them in his present condition.

Early in the morning—it was still almost night—Gregor had the opportunity of testing the strength of the resolutions he had just made, for his sister, almost fully dressed, opened the door from the foyer and looked in eagerly. She did not see him right away, but when she caught sight of him under the couch—God, he had to be somewhere, he couldn't just fly away—she became so frightened that she lost control of herself and slammed the door shut again. But, as if she felt sorry for her behavior, she immediately opened the door again and came in on tiptoe, as if she were visiting someone seriously ill or perhaps even a stranger. Gregor had pushed his head forward just to the edge of the couch and was watching her. Would she notice that he had left the milk standing, and not because he hadn't been hungry, and would she bring in a dish of something he'd like better? If she were not going to do it of her own free will, he would rather starve than call it to her attention, although, really, he felt an enormous urge to shoot out from under the couch, throw himself at his sister's feet, and beg her for something good to eat. But his sister noticed at once, to her astonishment, that the bowl was still full, only a little milk was spilled around it; she picked it up immediately—not with her bare hands, of course, but with a rag—and carried it out. Gregor was extremely curious to know what she would bring him instead, and he racked his brains on the subject. But he would never have been able to guess what his sister, in the goodness of her heart, actually did. To find out his likes and dislikes, she brought him a wide assortment of things, all spread out on an old newspaper: old, half-rotten vegetables; bones left over from the evening meal, caked with congealed white sauce; some raisins and almonds; a piece of cheese, which two days before Gregor had declared inedible; a plain slice of bread, a slice of bread and butter, and one with butter and salt. In addition to all this she put down some water in the bowl apparently permanently earmarked for Gregor's use. And out of a sense of delicacy, since she knew that Gregor would not eat in front of her, she left hurriedly and even turned the key, just so that Gregor should know that he might make himself as comfortable as he wanted. Gregor's legs began whirring now that he was going to eat. Besides, his bruises must have completely healed, since he no longer felt any handicap, and marveling at this he thought how, over a month ago, he had cut his finger very slightly with a knife and how this wound was still hurting him only the day before yesterday. "Have I become less sensitive?" he thought, already sucking greedily at the cheese, which had immediately and forcibly attracted him ahead of all the other dishes. One right after the other, and with eyes streaming with tears of contentment, he devoured the cheese, the vegetables, and the sauce; the fresh foods, on the other hand, he did not care for; he couldn't even stand their smell and even dragged the things he wanted to eat a bit farther away. He had finished with everything long since and was just lying lazily at the same spot when his sister slowly turned the key as a sign for him to withdraw. That immediately startled him, although he was almost asleep, and he scuttled under the couch again. But it took great self-control for him to stay under the couch even for the short time his sister was in the room, since his body had become a little bloated from the heavy meal, and in his cramped position he could hardly breathe. In between slight attacks of suffocation he watched with bulging eyes as his unsuspecting sister took a broom and swept up, not only his leavings, but even the foods which Gregor had left completely untouched—as if they too were no longer usable—and dumping everything hastily into a pail, which she covered with a wooden lid, she carried everything out. She had hardly turned her back when Gregor came out from under the couch, stretching and puffing himself up.

This, then, was the way Gregor was fed each day, once in the morning, when his parents and the maid[12] were still asleep, and a second time in the afternoon after everyone had had dinner, for then his parents took a short nap again, and the maid could be sent out by his sister on some errand. Certainly they did not want him to starve either, but perhaps they would not have been able to stand knowing any more about his meals than from hearsay, or perhaps his sister wanted to spare them even what was possibly only a minor torment, for really, they were suffering enough as it was.

Gregor could not find out what excuses had been made to get rid of the doctor and the locksmith on that first morning, for since the others could not understand what he said, it did not occur to any of them, not even to his sister, that he could understand what they said, and so he had to be satisfied, when his sister was in the room, with only occasionally hearing her sighs and appeals to the saints.[13] It was only later, when she had begun to get used to everything—there could never, of course, be any question of a complete adjustment—that Gregor sometimes caught a remark which was meant to be friendly or could be interpreted as such. "Oh, he liked what he had today," she would say when Gregor had tucked away a good helping, and in the opposite case, which gradually occurred more and more frequently, she used to say, almost sadly, "He's left everything again."

But if Gregor could not get any news directly, he overheard a great deal from the neighboring rooms, and as soon as he heard voices, he would immediately run to the door concerned and press his whole body against it. Especially in the early days, there was no conversation that was not somehow about him, if only implicitly. For two whole days there were family consultations at every mealtime about how they should cope; this was also the topic of discussion between meals, for at least two members of the family were always at home, since no one probably wanted to stay home alone and it was impossible to leave the apartment completely empty. Besides, on the very first day the maid—it was not completely clear what and how much she knew of what had happened—had begged his mother on bended knees to dismiss her immediately; and when she said good-bye a quarter of an hour later, she thanked them in tears for the dismissal, as if for the greatest favor that had ever been done to her in this house, and made a solemn vow, without anyone asking her for it, not to give anything away to anyone.

Now his sister, working with her mother, had to do the cooking too; of course that did not cause her much trouble, since they hardly ate anything. Gregor was always hearing one of them pleading in vain with one of the others to eat and getting no answer except, "Thanks, I've had enough," or something similar. They did not seem to drink anything either. His sister often asked her father if he wanted any beer and gladly offered to go out for it herself; and when he did not answer, she said, in order to remove any hesitation on his part, that she could also send the janitor's wife to get it, but then his father finally answered with a definite "No," and that was the end of that.

In the course of the very first day his father explained the family's financial situation and prospects to both the mother and the sister. From time to time he got up from the table to get some kind of receipt or notebook out of the little strongbox he had rescued from the collapse of his business five years before. Gregor heard him open the complicated lock and secure it again after taking out what he had been looking for. These explanations by his father were to some extent the first pleasant news Gregor had heard since his imprisonment. He had always believed that his father had not been able to save a penny from the business, at least his father had never told him anything to the contrary, and Gregor, for his part, had never asked him any questions. In those days Gregor's sole concern had been to do everything in his power to make the family forget as quickly as possible the business disaster which had plunged everyone into a state of total despair. And so he had begun to work with special ardor and had risen almost overnight from stock clerk to traveling salesman, which of course had opened up very different money-making possibilities, and in no time his successes on the job were transformed, by means of commissions, into hard cash that could be plunked down on the table at home in front of his astonished and delighted family. Those had been wonderful times, and they had never returned, at least not with the same glory, although later on Gregor earned enough money to meet the expenses of the entire family and actually did so. They had just gotten used to it, the family as well as Gregor, the money was received with thanks and given with pleasure, but no special feeling of warmth went with it any more. Only his sister had remained close to Gregor, and it was his secret plan that she, who, unlike him, loved music and could play the violin movingly, should be sent next year to the Conservatory, regardless of the great expense involved, which could surely be made up for in some other way. Often during Gregor's short stays in the city, the Conservatory would come up in his conversations with his sister, but always merely as a beautiful dream which was not supposed to come true, and his parents were not happy to hear even these innocent allusions; but Gregor had very concrete ideas on the subject and he intended solemnly to announce his plan on Christmas Eve.

Thoughts like these, completely useless in his present state, went through his head as he stood glued to the door, listening. Sometimes out of general exhaustion he could not listen any more and let his head bump carelessly against the door, but immediately pulled it back again, for even the slight noise he made by doing this had been heard in the next room and made them all lapse into silence. "What's he carrying on about in there now?" said his father after a while, obviously turning toward the door, and only then would the interrupted conversation gradually be resumed.

Gregor now learned in a thorough way—for his father was in the habit of often repeating himself in his explanations, partly because he himself had not dealt with these matters for a long time, partly, too, because his mother did not understand everything the first time around—that in spite of all their misfortunes a bit of capital, a very little bit, certainly, was still intact from the old days, which in the meantime had increased a little through the untouched interest. But besides that, the money Gregor had brought home every month—he had kept only a few dollars for himself—had never been completely used up and had accumulated into a tidy principal. Behind his door Gregor nodded emphatically, delighted at this unexpected foresight and thrift. Of course he actually could have paid off more of his father's debt to the boss with this extra money, and the day on which he could have gotten rid of his job would have been much closer, but now things were undoubtedly better the way his father had arranged them.

Now this money was by no means enough to let the family live off the interest; the principal was perhaps enough to support the family for one year, or at the most two, but that was all there was. So it was just a sum that really should not be touched and that had to be put away for a rainy day; but the money to live on would have to be earned. Now his father was still healthy, certainly, but he was an old man who had not worked for the past five years and who in any case could not be expected to undertake too much; during these five years, which were the first vacation of his hardworking yet unsuccessful life, he had gained a lot of weight and as a result had become fairly sluggish. And was his old mother now supposed to go out and earn money, when she suffered from asthma, when a walk through the apartment was already an ordeal for her, and when she spent every other day lying on the sofa under the open window, gasping for breath? And was his sister now supposed to work—who for all her seventeen years was still a child and whom it would be such a pity to deprive of the life she had led until now, which had consisted of wearing pretty clothes, sleeping late, helping in the house, enjoying a few modest amusements, and above all playing the violin? At first, whenever the conversation turned to the necessity of earning money, Gregor would let go of the door and throw himself down on the cool leather sofa which stood beside it, for he felt hot with shame and grief.

Often he lay there the whole long night through, not sleeping a wink and only scrabbling on the leather for hours on end. Or, not balking at the huge effort of pushing an armchair to the window, he would crawl up to the windowsill and, propped up in the chair, lean against the window, evidently in some sort of remembrance of the feeling of freedom he used to have from looking out the window. For, in fact, from day to day he saw things even a short distance away less and less distinctly; the hospital opposite, which he used to curse because he saw so much of it, was now completely beyond his range of vision, and if he had not been positive that he was living in Charlotte Street—a quiet but still very much a city street—he might have believed that he was looking out of his window into a desert where the gray sky and the gray earth were indistinguishably fused. It took his observant sister only twice to notice that his armchair was standing by the window, for her to push the chair back to the same place by the window each time she had finished cleaning the room, and from then on she even left the inside casement of the window open.

If Gregor had only been able to speak to his sister and thank her for everything she had to do for him, he could have accepted her services more easily; as it was, they caused him pain. Of course his sister tried to ease the embarrassment of the whole situation as much as possible, and as time went on, she naturally managed it better and better, but in time Gregor, too, saw things much more clearly. Even the way she came in was terrible for him. Hardly had she entered the room than she would run straight to the window without taking time to close the door—though she was usually so careful to spare everyone the sight of Gregor's room—then tear open the casements with eager hands, almost as if she were suffocating, and remain for a little while at the window even in the coldest weather, breathing deeply. With this racing and crashing she frightened Gregor twice a day; the whole time he cowered under the couch, and yet he knew very well that she would certainly have spared him this if only she had found it possible to stand being in a room with him with the window closed.

One time—it must have been a month since Gregor's metamorphosis, and there was certainly no particular reason any more for his sister to be astonished at Gregor's appearance—she came a little earlier than usual and caught Gregor still looking out the window, immobile and so in an excellent position to be terrifying. It would not have surprised Gregor if she had not come in, because his position prevented her from immediately opening the window, but not only did she not come in, she even sprang back and locked the door; a stranger might easily have thought that Gregor had been lying in wait for her, wanting to bite her. Of course Gregor immediately hid under the couch, but he had to wait until noon before his sister came again, and she seemed much more uneasy than usual. He realized from this that the sight of him was still repulsive to her and was bound to remain repulsive to her in the future, and that she probably had to overcome a lot of resistance not to run away at the sight of even the small part of his body that jutted out from under the couch. So, to spare her even this sight, one day he carried the sheet on his back to the couch—the job took four hours—and arranged it in such a way that he was now completely covered up and his sister could not see him even when she stooped. If she had considered this sheet unnecessary, then of course she could have removed it, for it was clear enough that it could not be for his own pleasure that Gregor shut himself off altogether, but she left the sheet the way it was, and Gregor thought that he had even caught a grateful look when one time he cautiously lifted the sheet a little with his head in order to see how his sister was taking the new arrangement.

During the first two weeks, his parents could not bring themselves to come in to him, and often he heard them say how much they appreciated his sister's work, whereas until now they had frequently been annoyed with her because she had struck them as being a little useless. But now both of them, his father and his mother, often waited outside Gregor's room while his sister straightened it up, and as soon as she came out she had to tell them in great detail how the room looked, what Gregor had eaten, how he had behaved this time, and whether he had perhaps shown a little improvement. His mother, incidentally, began relatively soon to want to visit Gregor, but his father and his sister at first held her back with reasonable arguments to which Gregor listened very attentively and of which he wholeheartedly approved. But later she had to be restrained by force, and then when she cried out, "Let me go to Gregor, he is my unfortunate boy! Don't you understand that I have to go to him?" Gregor thought that it might be a good idea after all if his mother did come in, not every day of course, but perhaps once a week; she could still do everything much better than his sister, who, for all her courage, was still only a child and in the final analysis had perhaps taken on such a difficult assignment only out of childish flightiness.

Gregor's desire to see his mother was soon fulfilled. During the day Gregor did not want to show himself at the window, if only out of consideration for his parents, but he couldn't crawl very far on his few square yards of floor space, either; he could hardly put up with just lying still even at night; eating soon stopped giving him the slightest pleasure, so, as a distraction, he adopted the habit of crawling crisscross over the walls and the ceiling. He especially liked hanging from the ceiling; it was completely different from lying on the floor; one could breathe more freely; a faint swinging sensation went through the body; and in the almost happy absentmindedness which Gregor felt up there, it could happen to his own surprise that he let go and plopped onto the floor. But now, of course, he had much better control of his body than before and did not hurt himself even from such a big drop. His sister immediately noticed the new entertainment Gregor had discovered for himself—after all, he left behind traces of his sticky substance wherever he crawled—and so she got it into her head to make it possible for Gregor to crawl on an altogether wider scale by taking out the furniture which stood in his way—mainly the chest of drawers and the desk. But she was not able to do this by herself; she did not dare ask her father for help; the maid would certainly not have helped her, for although this girl, who was about sixteen, was bravely sticking it out after the previous cook[14] had left, she had asked for the favor of locking herself in the kitchen at all times and of only opening the door on special request. So there was nothing left for his sister to do except to get her mother one day when her father was out. And his mother did come, with exclamations of excited joy, but she grew silent at the door of Gregor's room. First his sister looked to see, of course, that everything in the room was in order; only then did she let her mother come in. Hurrying as fast as he could, Gregor had pulled the sheet down lower still and pleated it more tightly—it really looked just like a sheet accidently thrown over the couch. This time Gregor also refrained from spying from under the sheet; he renounced seeing his mother for the time being and was simply happy that she had come after all. "Come on, you can't see him," his sister said, evidently leading her mother in by the hand. Now Gregor could hear the two frail women moving the old chest of drawers—heavy for anyone—from its place and his sister insisting on doing the harder part of the job herself, ignoring the warnings of her mother, who was afraid that she would overexert herself. It went on for a long time. After struggling for a good quarter of an hour, his mother said that they had better leave the chest where it was, because, in the first place, it was too heavy, they would not finish before his father came, and with the chest in the middle of the room, Gregor would be completely barricaded; and, in the second place, it was not at all certain that they were doing Gregor a favor by removing his furniture. To her the opposite seemed to be the case; the sight of the bare wall was heartbreaking; and why shouldn't Gregor also have the same feeling, since he had been used to his furniture for so long and would feel abandoned in the empty room. "And doesn't it look," his mother concluded very softly—in fact she had been almost whispering the whole time, as if she wanted to avoid letting Gregor, whose exact whereabouts she did not know, hear even the sound of her voice, for she was convinced that he did not understand the words—"and doesn't it look as if by removing his furniture we were showing him that we have given up all hope of his getting better and are leaving him to his own devices without any consideration? I think the best thing would be to try to keep the room exactly the way it was before, so that when Gregor comes back to us again, he'll find everything unchanged and can forget all the more easily what's happened in the meantime."

When he heard his mother's words, Gregor realized that the monotony of family life, combined with the fact that not a soul had addressed a word directly to him, must have addled his brain in the course of the past two months, for he could not explain to himself in any other way how in all seriousness he could have been anxious to have his room cleared out. Had he really wanted to have his warm room, comfortably fitted with furniture that had always been in the family, changed into a cave, in which, of course, he would be able to crawl around unhampered in all directions but at the cost of simultaneously, rapidly, and totally forgetting his human past? Even now he had been on the verge of forgetting, and only his mother's voice, which he had not heard for so long, had shaken him up. Nothing should be removed; everything had to stay; he could not do without the beneficial influence of the furniture on his state of mind; and if the furniture prevented him from carrying on this senseless crawling around, then that was no loss but rather a great advantage.

But his sister unfortunately had a different opinion; she had become accustomed, certainly not entirely without justification, to adopt with her parents the role of the particularly well-qualified expert whenever Gregor's affairs were being discussed; and so her mother's advice was now sufficient reason for her to insist, not only on the removal of the chest of drawers and the desk, which was all she had been planning at first, but also on the removal of all the furniture with the exception of the indispensable couch. Of course it was not only childish defiance and the self-confidence she had recently acquired so unexpectedly and at such a cost that led her to make this demand; she had in fact noticed that Gregor needed plenty of room to crawl around in; and on the other hand, as best she could tell, he never used the furniture at all. Perhaps, however, the romantic enthusiasm of girls her age, which seeks to indulge itself at every opportunity, played a part, by tempting her to make Gregor's situation even more terrifying in order that she might do even more for him. Into a room in which Gregor ruled the bare walls all alone, no human being except Grete was ever likely to set foot.

And so she did not let herself be swerved from her decision by her mother, who, besides, from the sheer anxiety of being in Gregor's room, seemed unsure of herself, soon grew silent, and helped her daughter as best she could to get the chest of drawers out of the room. Well, in a pinch Gregor could do without the chest, but the desk had to stay. And hardly had the women left the room with the chest, squeezing against it and groaning, than Gregor stuck his head out from under the couch to see how he could feel his way into the situation as considerately as possible. But unfortunately it had to be his mother who came back first, while in the next room Grete was clasping the chest and rocking it back and forth by herself, without of course budging it from the spot. His mother, however, was not used to the sight of Gregor, he could have made her ill, and so Gregor, frightened, scuttled in reverse to the far end of the couch but could not stop the sheet from shifting a little at the front. That was enough to put his mother on the alert. She stopped, stood still for a moment, and then went back to Grete.

Although Gregor told himself over and over again that nothing special was happening, only a few pieces of furniture were being moved, he soon had to admit that this coming and going of the women, their little calls to each other, the scraping of the furniture along the floor had the effect on him of a great turmoil swelling on all sides, and as much as he tucked in his head and his legs and shrank until his belly touched the floor, he was forced to admit that he would not be able to stand it much longer. They were clearing out his room; depriving him of everything that he loved; they had already carried away the chest of drawers, in which he kept the fretsaw and other tools; were now budging the desk firmly embedded in the floor, the desk he had done his homework on when he was a student at business college, in high school, yes, even in public school—now he really had no more time to examine the good intentions of the two women, whose existence, besides, he had almost forgotten, for they were so exhausted that they were working in silence, and one could hear only the heavy shuffling of their feet.

And so he broke out—the women were just leaning against the desk in the next room to catch their breath for a minute—changed his course four times, he really didn't know what to salvage first, then he saw hanging conspicuously on the wall, which was otherwise already bare, the picture of the lady all dressed in furs, hurriedly crawled up on it and pressed himself against the glass, which gave a good surface to stick to and soothed his hot belly. At least no one would take away this picture while Gregor completely covered it up. He turned his head toward the living-room door to watch the women when they returned.

They had not given themselves much of a rest and were already coming back; Grete had put her arm around her mother and was practically carrying her. "So what should we take now?" said Grete and looked around. At that her eyes met Gregor's as he clung to the wall. Probably only because of her mother's presence she kept her self-control, bent her head down to her mother to keep her from looking around, and said, though in a quavering and thoughtless voice: "Come, we'd better go back into the living room for a minute." Grete's intent was clear to Gregor, she wanted to bring his mother into safety and then chase him down from the wall. Well, just let her try! He squatted on his picture and would not give it up. He would rather fly in Grete's face.

But Grete's words had now made her mother more anxious than ever; she stepped to one side, caught sight of the gigantic brown blotch on the flowered wallpaper, and before it really dawned on her that what she saw was Gregor, cried in a hoarse, bawling voice: "Oh, God, oh, God!"; and as if giving up completely, she fell with outstretched arms across the couch and did not stir. "You, Gregor!" cried his sister with raised fist and piercing eyes. These were the first words she had addressed directly to him since his metamorphosis. She ran into the next room to get some kind of spirits to revive her mother; Gregor wanted to help too—there was time to rescue the picture—but he was stuck to the glass and had to tear himself loose by force; then he too ran into the next room, as if he could give his sister some sort of advice, as in the old days; but then had to stand behind her doing nothing while she rummaged among various little bottles; moreover, when she turned around she was startled, a bottle fell on the floor and broke, a splinter of glass wounded Gregor in the face, some kind of corrosive medicine flowed around him; now without waiting any longer, Grete grabbed as many little bottles as she could carry and ran with them inside to her mother; she slammed the door behind her with her foot. Now Gregor was cut off from his mother, who was perhaps near death through his fault; he could not dare open the door if he did not want to chase away his sister, who had to stay with his mother; now there was nothing for him to do except wait; and tormented by self-reproaches and worry, he began to crawl, crawled over everything, walls, furniture, and ceiling, and finally in desperation, as the whole room was beginning to spin, fell down onto the middle of the big table.

A short time passed; Gregor lay there prostrate; all around, things were quiet, perhaps that was a good sign. Then the doorbell rang. The maid, of course, was locked up in her kitchen, and so Grete had to answer the door. His father had come home. "What's happened?" were his first words; Grete's appearance must have told him everything. Grete answered in a muffled voice, her face was obviously pressed against her father's chest: "Mother fainted, but she's better now. Gregor's broken out." "I knew it," his father said. "I kept telling you, but you women don't want to listen." It was clear to Gregor that his father had put the worst interpretation on Grete's all-too-brief announcement and assumed that Gregor was guilty of some outrage. Therefore Gregor now had to try to calm his father down, since he had neither the time nor the ability to enlighten him. And so he fled to the door of his room and pressed himself against it for his father to see, as soon as he came into the foyer, that Gregor had the best intentions of returning to his room immediately and that it was not necessary to drive him back; if only the door were opened for him, he would disappear at once.

But his father was in no mood to notice such subtleties; "Ah!" he cried as he entered, in a tone that sounded as if he were at once furious and glad. Gregor turned his head away from the door and lifted it toward his father. He had not really imagined his father looking like this, as he stood in front of him now; admittedly Gregor had been too absorbed recently in his newfangled crawling to bother as much as before about events in the rest of the house and should really have been prepared to find some changes. And yet, and yet—was this still his father? Was this the same man who in the old days used to lie wearily buried in bed when Gregor left on a business trip; who greeted him on his return in the evening, sitting in his bathrobe in the armchair, who actually had difficulty getting to his feet but as a sign of joy only lifted up his arms; and who, on the rare occasions when the whole family went out for a walk, on a few Sundays in June and on the major holidays, used to shuffle along with great effort between Gregor and his mother, who were slow walkers themselves, always a little more slowly than they, wrapped in his old overcoat, always carefully planting down his crutch-handled cane, and, when he wanted to say something, nearly always stood still and assembled his escort around him? Now, however, he was holding himself very erect, dressed in a tight-fitting blue uniform with gold buttons, the kind worn by messengers at banking concerns; above the high stiff collar of the jacket his heavy chin protruded; under his bushy eyebrows his black eyes darted bright, piercing glances; his usually rumpled white hair was combed flat, with a scrupulously exact, gleaming part. He threw his cap—which was adorned with a gold monogram, probably that of a bank—in an arc across the entire room onto the couch, and with the tails of his long uniform jacket slapped back, his hands in his pants pockets, went for Gregor with a sullen look on his face. He probably did not know himself what he had in mind; still he lifted his feet unusually high off the floor, and Gregor staggered at the gigantic size of the soles of his boots. But he did not linger over this, he had known right from the first day of his new life that his father considered only the strictest treatment called for in dealing with him. And so he ran ahead of his father, stopped when his father stood still, and scooted ahead again when his father made even the slightest movement. In this way they made more than one tour of the room, without anything decisive happening; in fact the whole movement did not even have the appearance of a chase because of its slow tempo. So Gregor kept to the floor for the time being, especially since he was afraid that his father might interpret a flight onto the walls or the ceiling as a piece of particular nastiness. Of course Gregor had to admit that he would not be able to keep up even this running for long, for whenever his father took one step, Gregor had to execute countless movements. He was already beginning to feel winded, just as in the old days he had not had very reliable lungs. As he now staggered around, hardly keeping his eyes open in order to gather all his strength for the running; in his obtuseness not thinking of any escape other than by running; and having almost forgotten that the walls were at his disposal, though here of course they were blocked up with elaborately carved furniture full of notches and points—at that moment a lightly flung object hit the floor right near him and rolled in front of him. It was an apple; a second one came flying right after it; Gregor stopped dead with fear; further running was useless, for his father was determined to bombard him. He had filled his pockets from the fruit bowl on the buffet and was now pitching one apple after another, for the time being without taking good aim. These little red apples rolled around on the floor as if electrified, clicking into each other. One apple, thrown weakly, grazed Gregor's back and slid off harmlessly. But the very next one that came flying after it literally forced its way into Gregor's back; Gregor tried to drag himself away, as if the startling, unbelievable pain might disappear with a change of place; but he felt nailed to the spot and stretched out his body in a complete confusion of all his senses. With his last glance he saw the door of his room burst open as his mother rushed out ahead of his screaming sister, in her chemise, for his sister had partly undressed her while she was unconscious in order to let her breathe more freely; saw his mother run up to his father and on the way her unfastened petticoats slide to the floor one by one; and saw as, stumbling over the skirts, she forced herself onto his father, and embracing him, in complete union with him—but now Gregor's sight went dim—her hands clasping his father's neck, begged for Gregor's life.

III

Gregor's serious wound, from which he suffered for over a month—the apple remained imbedded in his flesh as a visible souvenir since no one dared to remove it—seemed to have reminded even his father that Gregor was a member of the family, in spite of his present pathetic and repulsive shape, who could not be treated as an enemy; that, on the contrary, it was the commandment of family duty to swallow their disgust and endure him, endure him and nothing more.

And now, although Gregor had lost some of his mobility probably for good because of his wound, and although for the time being he needed long, long minutes to get across his room, like an old war veteran—crawling above ground was out of the question—for this deterioration of his situation he was granted compensation which in his view was entirely satisfactory: every day around dusk the living-room door—which he was in the habit of watching closely for an hour or two beforehand—was opened, so that, lying in the darkness of his room, invisible from the living room, he could see the whole family sitting at the table under the lamp and could listen to their conversation, as it were with general permission; and so it was completely different from before.

Of course these were no longer the animated conversations of the old days, which Gregor used to remember with a certain nostalgia in small hotel rooms when he'd had to throw himself wearily into the damp bedding. Now things were mostly very quiet. Soon after supper his father would fall asleep in his armchair; his mother and sister would caution each other to be quiet; his mother, bent low under the light, sewed delicate lingerie for a clothing store; his sister, who had taken a job as a salesgirl, was learning shorthand and French in the evenings in order to attain a better position some time in the future. Sometimes his father woke up, and as if he had absolutely no idea that he had been asleep, said to his mother, "Look how long you're sewing again today!" and went right back to sleep, while mother and sister smiled wearily at each other.

With a kind of perverse obstinacy his father refused to take off his official uniform even in the house;[15] and while his robe hung uselessly on the clothes hook, his father dozed, completely dressed, in his chair, as if he were always ready for duty and were waiting even here for the voice of his superior. As a result his uniform, which had not been new to start with, began to get dirty in spite of all the mother's and sister's care, and Gregor would often stare all evening long at this garment, covered with stains and gleaming with its constantly polished gold buttons, in which the old man slept most uncomfortably and yet peacefully.

As soon as the clock struck ten, his mother tried to awaken his father with soft encouraging words and then persuade him to go to bed, for this was no place to sleep properly, and his father badly needed his sleep, since he had to be at work at six o'clock. But with the obstinacy that had possessed him ever since he had become a messenger, he always insisted on staying at the table a little longer, although he invariably fell asleep and then could be persuaded only with the greatest effort to exchange his armchair for bed. However much mother and sister might pounce on him with little admonitions, he would slowly shake his head for a quarter of an hour at a time, keeping his eyes closed, and would not get up. Gregor's mother plucked him by the sleeves, whispered blandishments into his ear, his sister dropped her homework in order to help her mother, but all this was of no use. He only sank deeper into his armchair. Not until the women lifted him up under his arms did he open his eyes, look alternately at mother and sister, and usually say, "What a life. So this is the peace of my old age." And leaning on the two women, he would get up laboriously, as if he were the greatest weight on himself, and let the women lead him to the door, where, shrugging them off, he would proceed independently, while Gregor's mother threw down her sewing, and his sister her pen, as quickly as possible so as to run after his father and be of further assistance.

Who in this overworked and exhausted family had time to worry about Gregor any more than was absolutely necessary? The household was stinted more and more; now the maid was let go after all;[16] a gigantic bony cleaning woman with white hair fluttering about her head came mornings and evenings to do the heaviest work; his mother took care of everything else, along with all her sewing. It even happened that various pieces of family jewelry, which in the old days his mother and sister had been overjoyed to wear at parties and celebrations, were sold, as Gregor found out one evening from the general discussion of the prices they had fetched. But the biggest complaint was always that they could not give up the apartment, which was much too big for their present needs, since no one could figure out how Gregor was supposed to be moved. But Gregor understood easily that it was not only consideration for him which prevented their moving, for he could easily have been transported in a suitable crate with a few air holes; what mainly prevented the family from moving was their complete hopelessness and the thought that they had been struck by a misfortune as none of their relatives and acquaintances had ever been hit. What the world demands of poor people they did to the utmost of their ability; his father brought breakfast for the minor officials at the bank, his mother sacrificed herself to the underwear of strangers, his sister ran back and forth behind the counter at the request of the customers; but for anything more than this they did not have the strength. And the wound in Gregor's back began to hurt anew when mother and sister, after getting his father to bed, now came back, dropped their work, pulled their chairs close to each other and sat cheek to cheek; when his mother, pointing to Gregor's room, said, "Close that door, Grete"; and when Gregor was back in darkness, while in the other room the women mingled their tears or stared dry-eyed at the table.

Gregor spent the days and nights almost entirely without sleep. Sometimes he thought that the next time the door opened he would take charge of the family's affairs again, just as he had done in the old days; after this long while there again appeared in his thoughts the boss and the manager, the salesman and the trainees, the handyman who was so dense, two or three friends from other firms, a chambermaid in a provincial hotel—a happy fleeting memory—a cashier in a millinery store, whom he had courted earnestly but too slowly—they all appeared, intermingled with strangers or people he had already forgotten; but instead of helping him and his family, they were all inaccessible, and he was glad when they faded away. At other times he was in no mood to worry about his family, he was completely filled with rage at his miserable treatment, and although he could not imagine anything that would pique his appetite, he still made plans for getting into the pantry to take what was coming to him, even if he wasn't hungry. No longer considering what she could do to give Gregor a special treat, his sister, before running to business every morning and afternoon, hurriedly shoved any old food into Gregor's room with her foot; and in the evening, regardless of whether the food had only been toyed with or—the most usual case—had been left completely untouched, she swept it out with a swish of the broom. The cleaning up of Gregor's room, which she now always did in the evenings, could not be done more hastily. Streaks of dirt ran along the walls, fluffs of dust and filth lay here and there on the floor. At first, whenever his sister came in, Gregor would place himself in those corners that were particularly offending, meaning by his position in a sense to reproach her. But he could probably have stayed there for weeks without his sister's showing any improvement; she must have seen the dirt as clearly as he did, but she had just decided to leave it. At the same time she made sure—with an irritableness that was completely new to her and which had in fact infected the whole family—that the cleaning of Gregor's room remain her province. One time his mother had submitted Gregor's room to a major housecleaning, which she managed only after employing a couple of pails of water—all this dampness, of course, irritated Gregor too and he lay prostrate, sour and immobile, on the couch—but his mother's punishment was not long in coming. For hardly had his sister noticed the difference in Gregor's room that evening than, deeply insulted, she ran into the living room and, in spite of her mother's imploringly uplifted hands, burst out in a fit of crying, which his parents—his father had naturally been startled out of his armchair—at first watched in helpless amazement; until they too got going; turning to the right, his father blamed his mother for not letting his sister clean Gregor's room; but turning to the left, he screamed at his sister that she would never again be allowed to clean Gregor's room; while his mother tried to drag his father, who was out of his mind with excitement, into the bedroom; his sister, shaken with sobs, hammered the table with her small fists; and Gregor hissed loudly with rage because it did not occur to any of them to close the door and spare him such a scene and a row.

But even if his sister, exhausted from her work at the store, had gotten fed up with taking care of Gregor as she used to, it was not necessary at all for his mother to take her place and still Gregor did not have to be neglected. For now the cleaning woman was there. This old widow, who thanks to her strong bony frame had probably survived the worst in a long life, was not really repelled by Gregor. Without being in the least inquisitive, she had once accidentally opened the door of Gregor's room, and at the sight of Gregor—who, completely taken by surprise, began to race back and forth although no one was chasing him—she had remained standing, with her hands folded on her stomach, marveling. From that time on she never failed to open the door a crack every morning and every evening and peek in hurriedly at Gregor. In the beginning she also used to call him over to her with words she probably considered friendly, like, "Come over here for a minute, you old dung beetle!" or "Look at that old dung beetle!" To forms of address like these Gregor would not respond but remained immobile where he was, as if the door had not been opened. If only they had given this cleaning woman orders to clean up his room every day, instead of letting her disturb him uselessly whenever the mood took her. Once, early in the morning—heavy rain, perhaps already a sign of approaching spring, was beating on the windowpanes—Gregor was so exasperated when the cleaning woman started in again with her phrases that he turned on her, of course slowly and decrepitly, as if to attack. But the cleaning woman, instead of getting frightened, simply lifted up high a chair near the door, and as she stood there with her mouth wide open, her intention was clearly to shut her mouth only when the chair in her hand came crashing down on Gregor's back. "So, is that all there is?" she asked when Gregor turned around again, and she quietly put the chair back in the corner.

Gregor now hardly ate anything anymore. Only when he accidentally passed the food laid out for him would he take a bite into his mouth just for fun, hold it in for hours, and then mostly spit it out again. At first he thought that his grief at the state of his room kept him off food, but it was the very changes in his room to which he quickly became adjusted. His family had gotten into the habit of putting in this room things for which they could not find any other place, and now there were plenty of these, since one of the rooms in the apartment had been rented to three boarders. These serious gentlemen—all three had long beards, as Gregor was able to register once through a crack in the door—were obsessed with neatness, not only in their room, but since they had, after all, moved in here, throughout the entire household and especially in the kitchen. They could not stand useless, let alone dirty junk. Besides, they had brought along most of their own household goods. For this reason many things had become superfluous, and though they certainly weren't salable, on the other hand they could not just be thrown out. All these things migrated into Gregor's room. Likewise the ash can and the garbage can from the kitchen. Whatever was not being used at the moment was just flung into Gregor's room by the cleaning woman, who was always in a big hurry; fortunately Gregor generally saw only the object involved and the hand that held it. Maybe the cleaning woman intended to reclaim the things as soon as she had a chance or else to throw out everything together in one fell swoop, but in fact they would have remained lying wherever they had been thrown in the first place if Gregor had not squeezed through the junk and set it in motion, at first from necessity, because otherwise there would have been no room to crawl in, but later with growing pleasure, although after such excursions, tired to death and sad, he did not budge again for hours.

Since the roomers sometimes also had their supper at home in the common living room, the living-room door remained closed on certain evenings, but Gregor found it very easy to give up the open door, for on many evenings when it was opened he had not taken advantage of it, but instead, without the family's noticing, had lain in the darkest corner of his room. But once the cleaning woman had left the living-room door slightly open, and it also remained opened a little when the roomers came in in the evening and the lamp was lit. They sat down at the head of the table where in the old days his father, his mother, and Gregor had eaten, unfolded their napkins, and picked up their knives and forks. At once his mother appeared in the doorway with a platter of meat, and just behind her came his sister with a platter piled high with potatoes. A thick vapor steamed up from the food. The roomers bent over the platters set in front of them as if to examine them before eating, and in fact the one who sat in the middle, and who seemed to be regarded by the other two as an authority, cut into a piece of meat while it was still on the platter, evidently to find out whether it was tender enough or whether it should perhaps be sent back to the kitchen. He was satisfied, and mother and sister, who had been watching anxiously, sighed with relief and began to smile.

The family itself ate in the kitchen. Nevertheless, before going into the kitchen, his father came into this room and, bowing once, cap in hand, made a turn around the table. The roomers rose as one man and mumbled something into their beards.

When they were alone again, they ate in almost complete silence. It seemed strange to Gregor that among all the different noises of eating he kept picking up the sound of their chewing teeth, as if this were a sign to Gregor that you needed teeth to eat with and that even with the best make of toothless jaws you couldn't do a thing. "I'm hungry enough," Gregor said to himself, full of grief, "but not for these things. Look how these roomers are gorging themselves, and I'm dying!"

On this same evening—Gregor could not remember having heard the violin during the whole time—the sound of violin playing came from the kitchen. The roomers had already finished their evening meal, the one in the middle had taken out a newspaper, given each of the two others a page, and now, leaning back, they read and smoked. When the violin began to play, they became attentive, got up, and went on tiptoe to the door leading to the foyer, where they stood in a huddle. They must have been heard in the kitchen, for his father called, "Perhaps the playing bothers you, gentlemen? It can be stopped right away." "On the contrary," said the middle roomer. "Wouldn't the young lady like to come in to us and play in here where it's much roomier and more comfortable?" "Oh, certainly," called Gregor's father, as if he were the violinist. The boarders went back into the room and waited. Soon Gregor's father came in with the music stand, his mother with the sheet music, and his sister with the violin. Calmly his sister got everything ready for playing; his parents—who had never rented out rooms before and therefore behaved toward the roomers with excessive politeness—did not even dare sit down on their own chairs; his father leaned against the door, his right hand inserted between two buttons of his uniform coat, which he kept closed; but his mother was offered a chair by one of the roomers, and since she left the chair where the roomer just happened to put it, she sat in a corner to one side.

His sister began to play. Father and mother, from either side, attentively followed the movements of her hands. Attracted by the playing, Gregor had dared to come out a little further and already had his head in the living room. It hardly surprised him that lately he was showing so little consideration for the others; once such consideration had been his greatest pride. And yet he would never have had better reason to keep hidden; for now, because of the dust which lay all over his room and blew around at the slightest movement, he too was completely covered with dust; he dragged around with him on his back and along his sides fluff and hairs and scraps of food; his indifference to everything was much too deep for him to have gotten on his back and scrubbed himself clean against the rug, as once he had done several times a day. And in spite of his state, he was not ashamed to inch out a little farther on the immaculate living-room floor.

Admittedly no one paid any attention to him. The family was completely absorbed by the violin-playing; the roomers, on the other hand, who at first had stationed themselves, hands in pockets, much too close behind his sister's music stand, so that they could all have followed the score, which certainly must have upset his sister, soon withdrew to the window, talking to each other in an undertone, their heads lowered, where they remained, anxiously watched by his father. It now seemed only too obvious that they were disappointed in their expectation of hearing beautiful or entertaining violin-playing, had had enough of the whole performance, and continued to let their peace be disturbed only out of politeness. Especially the way they all blew the cigar smoke out of their nose and mouth toward the ceiling suggested great nervousness. And yet his sister was playing so beautifully. Her face was inclined to one side, sadly and probingly her eyes followed the lines of music. Gregor crawled forward a little farther, holding his head close to the floor, so that it might be possible to catch her eye. Was he an animal, that music could move him so? He felt as if the way to the unknown nourishment he longed for were coming to light. He was determined to force himself on until he reached his sister, to pluck at her skirt, and to let her know in this way that she should bring her violin into his room, for no one here appreciated her playing the way he would appreciate it. He would never again let her out of his room—at least not for as long as he lived; for once, his nightmarish looks would be of use to him; he would be at all the doors of his room at the same time and hiss and spit at the aggressors; his sister, however, should not be forced to stay with him, but would do so of her own free will; she should sit next to him on the couch, bending her ear down to him, and then he would confide to her that he had had the firm intention of sending her to the Conservatory, and that, if the catastrophe had not intervened, he would have announced this to everyone last Christmas—certainly Christmas had come and gone?—without taking notice of any objections. After this declaration his sister would burst into tears of emotion, and Gregor would raise himself up to her shoulder and kiss her on the neck which, ever since she started going out to work, she kept bare, without a ribbon or collar.

"Mr. Samsa!" the middle roomer called to Gregor's father and without wasting another word pointed his index finger at Gregor, who was slowly moving forward. The violin stopped, the middle roomer smiled first at his friends, shaking his head, and then looked at Gregor again. Rather than driving Gregor out, his father seemed to consider it more urgent to start by soothing the roomers although they were not at all upset, and Gregor seemed to be entertaining them more than the violin-playing. He rushed over to them and tried with outstretched arms to drive them into their room and at the same time with his body to block their view of Gregor. Now they actually did get a little angry—it was not clear whether because of his father's behavior or because of their dawning realization of having had without knowing it such a next-door neighbor as Gregor. They demanded explanations from his father; in their turn they raised their arms, plucked excitedly at their beards, and, dragging their feet, backed off toward their room. In the meantime his sister had overcome the abstracted mood into which she had fallen after her playing had been so suddenly interrupted; and all at once, after holding violin and bow for a while in her slackly hanging hands and continuing to follow the score as if she were still playing, she pulled herself together, laid the instrument on the lap of her mother—who was still sitting in her chair, fighting for breath, her lungs violently heaving—and ran into the next room, which the roomers, under pressure from her father, were nearing more quickly than before. One could see the covers and bolsters on the beds, obeying his sister's practiced hands, fly up and arrange themselves. Before the boarders had reached the room, she had finished turning down the beds and had slipped out. Her father seemed once again to be gripped by his perverse obstinacy to such a degree that he completely forgot any respect still due his tenants. He drove them on and kept on driving until, already at the bedroom door, the middle boarder stamped his foot thunderingly and thus brought him to a standstill. "I herewith declare," he said, raising his hand and casting his eyes around for Gregor's mother and sister too, "that in view of the disgusting conditions prevailing in this apartment and family"—here he spat curtly and decisively on the floor—"I give notice as of now. Of course I won't pay a cent for the days I have been living here, either; on the contrary, I shall consider taking some sort of action against you with claims that—believe me—will be easy to substantiate." He stopped and looked straight in front of him, as if he were expecting something. And in fact his two friends at once chimed in with the words, "We too give notice as of now." Thereupon he grabbed the doorknob and slammed the door with a bang.

Gregor's father, his hands groping, staggered to his armchair and collapsed into it; it looked as if he were stretching himself out for his usual evening nap, but the heavy drooping of his head, as if it had lost all support, showed that he was certainly not asleep. All this time Gregor had lain quietly at the spot where the roomers had surprised him. His disappointment at the failure of his plan—but perhaps also the weakness caused by so much fasting—made it impossible for him to move. He was afraid with some certainty that in the very next moment a general debacle would burst over him, and he waited. He was not even startled by the violin as it slipped from under his mother's trembling fingers and fell off her lap with a reverberating clang.

"My dear parents," said his sister and by way of an introduction pounded her hand on the table, "things can't go on like this. Maybe you don't realize it, but I do. I won't pronounce the name of my brother in front of this monster, and so all I say is: we have to try to get rid of it. We've done everything humanly possible to take care of it and to put up with it; I don't think anyone can blame us in the least."

"She's absolutely right," said his father to himself. His mother, who still could not catch her breath, began to cough dully behind her hand, a wild look in her eyes.

His sister rushed over to his mother and held her forehead. His father seemed to have been led by Grete's words to more definite thoughts, had sat up, was playing with the cap of his uniform among the plates which were still lying on the table from the roomers' supper, and from time to time looked at Gregor's motionless form.

"We must try to get rid of it," his sister now said exclusively to her father, since her mother was coughing too hard to hear anything. "It will be the death of you two, I can see it coming. People who already have to work as hard as we do can't put up with this constant torture at home, too. I can't stand it anymore either." And she broke out crying so bitterly that her tears poured down onto her mother's face, which she wiped off with mechanical movements of her hand.

"Child," said her father kindly and with unusual understanding, "but what can we do?"

Gregor's sister only shrugged her shoulders as a sign of the bewildered mood that had now gripped her as she cried, in contrast with her earlier confidence.

"If he could understand us," said her father, half questioning; in the midst of her crying Gregor's sister waved her hand violently as a sign that that was out of the question.

"If he could understand us," his father repeated and by closing his eyes, absorbed his daughter's conviction of the impossibility of the idea, "then maybe we could come to an agreement with him. But the way things are——"

"It has to go," cried his sister. "That's the only answer, Father. You just have to try to get rid of the idea that it's Gregor. Believing it for so long, that is our real misfortune. But how can it be Gregor? If it were Gregor, he would have realized long ago that it isn't possible for human beings to live with such a creature, and he would have gone away of his own free will. Then we wouldn't have a brother, but we'd be able to go on living and honor his memory. But as things are, this animal persecutes us, drives the roomers away, obviously wants to occupy the whole apartment and for us to sleep in the gutter. Look, Father," she suddenly shrieked, "he's starting in again!" And in a fit of terror that was completely incomprehensible to Gregor, his sister abandoned even her mother, literally shoved herself off from her chair, as if she would rather sacrifice her mother than stay near Gregor, and rushed behind her father, who, upset only by her behavior, also stood up and half-lifted his arms in front of her as if to protect her.

But Gregor had absolutely no intention of frightening anyone, let alone his sister. He had only begun to turn around in order to trek back to his room; certainly his movements did look peculiar, since his ailing condition made him help the complicated turning maneuver along with his head, which he lifted up many times and knocked against the floor. He stopped and looked around. His good intention seemed to have been recognized; it had only been a momentary scare. Now they all watched him, silent and sad. His mother lay in her armchair, her legs stretched out and pressed together, her eyes almost closing from exhaustion; his father and his sister sat side by side, his sister had put her arm around her father's neck.

Now maybe they'll let me turn around, Gregor thought, and began his labors again. He could not repress his panting from the exertion, and from time to time he had to rest. Otherwise no one harassed him; he was left completely on his own. When he had completed the turn, he immediately began to crawl back in a straight line. He was astonished at the great distance separating him from his room and could not understand at all how, given his weakness, he had covered the same distance a little while ago almost without realizing it. Constantly intent only on rapid crawling, he hardly noticed that not a word, not an exclamation from his family interrupted him. Only when he was already in the doorway did he turn his head—not completely, for he felt his neck stiffening; nevertheless he still saw that behind him nothing had changed except that his sister had stood up. His last glance ranged over his mother, who was now fast asleep.

He was hardly inside his room when the door was hurriedly

slammed shut, firmly bolted, and locked. Gregor was so frightened at the sudden noise behind him that his little legs gave way under him. It was his sister who had been in such a hurry. She had been standing up straight, ready and waiting, then she had leaped forward nimbly, Gregor had not even heard her coming, and she cried "Finally!" to her parents as she turned the key in the lock.

"And now?" Gregor asked himself, looking around in the darkness. He soon made the discovery that he could no longer move at all. It did not surprise him; rather, it seemed unnatural that until now he had actually been able to propel himself on these thin little legs. Otherwise he felt relatively comfortable. He had pains, of course, throughout his whole body, but it seemed to him that they were gradually getting fainter and fainter and would finally go away altogether. The rotten apple in his back and the inflamed area around it, which were completely covered with fluffy dust, already hardly bothered him. He thought back on his family with deep emotion and love. His conviction that he would have to disappear was, if possible, even firmer than his sister's. He remained in this state of empty and peaceful reflection until the tower clock struck three in the morning. He still saw that outside the window everything was beginning to grow light. Then, without his consent, his head sank down to the floor, and from his nostrils streamed his last weak breath.

When early in the morning the cleaning woman came—in sheer energy and impatience she would slam all the doors so hard although she had often been asked not to, that once she had arrived, quiet sleep was no longer possible anywhere in the apartment—she did not at first find anything out of the ordinary on paying Gregor her usual short visit. She thought that he was deliberately lying motionless, pretending that his feelings were hurt; she credited him with unlimited intelligence. Because she happened to be holding the long broom, she tried from the doorway to tickle Gregor with it. When this too produced no results, she became annoyed and jabbed Gregor a little, and only when she had shoved him without any resistance to another spot did she begin to take notice. When she quickly became aware of the true state of things, she opened her eyes wide, whistled softly, but did not dawdle; instead, she tore open the door of the bedroom and shouted at the top of her voice into the darkness: "Come and have a look, it's croaked; it's lying there, dead as a doornail!"

The couple Mr. and Mrs. Samsa sat up in their marriage bed and had a struggle overcoming their shock at the cleaning woman before they could finally grasp her message. But then Mr. and Mrs. Samsa hastily scrambled out of bed, each on his side, Mr. Samsa threw the blanket around his shoulders, Mrs. Samsa came out in nothing but her nightgown; dressed this way, they entered Gregor's room. In the meantime the door of the living room had also opened, where Grete had been sleeping since the roomers had moved in; she was fully dressed, as if she had not been asleep at all; and her pale face seemed to confirm this. "Dead?" said Mrs. Samsa and looked inquiringly at the cleaning woman, although she could scrutinize everything for herself and could recognize the truth even without scrutiny. "I'll say," said the cleaning woman, and to prove it she pushed Gregor's corpse with her broom a good distance sideways. Mrs. Samsa made a movement as if to hold the broom back but did not do it. "Well," said Mr. Samsa, "now we can thank God!" He crossed himself,[17] and the three women followed his example. Grete, who never took her eyes off the corpse, said, "Just look how thin he was. Of course he didn't eat anything for such a long time. The food came out again just the way it went in." As a matter of fact,

Gregor's body was completely flat and dry; this was obvious now for the first time, really, since the body was no longer raised up by his little legs and nothing else distracted the eye.

"Come in with us for a little while, Grete," said Mrs. Samsa with a melancholy smile, and Grete, not without looking back at the corpse, followed her parents into their bedroom. The cleaning woman shut the door and opened the window wide. Although it was early in the morning, there was already some mildness mixed in with the fresh air. After all, it was already the end of March.

The three boarders came out of their room and looked around in astonishment for their breakfast; they had been forgotten. "Where's breakfast?" the middle roomer grumpily asked the cleaning woman. But she put her finger to her lips and then hastily and silently beckoned the boarders to follow her into Gregor's room. They came willingly and then stood, their hands in the pockets of their somewhat shabby jackets, in the now already very bright room, surrounding Gregor's corpse.

At that point the bedroom door opened, and Mr. Samsa appeared in his uniform, his wife on one arm, his daughter on the other. They all looked as if they had been crying; from time to time Grete pressed her face against her father's sleeve.

"Leave my house immediately," said Mr. Samsa and pointed to the door, without letting go of the women. "What do you mean by that?" said the middle roomer, somewhat nonplussed, and smiled with a sugary smile. The two others held their hands behind their back and incessantly rubbed them together, as if in joyful anticipation of a big argument, which could only turn out in their favor. "I mean just what I say," answered Mr. Samsa and with his two companions marched in a straight line toward the roomer. At first the roomer stood still and looked at the floor, as if the thoughts inside his head were fitting themselves together in a new order. "So, we'll go, then," he said and looked up at Mr. Samsa as if, suddenly overcome by a fit of humility, he were asking for further permission even for this decision. Mr. Samsa merely nodded briefly several times, his eyes wide open. Thereupon the roomer actually went immediately into the foyer, taking long strides; his two friends had already been listening for a while, their hands completely still, and now they went hopping right after him, as if afraid that Mr. Samsa might get into the foyer ahead of them and interrupt the contact with their leader. In the foyer all three took their hats from the coatrack, pulled their canes from the umbrella stand, bowed silently, and left the apartment. In a suspicious mood which proved completely unfounded, Mr. Samsa led the two women out onto the landing; leaning over the banister, they watched the three roomers slowly but steadily going down the long flight of stairs, disappearing on each landing at a particular turn of the stairway and a few moments later emerging again; the farther down they got, the more the Samsa family's interest in them wore off, and when a butcher's boy with a carrier on his head came climbing up the stairs with a proud bearing, toward them and then up on past them, Mr. Samsa and the women quickly left the banister and all went back, as if relieved, into their apartment.

They decided to spend this day resting and going for a walk; they not only deserved a break in their work, they absolutely needed one. And so they sat down at the table and wrote three letters of excuse, Mr. Samsa to the management of the bank, Mrs. Samsa to her employer, and Grete to the store owner. While they were writing, the cleaning woman came in to say that she was going, since her morning's work was done. The three letter writers at first simply nodded without looking up, but as the cleaning woman still kept lingering, they looked up, annoyed. "Well?" asked Mr. Samsa. The cleaning woman stood smiling in the doorway, as if she had some great good news to announce to the family but would do so only if she were thoroughly questioned. The little ostrich feather which stood almost upright on her hat and which had irritated Mr. Samsa the whole time she had been with them swayed lightly in all directions. "What do you want?" asked Mrs. Samsa, who inspired the most respect in the cleaning woman. "Well," the cleaning woman answered, and for good-natured laughter could not immediately go on, "look, you don't have to worry about getting rid of the stuff next door. It's already been taken care of." Mrs. Samsa and Grete bent down over their letters, as if to continue writing; Mr. Samsa, who noticed that the cleaning woman was now about to start describing everything in detail, stopped her with a firmly outstretched hand. But since she was not going to be permitted to tell her story, she remembered that she was in a great hurry, cried, obviously insulted, "So long, everyone," whirled around wildly, and left the apartment with a terrible slamming of doors.

"We'll fire her tonight," said Mr. Samsa, but did not get an answer from either his wife or his daughter, for the cleaning woman seemed to have ruined their barely regained peace of mind. They got up, went to the window, and stayed there, holding each other tight. Mr. Samsa turned around in his chair toward them and watched them quietly for a while. Then he called, "Come on now, come over here. Stop brooding over the past. And have a little consideration for me, too." The women obeyed him at once, hurried over to him, fondled him, and quickly finished their letters.

Then all three of them left the apartment together, something they had not done in months, and took the trolley into the open country on the outskirts of the city. The car, in which they were the only passengers, was completely filled with warm sunshine. Leaning back comfortably in their seats, they discussed their prospects for the time to come, and it seemed on closer examination that these weren't bad at all, for all three positions—about which they had never really asked one another in any detail—were exceedingly advantageous and especially promising for the future. The greatest immediate improvement in their situation would come easily, of course, from a change in apartments; they would now take a smaller and cheaper apartment, but one better situated and in every way simpler to manage than the old one, which Gregor had picked for them. While they were talking in this vein, it occurred almost simultaneously to Mr. and Mrs. Samsa, as they watched their daughter becoming livelier and livelier, that lately, in spite of all the troubles which had turned her cheeks pale, she had blossomed into a good-looking, shapely girl. Growing quieter and communicating almost unconsciously through glances, they thought that it would soon be time, too, to find her a good husband. And it was like a confirmation of their new dreams and good intentions when at the end of the ride their daughter got up first and stretched her young body.

Backgrounds

Franz Kafka

From Wedding Preparations in the Country

And besides, can't I do it the way I always did as a child when dangerous matters were involved. I don't even have to go to the country myself, it isn't necessary. I'll send [only] my clothed body. [So I shall send this clothed body.] If it staggers to the door on the way out of my room, the staggering will indicate not fear but its nullity. It is also not a sign of excitement if it stumbles on the stairs, if it goes to the country sobbing, and eats its dinner there in tears. For I, I am meanwhile lying in my bed, all covered up with a yellow-brown blanket, exposed to the breeze that blows in through the barely opened window. . . .

As I lie in bed I assume the shape of a big beetle, a stag beetle or a June beetle, I think. . . .

The form of a big beetle, yes. Then I would pretend it were a matter of hibernating, and I would press my little legs against my bulging body. And I whisper a few words. These are instructions to my sad body, which stands close beside me, bent over. Soon I have finished, it bows, it goes swiftly, and it will do everything the best way possible while I rest.

Letters and Diaries

To Max Brod[1]

October 8, 1912

Dearest Max,

After I had been writing well during the night from Sunday to Monday—I could have gone on writing through the night, and all day, and all night and all day, and finally flown away—and certainly could have written well today too—one page, really only the last dying breath of yesterday's ten, is actually finished—I have to stop for the following reason: My brother-in-law, the factory owner—something which I, in my happy absent-mindedness [*glückliche Zerstreutheit*],[2] had hardly paid attention to—went away early this morning on a business trip that will last ten days to two weeks. While he is away, the factory is really entirely in the hands of the manager; and no employer, least of all one so nervous as my father, would doubt that the most complete fraud is now being perpetrated in the factory. By the way, I also think so, not so much, of course, because of worry about the money but because of ignorance and pangs of conscience.
But, finally, even someone not involved, so far as I can imagine such a person, couldn't doubt very much that my father's fears are justified, even though I may also not forget that in the last analysis *I* cannot see at all why a

factory manager from Germany, even during the absence of my brother-in-law, to whom he is vastly superior in all technical and organizational questions, should not be able to keep things running in the same orderly way as before, since, after all, we are human beings and not thieves. [. . .]

When I maintained to you once recently that nothing from the outside could disturb my writing (I wasn't boasting, of course; just consoling myself), I was thinking only of how my mother whimpers to me almost every evening that I really should have a look at the factory once in a while for my father's peace of mind and how, for his part too, my father has said the same thing, only much nastier, with looks and in other indirect ways. Pleading with me and reproaching me in this way isn't, of course, for the most part, something stupid, since a supervision of my brother-in-law would certainly do him and the factory a lot of good; only—and in this lay the undeniable stupidity of all this talk—I can't carry through this sort of a supervision even in my most lucid moments.

But it's not a question of this for the next two weeks, when all that is needed is for any pair of eyes, even if only mine, to wander about over the factory. And one can't have the slightest objection to their making this demand precisely of me, for in everyone's opinion I am mainly responsible [bear the most guilt, *trage . . . die Hauptschuld*] for founding the factory—to me, of course, it seems that I must have been dreaming when I took over this responsibility [debt, *Schuld*]—and besides there is no one here besides me who could go to the factory, since my parents, whose going is out of the question anyway for other reasons, are right now in the middle of their busiest season (the business also seems to be doing better in the new locale), and today, for example, my mother didn't even come home for lunch.

And so, when this evening my mother started in again with the old complaint and, besides referring to my father's getting embittered and sick on account of me [through my fault, *durch meine Schuld*], also brought up this new argument of my brother-in-law's business trip and the complete abandonment of the factory, and when my younger sister too, who at other times does after all back me up with the true feeling that has recently gone over from me to her, in the same breath abandoned me,[3] with a monstrous lack of judgment, right in front of my mother, and when a wave of bitterness—I don't know if it was only gall—went through my whole body, I saw with perfect clarity that the only alternatives I now had were either waiting until everyone had gone to bed and then jumping out of the window or of going to the factory and sitting in my brother-in-law's office every day for the next two weeks. The first would make it possible for me to cast off all responsibility both for interrupting my writing and for abandoning the factory, the second would certainly interrupt my writing—I can't just rub fourteen nights' sleep out of my eyes—and leave me, if I had enough strength of will and hope, with the prospect of perhaps being able to begin again in two weeks where I left off today.

And so I didn't jump out of the window, and even the temptation of turning this letter into a letter of farewell (my ideas for it are running in a different direction) is not very strong. I stood at the window for a long time and pressed myself against the pane, and several times I felt like frightening the toll collector on the bridge with my fall. But the whole time I felt myself too solid for this decision to dash myself to pieces on the pavement to penetrate me to the right, crucial depth. It also seemed to me that staying alive—even when one talks of nothing, nothing, but an interruption—interrupts my writing less than my death, and that between the beginning of my novel[4] and its continuation in two weeks, I shall somehow move about at the heart of my novel and live in it right in the factory, right in the face of my contented parents.

I put the whole story before you, my dearest Max, not perhaps for judgment, for you really can't pass judgment on it, but since I had firmly resolved to jump without a letter of farewell—before the end one is surely allowed to be tired—I wanted, since I am going to walk back into my room again as its occupant, to write you instead a long letter of meeting again, and here it is. And now a final kiss and good night, so that tomorrow I can be boss of a factory, as they want.

Your Franz

Tuesday, half-past one o'clock, October 1912

And yet—something I may not conceal either—now that it is morning, I hate them all, each in turn, and think that during these two weeks I shall hardly manage words of greeting for them. But hate—and this will once more go against me—surely belongs more outside the window than quietly sleeping in bed. I am far less sure than I was last night.[5]

To Felice Bauer[6]

November 17, 1912

Dearest, [. . .] I was simply too miserable to get out of bed. It also seemed to me that last night my novel[7] got much worse, and I lay in the lowest depths. [. . .] I'll write you again today, even though I still have to run around a lot and shall write down a short story that occurred to me during my misery in bed and oppresses me with inmost intensity.[8]

To Felice Bauer[9]

Night of November 17–18, 1912

Dearest, it is now 1:30 in the morning, the story I proclaimed is a long way from being finished, not a line of the novel has been written today, I am going to bed with little enthusiasm. If only I had the night free and without lifting pen from paper could write right through it till morning! That would be a lovely night.

To Felice Bauer[10]

November 18, 1912

I was just sitting down to yesterday's story with an infinite longing to pour myself into it, obviously stimulated by my despair. Harassed by so much, uncertain of you, completely incapable of coping with the office, in view of the novel's being at a standstill for a day with a wild desire to continue the new, equally cautionary story, for several days and nights worrisomely close to complete insomnia, and with some less important but still upsetting and irritating things in my head—in a word, when I went for my evening walk today, which is already down to half an hour, [. . .] I firmly decided that my only salvation was to write to a man in Silesia whom I got to know fairly well this summer and who, for entire long afternoons, tried to convert me to Jesus.

TO FELICE BAUER[11]

November 23, 1912

It is very late at night. I have put aside my little story, on which I really haven't done anything at all for two evenings now and which in the stillness is beginning to develop into a bigger story. Give it to you to read? How shall I do that, even if it were already finished? It is written quite illegibly, and even if that weren't an obstacle—for up until now I certainly haven't spoiled you with beautiful handwriting—I still don't want to send you anything to read. I want to read it aloud to you. Yes, that would be fine, to read this story aloud to you and be forced to hold your hand, for the story is a little horrible. It is called *The Metamorphosis*, it would give you a real scare [. . .]. I am too depressed now, and perhaps I shouldn't have written to you at all. But today the hero of my little story also had a very bad time, and yet this is only the latest rung of his misfortune, which is now becoming permanent.

TO FELICE BAUER[12]

November 24, 1912

What sort of exceptionally repulsive story is this, which I am now once again putting aside in order to refresh myself with thoughts of you. It has already advanced a bit past the halfway mark, and on the whole I am not dissatisfied with it; but it is infinitely repulsive; and such things, you see, rise up from the same heart in which you dwell and which you put up with as your dwelling place. But don't be unhappy about this, for who knows, the more I write and the more I free myself, the purer and more worthy of you I may become, but no doubt there is still a lot more of me to be gotten rid of, and the nights can never be long enough for this business which, incidentally, is extremely voluptuous.

To Felice Bauer[13]

November 24, 1912

Now that I've mentioned the trip to Kratzau, I can't get this annoying thought out of my head. My little story would certainly have been finished tomorrow, but now I have to leave at 6 tomorrow evening, arrive at Reichenberg at 10, and go on to Kratzau at 7 the next morning to appear in court.

To Felice Bauer[14]

November 25, 1912

Well, today, dearest, I have to put aside my story, which I didn't work on today nearly as much as yesterday, and on account of the damned Kratzau trip shelve it for a day or two. I'm so unhappy about this, even if, as I hope, the story won't suffer too much, though I still need another 3–4 evenings to finish it. By not "suffering too much," I mean that the story is, unfortunately, already damaged by my method of working on it. This kind of story should be written with at most one interruption, in two ten-hour bouts: then it would have the natural thrust and charge it had in my head last Sunday. But I don't have twice ten hours at my disposal. So one has to try to do the best one can, since the best has been denied to one. What a pity that I can't read it to you—a great pity—for example, every Sunday morning. Not in the afternoon, I wouldn't have time then, that's when I have to write to you.

To Felice Bauer[15]

November 26, 1912

It was a horrible trip, dearest. [. . .] One should never travel: better be insubordinate at the office if there's work to be done at home that requires all one's strength. This eternal worry, which, incidentally, I still have now, that the trip will harm my little story, that I won't be able to write any more, etc.

To Felice Bauer[16]

November 27, 1912

I sit here all alone in the night, and, as today and yesterday, haven't written particularly well—the story lurches forward rather drearily and monotonously, and the requisite clarity illuminates it only for moments. [. . .] Now, however, I was firmly determined to use [the Christmas vacation] just for my novel and perhaps even to finish it. Today, when the novel has lain quiet for over a week—and the new story, though nearing its end, has been trying to convince me for the past two days that I have gotten stuck—I really should have to keep to that decision even more firmly.

To Felice Bauer[17]

December 1, 1912

After concluding the struggle with my little story—a third section, however, quite definitely [. . .] the last, has begun to take shape—I must absolutely say good night to you, dearest.

To Felice Bauer[18]

December 1, 1912

Just a few words, it's late, very late, and tomorrow there's a lot of work to be done; I've finally caught fire a bit with my little story, my heart wants to drive me with its beating further into it. However, I must try to get myself out of it as best I can, and since this will be hard work, and it will be hours before I get to sleep. I must hurry to bed. [. . .] Dearest, I wish I could still say something amusing, but nothing occurs to me naturally; furthermore, on the last page of my story open before me, all 4 characters are crying or at any rate are in a most mournful mood.

To Felice Bauer[19]

December 3, 1912

I really should have kept on writing all night long. It would have been my duty, for I'm right at the end of my little story, and uniformity and the fire of consecutive hours would do this ending an unbelievable amount of good. Who knows, besides, whether I shall still be able to write tomorrow after the reading,[20] which I'm cursing now. Nevertheless—I'm stopping, I won't risk it. As a result of my writing, which I haven't been doing by any means for long with this sort of coherence and regularity, I have turned from being a by no means exemplary but in some ways still quite useful employee [. . .] into a horror for my boss. My desk in the office was certainly never orderly, but now it is piled high with a chaotic heap of papers and files. I have a rough idea of whatever lies on top, but I suspect nothing down below except terrors. Sometimes I think I can almost hear myself being ground to bits by my writing, on the one hand, and by the office, on the other. Then, again, there are times when I keep them both relatively well-balanced, especially when at home I've written badly, but I'm afraid I am gradually losing this ability (I don't mean of writing badly).

To Felice Bauer[21]

Night of December 4–5, 1912

Oh dearest, infinitely beloved, it is really too late now for my little story, just as I feared it would be; it will stare up at the sky unfinished until tomorrow night.

To Felice Bauer[22]

Presumably during the night of December 5–6, 1912

Cry, dearest, cry, the time for crying has come! The hero of my little story died a little while ago. If it is of any comfort to you, learn now that he died peaceably enough and reconciled with everything. The story itself is not yet completely finished: I'm no longer in the right mood for it now, and I am leaving the ending for tomorrow. It is also already very late, and I had enough to do to get over yesterday's disturbance.[23] It's a pity that in many passages of the story my states of exhaustion and other interruptions and extraneous worries are clearly inscribed; it could certainly have been done more purely: this can be seen precisely from the charming pages. That is exactly this persistently nagging feeling: I myself, I, with the creative powers that I feel in me, quite apart from their strength and endurance, could in more favorable circumstances of life have achieved a purer, more compelling, better organized work than the one which now exists. It is the one feeling that no amount of reason can dissuade me of, despite the fact, of course, that it is none other than reason that is right—which says that, just as there are no circumstances other than real ones, one cannot take any other ones into account, either. However that may be, I hope to finish the story tomorrow and the day after tomorrow throw myself back onto the novel.[24]

To Felice Bauer[25]

December 6–7, 1912

Dearest, listen now: my little story is finished, but today's ending does not make me happy at all; it really could have been better, no doubt about that.

To Felice Bauer[26]

March 1, 1913

Just a few words, dearest. A lovely evening at Max's. I read myself into a frenzy with my story. Then we let ourselves go and laughed a lot.

Diary[27]

October 20, 1913

I have been reading *The Metamorphosis* at home, and I find it bad.

Diary[28]

January 19, 1914

Great antipathy to *The Metamorphosis.* Unreadable ending. Imperfect almost to the core. It would have been much better if I had not been interrupted at the time by the business trip.

To Grete Bloch[29]

April 21, 1914

Whether you might look forward to the "story" [*The Metamorphosis*]? I don't know, you did not like "The Stoker."[30] Still the "story" is looking forward to you, there's no doubt about that. Incidentally, the heroine's name is Grete, and she does not dishonor you, at least not in the first part. Later on, though, when the torment becomes too great, she gives up and starts a life of her own, abandoning the one who needs her. An old story, by the way, more than a year old; at that time I hadn't begun to appreciate the name Grete and learned to do so only in the course of writing the story.

Diary[31]

August 6, 1914

From the standpoint of literature my fate is very simple. The sense for the representation of my dreamlike inner life has rendered everything else trivial, and it has withered in a terrible way and does not stop withering. Nothing else can ever satisfy me. But my strength for that representation is not to be counted on, perhaps it has already vanished forever, perhaps it actually will come over me once again; the circumstances of my life by no means favor its return. And so I waver, fly incessantly to the summit of the mountain but can keep myself on top for hardly a moment. Others waver too, but in lesser regions, with greater powers; if they threaten to fall, they are caught up by the kinsman who walks beside them for this purpose. But I waver on the heights; it is not a death, alas, but the eternal torments of dying.

To Kurt Wolff Publishing Company[32]

Dear Sir, You recently wrote that Ottomar Starke is going to do an illustration for the title page of *The Metamorphosis*. Now I have had a slight [. . .] probably wholly unnecessary shock. It occurred to me that Starke [. . .]might want, let us say, to draw the insect itself. Not that, please, not that! I don't want to restrict his authority but only to make this request from my own naturally better knowledge of the story. The insect itself cannot be drawn. It cannot even be shown at a distance. [. . .] If I might make suggestions for an illustration, I would choose such scenes as the parents and the office manager in front of the closed door or, even better, the parents and the sister in the room with the lights on, while the door to the totally dark adjoining room is open.

To Felice Bauer[33]

October 7, 1916

Dearest, [. . .] Incidentally, won't you tell me what I really am? In the latest issue of the *Neue Rundschau, The Metamorphosis* is mentioned and rejected on reasonable grounds; then there are these lines, more or less: "There is something *ur*-German about K's art of narration."[34] In Max's essay, on the other hand, "K's narratives are among the most Jewish documents of our time." A painful case. Am I a circus rider on 2 horses? Unfortunately, I'm not a rider, but lie prostrate on the ground.

To Felice Bauer[35]

December 7, 1916

Incidentally, in Prague I also remembered Rilke's words.[36] After some very kind things about "The Stoker" he said that neither in *The Metamorphosis* nor in "In the Penal Colony" had the same rigor [*Konsequenz*] been achieved. This remark is not immediately understandable, but it is perceptive.

Letter to His Father[37]

November 1919

[Kafka imagines his father speaking to him.]

You have in fact gotten it into your head to live completely off me. I admit that we are fighting with each other, but there are two kinds of fighting. The chivalrous fight, where the powers of independent opponents compete with each other: each is his own man, loses on his own, wins on his own. And the fight of the vermin, which not only stings but also sucks blood for its self-preservation. That is after all what the real professional soldier is, and that's what you are. You are unfit for life; but in order to be able to settle down in it comfortably, without worries and without self-reproaches, you prove that I took all your fitness for life out of you and put it into my pocket. What does it matter to you now if you're unfit for life: it's my responsibility. But you calmly stretch yourself out and let yourself be dragged body and soul through life by me.

Letter to Elli Hermann[38]

Fall 1921

What Swift means [by the sentence "Parents are the last of all others to be trusted with the education of their own children"][39] is:

Every typical family at first represents only an animal connection, to a certain extent a single organism, a single bloodstream. Thus, thrown back only upon itself, it cannot get beyond itself; it cannot create a new human being only from itself; if it tries to do so through family education, it is a kind of spiritual incest.

The family, then, is an organism, but an extremely complicated and unstable one; like every organism it too continually strives for equilibrium. To the extent that this striving for equilibrium goes on between parents and children, [. . .] it is called education. Why it is called that is incomprehensible, for there is no trace here of real education, that is, the calm, selflessly-loving unfolding of the abilities of a developing human being or even the calm tolerance of its independent unfolding. Rather, it is precisely only the mostly convulsive attempt of an animal organism to achieve equilibrium—one that for many years at least has been condemned to the most acute instability and which in distinction to the individual human animal can be called the family animal.

The reason for the absolute impossibility of immediately achieving a just equilibrium (and only a just equilibrium is a true equilibrium, only it can endure) within this family animal is the unequal rank of its parts, that is, the monstrous dominance of the parent pair over the children for many years. As a result, while their children are growing up, the parents arrogate to themselves the sole prerogative of representing the family not only to the outside world but also within the inner spiritual organization: thus they deprive their children, step by step, of the right to their own personality and from then on can make them incapable of ever asserting this right in a healthy way, a misfortune which can later befall the parents not much less gravely than the children.

The essential difference between real education and family education is that the first is a human affair, the second a family affair. In the human world every individual has his place or at least the possibility of being destroyed in his own fashion, but in a family in the clutches of the parents, only quite particular kinds of individuals have a place—those who conform to quite particular demands and furthermore to the deadlines imposed by the parents. If they don't conform, they are not, say, cast out—that would be very fine, but it is impossible, for after all we are dealing with an organism—but are instead cursed or devoured or both. This devouring doesn't happen physically as in the case of the old archetype of the parent in Greek mythology (Kronos, who gobbled up his sons—that most honest of fathers), but perhaps Kronos preferred his method to the usual ones precisely out of pity for his children.

LETTER TO MAX BROD[40]

July 5, 1922

I am, to put it first quite generally, afraid of the trip. [. . .] But it is not fear of the trip itself. [. . .] Rather, it is the fear of change, fear of attracting the attention of the gods to myself by an act great for my condition.

When during last night's sleepless night I let everything run back and forth again and again between my aching temples, I once more became aware of what I had almost forgotten in the relative calm of the past days—what a weak or even nonexistent ground I live on, over a darkness out of which the dark power emerges when it wills and, without bothering about my stammering, destroys my life. Writing maintains me, but isn't it more correct to say that it maintains this sort of life? Of course I don't mean by this that my life is better when I don't write. Rather it is much worse then and wholly intolerable and must end in madness. But that [is true], of course, only under the condition that I, as is actually the case, even when I don't write, am a writer; and a writer who doesn't write is, to be sure, a monster [*Unding*] asking for madness.

But what is it to be a writer? Writing is a sweet, wonderful reward, but its price? During the night the answer was transparently clear to me: it is the reward for service to the devil. This descent to the dark powers, this unbinding of spirits by nature bound, dubious embraces and whatever else may go on below, of which one no longer knows anything above ground, when in the sunlight one writes stories. Perhaps there is another kind of writing, I know only this one; in the night, when anxiety does not let me sleep, I know only this. And what is devilish in it seems to me quite clear. It is vanity and the craving for enjoyment, which is forever whirring around one's own form or even another's—the movement then multiplies itself, it becomes a solar system of vanities—and enjoys it. What a naive person sometimes wishes: "I would like to die and watch the others cry over me," is what such a writer constantly experiences: he dies (or he does not live) and continually cries over himself. From this comes a terrible fear of death, which does not have to manifest itself as the fear of death but can also emerge as the fear of change [. . .].

The reasons for his fear of death can be divided into two main groups. First, he is terribly afraid of dying because he hasn't yet lived. By this I don't mean that to live, wife and child and field and cattle are necessary. What is necessary for life is only the renunciation of self-delight: to move into the house instead of admiring it and decking it with wreathes. Countering this, one could say that that is fate and put into no man's hands. But then why does one feel remorse, why doesn't the remorse stop? To make oneself more beautiful, more tasty? That too. But why, over and beyond this, in such nights, is the keyword always: I could live, but I do not.

The second main reason—perhaps there is only the one, at the moment I can't quite tell the two apart—is the consideration: "What I have played at will really happen. I have not ransomed myself by writing. All my life I have been dead, and now I shall really die. My life was sweeter than that of the others, my death will be that much more terrible. The writer in me of course will die at once, for such a figure has no basis, has no substance, isn't even of dust; it is only a little bit possible in the maddest earthly life, it is only a construction of the craving for enjoyment. This is the writer. But I myself cannot live on, as indeed I have not lived, I have remained clay, I have not turned the spark into a fire but used it only for the illumination of my corpse." It will be a peculiar burial: the writer, hence, a thing without existence, consigns the old corpse, corpse from the beginning, to the grave. I am enough of a writer to want to enjoy it with all my sense, in total self-forgetfulness—not wakefulness, self-forgetfulness is the first prerequisite of literature—or what amounts to the same thing, to want to tell the story of it, but that won't happen any more. But why do I speak only of real dying? It is after all the same thing in life. I sit here in the comfortable position of the writer, ready for anything beautiful, and must watch idly—for what can I do besides write—as my real self, this poor defenseless being (the writer's existence is an argument against the soul, for the soul has evidently abandoned the real self, but has only become a writer, has not been able to get any further; ought its parting from the self be able to weaken the soul so much?) for any old reason, now, for a little trip [. . .], is pinched, thrashed, and almost ground to bits by the devil. What right have I to be shocked, I who was not at home, when the house suddenly collapses; for do I know what preceded the collapse, didn't I wander off, abandoning the house to all the powers of evil?

Critical Essays

The I Without a Self

W. H. Auden

The joys of this life are not its own, but our dread of ascending to a higher life: the torments of this life are not its own, but our self-torment because of that dread.

Franz Kafka

Kafka is a great, perhaps the greatest, master of the pure parable, a literary genre about which a critic can say very little worth saying. The reader of a novel, or the spectator at a drama, though novel and drama may also have a parabolic significance, is confronted by a feigned history, by characters, situations, actions which, though they may be analogous to his own, are not identical. Watching a performance of *Macbeth*, for example, I see particular historical persons involved in a tragedy of their own making: I may compare Macbeth with myself and wonder what I should have done and felt had I been in his situation, but I remain a spectator, firmly fixed in my own time and place. But I cannot read a pure parable in this way. Though the hero of a parable may be given a proper name (often, though, he may just be called "a certain man" or "K") and a definite historical and geographical setting, these particulars are irrelevant to the meaning of parable. To find out what, if anything, a parable means, I have to surrender my objectivity and identify myself with what I read. The "meaning" of a parable, in fact, is different for every reader. In consequence there is nothing a critic can do to "explain" it to others. Thanks to his superior knowledge of artistic and social history, of language, of human nature even, a good critic can make others see things in a novel or a play which, but for him, they would never have seen for themselves. But if he tries to interpret a parable, he will only reveal himself. What he writes will be a description of what the parable has done to him; of what it may do to others he does not and cannot have any idea.

Sometimes in real life one meets a character and thinks, "This man comes straight out of Shakespeare or Dickens," but nobody ever met a Kafka character. On the other hand, one can have experiences which one recognizes as Kafkaesque, while one would never call an experience of one's own Dickensian or Shakespearian. During the war, I had spent a long and tiring day in the Pentagon. My errand done, I hurried down long corridors eager to get home, and came to a turnstile with a guard standing beside it. "Where are you going?" said the guard. "I'm trying to get out," I replied. "You are out," he said. For the moment I felt I was K.

In the case of the ordinary novelist or playwright, a knowledge of his personal life and character contributes almost nothing to one's understanding of his work, but in the case of a writer of parables like Kafka, biographical information is, I believe, a great help, at least in a negative way, by preventing one from making false readings. (The "true" readings are always many.)

In the new edition of Max Brod's biography, he describes a novel by a Czech writer, Božvena Něvmcová (1820–1862), called *The Grandmother.* The setting is a village in the Riesengebirge which is dominated by a castle. The villagers speak Czech, the inhabitants of the castle German. The Duchess who owns the castle is kind and good, but she is often absent on her travels and between her and the peasants are interposed a horde of insolent household servants and selfish, dishonest officials, so that the Duchess has no idea of what is really going on in the village. At last the heroine of the story succeeds in getting past the various barriers to gain a personal audience with the Duchess, to whom she tells the truth, and all ends happily.

What is illuminating about this information is that the castle officials in Něvmcová are openly presented as being evil, which suggests that those critics who have thought of the inhabitants of Kafka's castle as agents of Divine Grace were mistaken, and that Erich Heller's reading is substantially correct.

> The castle of Kafka's novel is, as it were, the heavily fortified garrison of a company of Gnostic demons, successfully holding an advanced position against the manoeuvres of an impatient soul. I do not know of any conceivable idea of divinity which could justify those interpreters who see in the castle the residence of "divine law and divine grace." Its officers are totally indifferent to good if they are not positively wicked. Neither in their decrees nor in their activities is there discernible any trace of love, mercy, charity or majesty. In their icy detachment they inspire no awe, but fear and revulsion.

Dr. Brod also publishes for the first time a rumor which, if true, might have occurred in a Kafka story rather than in his life, namely, that, without his knowledge, Kafka was the father of a son who died in 1921 at the age of seven. The story cannot be verified since the mother was arrested by the Germans in 1944 and never heard of again.

Remarkable as *The Trial* and *The Castle* are, Kafka's finest work, I think, is to be found in the volume *The Great Wall of China*, all of it written during the last six years of his life. The world it portrays is still the world of his earlier books and one cannot call it euphoric, but the tone is lighter. The sense of appalling anguish and despair which make stories like "The Penal Colony" almost unbearable, has gone. Existence may be as difficult and frustrating as ever, but the characters are more humorously resigned to it.

Of a typical story one might say that it takes the formula of the heroic Quest and turns it upside down. In the traditional Quest, the goal—a Princess, the Fountain of Life, etc.—is known to the hero before he starts. This goal is far distant and he usually does not know in advance the way thither nor the dangers which beset it, but there are other beings who know both and give him accurate directions and warnings. Moreover the goal is publicly recognizable as desirable. Everybody would like to achieve it, but it can only be reached by the Predestined Hero. When three brothers attempt the Quest in turn, the first two are found wanting and fail because of their arrogance and self-conceit, while the youngest succeeds, thanks to his humility and kindness of heart. But the youngest, like his two elders, is always perfectly confident that he will succeed.

In a typical Kafka story, on the other hand, the goal is peculiar to the hero himself: he has no competitors. Some beings whom he encounters try to help him, more are obstructive, most are indifferent, and none has the faintest notion of the way. As one of the aphorisms puts it: "There is a goal but no way; what we call the way is mere wavering." Far from being confident of success, the Kafka hero is convinced from the start that he is doomed to fail, as he is also doomed, being who he is, to make prodigious and unending efforts to reach it. Indeed, the mere desire to reach the goal is itself a proof, not that he is one of the Elect, but that he is under a special curse.

> Perhaps there is only one cardinal sin: impatience. Because of impatience we were driven out of Paradise, because of impatience we cannot return.
>
> Theoretically, there exists a perfect possibility of happiness: to believe in the indestructible element in oneself and not strive after it.

In all previous versions of the Quest, the hero knows what he ought to do and his one problem is "Can I do it?" Odysseus knows he must not listen to the song of the sirens, a knight in quest of the Sangreal knows he must remain chaste, a detective knows he must distinguish between truth and falsehood. But for K the problem is "What ought I to do?" He is neither tempted, confronted with a choice between good and evil, nor carefree, content with the sheer exhilaration of motion. He is certain that it matters enormously what he does *now*, without knowing at all what that ought to be. If he *guesses* wrong, he must not only suffer the same consequences as if he had *chosen* wrong, but also feel the same responsibility. If the instructions and advice he receives seem to him absurd or contradictory, he cannot interpret this as evidence of malice or guilt in others; it may well be proof of his own.

The traditional Quest Hero has *arete*, either manifest, like Odysseus, or concealed, like the fairy tale hero; in the first case, successful achievement of the Quest adds to his glory, in the second it reveals that the apparent nobody is a glorious hero: to become a hero, in the traditional sense, means acquiring the right, thanks to one's exceptional gifts and deeds, to say *I*. But K is an *I* from the start, and in this fact alone, that he exists, irrespective of any gifts or deeds, lies his guilt.

If the K of *The Trial* were innocent, he would cease to be K and become nameless like the fawn in the wood in *Through the Looking-Glass*. In *The Castle, K*, the letter, wants to become a word, *land-surveyor*, that is to say, to acquire a self like everybody else but this is precisely what he is not allowed to acquire.

The world of the traditional Quest may be dangerous, but it is open: the hero can set off in any direction he fancies. But the Kafka world is closed; though it is almost devoid of sensory properties, it is an intensely physical world. The objects and faces in it may be vague, but the reader feels himself hemmed in by their suffocating presence: in no other imaginary world, I think, is everything so *heavy*. To take a single step exhausts the strength. The hero feels himself to be a prisoner and tries to escape but perhaps imprisonment is the proper state for which he was created, and freedom would destroy him.

> The more horse you yoke, the quicker everything will go—not the rending of the block from its foundation, which is impossible, but the snapping of the traces and with that the gay and empty journey.

The narrator hero of "The Burrow" for example, is a beast of unspecified genus, but, presumably, some sort of badger-like animal, except that he is carnivorous. He lives by himself without a mate and never encounters any other member of his own species. He also lives in a perpetual state of fear lest he be persued and attacked by other animals—"My enemies are countless," he says—but we never learn what they may be like and we never actually encounter one. His preoccupation is with the burrow which has been his lifework. Perhaps, when he first began excavating this, the idea of a burrow-fortress was more playful than serious, but the bigger and better the burrow becomes, the more he is tormented by the question: "Is it possible to construct the absolutely impregnable burrow?" This is a torment because he can never be certain that there is not some further precaution of which he has not thought. Also the burrow he has spent his life constructing has become a precious thing which he must defend as much as he would defend himself.

> One of my favorite plans was to isolate the Castle Keep from its surroundings, that is to say to restrict the thickness of the walls to about my own height, and leave a free space of about the same width all around the Castle Keep . . . I had always pictured this free space, and not without reason, as the loveliest imaginable haunt. What a joy to lie pressed against the rounded outer wall, pull oneself up, let oneself slide down again, miss one's footing and find oneself on firm earth, and play all these games literally upon the Castle Keep and not inside it; to avoid the Castle Keep, to rest one's eyes from it whenever one wanted, to postpone the joy of seeing it until later and yet not have to do without it, but literally hold it safe between one's claws . . .

He begins to wonder if, in order to defend it, it would not be better to hide in the bushes outside near its hidden entrance and keep watch. He considers the possibility of enlisting the help of a confederate to share the task of watching, but decides against it.

> . . . would he not demand some counter-service from me; would he not at least want to see the burrow? That in itself, to let anyone freely into my burrow, would be exquisitely painful to me. I built it for myself, not for visitors, and I think I would refuse to admit him . . . I simply could not admit him, for either I must let him go in first by himself, which is simply unimaginable, or we must both descend at the same time, in which case the advantage I am supposed to derive from him, that of being kept watch over, would be lost. And what trust can I really put in him? . . . It is comparatively easy to trust any one if you are supervising him or at least supervise him; perhaps it is possible to trust some one at a distance; but completely to trust some one outside the burrow when you are inside the burrow, that is, in a different world, that, it seems to me, is impossible.

One morning he is awakened by a faint whistling noise which he cannot identify or locate. It might be merely the wind, but it might be some enemy. From now on, he is in the grip of a hysterical anxiety. Does this strange beast, if it is a beast, know of his existence and, if so, what does it know. The story breaks off without a solution. Edwin Muir has suggested that the story would have ended with the appearance of the invisible enemy to whom the hero would succumb. I am doubtful about this. The whole point of the parable seems to be that the reader is never to know if the narrator's subjective fears have any objective justification.

The more we admire Kafka's writings, the more seriously we must reflect upon his final instructions that they should be destroyed. At first one is tempted to see in this request a fantastic spiritual pride, as if he had said to himself: "To be worthy of me, anything I write must be absolutely perfect. But no piece of writing, however excellent, can be perfect. Therefore, let what I have written be destroyed as unworthy of me." But everything which Dr. Brod and other friends tell us about Kafka as a person makes nonsense of this explanation.

It seems clear that Kafka did not think of himself as an artist in the traditional sense, that is to say, as a being dedicated to a particular function, whose personal existence is accidental to his artistic productions. If there ever was a man of whom it could be said that he "hungered and thirsted after righteousness," it was Kafka. Perhaps he came to regard what he had written as a personal device he had employed in his search for God. "Writing," he once wrote, "is a form of prayer," and no person whose prayers are genuine, desires them to be overheard by a third party. In another passage, he describes his aim in writing thus:

> Somewhat as if one were to hammer together a table with painful and methodical technical efficiency, and simultaneously do nothing at all, and not in such a way that people could say: "Hammering a table together is nothing to him," but rather "Hammering a table together is really hammering a table together to him, but at the same time it is nothing," whereby certainly the hammering would have become still bolder, still surer, still more real, and if you will, still more senseless.

But whatever the reasons, Kafka's reluctance to have his work published should at least make a reader wary of the way in which he himself reads it. Kafka may be one of those writers who are doomed to be read by the wrong public. Those on whom their effect would be most beneficial are repelled and on those whom they most fascinate their effect may be dangerous, even harmful.

I am inclined to believe that one should only read Kafka when one is in a eupeptic state of physical and mental health and, in consequence, tempted to dismiss any scrupulous heart-searching as a morbid fuss. When one is in low spirits, one should probably keep away from him, for, unless introspection is accompanied, as it always was in Kafka, by an equal passion for the good life, it all too easily degenerates into a spineless narcissistic fascination with one's own sin and weakness.

No one who thinks seriously about evil and suffering can avoid entertaining as a possibility the gnostic-manichean notion of the physical world as intrinsically evil, and some of Kafka's sayings come perilously close to accepting it.

> There is only a spiritual world; what we call the physical world is the evil in the spiritual one.
>
> The physical world is not an illusion, but only its evil which, however, admittedly constitutes our picture of the physical world.

Kafka's own life and his writings as a whole are proof that he was not a gnostic at heart, for the true gnostic can always be recognized by certain characteristics. He regards himself as a member of a spiritual elite and despises all earthly affections and social obligations. Quite often, he also allows himself an anarchic immorality in his sexual life, on the grounds that, since the body is irredeemable, a moral judgment cannot be applied to its actions.

Neither Kafka, as Dr. Brod knew him, nor any of his heroes show a trace of spiritual snobbery nor do they think of the higher life they search for as existing in some other-world sphere: the distinction they draw between *this* world and *the* world does not imply that there are two different worlds, only that our habitual conceptions of reality are not the true conception.

Perhaps, when he wished his writings to be destroyed, Kafka foresaw the nature of too many of his admirers.

"I Always Wanted You to Admire My Fasting"; or, Looking at Kafka

Philip Roth

To the Students of English 275, University of Pennsylvania, Fall 1972

"I always wanted you to admire my fasting," said the hunger artist. "We do admire it," said the overseer, affably. "But you shouldn't admire it," said the hunger artist. "Well then we don't admire it," said the overseer, "but why shouldn't we admire it?" "Because I have to fast, I can't help it," said the hunger artist. "What a fellow you are," said the overseer, "and why can't you help it?" "Because," said the hunger artist, lifting his head a little and speaking, with his lips pursed, as if for a kiss, right into the overseer's ear, so that no syllable might be lost, "because I couldn't find the food I liked. If I had found it, believe me, I should have made no fuss and stuffed myself like you or anyone else." These were his last words, but in his dimming eyes remained the firm though no longer proud persuasion that he was still continuing to fast.

—Franz Kafka, *"A Hunger Artist"*

1

I am looking, as I write of Kafka, at the photograph taken of him at the age of forty (my age)—it is 1924, as sweet and hopeful a year as he may ever have known as a man, and the year of his death. His face is sharp and skeletal, a burrower's face: pronounced cheekbones made even more conspicuous by the absence of sideburns; the ears shaped and angled on his head like angel wings; an intense, creaturely gaze of startled composure—enormous fears, enormous control; a black towel of Levantine hair pulled close around the skull the only sensuous feature; there is a familiar Jewish flare in the bridge of the nose, the nose itself is long and weighted slightly at the tip—the nose of half the Jewish boys who were my friends in high school. Skulls chiseled like this one were shoveled by the thousands from the ovens; had he lived, his would have been among them, along with the skulls of his three younger sisters.

Of course it is no more horrifying to think of Franz Kafka in Auschwitz than to think of anyone in Auschwitz—it is just horrifying in its own way. But he died too soon for the holocaust. Had he lived, perhaps he would have escaped with his good friend Max Brod, who found refuge in Palestine, a citizen of Israel until his death there in 1968. But *Kafka* escaping? It seems unlikely for one so fascinated by entrapment and careers that culminate in anguished death. Still, there is Karl Rossmann, his American greenhorn. Having imagined Karl's escape to America and his mixed luck here, could not Kafka have found a way to execute an escape for himself? The New School for Social Research in New York becoming *his* Great Nature Theatre of Oklahoma? Or perhaps, through the influence of Thomas Mann, a position in the German department at Princeton . . . But then, had Kafka lived, it is not at all certain that the books of his which Mann celebrated from *his* refuge in New Jersey would ever have been published; eventually Kafka might either have destroyed those manuscripts that he had once bid Max Brod to dispose of at his death or, at the least, continued to keep them his secret. The Jewish refugee arriving in America in 1938 would not then have been Mann's "religious humorist" but a frail and bookish fifty-five-year-old bachelor, formerly a lawyer for a government insurance firm in Prague, retired on a pension in Berlin at the time of Hitler's rise to power—an author, yes, but of a few eccentric stories, mostly about animals, stories no one in America had ever heard of and only a handful in Europe had read; a homeless K., but without K.'s willfulness and purpose, a homeless Karl, but without Karl's youthful spirit and resilience; just a Jew lucky enough to have escaped with his life, in his possession a suitcase containing some clothes, some family photos, some Prague mementos, and the manuscripts, still unpublished and in pieces, of *Amerika, The Trial, The Castle*, and (stranger things happen) three more fragmented novels, no less remarkable than the bizarre masterworks that he keeps to himself out of oedipal timidity, perfectionist madness, and insatiable longings for solitude and spiritual purity.

July 1923: Eleven months before he will die in a Vienna sanatorium, Kafka somehow finds the resolve to leave Prague and his father's home for good. Never before has he even remotely succeeded in living apart, independent of his mother, his sisters, and his father, nor has he been a writer other than in those few hours when he is not working in the legal department of the Workers' Accident Insurance Office in Prague; since taking his law degree at the university, he has been by all reports the most dutiful and scrupulous of employees, though he finds the work tedious and enervating. But in June of 1923—having some months earlier been pensioned from his job because of his illness—he meets a young Jewish girl of nineteen at a seaside resort in Germany, Dora Dymant, an employee at the vacation camp of the Jewish People's Home of Berlin. Dora has left her Orthodox Polish family to make a life of her own (at half Kafka's age); she and Kafka—who has just turned forty—fall in love . . . Kafka has by now been engaged to two somewhat more conventional Jewish girls—twice to one of them—hectic, anguished engagements wrecked largely by his fears. "I am mentally incapable of marrying," he writes his father in the forty-five-page letter he gave to his mother to deliver. ". . . the moment I make up my mind to marry I can no longer sleep, my head burns day and night, life can no longer be called life." He explains why. "Marrying is barred to me," he tells his father, "because it is your domain. Sometimes I imagine the map of the world spread out and you stretched diagonally across it. And I feel as if I could consider living in only those regions that are not covered by you or are not within your reach. And in keeping with the conception I have of your magnitude, these are not many and not very comforting regions—and marriage is not among them." The letter explaining what is wrong between this father and this son is dated November 1919; the mother thought it best not even to deliver it, perhaps for lack of courage, probably, like the son, for lack of hope.

During the following two years, Kafka attempts to wage an affair with Milena Jesenská-Pollak, an intense young woman of twenty-four who has translated a few of his stories into Czech and is most unhappily married in Vienna; his affair with Milena, conducted feverishly, but by and large through the mails, is even more demoralizing to Kafka than the fearsome engagements to the nice Jewish girls. They aroused only the paterfamilias longings that he dared not indulge, longings inhibited by his exaggerated awe of his father—"spellbound," says Brod, "in the family circle"—and the hypnotic spell of his own solitude; but the Czech Milena, impetuous, frenetic, indifferent to conventional restraints, a woman of appetite and anger, arouses more elemental yearnings and more elemental fears. According to a Prague critic, Rio Preisner, Milena was "psychopathic"; according to Margaret Buber-Neumann, who lived two years beside her in the German concentration camp where Milena died following a kidney operation in 1944, she was powerfully sane, extraordinarily humane and courageous. Milena's obituary for Kafka was the only one of consequence to appear in the Prague press; the prose is strong, so are the claims she makes for Kafka's accomplishment. She is still only in her twenties, the dead man is hardly known as a writer beyond his small circle of friends—yet Milena writes: "His knowledge of the world was exceptional and deep, and he was a deep and exceptional world in himself.... [He had] a delicacy of feeling bordering on the miraculous and a mental clarity that was terrifyingly uncompromising, and in turn he loaded on to his illness the whole burden of his mental fear of life. . . . He wrote the most important books in recent German literature." One can imagine this vibrant young woman stretched diagonally across the bed, as awesome to Kafka as his own father spread out across the map of the world. His letters to her are disjointed, unlike anything else of his in print; the word "fear" appears on page after page. "We are both married, you in Vienna, I to my Fear in Prague." He yearns to lay his head upon her breast; he calls her "Mother Milena"; during at least one of their two brief rendezvous, he is hopelessly impotent. At last he has to tell her to leave him be, an edict that Milena honors, though it leaves her hollow with grief. "Do not write," Kafka tells her, "and let us not see each other; I ask you only to quietly fulfill this request of mine; only on those conditions is survival possible for me; everything else continues the process of destruction."

Then, in the early summer of 1923, during a visit to his sister, who is vacationing with her children by the Baltic Sea, he finds young Dora Dymant, and within a month Franz Kafka has gone off to live with her in two rooms in a suburb of Berlin, out of reach at last of the "claws" of Prague and home. How can it be? How can he, in his illness, have accomplished so swiftly and decisively the leave-taking that was beyond him in his healthiest days? The impassioned letter writer who could equivocate interminably about which train to catch to Vienna to meet with Milena (if he should meet with her for the weekend at all); the bourgeois suitor in the high collar, who, during his drawn-out agony of an engagement with the proper Fräulein Bauer, secretly draws up a memorandum for himself, countering the arguments "for" marriage with the arguments "against"; the poet of the ungraspable and the unresolved, whose belief in the immovable barrier separating the wish from its realization is at the heart of his excruciating visions of defeat; the Kafka whose fiction refutes every easy, touching, humanish daydream of salvation and justice and fulfillment with densely imagined counterdreams that mock all solutions and escapes—this Kafka *escapes.* Overnight! K. penetrates the Castle walls—Joseph K. evades his indictment—"a breaking away from it altogether, a mode of living completely outside the jurisdiction of the Court." Yes, the possibility of which Joseph K. has just a glimmering in the Cathedral, but can neither fathom nor effectuate—"not . . . some influential manipulation of the case, but . . . a circumvention of it"—Kafka realizes in the last year of his life.

Was it Dora Dymant or was it death that pointed the new way? Perhaps it could not have been one without the other. We know that the "illusory emptiness" at which K. gazed, upon first entering the village and looking up through the mist and the darkness to the Castle, was no more vast and incomprehensible than the idea of himself as husband and father was to the young Kafka; but now, it seems, the prospect of a Dora forever, of a wife, home, and children everlasting, is no longer the terrifying, bewildering prospect it would once have been, for now "everlasting" is undoubtedly not much more than a matter of months. Yes, the dying Kafka is determined to marry, and writes to Dora's Orthodox father for his daughter's hand. But the imminent death that has resolved all contradictions and uncertainties in Kafka is the very obstacle placed in his path by the young girl's father. The request of the dying man Franz Kafka to bind to him in his invalidism the healthy young girl Dora Dymant is—denied!

If there is not one father standing in Kafka's way, there is another—and another behind him. Dora's father, writes Max Brod in his biography of Kafka, "set off with [Kafka's] letter to consult the man he honored most, whose authority counted more than anything else for him, the 'Gerer Rebbe.' The rabbi read the letter, put it to one side, and said nothing more than the single syllable, 'No.'" *No.* Klamm himself could have been no more abrupt—or any more removed from the petitioner. *No.* In its harsh finality, as telling and inescapable as the curselike threat delivered by his father to Georg Bendemann, that thwarted fiancé: "Just take your bride on your arm and try getting in my way. I'll sweep her from your very side, you don't know how!" *No.* Thou shalt not have, say the fathers, and Kafka agrees that he shall not. The habit of obedience and renunciation; also, his own distaste for the diseased and reverence for strength, appetite, and health. "'Well, clear this out now!' said the overseer, and they buried the hunger artist, straw and all. Into the cage they put a young panther. Even the most insensitive felt it refreshing to see this wild creature leaping around the cage that had so long been dreary. The panther was all right. The food he liked was brought him without hesitation by the attendants; he seemed not even to miss his freedom; his noble body, furnished almost to the bursting point with all that it needed, seemed to carry freedom around with it too; somewhere in his jaws it seemed to lurk; and the joy of life streamed with such ardent passion from his throat that for the onlookers it was not easy to stand the shock of it. But they braced themselves, crowded round the cage, and did not want ever to move away." So no is no; he knew as much himself. A healthy young girl of nineteen cannot, *should* not, be given in matrimony to a sickly man twice her age, who spits up blood ("I sentence you," cries Georg Bendemann's father, "to death by drowning!") and shakes in his bed with fevers and chills. What sort of un-Kafka-like dream had Kafka been dreaming?

And those nine months spent with Dora have still other "Kafkaesque" elements: a fierce winter in quarters inadequately heated; the inflation that makes a pittance of his own meager pension, and sends into the streets of Berlin the hungry and needy whose suffering, says Dora, turns Kafka "ash-gray"; and his tubercular lungs, flesh transformed and punished. Dora cares for the diseased writer as devotedly and tenderly as Gregor Samsa's sister does for her brother, the bug. Gregor's sister plays the violin so beautifully that Gregor "felt as if the way were opening before him to the unknown nourishment he craved"; he dreams, in his condition, of sending his gifted sister to the Conservatory! Dora's music is Hebrew, which she reads aloud to Kafka, and with such skill that, according to Brod, "Franz recognized her dramatic talent; on his advice and under his direction she later educated herself in the art . . ."

Only Kafka is hardly vermin to Dora Dymant, *or to himself.* Away from Prague and his father's home, Kafka, at forty, seems at last to have been delivered from the self-loathing, the self-doubt, and those guilt-ridden impulses to dependence and self-effacement that had nearly driven him mad throughout his twenties and thirties; all at once he seems to have shed the pervasive sense of hopeless despair that informs the great punitive fantasies of *The Trial*, "In the Penal Colony," and *The Metamorphosis.* Years earlier, in Prague, he had directed Max Brod to destroy all his papers, including three unpublished novels, upon his death; now, in Berlin, when Brod introduces him to a German publisher interested in his work, Kafka consents to the publication of a volume of four stories, and consents, says Brod, "without much need of long arguments to persuade him." With Dora to help, he diligently resumes the study of Hebrew; despite his illness and the harsh winter, he travels to the Berlin Academy for Jewish Studies to attend a series of lectures on the Talmud—a very different Kafka from the estranged melancholic who once wrote in his diary, "What have I in common with the Jews? I have hardly anything in common with myself and should stand very quietly in a corner, content that I can breathe." And to further mark the change, there is ease and happiness with a woman: with this young and adoring companion, he is playful, he is pedagogical, and, one would guess, in light of his illness (*and* his happiness), he is chaste. If not a husband (such as he had striven to be to the conventional Fräulein Bauer), if not a lover (as he struggled hopelessly to be with Milena), he would seem to have become something no less miraculous in his scheme of things: a father, a kind of father to this sisterly, mothering daughter. *As Franz Kafka awoke one morning from uneasy dreams he found himself transformed in his bed into a father, a writer, and a Jew.*

"I have completed the construction of my burrow," begins the long, exquisite, and tedious story that he wrote that winter in Berlin, "and it seems to be successful. . . . Just the place where, according to my calculations, the Castle Keep should be, the soil was very loose and sandy and had literally to be hammered and pounded into a firm state to serve as a wall for the beautifully vaulted chamber. But for such tasks the only tool I possess is my forehead. So I had to run with my forehead thousands and thousands of times, for whole days and nights, against the ground, and I was glad when the blood came, for that was proof that the walls were beginning to harden; in that way, as everybody must admit, I richly paid for my Castle Keep."

"The Burrow" is the story of an animal with a keen sense of peril whose life is organized around the principle of defense, and whose deepest longings are for security and serenity; with teeth and claws—*and* forehead—the burrower constructs an elaborate and ingeniously intricate system of underground chambers and corridors that are designed to afford it some peace of mind; however, while this burrow does succeed in reducing the sense of danger from without, its maintenance and protection are equally fraught with anxiety: "these anxieties are different from ordinary ones, prouder, richer in content, often long repressed, but in their destructive effects they are perhaps much the same as the anxieties that existence in the outer world gives rise to." The story (whose ending is lost) terminates with the burrower fixated upon distant subterranean noises that cause it "to assume the existence of a great beast," itself burrowing in the direction of the Castle Keep.

Another grim tale of entrapment, and of obsession so absolute that no distinction is possible between character and predicament. Yet this fiction imagined in the last "happy" months of his life is touched by a spirit of personal reconciliation and sardonic self-acceptance, by a tolerance of one's own brand of madness, that is not apparent in *The Metamorphosis.* The piercing masochistic irony of the earlier animal story—as of "The Judgment" and *The Trial*—has given way here to a critique of the self and its preoccupations that, though bordering on mockery, no longer seeks to resolve itself in images of the uttermost humiliation and defeat... Yet there is more here than a metaphor for the insanely defended ego, whose striving for invulnerability produces a defensive system that must in its turn become the object of perpetual concern—there is also a very unromantic and hardheaded fable about how and why art is made, a portrait of the artist in all his ingenuity, anxiety, isolation, dissatisfaction, relentlessness, obsessiveness, secretiveness, paranoia, and self-addiction, a portrait of the magical thinker at the end of his tether, Kafka's Prospero . . . It is an endlessly suggestive story, this story of life in a hole. For, finally, remember the proximity of Dora Dymant during the months that Kafka was at work on "The Burrow" in the two underheated rooms that were their illicit home. Certainly a dreamer like Kafka need never have entered the young girl's body for her tender presence to kindle in him a fantasy of a hidden orifice that promises "satisfied desire," "achieved ambition," and "profound slumber," but that, once penetrated and in one's possession, arouses the most terrifying and heartbreaking fears of retribution and loss. "For the rest I try to unriddle the beast's plans. Is it on its wanderings, or is it working on its own burrow? If it is on its wanderings then perhaps an understanding with it might be possible. If it should really break through to the burrow I shall give it some of my stores and it will go on its way again. It will go on its way again, a fine story! Lying in my heap of earth I can naturally dream of all sorts of things, even of an understanding with the beast, though I know well enough that no such thing can happen, and that at the instant when we see each other, more, at the moment when we merely guess at each other's presence, we shall blindly bare our claws and teeth . . ."

He died of tuberculosis of the lungs and larynx on June 3,

1924, a month before his forty-first birthday. Dora, inconsolable, whispers for days afterward, "My love, my love, my good one..."

2

1942. I am nine; my Hebrew-school teacher, Dr. Kafka, is fifty-nine. To the little boys who must attend his "four-to-five" class each afternoon, he is known—in part because of his remote and melancholy foreignness, but largely because we vent on him our resentment at having to learn an ancient calligraphy at the very hour we should be out screaming our heads off on the ball field—he is known as Dr. Kishka. Named, I confess, by me. His sour breath, spiced with intestinal juices by five in the afternoon, makes the Yiddish word for "insides" particularly telling, I think. Cruel, yes, but in truth I would have cut out my tongue had I ever imagined the name would become legend. A coddled child, I do not yet think of myself as persuasive, or, quite yet, as a literary force in the world. My jokes don't hurt, how could they, I'm so adorable. And if you don't believe me, just ask my family and the teachers in my school. Already at nine, one foot in college, the other in the Catskills. Little borscht-belt comic that I am outside the classroom, I amuse my friends Schlossman and Ratner on the dark walk home from Hebrew school with an imitation of Kishka, his precise and finicky professorial manner, his German accent, his cough, his gloom. "Doctor *Kishka*!" cries Schlossman, and hurls himself savagely against the newsstand that belongs to the candy-store owner whom Schlossman drives just a little crazier each night. "Doctor Franz—Doctor Franz—Doctor Franz—*Kishka*!" screams Ratner, and my chubby little friend who lives upstairs from me on nothing but chocolate milk and Mallomars does not stop laughing until, as is his wont (his mother has asked me "to keep an eye on him" for just this reason), he wets his pants. Schlossman takes the occasion of Ratner's humiliation to pull the little boy's paper out of his notebook and wave it in the air—it is the assignment Dr. Kafka has just returned to us, graded; we were told to make up an alphabet of our own, out of straight lines and curved lines and dots. "That is all an alphabet is," he had explained. "That is all Hebrew is. That is all English is. Straight lines and curved lines and dots." Ratner's alphabet, for which he received a C, looks like twenty-six skulls strung in a row. I received my A for a curlicued alphabet, inspired largely (as Dr. Kafka seems to have surmised, given his comment at the top of the page) by the number eight. Schlossman received an F for forgetting even to do it—and a lot he seems to care. He is content—he is *overjoyed*—with things as they are. Just waving a piece of paper in the air and screaming, "Kishka! Kishka!" makes him deliriously happy. We should all be so lucky.

At home, alone in the glow of my goose-necked "desk" lamp (plugged after dinner into an outlet in the kitchen, my study), the vision of our refugee teacher, sticklike in a fraying three-piece blue suit, is no longer very funny—particularly after the entire beginners' Hebrew class, of which I am the most studious member, takes the name Kishka to its heart. My guilt awakens redemptive fantasies of heroism, I have them often about the "Jews in Europe." I must save him. If not me, who? The demonic Schlossman? The babyish Ratner? And if not now, when? For I have learned in the ensuing weeks that Dr. Kafka lives in a room in the house of an elderly Jewish lady on the shabby lower stretch of Avon Avenue, where the trolley still runs and the poorest of Newark's Negroes shuffle meekly up and down the street, for all they seem to know, still back in Mississippi. A *room*. And *there*!

My family's apartment is no palace, but it is ours at least, so long as we pay the $38.50 a month in rent; and though our neighbors are not rich, they refuse to be poor and they refuse to be meek. Tears of shame and sorrow in my eyes, I rush into the living room to tell my parents what I have heard (though not that I heard it during a quick game of "aces up" played a minute before class against the synagogue's rear wall—worse, played directly beneath a stained-glass window embossed with the names of the dead): "My Hebrew teacher lives in a *room*."

My parents go much further than I could imagine anybody going in the real world. Invite him to dinner, my mother says. *Here?* Of course here—Friday night; I'm sure he can stand a home-cooked meal, she says, and a little pleasant company. Meanwhile, my father gets on the phone to call my Aunt Rhoda, who lives with my grandmother and tends her and her potted plants in the apartment house at the corner of our street. For nearly two decades my father has been introducing my mother's "baby" sister, now forty, to the Jewish bachelors and widowers of north Jersey. No luck so far. Aunt Rhoda, an "interior decorator" in the dry-goods department of the Big Bear, a mammoth merchandise and produce market in industrial Elizabeth, wears falsies (this information by way of my older brother) and sheer frilly blouses, and family lore has it that she spends hours in the bathroom every day applying powder and sweeping her stiffish hair up into a dramatic pile on her head; but despite all this dash and display, she is, in my father's words, "still afraid of the facts of life." He, however, is undaunted, and administers therapy regularly and gratis: "Let 'em squeeze ya, Rhoda—it *feels* good!" I am his flesh and blood, I can reconcile myself to such scandalous talk in our kitchen—*but what will Dr. Kafka think?* Oh, but it's too late to do anything now. The massive machinery of matchmaking has been set in motion by my undiscourageable father, and the smooth engines of my proud homemaking mother's hospitality are already purring away. To throw my body into the works in an attempt to bring it all to a halt—well, I might as well try to bring down the New Jersey Bell Telephone Company by leaving our receiver off the hook. Only Dr. Kafka can save me now. But to my muttered invitation, he replies, with a formal bow that turns me scarlet—who has ever seen a person do such a thing outside of a movie house?—he replies that he would be *honored* to be my family's dinner guest. "My aunt," I rush to tell him, "will be there too." It appears that I have just said something mildly humorous; odd to see Dr. Kafka smile. Sighing, he says, "I will be delighted to meet her." Meet her? He's supposed to *marry* her. How do I warn him? And how do I warn Aunt Rhoda (a very great admirer of me and my marks) about his sour breath, his roomer's pallor, his Old World ways, so at odds with her up-to-dateness? My face feels as if it will ignite of its own—and spark the fire that will engulf the synagogue, Torah and all—when I see Dr. Kafka scrawl our address in his notebook, and beneath it, some words *in German*. "Good night, Dr. Kafka!" "Good night, and thank you, thank you." I turn to run, I go, but not fast enough: out on the street I hear Schlossman—that fiend!—announcing to my classmates, who are punching one another under the lamplight down from the synagogue steps (where a card game is also in progress, organized by the bar mitzvah boys): "Roth invited Kishka to his *house*! To *eat*!"

Does my father do a job on Kafka! Does he make a sales pitch for familial bliss! What it means to a man to have two fine boys and a wonderful wife! Can Dr. Kafka imagine what it's like? The thrill? The satisfaction? The pride? He tells our visitor of the network of relatives on his mother's side that are joined in a "family association" of over two hundred people located in seven states, including the state of Washington! Yes, relatives even in the Far West: here are their photographs, Dr. Kafka; this is a beautiful book we published entirely on our own for five dollars a copy, pictures of every member of the family, including infants, and a family history by "Uncle" Lichtblau, the eighty-five-year-old patriarch of the clan. This is our family newsletter, which is published twice a year and distributed nationwide to all the relatives. This, in the frame, is the menu from the banquet of the family association, held last year in a ballroom of the "Y" in Newark, in honor of my father's mother on her seventy-fifth birthday. My mother, Dr. Kafka learns, has served *six consecutive years* as the secretary-treasurer of the family association. My father has served a two-year term as president, as have each of his three brothers. We now have fourteen boys in the family in uniform. Philip writes a letter on V-mail stationery to five of his cousins in the army every single month. "Religiously," my mother puts in, smoothing my hair. "I firmly believe," says my father, "that the family is the cornerstone of everything."

Dr. Kafka, who has listened with close attention to my father's spiel, handling the various documents that have been passed to him with great delicacy and poring over them with a kind of rapt absorption that reminds me of myself over the watermarks of my stamps, now for the first time expresses himself on the subject of family; softly he says, "I agree," and inspects again the pages of our family book. "Alone," says my father, in conclusion, "alone, Dr. Kafka, is a stone." Dr. Kafka, setting the book gently down upon my mother's gleaming coffee table, allows with a nod that that is so. My mother's fingers are now turning in the curls behind my ears; not that I even know it at the time, or that she does. Being stroked is my life; stroking me, my father, and my brother is hers.

My brother goes off to a Boy Scout meeting, but only after my father has him stand in his neckerchief before Dr. Kafka and describe to him the skills he has mastered to earn each of his badges. I am invited to bring my stamp album into the living room and show Dr. Kafka my set of triangular stamps from Zanzibar. "Zanzibar!" says my father rapturously, as though I, not even ten, have already been there and back. My father accompanies Dr. Kafka and me into the "sun parlor," where my tropical fish swim in the aerated, heated, and hygienic paradise I have made for them with my weekly allowance and my Hanukkah *gelt.* I am encouraged to tell Dr. Kafka what I know about the temperament of the angelfish, the function of the catfish, and the family life of the black mollie. I know quite a bit. "All on his own he does that," my father says to Kafka. "He gives me a lecture on one of those fish, it's seventh heaven, Dr. Kafka." "I can imagine," Kafka replies.

Back in the living room my Aunt Rhoda suddenly launches into a rather recondite monologue on "Scotch plaids," intended, it would appear, for the edification of my mother alone. At least she looks fixedly at my mother while she delivers it. I have not yet seen her look directly at Dr. Kafka; she did not even turn his way at dinner when he asked how many employees there were at the Big Bear. "How would I know?" she had replied, and then continued right on conversing with my mother, about a butcher who would take care of her "under the counter" if she could find him nylons for his wife. It never occurs to me that she will not look at Dr. Kafka because she is shy—nobody that dolled up could, in my estimation, be shy. I can only think that she is outraged. *It's his breath. It's his accent. It's his age.*

I'm wrong—it turns out to be what Aunt Rhoda calls his "superiority complex." "Sitting there, sneering at us like that," says my aunt, somewhat superior now herself. "Sneering?" repeats my father, incredulous. "Sneering and laughing, yes!" says Aunt Rhoda. My mother shrugs. "*I* didn't think he was laughing." "Oh, don't worry, by himself there he was having a very good time—*at our expense.* I know the European-type man. Underneath they think they're all lords of the manor," Rhoda says. "You know something, Rhoda?" says my father, tilting his head and pointing a finger, "I think you fell in love." "With *him*? Are you *crazy*?" "He's too quiet for Rhoda," my mother says. "I think maybe he's a little bit of a wallflower. Rhoda is a very lively person, she needs lively people around her." "Wallflower? He's not a wallflower! He's a gentleman, that's all. And he's lonely," my father says assertively, glaring at my mother for going over his head like this *against* Kafka. My Aunt Rhoda is forty years old—it is not exactly a shipment of brand-new goods that he is trying to move. "He's a gentleman, he's an educated man, and I'll tell you something, he'd give his eyeteeth to have a nice home and a wife." "Well," says my Aunt Rhoda, "let him find one then, if he's so educated. Somebody who's his equal, who he doesn't have to look down his nose at with his big sad refugee eyes!" "Yep, she's in love," my father announces, squeezing Rhoda's knee in triumph. "With him?" she cries, jumping to her feet, taffeta crackling around her like a bonfire. "With *Kafka*?" she snorts. "I wouldn't give an old man like him the time of day!"

Dr. Kafka calls and takes my Aunt Rhoda to a movie. I am astonished, both that he calls and that she goes; it seems there is more desperation in life than I have come across yet in my fish tank. Dr. Kafka takes my Aunt Rhoda to a play performed at the "Y." Dr. Kafka eats Sunday dinner with my grandmother and my Aunt Rhoda and, at the end of the afternoon, accepts with that formal bow of his the mason jar of barley soup that my grandmother presses him to carry back to his room with him on the No. 8 bus. Apparently he was very taken with my grandmother's jungle of potted plants—and she, as a result, with him. Together they spoke in Yiddish about gardening. One Wednesday morning, only an hour after the store has opened for the day, Dr. Kafka shows up at the dry-goods department of the Big Bear; he tells Aunt Rhoda that he just wants to see where she works. That night he writes in his diary: "With the customers she is forthright and cheery, and so managerial about 'taste' that when I hear her explain to a chubby young bride why green and blue do not 'go,' I am myself ready to believe that Nature is in error and R. is correct."

One night, at ten, Dr. Kafka and Aunt Rhoda come by unexpectedly, and a small impromptu party is held in the kitchen—coffee and cake, even a thimbleful of whiskey all around, to celebrate the resumption of Aunt Rhoda's career on the stage. I have only heard tell of my aunt's theatrical ambitions. My brother says that when I was small she used to come to entertain the two of us on Sundays with her puppets—she was at that time employed by the W.P.A. to travel around New Jersey and put on marionette shows in schools and even in churches; Aunt Rhoda did all the voices and, with the help of a female assistant, manipulated the manikins on their strings. Simultaneously she had been a member of the Newark Collective Theater, a troupe organized primarily to go around to strike groups to perform *Waiting for Lefty.* Everybody in Newark (as I understood it) had had high hopes that Rhoda Pilchik would go on to Broadway—everybody except my grandmother. To me this period of history is as difficult to believe in as the era of the lake dwellers, which I am studying in school; people say it was once so, so I believe them, but nonetheless it is hard to grant such stories the status of the real, given the life I see around me.

Yet my father, a very avid realist, is in the kitchen, schnapps glass in hand, toasting Aunt Rhoda's success. She has been awarded one of the starring roles in the Russian masterpiece *The Three Sisters,* to be performed six weeks hence by the amateur group at the Newark "Y." Everything, announces Aunt Rhoda, everything she owes to Franz and his encouragement. One conversation—"One!" she cries gaily—and Dr. Kafka had apparently talked my grandmother out of her lifelong belief that actors are not serious human beings. And what an actor *he* is, in his own right, says Aunt Rhoda. How he had opened her eyes to the meaning of things, by reading her the famous Chekhov play—yes, read it to her from the opening line to the final curtain, all the parts, and actually left her in tears. Here Aunt Rhoda says, "Listen, listen—this is the first line of the play—it's the key to everything. Listen—I just think about what it was like the night Pop passed away, how I wondered and wondered what would become of us, what would we all do—and, and, *listen*—"

"We're listening," laughs my father. So am *I* listening, from my bed.

Pause; she must have walked to the center of the kitchen linoleum. She says, sounding a little surprised, " 'It's just a year ago today that father died.' "

"Shhh," warns my mother, "you'll give the little one nightmares."

I am not alone in finding my aunt a "changed person" during the weeks of rehearsal. My mother says this is just what she was like as a little girl. "Red cheeks, always those hot, red cheeks—and everything exciting, even taking a bath." "She'll calm down, don't worry," says my father, "and then he'll pop the question." "Knock on wood," says my mother. "Come on," says my father, "he knows what side his bread is buttered on—he sets foot in this house, he sees what a family is all about, and believe me, he's licking his chops. Just look at him when he sits in that club chair. This is his dream come true." "Rhoda says that in Berlin, before Hitler, he had a young girl friend, years and years it went on, and then she left him. For somebody else. She got tired of waiting."

"Don't worry," says my father, "when the time comes I'll give him a little nudge. He ain't going to live forever, either, and he knows it."

Then one weekend, as a respite from the "strain" of nightly rehearsals—which Dr. Kafka regularly visits, watching in his hat and coat at the back of the auditorium until it is time to accompany Aunt Rhoda home—they take a trip to Atlantic City. Ever since he arrived on these shores Dr. Kafka has wanted to see the famous boardwalk and the horse that dives from the high board. But in Atlantic City something happens that I am not allowed to know about; any discussion of the subject conducted in my presence is in Yiddish. Dr. Kafka sends Aunt Rhoda four letters in three days. She comes to us for dinner and sits till midnight crying in our kitchen. She calls the "Y" on our phone to tell them (weeping) that her mother is still ill and she cannot come to rehearsal again—she may even have to drop out of the play. No, she can't, she can't, her mother is too ill, she herself is too upset! goodbye! Then back to the kitchen table to cry. She wears no pink powder and no red lipstick, and her stiff brown hair, down, is thick and spiky as a new broom.

My brother and I listen from our bedroom, through the door that silently he has pushed ajar.

"Have you ever?" says Aunt Rhoda, weeping. "Have you *ever*?"

"Poor soul," says my mother.

"*Who?*" I whisper to my brother. "Aunt Rhoda or—"

"Shhhh!" he says. "Shut *up*!"

In the kitchen my father grunts. "Hmm. Hmm." I hear him getting up and walking around and sitting down again—and then grunting. I am listening so hard that I can hear the letters being folded and unfolded, stuck back into their envelopes, then removed to be puzzled over one more time.

"Well?" demands Aunt Rhoda. "*Well?*"

"Well what?" answers my father.

"Well, what do you want to say *now*?"

"He's *meshugeh*," admits my father. "Something is wrong with him all right."

"But," sobs Aunt Rhoda, "no one would believe me when *I* said it!"

"Rhody, Rhody," croons my mother in that voice I know from those times that I have had to have stitches taken, or when I have awakened in tears, somehow on the floor beside my bed. "Rhody, don't be hysterical, darling. It's over, kitten, it's all over."

I reach across to my brother's twin bed and tug on the blanket. I don't think I've ever been so confused in my life, not even by death. The speed of things! Everything good undone in a moment! By what? *"What?"* I whisper. *"What is it?"*

My brother, the Boy Scout, smiles leeringly and, with a fierce hiss that is no answer and enough answer, addresses my bewilderment: "Sex!"

Years later, a junior at college, I receive an envelope from home containing Dr. Kafka's obituary, clipped from *The Jewish News*, the tabloid of Jewish affairs that is mailed each week to the homes of the Jews of Essex County. It is summer, the semester is over, but I have stayed on at school, alone in my room in the town, trying to write short stories. I am fed by a young English professor and his wife in exchange for baby-sitting; I tell the sympathetic couple, who are also loaning me the money for my rent, why it is I can't go home. My tearful fights with my father are all I can talk about at their dinner table. "Keep him away from me!" I scream at my mother. "But, darling," she asks me, "what is going on? What is this all about?"—the very same question with which I used to plague my older brother, asked now of me and out of the same bewilderment and innocence. "He *loves* you," she explains.

But that, of all things, seems to me precisely what is blocking my way. Others are crushed by paternal criticism—I find myself oppressed by his high opinion of me! Can it possibly be true (and can I possibly admit) that I am coming to hate him for loving me so? praising me so? But that makes no sense—the ingratitude! the stupidity! the contrariness! Being loved is so obviously a blessing, *the* blessing, praise such a rare bequest. Only listen late at night to my closest friends on the literary magazine and in the drama society—they tell horror stories of family life to rival *The Way of All Flesh*, they return shell-shocked from vacations, drift back to school as though from the wars. What they would give to be in my golden slippers! "What's going on?" my mother begs me to tell her; but how can I, when I myself don't fully believe that this is happening to us, or that I am the one who is making it happen. That they, who together cleared all obstructions from my path, should seem now to be my final obstruction! No wonder my rage must filter through a child's tears of shame, confusion, and loss. All that we have constructed together over the course of two century-long decades, and look how I must bring it down—in the name of this tyrannical need that I call my "independence"! My mother, keeping the lines of communication open, sends a note to me at school: "We miss you"—and encloses the brief obituary notice. Across the margin at the bottom of the clipping, she has written (in the same hand with which she wrote notes to my teachers and signed my report cards, in that very same handwriting that once eased my way in the world), "Remember poor Kafka, Aunt Rhoda's beau?"

"Dr. Franz Kafka," the notice reads, "a Hebrew teacher at the Talmud Torah of the Schley Street Synagogue from 1939 to 1948, died on June 3 in the Deborah Heart and Lung Center in Browns Mills, New Jersey. Dr. Kafka had been a patient there since 1950. He was 70 years old. Dr. Kafka was born in Prague,

Czechoslovakia, and was a refugee from the Nazis. He leaves no survivors."

He also leaves no books: no *Trial*, no *Castle*, no Diaries. The dead man's papers are claimed by no one, and disappear—all except those four "*meshugeneh*" letters that are, to this day, as far as I know, still somewhere in among the memorabilia accumulated by my spinster aunt, along with a collection of Broadway Playbills, sales citations from the Big Bear, and transatlantic steamship stickers.

Thus all trace of Dr. Kafka disappears. Destiny being destiny, how could it be otherwise? Does the Land Surveyor reach the Castle? Does K. escape the judgment of the Court, or Georg Bendemann the judgment of his father? "'Well, clear this out now!' said the overseer, and they buried the hunger artist, straw and all." No, it simply is not in the cards for Kafka ever to become *the* Kafka—why, that would be stranger even than a man turning into an insect. No one would believe it, Kafka least of all.

Franz Kafka

ON THE TENTH ANNIVERSARY OF HIS DEATH

Walter Benjamin

Potemkin

It is related that Potemkin suffered from states of depression which recurred more or less regularly. At such times no one was allowed to go near him, and access to his room was strictly forbidden. This malady was never mentioned at court, and in particular it was known that any allusion to it incurred the disfavor of Empress Catherine. One of the Chancellor's depressions lasted for an extraordinary length of time and brought about serious difficulties; in the offices documents piled up that required Potemkin's signature, and the Empress pressed for their completion. The high officials were at their wits' end. One day an unimportant little clerk named Shuvalkin happened to enter the anteroom of the Chancellor's palace and found the councillors of state assembled there, moaning and groaning as usual. "What is the matter, Your Excellencies?" asked the obliging Shuvalkin. They explained things to him and regretted that they could not use his services. "If that's all it is," said Shuvalkin, "I beg you to let me have those papers." Having nothing to lose, the councillors of state let themselves be persuaded to do so, and with the sheaf of documents under his arm, Shuvalkin set out, through galleries and corridors, for Potemkin's bedroom. Without stopping or bothering to knock, he turned the door-handle; the room was not locked. In semidarkness Potemkin was sitting on his bed in a threadbare nightshirt, biting his nails. Shuvalkin stepped up to the writing desk, dipped a pen in ink, and without saying a word pressed it into Potemkin's hand while putting one of the documents on his knees. Potemkin gave the intruder a vacant stare; then, as though in his sleep, he started to sign—first one paper, then a second, finally all of them. When the last signature had been affixed, Shuvalkin took the papers under his arm and left the room without further ado, just as he had entered it. Waving the papers triumphantly, he stepped into the anteroom. The councillors of state rushed toward him and tore the documents out of his hands. Breathlessly they bent over them. No one spoke a word; the whole group seemed paralyzed. Again Shuvalkin came closer and solicitously asked why the gentlemen seemed so upset. At that point he noticed the signatures. One document after another was signed Shuvalkin . . . Shuvalkin . . . Shuvalkin. . . .

This story is like a herald racing two hundred years ahead of Kafka's work. The enigma which beclouds it is Kafka's enigma. The world of offices and registries, of musty, shabby, dark rooms, is Kafka's world. The obliging Shuvalkin, who makes light of everything and is finally left empty-handed, is Kafka's K. Potemkin, who vegetates, somnolent and unkempt, in a remote, inaccessible room, is an ancestor of those holders of power in Kafka's works who live in the attics as judges or in the castle as secretaries; no matter how highly placed they may be, they are always fallen or falling men, although even the lowest and seediest of them, the doorkeepers and the decrepit officials, may abruptly and strikingly appear in the fullness of their power.

Why do they vegetate? Could they be the descendants of the figures of Atlas that support globes with their shoulders? Perhaps that is why each has his head "so deep on his chest that one can hardly see his eyes," like the Castellan in his portrait, or Klamm when he is alone. But it is not the globe they are carrying; it is just that even the most commonplace things have their weight. "His fatigue is that of the gladiator after the fight; his job was the whitewashing of a corner in the office!" Georg Lukács once said that in order to make a decent table nowadays, a man must have the architectural genius of a Michelangelo. If Lukács thinks in terms of ages, Kafka thinks in terms of cosmic epochs. The man who whitewashes has epochs to move, even in his most insignificant movement. On many occasions and often for strange reasons Kafka's figures clap their hands. Once the casual remark is made that these hands are "really steam hammers."

We encounter these holders of power in constant, slow movement, rising or falling. But they are at their most terrible when they rise from the deepest decay—from the fathers. The son calms his spiritless, senile father whom he has just gently put to bed: " 'Don't worry, you are well covered up.' 'No,' cried his father, cutting short the answer, threw the blanket off with such strength that it unfolded fully as it flew, and stood up in bed. Only one hand lightly touched the ceiling to steady him. 'You wanted to cover me up, I know, my little scamp, but I'm not all covered up yet. And even if this is all the strength I have left, it's enough for you, too much for you. . . . But thank goodness a father does not need to be taught how to see through his son.' . . . And he stood up quite unsupported and kicked his legs out. He beamed with insight. . . . 'So now you know what else there was in the world besides yourself; until now you have known only about yourself! It is true, you were an innocent child, but it is even more true that you have been a devilish person!' " As the father throws off the burden of the blanket, he also throws off a cosmic burden. He has to set cosmic ages in motion in order to turn the age-old father-son relationship into a living and consequential thing. But what consequences! He sentences his son to death by drowning. The father is the one who punishes; guilt attracts him as it does the court officials. There is much to indicate that the world of the officials and the world of the fathers are the same to Kafka. The similarity does not redound to this world's credit; it consists of dullness, decay, and dirt. The father's uniform is stained all over; his underwear is dirty. Filth is the element of the officials. "She could not understand why there were office hours for the public in the first place. 'To get some dirt on the front staircase'—this is how her question was once answered by an official, who was probably annoyed, but it made a lot of sense to her." Uncleanness is so much the attribute of officials that one could almost regard them as enormous parasites. This, of course, does not refer to the economic context, but to the forces of reason and humanity from which this clan makes a living. In the same way the fathers in Kafka's strange families batten on their sons, lying on top of them like giant parasites. They not only prey upon their strength, but gnaw away at the sons' right to exist. The fathers punish, but they are at the same time the accusers. The sin of which they accuse their sons seems to be a kind of original sin. The definition of it which Kafka has given applies to the sons more than to anyone else: "Original sin, the old injustice committed by man, consists in the complaint unceasingly made by man that he has been the victim of an injustice, the victim of original sin." But who is accused of this inherited sin—the sin of having produced an heir—if not the father by the son? Accordingly the son would be the sinner. But one must not conclude from Kafka's definition that the accusation is sinful because it is false. Nowhere does Kafka say that it is made wrongfully. A never-ending process is at work here, and no cause can appear in a worse light than the one for which the father enlists the aid of these officials and court offices. A boundless corruptibility is not their worst feature, for their essence is such that their venality is the only hope held out to the human spirit facing them. The courts, to be sure, have lawbooks at their disposal, but people are not allowed to see them. "It is characteristic of this legal system," conjectures K., "that one is sentenced not only in innocence but also in ignorance." Laws and definite norms remain unwritten in the prehistoric world. A man can transgress them without suspecting it and thus become subject to atonement. But no matter how hard it may hit the unsuspecting, the transgression in the sense of the law is not accidental but fated, a destiny which appears here in all its ambiguity. In a cursory investigation of the idea of fate in antiquity Hermann Cohen came to a "conclusion that becomes inescapable": "the very rules of fate seem to be what causes and brings about the breaking away from them, the defection." It is the same way with the legal authorities whose proceedings are directed against K. It takes us back far beyond the time of the giving of the Law on twelve tablets to a prehistoric world, written law being one of the first victories scored over this world. In Kafka the written law is contained in books, but these are secret; by basing itself on them the prehistoric world exerts its rule all the more ruthlessly.

In Kafka's works, the conditions in offices and in families have multifarious points of contact. In the village at the foot of Castle Hill people use an illuminating saying. "'We have a saying here that you may be familiar with: Official decisions are as shy as young girls.' 'That's a sound observation,' said K., 'a sound observation. Decisions may have even other characteristics in common with girls.'" The most remarkable of these qualities is the willingness to lend oneself to anything, like the shy girls whom

K. meets in *The Castle* and *The Trial*, girls who indulge in unchastity in the bosom of their family as they would in a bed. He encounters them at every turn; the rest give him as little trouble as the conquest of the barmaid. "They embraced each other; her little body burned in K.'s hands; in a state of unconsciousness which K. tried to master constantly but fruitlessly, they rolled a little way, hit Klamm's door with a thud, and then lay in the little puddles of beer and the other refuse that littered the floor. Hours passed . . . in which K. constantly had the feeling that he was losing his way or that he had wandered farther than anyone had ever wandered before, to a place where even the air had nothing in common with his native air, where all this strangeness might choke one, yet a place so insanely enchanting that one could not help but go on and lose oneself even further." We shall have more to say about this strange place. The remarkable thing is that these whorelike women never seem to be beautiful. Rather, beauty appears in Kafka's world only in the most obscure places—among the accused persons, for example. "This, to be sure, is a strange phenomenon, a natural law, as it were. . . . It cannot be guilt that makes them attractive . . . nor can it be the just punishment which makes them attractive in anticipation . . . so it must be the mere charges brought against them that somehow show on them."

From *The Trial* it may be seen that these proceedings usually are hopeless for those accused—hopeless even when they have hopes of being acquitted. It may be this hopelessness that brings out the beauty in them—the only creatures in Kafka thus favored. At least this would be very much in keeping with a conversation which Max Brod has related. "I remember," Brod writes, "a conversation with Kafka which began with present-day Europe and the decline of the human race. 'We are nihilistic thoughts, suicidal thoughts that come into God's head,' Kafka said. This reminded me at first of the Gnostic view of life: God as the evil demiurge, the world as his Fall. 'Oh no,' said Kafka, 'our world is only a bad mood of God, a bad day of his.' 'Then there is hope outside this manifestation of the world that we know.' He smiled. 'Oh, plenty of hope, an infinite amount of hope—but not for us.'" These words provide a bridge to those extremely strange figures in Kafka, the only ones who have escaped from the family circle and for whom there may be hope. These are not the animals, not even those hybrids or imaginary creatures like the Cat Lamb or Odradek; they all still live under the spell of the family. It is no accident that Gregor Samsa wakes up as a bug in his parental home and not somewhere else, and that the peculiar animal which is half kitten, half lamb, is inherited from the father; Odradek likewise is the concern of the father of the family. The "assistants," however, are outside this circle.

These assistants belong to a group of figures which recurs through Kafka's entire work. Their tribe includes the confidence man who is unmasked in "Meditation"; the student who appears on the balcony at night as Karl Rossmann's neighbor; and the fools who live in that town in the south and never get tired. The twilight in which they exist is reminiscent of the uncertain light in which the figures in the short prose pieces of Robert Walser appear [the author of *Der Gehülfe, The Assistant,* a novel Kafka was very fond of]. In Indian mythology there are the *gandharvas,* celestial creatures, beings in an unfinished state. Kafka's assistants are of that kind: neither members of, nor strangers to, any of the other groups of figures, but, rather, messengers from one to the other. Kafka tells us that they resemble Barnabas, who is a messenger. They have not yet been completely released from the womb of nature, and that is why they have "settled down on two old women's skirts on the floor in a corner. It was . . . their ambition . . . to use up as little space as possible. To that end they kept making various experiments, folding their arms and legs, huddling close together; in the darkness all one could see in their corner was one big ball." It is for them and their kind, the unfinished and the bunglers, that there is hope.

What may be discerned, subtly and informally, in the activities of these messengers is law in an oppressive and gloomy way for this whole group of beings. None has a firm place in the world, firm, inalienable outlines. There is not one that is not either rising or falling, none that is not trading qualities with its enemy or neighbor, none that has not completed its period of time and yet is unripe, none that is not deeply exhausted and yet is only at the beginning of a long existence. To speak of any order or hierarchy is impossible here. Even the world of myth of which we think in this context is incomparably younger than Kafka's world, which has been promised redemption by the myth. But if we can be sure of one thing, it is this: Kafka did not succumb to its temptation. A latter-day Ulysses, he let the Sirens go by "his gaze which was fixed on the distance, the Sirens disappeared as it were before his determination, and at the very moment when he was closest to them he was no longer aware of them." Among Kafka's ancestors in the ancient world, the Jews and the Chinese, whom we shall encounter later, this Greek one should not be forgotten. Ulysses, after all, stands at the dividing line between myth and fairy tale. Reason and cunning have inserted tricks into myths; their forces cease to be invincible. Fairy tales are the traditional stories about victory over these forces, and fairy tales for dialecticians are what Kafka wrote when he went to work on legends. He inserted little tricks into them; then he used them as proof "that inadequate, even childish measures may also serve to rescue one." With these words he begins his story about the "Silence of the Sirens." For Kafka's Sirens are silent; they have "an even more terrible weapon than their song . . . their silence." This they used on Ulysses. But he, so Kafka tells us, "was so full of guile, was such a fox that not even the goddess of fate could pierce his armor. Perhaps he had really noticed, although here the human understanding is beyond its depths, that the Sirens were silent, and opposed the aforementioned pretense to them and the gods merely as a sort of shield."

Kafka's Sirens are silent. Perhaps because for Kafka music and singing are an expression or at least a token of escape, a token of hope which comes to us from that intermediate world—at once unfinished and commonplace, comforting and silly—in which the assistants are at home. Kafka is like the lad who set out to learn what fear was. He has got into Potemkin's palace and finally, in the depths of its cellar, has encountered Josephine, the singing mouse, whose tune he describes: "Something of our poor, brief childhood is in it, something of lost happiness which can never be found again, but also something of active present-day life, of its small gaieties, unaccountable and yet real and unquenchable."

A Childhood Photograph

There is a childhood photograph of Kafka, a rarely touching portrayal of the "poor, brief childhood." It was probably made in one of those nineteenth-century studios whose draperies and palm trees, tapestries and easels placed them somewhere between a torture chamber and a throne room. At the age of approximately six the boy is presented in a sort of greenhouse setting, wearing a tight, heavily lace-trimmed, almost embarrassing child's suit. Palm branches loom in the background. And as if to make these upholstered tropics still more sultry and sticky, the model holds in his left hand an oversized, wide-brimmed hat of the type worn by Spaniards. Immensely sad eyes dominate the landscape prearranged for them, and the auricle of a big ear seems to be listening for its sounds.

The ardent "wish to become a Red Indian" may have consumed this great sadness at some point. "If one were only an Indian, instantly alert, and on a racing horse, leaning against the wind, kept on quivering briefly over the quivering ground, until one shed one's spurs, for there were no spurs, threw away the reins, for there were no reins, and barely saw the land before one as a smoothly mown heath, with the horse's neck and head already gone." A great deal is contained in this wish. Its fulfillment, which he finds in America, yields up its secret. That *Amerika* is a very special case is indicated by the name of its hero. While in the earlier novels the author never addressed himself otherwise than with a mumbled initial, here he experiences a rebirth on a new continent with a full name. He has this experience in the Nature Theater of Oklahoma. "At a street corner Karl saw a poster with the following announcement: The Oklahoma Theater will engage members for its company today at Clayton Racetrack from 6 a.m. until midnight. The great Theater of Oklahoma calls you! The one and only call is today! If you miss your chance now, you miss it forever! If you think of your future, you should be one of us! Everyone is welcome! If you want to be an artist, come forward! Our Theater can use everyone and find the right place for everyone! If you decide to join us, we congratulate you here and now! But hurry, so that you get in before midnight! At twelve o'clock the doors will be shut and never opened again! A curse on those who do not believe in us! Set out for Clayton!" The reader of this announcement is Karl Rossmann, the third and happier incarnation of K., the hero of Kafka's novels. Happiness awaits him at the Nature Theater of Oklahoma, which is really a racetrack, just as "unhappiness" had once beset him on the narrow rug in his room on which he ran about "as on a racetrack." Ever since Kafka wrote his "reflections for gentleman jockeys," ever since he made the "new attorney" mount the courthouse steps, lifting his legs high, with a tread that made the marble ring, ever since he made his "children on a country road" amble through the countryside with large steps and folded arms, this figure had been familiar to him; and even Karl Rossmann, "distracted by his sleepiness," may often make "too high, time-consuming, and useless leaps." Thus it can only be a racetrack on which he attains the object of his desire.

This racetrack is at the same time a theater, and this poses a puzzle. The mysterious place and the entirely unmysterious, transparent, pure figure of Karl Rossmann are congruous, however. For Karl Rossmann is transparent, pure, without character as it were in the same sense in which Franz Rosenzweig says in his *Star of Redemption* that in China people, in their spiritual aspects, are "as it were devoid of individual character; the idea of the wise man, of which Confucius is the classic incarnation, blurs any individuality of character; he is the truly characterless man, namely, the average man. . . . What distinguishes a Chinese is something quite different from character: a very elemental purity of feeling." No matter how one may convey it intellectually, this purity of feeling may be a particularly sensitive measurement of gestic behavior; the Nature Theater of Oklahoma in any case harks back to the Chinese theater, which is a gestic theater. One of the most significant functions of this theater is to dissolve happenings into their gestic components. One can go even further and say that a good number of Kafka's shorter studies and stories are seen in their full light only when they are, so to speak, put on as acts in the "Nature Theater of Oklahoma." Only then will one recognize with certainty that Kafka's entire work constitutes a code of gestures which surely had no definite symbolic meaning for the author from the outset; rather, the author tried to derive such a meaning from them in ever-changing contexts and experimental groupings. The theater is the logical place for such groupings. In an unpublished commentary on "A Fratricide," Werner Kraft perceptively identified the events in this little story as scenic events. "The play is ready to begin, and it is actually announced by a bell. This comes about in a very natural way. Wese leaves the building in which his office is located. But this doorbell, so we are expressly told, is 'too loud for a doorbell; it rings out over the town and up to heaven.'" Just as this bell, which is too loud for a doorbell, rings out toward heaven, the gestures of Kafka's figures are too powerful for our accustomed surroundings and break out into wider areas. The greater Kafka's mastery became, the more frequently did he eschew adapting these gestures to common situations or explaining them. "It is strange behavior," we read in *The Metamorphosis,* "to sit on the desk and talk down at the employee, who, furthermore, must come quite close because his boss is hard of hearing." *The Trial* has already left such motivations far behind. In the penultimate chapter, K. stops at the first rows in the Cathedral, "but the priest seemed to consider the distance still too great; he stretched out an arm and pointed with his sharply bent forefinger to a spot right in front of the pulpit. K. followed this direction too; at that place he had to bend his head far back to see the priest at all."

Max Brod has said: "The world of those realities that were important for him was invisible." What Kafka could see least of all was the *gestus.* Each gesture is an event—one might even say, a drama—in itself. The stage on which this drama takes place is the World Theater which opens up toward heaven. On the other hand, this heaven is only background; to explore it according to its own laws would be like framing the painted backdrop of the stage and hanging it in a picture gallery. Like El Greco, Kafka tears open the sky behind every gesture; but as with El Greco—who was the patron saint of the Expressionists—the gesture remains the decisive thing, the center of the event. The people who have assumed responsibility for the knock at the manor gate walk doubled up with fright. This is how a Chinese actor would portray terror, but no one would give a start. Elsewhere K. himself does a bit of acting. Without being fully conscious of it, "slowly . . . with his eyes not looking down but cautiously raised upwards he took one of the papers from the desk, put it on the palm of his hand and gradually raised it up to the gentlemen while getting up himself. He had nothing definite in mind, but acted only with the feeling that this was what he would have to do once he had completed the big petition which was to exonerate him completely." This animal gesture combines the utmost mysteriousness with the utmost simplicity. It is possible to read Kafka's animal stories for quite a while without realizing that they are not about human beings at all. When one encounters the name of the creature—monkey, dog, mole—one looks up in fright and realizes that one is already far away from the continent of man. But it is always Kafka; he divests the human gesture of its traditional supports and then has a subject for reflection without end.

Strangely enough, these reflections are endless even when their point of departure is one of Kafka's philosophical tales. Take, for example, the parable "Before the Law." The reader who read it in *A Country Doctor* may have been struck by the cloudy spot in it. But would it have led him to the never-ending series of reflections traceable to this parable at the place where Kafka undertakes to interpret it? This is done by the priest in *The Trial*, and at such a significant moment that it looks as if the novel were nothing but the unfolding of the parable. The word "unfolding" has a double meaning. A bud unfolds into a blossom, but the boat which one teaches children to make by folding paper unfolds into a flat sheet of paper. This second kind of "unfolding" is really appropriate to the parable; it is the reader's pleasure to smooth it out so that he has the meaning on the palm of his hand. Kafka's parables, however, unfold in the first sense, the way a bud turns into a blossom. That is why their effect resembles poetry. This does not mean that his prose pieces belong entirely in the tradition of Western prose forms; they have, rather, a similar relationship to doctrine as the Haggadah does to the Halakah. They are not parables, and yet they do not want to be taken at their face value; they lend themselves to quotation and can be told for purposes of clarification. But do we have the doctrine which Kafka's parables interpret and which K.'s postures and the gestures of his animals clarify? It does not exist; all we can say is that here and there we have an allusion to it. Kafka might have said that these are relics transmitting the doctrine, although we could regard them just as well as precursors preparing the doctrine. In every case it is a question of how life and work are organized in human society. This question increasingly occupied Kafka as it became impenetrable to him. If Napoleon, in his famous conversation with Goethe at Erfurt, substituted politics for fate, Kafka, in a variation of this statement, could have defined organization as destiny. He faces it not only in the extensive hierarchy of officialdom in *The Trial* and *The Castle*, but even more concretely in the difficult and incalculable construction plans whose venerable model he dealt with in *The Great Wall of China*.

"The wall was to be a protection for centuries; accordingly, the most scrupulous care in the construction, the application of the architectural wisdom of all known ages and peoples, a constant sense of personal responsibility on the part of the builders were indispensable prerequisites for the work. To be sure, for the menial tasks ignorant day laborers from the populace, men, women, and children, whoever offered his services for good money, could be used; but for the supervision even of every four day laborers a man trained in the building trade was required.... We—and here I speak in the name of many people—did not really know ourselves until we had carefully scrutinized the decrees of the high command; then we discovered that without this leadership neither our book learning nor our common sense would have sufficed for the humble tasks which we performed in the great whole." This organization resembles fate. Metchnikoff, who has outlined this in his famous book *La Civilisation et les grands fleuves historiques* [*Civilization and the Great Historical Rivers*], uses language that could be Kafka's. "The canals of the Yangtze and the dams of the Yellow River," he writes, "are in all likelihood the result of the skillfully organized joint labor of ... generations. The slightest carelessness in the digging of a ditch or the buttressing of a dam, the least bit of negligence or selfish behavior on the part of an individual or a group of men in the maintenance of the common hydraulic wealth becomes, under such unusual circumstances, the source of social evils and far-reaching social calamity. Consequently, a life-giving river requires on pain of death a close and permanent solidarity between groups of people that frequently are alien or even hostile to one another; it sentences everyone to labors whose common usefulness is revealed only by time and whose design quite often remains utterly incomprehensible to an ordinary man."

Kafka wished to be numbered among ordinary men. He was pushed to the limits of understanding at every turn, and he liked to push others to them as well. At times he seems to come close to saying with Dostoevsky's Grand Inquisitor: "So we have before us a mystery which we cannot comprehend. And precisely because it is a mystery we have had the right to preach it, to teach the people that what matters is neither freedom nor love, but the riddle, the secret, the mystery to which they have to bow—without reflection and even against their conscience." Kafka did not always evade the temptations of mysticism. There is a diary entry concerning his encounter with Rudolf Steiner; in its published form at least it does not reflect Kafka's attitude toward him. Did he avoid taking a stand? His way with his own writings certainly does not exclude this possibility. Kafka had a rare capacity for creating parables for himself. Yet his parables are never exhausted by what is explainable; on the contrary, he took all conceivable precautions against the interpretation of his writings. One has to find one's way in them circumspectly, cautiously, and warily. One must keep in mind Kafka's way of reading as exemplified in his interpretation of the above-mentioned parable. His testament is another case in point. Given its background, the directive in which Kafka ordered the destruction of his literary remains is just as unfathomable, to be weighed just as carefully as the answers of the doorkeeper before the law. Perhaps Kafka, whose every day on earth brought him up against insoluble behavior problems and undecipherable communications, in death wished to give his contemporaries a taste of their own medicine.

Kafka's world is a world theater. For him, man is on the stage from the very beginning. The proof of the pudding is the fact that everyone is accepted by the Nature Theater of Oklahoma. What the standards for admission are cannot be determined. Dramatic talent, the most obvious criterion, seems to be of no importance. But this can be expressed in another way: all that is expected of the applicants is the ability to play themselves. It is no longer within the realm of possibility that they could, if necessary, be what they claim to be. With their roles these people look for a position in the Nature Theater just as Pirandello's six characters sought an author. For all of them this place is the last refuge, which does not preclude it from being their salvation. Salvation is not a premium on existence, but the last way out for a man whose path, as Kafka puts it, is "blocked . . . by his own frontal bone." The law of this theater is contained in a sentence tucked away in "A Report to an Academy": "I imitated people because I was looking for a way out, and for no other reason." Before the end of his trial, K. seems to have an intimation of these things. He suddenly turns to the two gentlemen wearing top hats who have come for him and asks them: " 'What theater are you playing at?' 'Theater?' asked one, the corners of his mouth twitching as he looked for advice to the other, who acted as if he were a mute struggling to overcome a stubborn disability." The men do not answer this question, but there is much to indicate that it has hit home.

At a long bench which has been covered with a white cloth all those who will henceforth be with the Nature Theater are fed. "They were all happy and excited." By way of celebration, extras act as angels. They stand on high pedestals that are covered with flowing raiments and have stairs inside—the makings of a country church fair, or maybe a children's festival, which may have eliminated the sadness from the eyes of the tightly laced, dressed-up boy we discussed above. But for the fact that their wings are tied on, these angels might be real. They have forerunners in Kafka's works. One of them is the impresario who climbs up on the luggage rack next to the trapeze artist beset by his "first sorrow," caresses him and presses his face against the artist's, "so that he was bathed by the trapeze artist's tears." Another, a guardian angel or guardian of the law, takes care of Schmar the murderer following the "fratricide" and leads him away, stepping lightly, with Schmar's "mouth pressed against the policeman's shoulder." Kafka's *Amerika* ends with the rustic ceremonies of Oklahoma. "In Kafka," said Soma Morgenstern, "there is the air of a village, as with all great founders of religions." Lao-tse's presentation of piousness is all the more pertinent here because Kafka has supplied its most perfect description in "The Next Village." "Neighboring countries may be within sight, so that the sounds of roosters and dogs may be heard in the distance. And yet people are said to die at a ripe old age without having traveled far." Thus Lao-tse. Kafka was a writer of parables, but he did not found a religion.

Let us consider the village at the foot of Castle Hill whence K.'s alleged employment as a land surveyor is so mysteriously and unexpectedly confirmed. In his Postscript to *The Castle* Brod mentioned that in depicting this village at the foot of Castle Hill Kafka had in mind a specific place, Zürau in the Erz Gebirge. We may, however, also recognize another village in it. It is the village in a Talmudic legend told by a rabbi in answer to the question why Jews prepare a festive evening meal on Fridays. The legend is about a princess languishing in exile, in a village whose language she does not understand, far from her compatriots. One day this princess receives a letter saying that her fiancé has not forgotten her and is on his way to her. The fiancé, so says the rabbi, is the Messiah; the princess is the soul; the village in which she lives in exile is the body. She prepares a meal for him because this is the only way in which she can express her joy in a village whose language she does not know. This village of the Talmud is right in Kafka's world. For just as K. lives in the village on Castle Hill, modern man lives in his body; the body slips away from him, is hostile toward him. It may happen that a man wakes up one day and finds himself transformed into vermin. Exile—his exile—has gained control over him. The air of this village blows about Kafka, and that is why he was not tempted to found a religion. The pigsty which houses the country doctor's horses; the stuffy back room in which Klamm, a cigar in his mouth, sits over a glass of beer; the manor gate, to knock against which brings ruin—all these are part of this village. The air in this village is not free of all the abortive and overripe elements that form such a putrid mixture. This is the air that Kafka had to breathe all his life. He was neither mantic nor the founder of a religion. How was he able to survive in this air?

The Little Hunchback

Some time ago it became known that Knut Hamsun was in the habit of expressing his views in an occasional letter to the editor of the local paper in the small town near which he lived. Years ago that town was the scene of the jury trial of a maid who had killed her infant child. She was sentenced to a prison term. Soon thereafter the local paper printed a letter from Hamsun in which he announced his intention of leaving a town which did not visit the supreme punishment on a mother who killed her newborn child—the gallows, or at least a life term of hard labor. A few years passed. *Growth of the Soil* appeared, and it contained the story of a maid who committed the same crime, suffered the same punishment, and, as is made clear to the reader, surely deserved no more severe one.

Kafka's posthumous reflections, which are contained in *The Great Wall of China*, recall this to mind. Hardly had this volume appeared when the reflections served as the basis for a Kafka criticism which concentrated on an interpretation of these reflections to the neglect of his real works. There are two ways to miss the point of Kafka's works. One is to interpret them naturally, the other is the supernatural interpretation. Both the psychoanalytic and the theological interpretations equally miss the essential points. The first kind is represented by Hellmuth Kaiser; the second, by numerous writers, such as H. J. Schoeps, Bernhard Rang, and Bernhard Groethuysen. To these last also belongs Willy Haas, although he has made revealing comments on Kafka in other contexts which we shall discuss later; such insights did not prevent him from interpreting Kafka's work after a theological pattern. "The powers above, the realm of grace," so Haas writes, "Kafka has depicted in his great novel *The Castle;* the powers below, the realm of the courts and of damnation, he has dealt with in his equally great novel *The Trial.* The earth between the two, earthly fate and its arduous demands, he attempted to present in strictly stylized form in a third novel, *Amerika.*" The first third of this interpretation has, since Brod, become the common property of Kafka criticism. Bernhard Rang writes in a similar vein: "To the extent that one may regard the Castle as the seat of grace, precisely these vain efforts and attempts mean, theologically speaking, that God's grace cannot be attained or forced by man at will and deliberately. Unrest and impatience only impede and confound the exalted stillness of the divine." This interpretation is a convenient one; but the further it is carried, the clearer it becomes that it is untenable. This is perhaps seen most clearly in a statement by Willy Haas. "Kafka goes back . . . to Kierkegaard as well as to Pascal; one may call him the only legitimate heir of these two. In all three there is an excruciatingly harsh basic religious theme: man is always in the wrong before God. . . . Kafka's upper world, his so-called Castle, with its immense, complex staff of petty and rather lecherous officials, his strange heaven plays a horrible game with people . . . and yet man is very much in the wrong even before this god." This theology falls far behind the doctrine of justification of

St. Anselm of Canterbury into barbaric speculations which do not even seem consistent with the text of Kafka's works. "Can an individual official forgive?" we read in *The Castle.* "This could only be a matter for the over-all authorities, but even they can probably not forgive but only judge." This road has soon led into a blind alley. "All this," says Denis de Rougemont, "is not the wretched situation of man without a god, but the wretched state of a man who is bound to a god he does not know, because he does not know Christ."

It is easier to draw speculative conclusions from Kafka's posthumous collection of notes than to explore even one of the motifs that appear in his stories and novels. Yet only these give some clue to the prehistoric forces that dominated Kafka's creativeness, forces which, to be sure, may justifiably be regarded as belonging to our world as well. Who can say under what names they appeared to Kafka himself? Only this much is certain: he did not know them and failed to get his bearings among them. In the mirror which the prehistoric world held before him in the form of guilt he merely saw the future emerging in the form of judgment. Kafka, however, did not say what it was like. Was it not the Last Judgment? Does it not turn the judge into the defendant? Is the trial not the punishment? Kafka gave no answer. Did he expect anything of this punishment? Or was he not rather concerned to postpone it? In the stories which Kafka left us, narrative art regains the significance it had in the mouth of Scheherazade: to postpone the future. In *The Trial* postponement is the hope of the accused man only if the proceedings do not gradually turn into the judgment. The patriarch himself is to benefit by postponement, even though he may have to trade his place in tradition for it. "I could conceive of another Abraham—to be sure, he would never get to be a patriarch or even an old-clothes dealer—, an Abraham who would be prepared to satisfy the demand for a sacrifice immediately, with the promptness of a waiter, but would be unable to bring it off because he cannot get away, being indispensable; the household needs him, there is always something or other to take care of, the house is never ready; but without having his house ready, without having something to fall back on, he cannot leave—this the Bible also realized, for it says: 'He set his house in order.' "

This Abraham appears "with the promptness of a waiter." Kafka could understand things only in the form of a *gestus*, and this *gestus* which he did not understand constitutes the cloudy part of the parables. Kafka's writings emanate from it. The way he withheld them is well known. His testament orders their destruction. This document, which no one interested in Kafka can disregard, says that the writings did not satisfy their author, that he regarded his efforts as failures, that he counted himself among those who were bound to fail. He did fail in his grandiose attempt to convert poetry into doctrine, to turn it into a parable and restore to it that stability and unpretentiousness which, in the face of reason, seemed to him to be the only appropriate thing for it. No other writer has obeyed the commandment "Thou shalt not make unto thee a graven image" so faithfully.

"It was as if the shame of it was to outlive him." With these words *The Trial* ends. Corresponding as it does to his "elemental purity of feeling," shame is Kafka's strongest gesture. It has a dual aspect, however. Shame is an intimate human reaction, but at the same time it has social pretensions. Shame is not only shame in the presence of others, but can also be shame one feels for them. Kafka's shame, then, is no more personal than the life and thought which govern it and which he has described thus: "He does not live for the sake of his own life, he does not think for the sake of his own thought. He feels as though he were living and thinking under the constraint of a family. . . . Because of this unknown family . . . he cannot be released." We do not know the make-up of this unknown family, which is composed of human beings and animals. But this much is clear: it is this family that forces Kafka to move cosmic ages in his writings. Doing this family's bidding, he moves the mass of historical happenings as Sisyphus rolled the stone. As he does so, its nether side comes to light; it is not a pleasant sight, but Kafka is capable of bearing it. "To believe in progress is not to believe that progress has already taken place. That would be no belief." Kafka did not consider the age in which he lived as an advance over the beginnings of time. His novels are set in a swamp world. In his works, created things appear at the stage which Bachofen has termed the hetaeric stage. The fact that it is now forgotten does not mean that it does not extend into the present. On the contrary: it is actual by virtue of this very oblivion. An experience deeper than that of an average person can make contact with it. "I have experience," we read in one of Kafka's earliest notes, "and I am not joking when I say that it is a seasickness on dry land." It is no accident that the first "Meditation" was made on a swing. And Kafka does not tire of expressing himself on the fluctuating nature of experiences. Each gives way and mingles with its opposite. "It was summer, a hot day," so begins "The Knock at the Manor Gate." "With my sister I was passing the gate of a great house on our way home. I don't remember whether she knocked on the gate out of mischief or in a fit of absent-mindedness, or merely shook her fist at it and did not knock at all." The very possibility of the third alternative puts the other two, which at first seemed harmless, in a different light. It is from the swampy soil of such experiences that Kafka's female characters rise. They are swamp creatures like Leni, "who stretches out the middle and ring fingers of her right hand between which the connecting web of skin reached almost to the top joint, short as the fingers were." "Fine times," so the ambivalent Frieda reminisces about her earlier life; "you never asked me about my past." This past takes us back to the dark, deep womb, the scene of the mating "whose untrammeled voluptuousness," to quote Bachofen, "is hateful to the pure forces of heavenly light and which justifies the term used by Arnobius, *luteae voluptates* [dirty voluptuousness]."

Only from this vantage point can the technique of Kafka the storyteller be comprehended. Whenever figures in the novels have anything to say to K., no matter how important or surprising it may be, they do so casually and with the implication that he must really have known it all along. It is as though nothing new was being imparted, as though the hero was just being subtly invited to recall to mind something that he had forgotten. This is how Willy Haas has interpreted the course of events in *The Trial*, and justifiably so. "The object of the trial," he writes, "indeed, the real hero of this incredible book is forgetting, whose main characteristic is the forgetting of itself.... Here it has actually become a mute figure in the shape of the accused man, a figure of the most striking intensity." It probably cannot be denied that "this mysterious center . . . derives from the Jewish religion." "Memory plays a very mysterious role as piousness. It is not an ordinary, but . . . the most profound quality of Jehovah that he remembers, that he retains an infallible memory 'to the third and fourth, even to the hundredth generation.' The most sacred . . . act of the . . . ritual is the erasing of sins from the book of memory."

What has been forgotten—and this insight affords us yet another avenue of access to Kafka's work—is never something purely individual. Everything forgotten mingles with what has been forgotten of the prehistoric world, forms countless, uncertain, changing compounds, yielding a constant flow of new, strange products. Oblivion is the container from which the inexhaustible intermediate world in Kafka's stories presses toward the light. "Here the very fullness of the world is considered as the only reality. All spirit must be concrete, particularized in order to have its place and *raison d'être.* The spiritual, if it plays a role at all, turns into spirits. These spirits become definite individuals, with names and a very special connection with the name of the worshiper. . . . Without any scruples their fullness is crammed into the fullness of the world. . . . The crowd of spirits is swelled without any concern . . . new ones are constantly added to the old ones, and all are distinguished from the others by their own names." All this does not refer to Kafka, but to—China. This is how Franz Rosenzweig describes the Chinese ancestor cult in his *Star of Redemption.* To Kafka, the world of his ancestors was as unfathomable as the world of realities was important for him, and we may be sure that, like the totem poles of primitive peoples, the world of ancestors took him down to the animals. Incidentally, Kafka is not the only writer for whom animals are the receptacles of the forgotten. In Tieck's profound story "Fair Eckbert," the forgotten name of a little dog, Strohmi, stands for a mysterious guilt. One can understand, then, that Kafka did not tire of picking up the forgotten from animals. They are not the goal, to be sure, but one cannot do without them. A case in point is the "hunger artist" who, "strictly speaking, was only an impediment on the way to the menagerie." Can one not see the animals in "The Burrow" or "The Giant Mole" ponder as they dig in? And yet this thinking is extremely flighty. Irresolutely it flits from one worry to the next, it nibbles at every anxiety with the fickleness of despair. Thus there are butterflies in Kafka, too. The guilt-ridden "Hunter Gracchus," who refuses to acknowledge his guilt, "has turned into a butterfly." "Don't laugh," says the hunter Gracchus. This much is certain: of all of Kafka's creatures, the animals have the greatest opportunity for reflection. What corruption is in the law, anxiety is in their thinking. It messes a situation up, yet it is the only hopeful thing about it. However, because the most forgotten alien land is one's own body, one can understand why Kafka called the cough that erupted from within him "the animal." It was the most advanced outpost of the great herd.

The strangest bastard which the prehistoric world has begotten with guilt in Kafka is Odradek [in "The Cares of a Family Man"]. "At first sight it looks like a flat, star-shaped spool for thread, and it really seems to have thread wound around it; to be sure, they probably are only old, broken-off bits of thread that are knotted and tangled together, of all sorts and colors. But it is not just a spool, for a small wooden cross-bar sticks out of the middle of the star, and another small rod is joined to it at a right angle. With the aid of this latter rod on one side and one of the extensions of the star on the other, the whole thing can stand upright as if on two legs." Odradek "stays alternately in the attic, on the staircase, in the corridors, and in the hall." So it prefers the same places as the court of law which investigates guilt. Attics are the places of discarded, forgotten objects. Perhaps the necessity to appear before a court of justice gives rise to a feeling similar to that with which one approaches trunks in the attic which have been locked up for years. One would like to put off this chore till the end of time, just as K. regards his written defense as suitable "for occupying one's senile mind some day during retirement."

Odradek is the form which things assume in oblivion. They are distorted. The "cares of a family man," which no one can identify, are distorted; the bug, of which we know all too well that it represents Gregor Samsa, is distorted; the big animal, half lamb, half kitten, for which "the butcher's knife" might be "a release," is distorted. These Kafka figures are connected by a long series of figures with the prototype of distortion, the hunchback. Among the images in Kafka's stories, none is more frequent than that of the man who bows his head far down on his chest: the fatigue of the court officials, the noise affecting the doormen in the hotel, the low ceiling facing the visitors in the gallery. In the *Penal Colony* those in power use an archaic apparatus which engraves letters with curlicues on the backs of guilty men, multiplying the stabs and piling up the ornaments to the point where the back of the guilty man becomes clairvoyant and is able to decipher the writing from which he must derive the nature of his unknown guilt. It is the back on which this is incumbent. It was always this way with Kafka. Compare this early diary entry: "In order to be as heavy as possible, which I believe to be an aid to falling asleep, I had crossed my arms and put my hands on my shoulders, so that I lay there like a soldier with his pack." Quite palpably, being loaded down is here equated with forgetting, the forgetting of a sleeping man. The same symbol occurs in the folksong "The Little Hunchback." This little man is at home in distorted life; he will disappear with the coming of the Messiah, of whom a great rabbi once said that he did not wish to change the world by force, but would only make a slight adjustment in it.

When I come into my room,
My little bed to make,
A little hunchback is in there,
With laughter does he shake.

This is the laughter of Odradek, which is described as sounding "something like the rustling in falling leaves."

When I kneel upon my stool
And I want to pray,
A hunchbacked man is in the room
And he starts to say:
My dear child, I beg of you,
Pray for the little hunchback too.

So ends the folksong. In his depth Kafka touches the ground which neither "mythical divination" nor "existential theology" supplied him with. It is the core of folk tradition, the German as well as the Jewish. Even if Kafka did not pray—and this we do not know—he still possessed in the highest degree what Malebranche called "the natural prayer of the soul": attentiveness. And in this attentiveness he included all living creatures, as saints include them in their prayers.

Sancho Panza

In a Hasidic village, so the story goes, Jews were sitting together in a shabby inn one Sabbath evening. They were all local people, with the exception of one person no one knew, a very poor, ragged man who was squatting in a dark corner at the back of the room. All sorts of things were discussed, and then it was suggested that everyone should tell what wish he would make if one were granted him. One man wanted money; another wished for a son-in-law; a third dreamed of a new carpenter's bench; and so everyone spoke in turn. After they had finished, only the beggar in his dark corner was left. Reluctantly and hesitantly he answered the question. "I wish I were a powerful king reigning over a big country. Then, some night while I was asleep in my palace, an enemy would invade my country, and by dawn his horsemen would penetrate to my castle and meet with no resistance. Roused from my sleep, I wouldn't have time even to dress and I would have to flee in my shirt. Rushing over hill and dale and through forests day and night, I would finally arrive safely right here at the bench in this corner. This is my wish." The others exchanged uncomprehending glances. "And what good would this wish have done you?" someone asked. "I'd have a shirt," was the answer.

This story takes us right into the milieu of Kafka's world. No one says that the distortions which it will be the Messiah's mission to set right someday affect only our space; surely they are distortions of our time as well. Kafka must have had this in mind, and in this certainty he made the grandfather in "The Next Village" say: "Life is astonishingly short. As I look back over it, life seems so foreshortened to me that I can hardly understand, for instance, how a young man can decide to ride over to the next village without being afraid that, quite apart from accidents, even the span of a normal life that passes happily may be totally insufficient for such a ride." This old man's brother is the beggar whose "normal" life that "passes happily" does not even leave him time for a wish, but who is exempted from this wish in the abnormal, unhappy life, that is, the flight which he attempts in his story, and exchanges the wish for its fulfillment.

Among Kafka's creatures there is a clan which reckons with the brevity of life in a peculiar way. It comes from the "city in the south . . . of which it was said: 'People live there who—imagine!—don't sleep!'—'And why not?'—'Because they don't get tired.'—'Why don't they?'—'Because they are fools.'—'Don't fools get tired?'—'How could fools get tired?' " One can see that the fools are akin to the indefatigable assistants. But there is more to this clan. It is casually remarked of the faces of the assistants that they seem to be those of "grown-ups, perhaps even students."

Actually, the students who appear in the strangest places in Kafka's works are the spokesmen for and leaders of this clan. "'But when do you sleep?' asked Karl, looking at the student in surprise. 'Oh, sleep!' said the student. 'I'll get some sleep when I'm finished with my studies.'" This reminds one of the reluctance with which children go to bed; after all, while they are asleep, something might happen that concerns them. "Don't forget the best!" We are familiar with this remark from a nebulous bunch of old stories, although it may not occur in any of them. But forgetting always involves the best, for it involves the possibility of redemption. "The idea of helping me is an illness and requires bed rest for a cure," ironically says the restlessly wandering ghost of the hunter Gracchus. While they study, the students are awake, and perhaps their being kept awake is the best thing about these studies. The hunger artist fasts, the doorkeeper is silent, and the students are awake. This is the veiled way in which the great rules of asceticism operate in Kafka.

Their crowning achievement is studying. Reverently Kafka unearths it from long-lost boyhood. "Not very unlike this—a long time ago—Karl had sat at home at his parents' table writing his homework, while his father read the newspaper or did bookkeeping and correspondence for some organization and his mother was busy sewing, drawing the thread high out of the material in her hand. To avoid disturbing his father, Karl used to put only his exercise book and his writing materials on the table, while he arranged the books he needed on chairs to the right and left of him. How quiet it had been there! How seldom strangers had entered that room!" Perhaps these studies had amounted to nothing. But they are very close to that nothing which alone makes it possible for something to be useful—that is, to the Tao. This is what Kafka was after with his desire "to hammer a table together with painstaking craftsmanship and, at the same time, to do nothing—not in such a way that someone could say 'Hammering is nothing to him,' but 'To him, hammering is real hammering and at the same time nothing,' which would have made the hammering even bolder, more determined, more real, and, if you like, more insane." This is the resolute, fanatical mien which students have when they study; it is the strangest mien imaginable. The scribes, the students, are out of breath; they fairly race along. "Often the official dictates in such a low voice that the scribe cannot even hear it sitting down; then he has to jump up, catch the dictation, quickly sit down again and write it down, then jump up again and so forth. How strange that is! It is almost incomprehensible!" It may be easier to understand this if one thinks of the actors in the Nature Theater. Actors have to catch their cues in a flash, and they resemble those assiduous people in other ways as well. Truly, for them "hammering is real hammering and at the same time nothing"—provided that this is part of their role. They study this role, and only a bad actor would forget a word or a movement. For the members of the Oklahoma troupe, however, the role is their earlier life; hence the "nature" in this Nature Theater. Its actors have been redeemed, but not so the student whom Karl watches silently on the balcony as he reads his book, "turning the pages, occasionally looking something up in another book which he always snatched up quick as a flash, and frequently making notes in a notebook, which he always did with his face surprisingly close to the paper."

Kafka does not grow tired of representing the *gestus* in this fashion, but he invariably does so with astonishment. K. has rightly been compared with the Good Soldier Schweik; the one is astonished at everything, the other at nothing. The invention of the film and the phonograph came in an age of maximum alienation of men from one another, of unpredictably intervening relationships which have become their only ones. Experiments have proved that a man does not recognize his own walk on the screen or his own voice on the phonograph. The situation of the subject in such experiments is Kafka's situation; this is what directs him to learning, where he may encounter fragments of his own existence, fragments that are still within the context of the role. He might catch hold of the lost *gestus* the way Peter Schlemihl caught hold of the shadow he had sold. He might understand himself, but what an enormous effort would be required! It is a tempest that blows from the land of oblivion, and learning is a cavalry attack against it. Thus the beggar on the corner bench rides toward his past in order to catch hold of himself in the figure of the fleeing king. This ride, which is long enough for a life, corresponds to life, which is too short for a ride—" . . . until one shed one's spurs, for there were no spurs, threw away the reins, for there were no reins, and barely saw the land before one as a smoothly mown heath, with the horse's neck and head already gone." This is the fulfillment of the fantasy about the blessed horseman who rushes toward the past on an untrammeled, happy journey, no longer a burden on his race horse. But accursed is the rider who is chained to his nag because he has set himself a goal for the future, even though it is as close as the coal cellar—accursed his animal, accursed both of them. "Seated on the bucket, my hands up on the handle, with the simplest kind of bridle, I propel myself with difficulty down the stairs; but once down below, my bucket ascends, superbly, superbly; camels lying flat on the ground do not rise any more handsomely as they shake themselves under the sticks of their drivers." There is no more hopeless vista than that of "the regions of the ice mountains" in which the bucket rider drops out of sight forever. From the "nethermost regions of death" blows the wind that is favorable to him, the same wind which so often blows from the prehistoric world in Kafka's works, and which also propels the boat of the hunter Gracchus. "At mysteries and sacrifices, among Greeks as well as barbarians," writes Plutarch, "it is taught that there must be two primary essences and two opposing forces, one of which points to the right and straight ahead, whereas the other turns around and drives back." Reversal is the direction of learning which transforms existence into writing. Its teacher is Bucephalus, "the new attorney," who takes the road back without the powerful Alexander—which means, rid of the onrushing conqueror. "His flanks free and unhampered by the thighs of a rider, under a quiet lamp far from the din of Alexander's battles, he reads and turns the pages of our old books."

Werner Kraft once wrote an interpretation of this story. After giving careful attention to every detail of the text, Kraft notes: "Nowhere else in literature is there such a powerful and penetrating criticism of the myth in its full scope." According to Kraft, Kafka does not use the word "justice," yet it is justice which serves as the point of departure for his critique of the myth. But once we have reached this point, we are in danger of missing Kafka by stopping here. Is it really the law which could thus be invoked against the myth in the name of justice? No, as a legal scholar Bucephalus remains true to his origins, except that he does not seem to be practicing law—and this is probably something new, in Kafka's sense, for both Bucephalus and the bar. The law which is studied and not practiced any longer is the gate to justice.

The gate to justice is learning. And yet Kafka does not dare attach to this learning the promises which tradition has attached to the study of the Torah. His assistants are sextons who have lost their house of prayer, his students are pupils who have lost the Holy Writ. Now there is nothing to support them on their "untrammeled, happy journey." Kafka, however, has found the law of his journey—at least on one occasion he succeeded in bringing its breathtaking speed in line with the slow narrative pace that he presumably sought all his life. He expressed this in a little prose piece which is his most perfect creation not only because it is an interpretation.

"Without ever boasting of it, Sancho Panza succeeded in the course of years, by supplying a lot of romances of chivalry and adventure for the evening and night hours, in so diverting from him his demon, whom he later called Don Quixote, that his demon thereupon freely performed the maddest exploits, which, however, lacking a preordained object, which Sancho Panza himself was supposed to have been, did no one any harm. A free man, Sancho Panza philosophically followed Don Quixote on his crusades, perhaps out of a sense of responsibility, and thus enjoyed a great and profitable entertainment to the end of his days."

Sancho Panza, a sedate fool and clumsy assistant, sent his rider on ahead; Bucephalus outlived his. Whether it is a man or a horse is no longer so important, if only the burden is removed from the back.

Kafka's *The Metamorphosis*: Metamorphosis of the Metaphor

Stanley Corngold

> What *is* literature? Where does it come from? What use is it? What questionable things! Add to this questionableness the further questionableness of what you say, and what you get is a monstrosity.
>
> Franz Kafka, *Dearest Father*

To judge from its critical reception, Franz Kafka's *The Metamorphosis* (*Die Verwandlung*) is the most haunting and universal of all his stories, and yet Kafka never claimed for it any special distinction. He never, for example, accorded it the importance he reserved for "The Judgment," a work it resembles but which it surpasses in depth and scope.[1] On the morning of September 23, 1912, after the night he spent composing "The Judgment," Kafka, with a fine elation, wrote in his diary: "Only *in this way* can writing be done, only with such coherence, with such a complete opening out of the body and the soul" (*DI,* 276). But throughout the period of the composition of *The Metamorphosis*—from November 17 to December 7, 1912—and until the beginning of the new year, his diary does not show an entry of any kind; and when it resumes on February 11, 1913, it is with an interpretation not of *The Metamorphosis* but of "The Judgment." The diary does finally acknowledge the new story, almost a year after its composition, with this remark: "I have been reading *The Metamorphosis* at home, and I find it bad" [78].

Kafka was especially disappointed with the conclusion of the story. On January 19, 1914, he wrote, "Great antipathy to *The Metamorphosis.* Unreadable ending" [78], and he blamed the botched conclusion on a business trip he was obliged to make just as he was well advanced into the piece. His annoyance and remorse at having to interrupt his work is vivid in the letters written at the time to his fiancée, Felice Bauer. These letters reveal Kafka's moods all during the composition of the story—moods almost entirely negative. The story originates "during my misery in bed and oppresses me with inmost intensity [*innerlichst bedrängt*]" (*BF,* 102) [71]. The tonality of the piece appears again as "despair" [72] and "monotony" [75]. On November 23 the story is said to be "a little horrible [*fürchterlich*]" (*BF,* 116) [73]; a day later, "exceptionally repulsive" [73]. A trace of liking and concern for *The Metamorphosis* appears in a later letter: "It's a pity that in many passages of the story my states of exhaustion and other interruptions and extraneous worries are clearly inscribed [*eingezeichnet*]; it could certainly have been done more purely [*reiner*]; this can be seen precisely from the charming [*süße*] pages" (*BF,* 160) [77]. But by this time Kafka has begun to consider *The Metamorphosis* more and more an interruption of the writing of the uncompleted novel that was to become *Amerika.* Finally, on the morning of December 7, he states the complaint that will recur: "My little story is finished, but today's ending does not make me happy at all; it really could have been better, no doubt about that" [77].

Kafka's own sense of *The Metamorphosis* compels us to consider the work essentially unfinished. The interruptions that set in so frequently past the midpoint of the story tend to shift the weight of its significance back toward its beginning. This view draws support from other evidence establishing what might be termed the general and fundamental priority of the beginning in Kafka's works. One thinks of the innumerable openings to stories scattered throughout the diaries and notebooks, suddenly appearing and as swiftly vanishing, leaving undeveloped the endless dialectical structures they contain. On October 16, 1921, Kafka explicitly invoked "the misery of having perpetually to begin, the lack of the illusion that anything is more than, or even as much as, a beginning" (*DII,* 193). For Dieter Hasselblatt, Kafka's prose "is in flight from the beginning, it does not strive toward the end: *initiofugal,* not final. And since it takes the impulse of its progression from what is set forth or what is just present at the outset, it cannot be completed. The end, the conclusion, is unimportant compared to the opening situation."[2]

One is directed, it would seem, by these empirical and theoretical considerations to formulate the overwhelming question of *The Metamorphosis* as the question of the meaning of its beginning. What fundamental intention inspires the opening sentence: "When Gregor Samsa woke up one morning from unsettling dreams, he found himself changed in his bed into a monstrous vermin [*ungeheueres Ungeziefer*]" (*M,* 3; *E,* 71) [3]? We shall do well to keep in mind, in the words of Edward Said, "the identity [of the beginning] as *radical* starting point; the intransitive and conceptual aspect, that which has no object but its own constant clarification."[3] Much of the action of *The Metamorphosis* consists of Kafka's attempt to come to terms with its beginning.

The opening recounts the transformation of a man into a monstrous, verminous bug; in the process, it appears to accomplish still another change: it metamorphoses a common figure of speech. This second transformation emerges in the light of the hypothesis proposed in 1947 by Günther Anders: "Kafka's sole point of departure is . . . *ordinary language.* . . . More precisely: *he draws from the resources on hand, the figurative nature* [*Bildcharakter*], *of language.* He takes metaphors at their word [*beim Wort*]. For example, because Gregor Samsa wants to live as an artist [i.e. as a *Luftmensch*—one who lives on air, lofty and free-floating], in the eyes of the highly respectable, hard-working world he is a 'nasty bug [*dreckiger Käfer*]': and so in *The Metamorphosis* he wakes up as a beetle whose ideal of happiness is to be sticking to the ceiling." For Anders, *The Metamorphosis* originates in the transformation of a familiar metaphor into a fictional being having the literal attributes of this figure. The story develops as aspects of the metaphor are enacted in minute detail. Anders's evidence for this view is furnished partly by his total understanding of Kafka: "What Kafka describes are . . . existing things, the world, as it appears to the stranger (namely strange)." Anders further adduces examples of everyday figures of speech which, taken literally, inspire stories and scenes in Kafka. "Language says, 'To feel it with your own body [*Am eignen Leibe etwas erfahren*]' when it wants to express the reality of experience. This is the basis of Kafka's *In the Penal Colony*, in which the criminal's punishment is not communicated to him by word of mouth, but is instead scratched into his body with a needle."[4]

Anders's hypothesis has been taken up in Walter Sokel's studies of *The Metamorphosis*. The notion of the "extended metaphor," which Sokel considers in an early essay to be "significant" and "interesting" though "insufficient as a total explanation of *The Metamorphosis*,"[5] reemerges in his *Writer in Extremis* as a crucial determinant of Expressionism: "The character Gregor Samsa has been transformed into a metaphor that states his essential self, and this metaphor in turn is treated like an actual fact.

Samsa does not call himself a cockroach; instead he wakes up to find himself one." Expressionistic prose, for Sokel, is defined precisely by such "extended metaphors, metaphoric visualizations of emotional situations, uprooted from any explanatory context."[6] In *Franz Kafka: Tragik und Ironie,* the factual character of the Kafkan metaphor is emphasized: "In Kafka's work, as in the dream, symbol is fact. . . . A world of pure significance, of naked expression, is represented deceptively as a sequence of empirical facts."[7] Finally, in his *Franz Kafka,* Sokel states the most advanced form of his understanding of Kafka's literalization of the metaphor:

> German usage applies the term *Ungeziefer* (vermin) to persons considered low and contemptible, even as our usage of "cockroach" describes a person deemed a spineless and miserable character. The traveling salesman Gregor Samsa, in Kafka's *Metamorphosis,* is "like a cockroach" because of his spineless and abject behavior and parasitic wishes. However, Kafka drops the word "like" and has the metaphor become reality when Gregor Samsa wakes up finding himself turned into a giant vermin. With this metamorphosis, Kafka reverses the original act of metamorphosis carried out by thought when it forms metaphor; for metaphor is always "metamorphosis." Kafka transforms metaphor back into his fictional reality, and this counter-metamorphosis becomes the starting point of his tale.[8]

The sequence of Sokel's reflections on Anders's hypothesis contains an important shift of emphasis. Initially, the force of *The Metamorphosis* is felt to lie in the choice and "extension" (dramatization) of the powerful metaphor. To support his view, Sokel cites Johannes Urzidil's recollection of a conversation with Kafka: "Once Kafka said to me: 'To be a poet means to be strong in metaphors. The greatest poets were always the most metaphorical ones. They were those who recognized the deep mutual concern, yes, even the identity of things between which nobody noticed the slightest connection before. It is the range and the scope of the metaphor which makes one a poet.' "[9] But in his later work Sokel locates the origin of Kafka's "poetry" not in the metamorphosis of reality accomplished by the metaphor but in the "counter-metamorphosis" accomplished by the transformation of the metaphor. Kafka's "taking over" figures from ordinary speech enacts a second metaphorization (*metapherá* = "a transfer")—one that concludes in the literalization and hence the metamorphosis of the metaphor.[10] This point once made, the genuine importance of Kafka's remarks to Urzidil stands revealed through their irony. In describing the poet as one "strong in metaphors," Kafka is describing writers other than himself; for he is the writer par excellence who came to detect in metaphorical language a crucial obstacle to his own enterprise.

Kafka's critique of the metaphor begins early, in the phantasmagoric story "Description of a Struggle" (1904–5). The first-person narrator addresses the supplicant—another persona of the author—with exaggerated severity:

> Now I realize, by God, that I guessed from the very beginning the state you are in. Isn't it something like a fever, a seasickness on dry land, a kind of leprosy? Don't you feel that it's this very feverishness which is preventing you from being properly satisfied with the genuine [*wahrhaftigen*] names of things, and that now, in your frantic haste, you're just pelting them with

> any old [*zufällige*] names? You can't do it fast enough. But hardly have you run away from them when you've forgotten the names you gave them. The poplar in the fields, which you've called the "Tower of Babel" because you didn't want to know it was a poplar, sways again without a name, so you have to call it "Noah in his cups." [*DS*, 60]

The weight of these accusations falls on the character who is dissatisfied with the "genuine" names of things and substitutes metaphors for them. His action is doubly arbitrary. First, the motive that prompts him to rename things—the act that generates figures—is arbitrary. His metaphors are the contingent product of a fever; or worse, they arise from deliberate bad faith, the refusal to accept the conventional bond of word and thing. Second, not a single one of his metaphors is any good, none leaves a permanent trace.

But what is also striking about this passage is its critique of "ordinary" as well as figurative names. With the irony of overstatement, the accusatory speaker calls the conventional link of name and thing "genuine," despite the fact that he does not appear to have at his disposal any such genuine names to identify the affliction of the supplicant. The speaker suffers from the same unhappy necessity of designating things by an enchainment of "any old" metaphors—such as "fever," "seasickness on dry land," "a kind of leprosy." Because (as Derrida says) "language is fundamentally metaphorical," figuring, in Heidegger's phrase, the "significations to which words accrue" as the significations within words, a critique of metaphor amounts logically to a critique of naming.[11] The exact difference between ordinary names and figurative names cannot be specified. Kafka's speaker, while seeing no advantage in replacing names with the figures of poetic language, at the same time cannot enact naming except by associating metaphors. Metaphors falsify, and they also invade "genuine" names.[12]

In a diary entry for December 27, 1911, Kafka recorded his despair of a particular attempt at metaphor. "An incoherent assumption is thrust like a board between the actual feeling and the metaphor of the description" (*DI,* 201). Kafka had begun this diary entry confidently, claiming to have found an image analogous to a moral sentiment. "My feeling when I write something that is wrong might be depicted as follows": A man stands before two holes in the ground, one to the right and one to the left; he is waiting for something that can rise up only out of the hole to the right. Instead, apparitions rise, one after the other, from the left; they try to attract his attention and finally even succeed in covering up the right-hand hole. At this stage of the construction, the materiality of the image predominates; as it is developed, however, so is the role of the spectator, who scatters these apparitions upward and in all directions in the hope "that after the false apparitions have been exhausted, the true will finally appear." But precisely at the point of conjuring up "truthful apparitions," the metaphorist feels most critically the inadequacy of this figurative language: "How weak this picture is." And he concludes with the complaint that between his sentiment and figurative language there is no true coherence (though he cannot, predictably, say this without having recourse to a figure of speech). Now what is crucial here is that an image that is mainly material has failed to represent the sentiment of writing; and though it has been replaced by one that introduces the consciousness of an observer, between the moral sentiment of writing and an act of perception there is also no true connection. If the writer finds it difficult to construct metaphors for "a feeling of falsity," how much greater must be his difficulty in constructing figures for genuine feelings, figures for satisfying the desire "to write all my anxiety entirely out of me, write it into the depths of the paper just as it comes out of the depths of me, or write it down in such a way that I could draw what I have written into me completely" (*DI,* 173).

Kafka's awareness of the limitations of metaphorical language continues to grow. The desire to represent a state of mind directly in language—in a form consubstantial with that consciousness—and hence to create symbols cannot be gratified. "For everything outside the phenomenal world, language can only be used allusively [as an allusion, *andeutungsweise*] but never even approximately in a comparative way [as a simile, *vergleichsweise*], since, corresponding as it does to the phenomenal world, it is concerned only with property and its relations" (*DF,* 40; *H,* 45). But try as language will to reduce itself to its allusive function, it continues to be dependent on the metaphor, on developing states of mind by means of material analogues. On December 6, 1921, Kafka wrote: "Metaphors are one among many things which make me despair of writing. Writing's lack of independence of the world, its dependence on the maid who tends the fire, on the cat warming itself by the stove; it is even dependent on the poor old human being warming himself by the stove. All these are independent activities ruled by their own laws; only writing is helpless, cannot live in itself, is a joke and a despair" (*DII,* 200–201). Indeed, the question arises of what truth even a language determinedly nonsymbolic—in Kafka's words, "allusive"—could possess. The parable employs language allusively, but in the powerful fable "On Parables" Kafka writes: "All these parables really set out to say merely that the incomprehensible is incomprehensible, and we know that already" (*GW,* 258). At this point, it is clear, the literary enterprise is seen in its radically problematical character. The growing desperation of

Kafka's critique of metaphorical language leads to the result—in the words of Maurice Blanchot—that at this time of Kafka's life "the exigency of the truth of this other world [of sheer inwardness determined on salvation] henceforth surpasses in his eyes the exigency of the work of art."[13] This situation suggests not the renunciation of writing but only the clearest possible awareness of its limitations, an awareness that emerges through Kafka's perplexity before the metaphor in the work of art and his despair of escaping it.

Kafka's "counter-metamorphosis" of the metaphor in *The Metamorphosis* is inspired by his fundamental objection to the metaphor. His purpose is accomplished—so Anders and Sokel propose—through the literalization of the metaphor. But is this true? What does it mean, exactly, to literalize a metaphor? The metaphor designates something (A) *as* something (B)—something in the quality of something not itself. To say that someone is a verminous bug is to designate a moral sensibility as something unlike itself, as a material sensation—complicated, of course, by the atmosphere of loathing that this sensation evokes. With I. A. Richards, I shall call the *tenor* of the metaphor (A), the thing designated, occulted, replaced, but otherwise established by the context of the figure; and the *vehicle* the metaphor proper, (B), that thing *as* which the tenor is designated.[14] If the metaphor is taken out of context, however, if it is taken literally, it no longer functions as a vehicle but as a name, directing us to (B) as an abstraction or an object in the world. Moreover, it directs us to (B) in the totality of its qualities and not, as does the vehicle, only to those qualities of (B) that can be assigned to (A).

This analysis will suggest the destructively paradoxical consequence of "taking the metaphor literally," supposing now that such a thing is possible. Reading the figure literally, we go to (B) as an object in the world in its totality; yet reading it metaphorically, we go to (B) only in its quality as a predicate of (A). As literalization proceeds, as we attempt to experience in (B) more and more qualities that can be accommodated by (A), we *metamorphose* (A). But if the metaphor is to be preserved and (A) and (B) are to remain unlike, we must stop before the metamorphosis is complete. If, now, the tenor—as in *The Metamorphosis*—is a human consciousness, the increasing literalization of the vehicle transforms the tenor into a monster.

This genesis of monsters occurs independently of the nature of the vehicle. The intent toward literalization of a metaphor linking a human consciousness and a material sensation produces a monster in every instance, no matter whether the vehicle is odious or not, whether we begin with the metaphor of a "louse" or of a man who is a "jewel" or a "rock." It now appears that Anders is not correct in suggesting that in *The Metamorphosis* literalization of the metaphor is actually accomplished; for then we should have not an indefinite monster but simply a bug. Indeed, the continual alteration of Gregor's body suggests on-going metamorphosis, the *process* of literalization in various directions and not its end state. Nor would Sokel's earlier formulation appear to be tenable: the metaphor is not treated "like an actual fact." Only the alien cleaning woman gives Gregor Samsa the factual, entomological identity of a "dung beetle," but precisely "to forms of address like these Gregor would not respond" (*M,* 45) [49]. The cleaning woman does not know that a metamorphosis has occurred, that within this insect shape there is a human consciousness—one superior at times to the ordinary consciousness of Gregor Samsa. It appears, then, that the metamorphosis in the Samsa household of man into vermin is unsettling not only because vermin are disturbing, or because the vivid representation of a human "louse" is disturbing, but because the indeterminate, fluid crossing of a human tenor and a material vehicle is in itself unsettling. Gregor is at one moment pure rapture and at another very nearly pure dung beetle, at times grossly human and at times airily buglike. In shifting incessantly the relation of Gregor's mind and body, Kafka shatters the suppositious unity of ideal tenor and bodily vehicle within the metaphor. This destruction must distress common sense, which defines itself by such "genuine" relations, such natural assertions of analogues between consciousness and matter, and in this way masks the knowledge of its own strangeness. The ontological legitimation for asserting analogues is missing in Kafka, who maintains the most ruthless division between the fire of the spirit and the "filth" of the world: "What we call the world of the senses is the Evil in the spiritual world" (*DF,* 39).

The distortion of the metaphor in *The Metamorphosis* is inspired by a radical aesthetic intention, which proceeds by destruction and results in creation—of a monster, virtually nameless, existing as an opaque sign.[15] "The name alone, revealed through a natural death, not the living soul, vouches for that in man which is immortal."[16] But what is remarkable in *The Metamorphosis* is that "the immortal part" of the writer accomplishes itself odiously, in the quality of an indeterminacy sheerly negative. The exact sense of his intention is captured in the *Ungeziefer,* a word that cannot be expressed by the English words "bug" or "vermin." *Ungeziefer* derives (as Kafka probably knew) from the late Middle High German word originally meaning "the unclean animal not suited for sacrifice."[17] If for Kafka "writing . . . [is] a form of prayer" (*DF,* 312), this act of writing reflects its own hopelessness. As a distortion of the "genuine" names of things, without significance as metaphor or as literal fact, the monster of *The Metamorphosis* is, like writing itself, a "fever" and a "despair."

Kafka's metamorphosis—through aberrant literalization—of the metaphor "this man is a vermin" appears to be an intricate and comprehensive act in which one can discern three orders of significance, all of which inform *The Metamorphosis.* These meanings emerge separately as one focuses critically on three facts: that the metaphor distorted is a familiar element of ordinary language; that, the distortion being incomplete, the body of the original metaphor maintains a shadow existence within the metamorphosis, and the body of *this* metaphor—a verminous bug—is negative and repulsive; and finally, that the source of the metamorphosis is, properly speaking, not the familiar metaphor but a radical aesthetic intention. Together these meanings interpenetrate in a dialectical way. For example, the aesthetic intention reflects itself in a monster but does so by distorting an initially monstrous metaphor; the outcome of its destroying a negative is itself a negative. These relations illuminate both Kafka's saying, "Doing the negative thing is imposed on us, an addition" (*DF,* 36–37), and his remark to Milena Jesenská-Pollak, "But even the truth of longing is not so much its truth, rather is it an expression of the lie of everything else" (*LM,* 200). For the sake of analysis, each of the three intents can be separated and discussed independently.

Kafka metamorphoses a figure of speech embedded in ordinary language. The intent is to make strange the familiar, not to invent the new; Kafka's diaries for the period around 1912 show that his created metaphors are more complex than "salesmen are vermin." To stress the estrangement of the monster from his familiar setting in the metaphor—the dirty bug—is to stress Gregor Samsa's estrangement from his identity in the family.

Gregor harks back to, yet defiantly resists, integration into the "ordinary language" of the family. The condition of the distorted metaphor, estranged from familiar speech, shapes the family drama of *The Metamorphosis*; the *Ungeziefer* is in the fullest sense of the word *ungeheue* (monstrous)—a being that cannot be accommodated in a family.[18]

Is it too odd an idea to see this family drama as the conflict between ordinary language and a being having the character of an indecipherable word? It will seem less odd, at any rate, to grasp the family life of the Samsas as a characteristic language. The family defines itself by the ease with which it enters into collusion on the question of Gregor. Divisions of opinion do arise—touching, say, on the severity of the treatment due Gregor—but issue at once into new decisions. The family's projects develop within the universe of their concerns, through transparent words and gestures that communicate without effort. At the end, images of family unity survive the story: the mother and father in complete union; mother, father, and daughter emerging arm in arm from the parents' bedroom to confront the boarders; mother and father "growing quieter and communicating almost unconsciously through glances" at the sight of their good-looking, shapely daughter (*M,* 58) [64].

Family language in *The Metamorphosis* has a precise symbolic correlative, Kimberly Sparks suggests, in the newspaper. The person in power at any moment reads or manipulates the newspaper.[19] Gregor has clipped the love object that hangs on his wall from an illustrated newspaper; his evening custom as head of the family had been to sit at the table and read the newspaper. It is a sorry comment on his loss of power and identity within the family that it is on newspaper that his first meal of garbage is served; the father, meanwhile, downcast for a while, fails to read the newspaper aloud to the family. When the boarders come to dominate the family, it is they who ostentatiously read the newspaper at the dinner table. The newspaper represents an order of efficient language from which Gregor is excluded.

The task of interpreting the monstrous noun that Gregor has become is more difficult; his transformation is essentially obscure and can be understood only through approximations. One such approximation is the *intelligible* transformation that also results in Gregor's becoming an opaque sign.

If Gregor had lost the ability to make himself understood by the others but had preserved his human shape, the family would have been inclined to interpret the change as temporary, would have encouraged Gregor to speak; the mere loss of language would not result in isolation and insignificance. But if Kafka wished to suggest the solitude resulting from the absolute loss of all significance, he had to present this condition as a consequence of the loss of the human form. The sense of Gregor's opaque body is thus to maintain him in a solitude without speech or intelligible gesture, in the solitude of an indecipherable sign. To put it another way: his body is the speech in which the impossibility of ordinary language expresses its own despair.

The conception of Gregor as a mutilated metaphor, uprooted from familiar language, brings another element of this family drama to light. The transformed metaphor preserves a trace of its original state. The consciousness of Gregor, like the uprooted metaphor, is defined by its reference to its former state: though Gregor cannot communicate, he continues to remember. This point underscores a feature of Kafka's metamorphosis which distinguishes it from the classical metamorphosis in Ovid,[20] where a human consciousness is converted into a natural object. *The Metamorphosis* converts a word having a quasi-natural identity, the rooted and familiar identity of ordinary speech, into a word having the character of a unique consciousness. The distorted word, without presence or future, suggests a mind dominated by nostalgia for its former life—a life of obscure habit and occupation rewarded by secure family ties.

Gregor's future is mainly obstructed by a particular form of the tyranny of nostalgia, by the "consideration" he shows his family (*M*, 23, 48) [25, 35]. Kafka's word *Rücksicht*, with its connotations of hindsight, of looking backward, is exactly right for Gregor: his consideration arises from his clinging to a mythic past—one that is, in fact, hopelessly lost (*E*, 96, 129). The play of Gregor's "consideration" reveals his family feeling as necessarily ambivalent, moving between extremes of solicitude and indifference.

The key passage has been pointed out by William Empson, though his interpretation of it is actually misleading. According to Empson, Kafka can only have been nodding when he wrote, in the scene of the sister's violin playing: "It hardly surprised [Gregor] that lately he was showing so little consideration for the others; once such consideration had been his greatest pride. . . . Now . . . his indifference to everything was much too deep for him to have gotten on his back and scrubbed himself clean against the carpet, as once he had done several times a day" (*M*, 48) [53]. "After the apple incident," Empson points out, "there could surely be no question of . . . this," for the apple fired at Gregor by his father has lodged in his back and caused a festering wound.[21] But Kafka's chiding Gregor for his indifference precisely at this point is not an "inconsistency." The moment teaches us to regard Gregor's consideration for the others as an aberration, an impulse opposite to his own most genuine concern, such as it is. It is in forgetting a useless consideration and pursuing the sound of the music that Gregor is able to discover his own condition, to perceive his irreducible strangeness. The abandonment of a *Rücksicht* that is bent on reintegration into ordinary life enables him for one moment (he did not formerly "understand" music) to imagine the music of the world in a finer tone. In our perspective this moment emerges as a restitution of language to Gregor, yet of a language fundamentally unlike the language he has lost. The character of the lost language is approximated by the abrupt fantasy of violence and incest following the violin music, into which Gregor's experience of music collapses. The language of music is degraded when it is made the means for the restitution of a family relationship.

Gregor's ambivalent relation to his family, inspired partly by the relationship between literary and conventional figurative language, suggests Kafka's own ambivalent feeling about intimacy. His ambivalence, centering as it does on an idea of renunciation, is spelled out in an early account of his love for the Yiddish actress Mrs. Tschissik. "A young man . . . declares to this woman his love to which he has completely fallen victim and . . . immediately renounces the woman. . . . Should I be grateful or should I curse the fact that despite all misfortune I can still feel love, an unearthly love but still for earthly objects?" (*DI*, 139). We know that Kafka at times thought the utmost a man might achieve was to found a family; he liked to quote the words attributed to Flaubert describing a family full of children: "*Ils sont dans le vrai* [they are living the truthful life]."[22] But he also wrote to Felice Bauer, "Rather put on blinkers and go my way to the limit than have the familiar pack [*das heimatliche Rudel*] mill around me and distract my gaze" (*DII*, 167, *Ta*, 514). The precarious existence that Kafka maintained outside "the house of life" required vigilant curbing of his nostalgia.

The separateness and nostalgia that inform Gregor's relation to his family (and reflect Kafka's ambivalent feelings about intimate relations) dramatize still more sharply Kafka's relation to the familiar language on which he drew. In "Description of a Struggle," Kafka alluded to that fevered soul who could not be contented with the genuine names of things but had to scatter arbitrary names over familiar things. But later in the same text the same fictional persona declares, "When as a child I opened my eyes after a brief afternoon nap, still not quite sure I was alive, I heard my mother up on the balcony asking in a natural tone of voice: 'What are you doing, my dear? Goodness, isn't it hot?' From the garden a woman answered: 'Me, I'm having my tea on the lawn [*Ich jause so im Grünen*].' They spoke casually and not very distinctly, as though this woman had expected the question, my mother the answer" (*DS*, 62; *B*, 44). In the model of a dialogue in ordinary language, Kafka communicates his early, intense longing for and insistence on wholeness and clarity—in Klaus Wagenbach's phrase, Kafka's "plain marveling at the magic of the simple." This is the simplicity of common speech in which names and things fit effortlessly together. Kafka's "idolatrous admiration of the truth, which grows more and more marked," Wagenbach continues, "is at the root of his decision to confine himself to the linguistic material offered him by his environment."[23] But Hermann Pongs foresees in this decision a dangerous end: the result of Kafka's confining himself to the juiceless, stilted language of Prague is Gregor Samsa's ongoing metamorphosis. "The fate of the animal voice, into which human sound is changed, becomes a terrible symptom of Kafka's being cut off from the substrata of the inner form of language. Kafka scholarship has brought to light the fact that the Prague German available to Kafka, homeless between Germans, Jews and Czechs in the region of Prague, was an already etiolated literary German obliged to do without any forces of rejuvenation through dialect."[24]

There is some truth in this statement, to which Kafka's frequent animadversions on the German of Prague testify (but then, of course, the fate of the animal voice is not a "symptom" but a conscious reflection of Kafka's alienation). "Yesterday," writes Kafka, "it occurred to me that I did not always love my mother as she deserved and as I could, only because the German language prevented it. The Jewish mother is no 'Mutter'" (*DI,* 111). In a letter to Max Brod composed in June 1921, Kafka discusses the predicament of the Jewish writer writing in German. The literary language of such a Jew he calls *mauscheln*, which ordinarily means "to speak German with a Yiddish accent": "This is not to say anything against *mauscheln*—in itself it is fine. It is an organic compound of bookish German [*Papierdeutsch*] and pantomime . . . and the product of a sensitive feeling for language which has recognized that in German only the dialects are really alive, and except for them, only the most individual High German, while all the rest, the linguistic middle ground, is nothing but embers which can be brought to a semblance of life only when excessively lively Jewish hands rummage through them" (*L,* 288; *Br,* 336–37). The middle ground of the German that Kafka heard around him was frequently not the object of his nostalgia but "clamor" (*DI,* 220) or inanity—"in the next room . . . they are talking about vermin" (*DI,* 258).

Now it is precisely through this act of "rummaging" about that Kafka names, elliptically and ironically, the kind of creative distortion to which he submitted the figures of the conventional idiom. That the metamorphic character of Kafka's relation to ordinary language is frequently misunderstood, however, is particularly clear from critics' speculations about the source of this act. Wagenbach suggests that Kafka's distortions are in fact the work of Prague German, which "of its own accord" provoked the counter-metamorphosis of metaphors. Kafka's native German,

Wagenbach writes, "always possessed a vestige of unfamiliarity; distance, too, vis-à-vis the individual word set in of its own accord. Removed from the leveling effect of everyday usage, words, metaphors, and verbal constructions recovered their original variety of meaning, became richer in images, richer in associative possibilities. As a result, in Kafka's work too on almost every page such chains of association are found arising from taking words with strict literalness."[25]

But it is as questionable to maintain that *of its own accord* Prague German proffered its metaphors literally as it is to maintain, as Martin Greenberg does, that Kafka's sociological situation determined his use of metaphor, that "thanks to his distance as a Prague Jew from the German language, he [was] able to see it in an 'analytic' way."[26] In the seven hundred closely printed pages of Kafka's letters to Felice Bauer—letters written, of course, in Prague German—Kafka is not tempted to rummage about in the metaphors of the conventional idiom, to take them literally, or to see them in an analytic way. In these letters Kafka achieves the most palpable intimacy, the native coldness of Prague German notwithstanding; indeed, so intimate is the world he conjures up and creates through language that it becomes for him as much of the married state as he can bear. It is not Prague German that imposes on Kafka his sense of the untruthfulness of the metaphor and hence the fundamental form of his writing; the source lies prior to his reflections on a particular kind and state of language.

Kafka, writers Martin Walser, "accomplished the metamorphosis of reality prior to the work, by reducing—indeed, destroying—his bourgeois-biographical personality for the sake of a development that has for its goal the personality of the poet; this poetic personality, the *poetica personalità,* establishes the form."[27] It is Kafka's literary consciousness, reflecting itself in the destruction of all intimacy even with itself, which from the beginning puts distance between Kafka and the world of Prague German. Tzvetan Todorov, too, stresses "the difference in the hierarchy of the two ideas [of figurative language and poetic language]: figurative language is a sort of potential stock inside language, while poetic language is already a construction, a utilization of this raw material. . . . Figurative language opposes transparent language in order to impose the presence of words; literary language opposes ordinary language in order to impose the presence of things"[28]—things unheard before, new realities, reflections of the poetic self.

Kafka's attachment to the everyday language of Prague is only one impetus in the thrust of his poetic consciousness toward its own truth. His language probes the depths of the imaginary—a depth that lies concealed within ordinary language but can be brought to light through the willful distortion of the figurative underlayer of ordinary language. The primitiveness of the vermin reflects Kafka's radical thrust toward origins. His destruction of his native personality for the sake of a poetic development destroys the privilege of inherited language.

Conceiving, then, the opening of *The Metamorphosis* as the metamorphosis of a familiar metaphor, we can identify minor and major movements of Kafka's spirit: the retrospective attachment to the familiar, and the movement of the spirit toward its own reality. As opposite movements, they cannot be accommodated within the metaphor that asserts an analogy between the spirit and the common life it negates. Only the metamorphosis destroying the metaphor establishes their distinction.

Our second approach to *Metamorphosis* stresses the presence in the fiction of Gregor Samsa of the residue of a real meaning, the real vermin in the conventional metaphor "the man is a vermin." This method opens a path to that whole range of criticism aiming to relate *The Metamorphosis* to empirical experiences and, by extension, to Kafka's personal life. Kafka, the approach stresses, has distorted but preserved through distortion the sense of a man debased in the way that vermin are debased. As Kafka incorporates in the story the empirical sense of a biting and sucking insect—so this argument proceeds—he incorporates as well his sense of his empirical self.[29] An essentially realistic tale of humiliation and neurosis reflects Kafka's tortured personality.

Innumerable attempts have been made to explain Gregor's debasement in terms of the ways in which a man can be humiliated. The Marxist critic Helmut Richter, for example, alludes to the deformed products of a mechanical work process, to Gregor the alienated salesman; Sokel, as a psychologist, stresses Gregor's intent to punish by means of his repulsiveness the family that had enslaved him. Hellmuth Kaiser views the metamorphosis as retribution for an Oedipal rebellion; the pathologist Wilfredo Dalmau Castañón sees it as the symptomatology of tuberculosis.[30] In most of these readings the evidence of Kafka's empirical personality is brought directly into court; the ne plus ultra[31] of this sort of criticism is an essay by Giuliano Baioni, which sees the metamorphosis as repeating Kafka's feeling of guilt and absolving him of it. Kafka is guilty and must be punished simply for being himself, for being his father's son, for hating his father, for getting engaged, for not loving enough, for being incapable of loving, for being a writer who is thinking about his father, for being a factory manager and not writing, and finally, for being an imperfect creature whose body is a foreign body and stands condemned by a Hasidic ideal of unity.[32] A critical bibliography of *The Metamorphosis* compiled in 1973 describes more than one hundred published critiques of an empirical or programmatic kind.[33] Though all are plausible, they are privative; Kafka, this most highly conscious of artists, implacable skeptic of psychoanalysis, never conceived of writing as enactment of or compensation for his troubled personality.

For Kafka, personal happiness is not the goal but a stake and as such alienable—a means, functioning essentially through its renunciation, to an altogether different elation (and anxiety), which is at the heart of literature, his "real life" (*DI,* 211). In a passage in *Amerika* written shortly before the composition of *The Metamorphosis*, Karl Rossman, as he plays the piano, feels "rising within him a sorrow which reached past the end of the song, seeking another end which it could not find" (*A,* 88).[34] "Art for the artist," said Kafka, "is only suffering, through which he releases himself for further suffering" (*J,* 28). In a letter to Max Brod of July 5, 1922, Kafka links his writing to the amelioration of his life in a merely concessive way: "I don't mean, of course, that my life is better when I don't write. Rather it is much worse then and wholly unbearable and has to end in madness" (*L,* 333) [83]. But this relation between not writing and madness obtains only because he is fundamentally a writer, and a writer who does not write is an absurdity (*Unding*) that would call down madness. The only madness that writing cures is the madness of not writing.

The attempt to interpret *The Metamorphosis* through Kafka's empirical personality suffers, by implication, from the difficulty of interpreting the vermin through the residual empirical sense of the metaphor of the vermin. The author of a monograph on the story, Jürg Schubiger, notes a concrete disparity between the form of the vermin and any bug that can be visualized:

> [The head] ends in "nostrils" and in strong jaws, which take the place of human jaws. Compared with

> what we are accustomed to in bugs, the head is unusually mobile. Not only can the creature lower and raise it, draw it in and stretch it out; he can even turn it so far to the side that he sees just what is going on behind him. . . . Statements about the weight of the creature . . . "two strong persons" would have been necessary to lift him out of bed (*M*, 8) [9] . . . are incompatible with Gregor's later ability to wander over the walls and ceiling; even with glue, a bug weighing at least seventy pounds cannot hang on the ceiling.

"And so," Schubiger concludes, "the bodily 'data' must not be understood as facts . . . they are bodily imaged questions and answers in the bug's dialogue with the world."[35] Kafka himself confirmed this conclusion when he specifically forbade his publisher to illustrate the first edition of *The Metamorphosis* with a drawing of the creature: "The insect itself cannot be depicted" (*L*, 115).

The importance within *The Metamorphosis* of the original metaphor "this man is a vermin" is not for Kafka the empirical identity of a bug. What is paramount is the form of the metaphor as such, which is then deformed; hence, any metaphor would do, with this provision (as formulated by Jacques Lacan): "Any conjunction of two signifiers would be equally sufficient to constitute a metaphor, except for the additional requirement of the greatest possible disparity of the images signified, needed for the production of the poetic spark, or in other words for there to be metaphoric creation."[36] In the most powerful metaphor, vehicle and tenor are poles apart; this power is appropriated by the act of aesthetic distortion. Kafka's metaphor is only impoverished when the tenor, a traveling salesman, is equated with Kafka's empirical personality as factory manager.

Lacan's insight helps, moreover, to clarify another crux. Anders originally saw the metaphor underlying *The Metamorphosis* as "This man, who wants to live as an artist, is a nasty bug." Dieter Hasselblatt has argued against this formulation, asserting, "Nowhere in the text is there any mention of the problem of the artist and society."[37] Of course it is true that Gregor Samsa is not an artist *manqué*.[38] But as the occasion of a metamorphosis, he becomes an aesthetic object—the unique correlative of a poetic intention. Indeed, Hasselblatt's own view of *The Metamorphosis* as the response of the everyday world to the inconceivable gives the work an essential bearing on the theme of poetic language. The empirical identity of the tenor, be it artist or any other man, is inconsequential because *Metamorphosis* is dominated by an aesthetic intent. The intent to literalize a metaphor produces a being wholly divorced from empirical reality.

The third approach focuses upon this aesthetic intent, which aims, through metamorphosis of the metaphor, to assert its own autonomy. We can no longer take our bearings from the empirical sense of the vermin. Yet neither are we obliged to abandon every attempt at interpreting the signifier. For Kafka has already established a link between the bug and the activity of writing itself. In his 1907 "Wedding Preparations in the Country" (*DF*, 2–31), of which only a fragment survives, Kafka conjures a hero, Eduard Raban, reluctant to take action in the world (he is supposed to go to the country to arrange his wedding). Raban dreams instead of autonomy, self-sufficiency, and omnipotence. For this transparent reflection of his early literary consciousness, Kafka finds the emblem of a beetle, about which there hovers an odd indeterminacy:

And besides, can't I do it the way I always did as a child when dangerous matters were involved. I don't even have to go to the country myself, it isn't necessary. I'll send [only] my clothed body. [So I shall send this clothed body.] If it staggers to the door on the way out of my room, the staggering will indicate not fear but its nullity. It is also not a sign of excitement if it stumbles on the stairs, if it goes to the country sobbing, and eats its dinner there in tears. For I, I am meanwhile lying in my bed, all covered up with a yellow-brown blanket, exposed to the breeze that blows in through the barely opened window. The carriages and people in the street move and walk hesitantly on shining ground, for I am still dreaming. Coachmen and pedestrians are shy, and every step they want to advance they ask as a favor from me, by looking at me. I encourage them, and they encounter no obstacle. . . .

As I lie in bed I assume the shape of a big beetle, a stag beetle or a June beetle, I think. . . .

The form of a big beetle, yes. Then I would pretend it were a matter of hibernating, and I would press my little legs against my bulging body. And I whisper a few words. These are instructions to my sad body, which stands close beside me, bent over. Soon I have finished, it bows, it goes swiftly and it will do everything the best way possible while I rest. [67]

The figure of the omnipotent bug is positive throughout this passage and suggests the inwardness of the act of writing rendered in its power and freedom, in its mystic exaltation, evidence of which abounds in Kafka's early diary entries:

> The special nature of my inspiration . . . is such that I can do everything, and not only what is directed to a definite piece of work. When I arbitrarily write a single sentence, for instance, "He looked out of the window," it already has perfection. (*DI,* 45)
>
> My happiness, my abilities, and every possibility of being useful in any way have always been in the literary field. And here I have, to be sure, experienced states . . . in which I completely dwelt in every idea, but also filled every idea, and in which I not only felt myself at my boundary, but at the boundary of the human in general. (*DI,* 58)
>
> Again it was the power of my dreams, shining forth into wakefulness even before I fall asleep, which did not let me sleep. In the evening and the morning my consciousness of the creative abilities in me is more than I can encompass. I feel shaken to the core of my being and can get out of myself whatever I desire. . . . It is a matter of . . . mysterious powers which are of an ultimate significance to me. (*DI,* 76)
>
> How everything can be said, how for everything, for the strangest fancies, there waits a great fire in which they perish and rise up again. (*DI,* 276)

But this is only one side of Kafka's poetic consciousness. The other is expressed through the narrator's hesitation in defining his trance by means of an objective correlative ("a stag beetle . . . I think"), which suggests beyond his particular distress the general impossibility of the metaphor's naming, by means of a material image, the being of an inward state and hence a doubt that will go to the root of writing itself. After 1912 there are few such positive emblems for the inwardness and solitude of the act of writing; this "beautiful" bug[39] is projected in ignorance; the truer emblem of the alien poetic consciousness which "has no basis, no substance" (*L*, 334) [84], which must suffer "the eternal torments of dying" (*DII*, 77) [79], becomes the vermin Gregor. The movement from the beautiful bug Raban to the monstrous bug Gregor marks an accession of self-knowledge—an increasing awareness of the poverty and shortcomings of writing.[40]

The direction of Kafka's reflection on literature is fundamentally defined, however, by "The Judgment," the story written immediately before *The Metamorphosis.* "The Judgment" struck Kafka as a breakthrough into his own style and produced an ecstatic notation in his diary. But later in his interpretation Kafka described the story in a somewhat more sinister tonality, as having "come out of me like a real birth, covered with filth and slime" (*DI*, 278). The image has the violence and inevitability of a natural process, but its filth and slime cannot fail to remind the reader of the strange birth that is the subject of Kafka's next story—the incubus trailing filth and slime through the household of its family.

Two major aspects of "The Judgment," I think, inspire in Kafka a sense of the authenticity of the story important enough for it to be commemorated in the figure of the vermin. First, the figure of the friend in Russia represents with the greatest clarity to date the negativity of the "business" of writing: the friend is said by the father to be "yellow enough to be thrown away" (*S*, 87). Second, "The Judgment," like *The Metamorphosis*, develops as the implications of a distorted metaphor are enacted: "The Judgment" metamorphoses the father's "judgment" or "estimate" into a fatal "verdict," a death "sentence."[41]

Kafka's awareness that "The Judgment" originates from the distortion of the metaphor dictates the conclusion of his "interpretation." The highly formal tonality of this structural analysis surprises the reader, following as it does on the organic simile of the sudden birth: "The friend is the link between father and son, he is their strongest common bond. Sitting alone at his window, Georg rummages voluptuously in this consciousness of what they have in common, believes he has his father within him, and would be at peace with everything if it were not for a fleeting, sad thoughtfulness. In the course of the story the father . . . uses the common bond of the friend to set himself up as Georg's antagonist" (*DI,* 278). This analysis employs the structural model of the metamorphosed metaphor. At first Georg considers the father *as* the friend, and his friend *as* the metaphor of the father. But Georg's doom is to take the metaphor literally, to suppose that by sharing the quality of the friend, he possesses the father in fact. In a violent countermovement the father distorts the initial metaphor, drawing the friend's existence into himself; and Georg, who now feels "what they have in common . . . only as something foreign, something that has become independent, that he has never given enough protection" (*DI,* 279), accepts his sentence.

It is this new art, generated from the distortion of relations modeled on the metaphor, that came to Kafka as an elation, a gross new birth, and a sentence. The aesthetic intention comes to light negatively when it must express itself through so tormented and elliptical a strategem as the metamorphosis of the metaphor. The restriction and misery of this art is the explicit subject of *The Metamorphosis;* the invention that henceforth shapes Kafka's existence as a writer is original, arbitrary, and fundamentally strange. In a later autobiographical note he writes: "All that he does seems to him, it is true, extraordinarily new, but also, because of the incredible spate of new things, extraordinarily amateurish, indeed scarcely tolerable, incapable of becoming history, breaking short the chain of the generations, cutting off for the first time at its most profound source the music of the world, which before him could at least be divined. Sometimes in his arrogance he has more anxiety for the world than for himself" (*GW*, 263–64). Kafka's pride in his separateness equals his nostalgia for "the music of the world." His tension defines the violently distorted metaphor Gregor Samsa, who, in responding to his sister's violin playing, causes this music to be broken off. That being who lives as a distortion of nature—and without a history and without a future still maintains a certain sovereignty—conjures up through the extremity of his separation the clearest possible idea of the music he cannot possess.

In the light of the beautiful beetle of "Wedding Preparations" and the trail of filth and mucus that "The Judgment" leaves behind, the vermin in *The Metamorphosis* is revealed as expressing a hermeneutical relation, as reflecting Kafka's sense of his literary destiny. But the negative character of this vermin, this judgment, still has to be clarified.[42] It is a seductive hypothesis to suppose that *The Metamorphosis* describes the fate of the writer who does not write, whose "business," like that of the Russian friend in "The Judgment," is not flourishing.

For this assumption there is a good deal of evidence in Kafka's letters. On November 1, 1912, two weeks before conceiving *The Metamorphosis*, Kafka wrote to Felice, with uncanny relevance to the story: "My life consists, and basically always has consisted, of attempts at writing, mostly unsuccessful. But when I didn't write, I was at once flat on the floor, fit for the dustbin" (*LF*, 20).[43] It is as a wholly literary being, albeit one who is foundering, that Kafka identifies himself with the corpse that will be swept out of the bedroom. On November 18, *The Metamorphosis* becomes a "cautionary tale" for the writer at a standstill: "I was just sitting down to yesterday's story with an infinite longing to pour myself into it, obviously stimulated by my despair. Harassed by so much, uncertain of you, completely incapable of coping with the office, in view of the novel's [*Amerika*'s] being at a standstill for a day with a wild desire to continue the new, equally cautionary [*mahnend*] story" (*LF,* 49; *BF,* 105) [92]. Several days after completing *The Metamorphosis,* Kafka wrote to Felice, "And don't talk about the greatness hidden in me, or do you think there is something great about spending a two-day interruption of my writing in permanent fear of never being able to write again, a fear, by the way, that this evening has proved to be not altogether unfounded?" (*LF,* 97).

This matter is given definite formulation in 1922, when Kafka finds an image for the danger of not writing that is powerfully reminiscent of the vermin's attempt to cling to his human past: "Since the existence of the writer is truly dependent upon his desk and if he wants to keep madness at bay he must never go far from his desk, he must hold on to it with his teeth" (*L,* 335). Here, then, as Erich Heller writes (in his edition of the letters to Felice), is Kafka's "curse: he is nothing when he cannot write." But he is also "in a different kind of nothingness, if, rarely enough, he believes he has written well [writing does 'accept' him, *ihn 'aufnimmt'*]" (*LF,* xvi; *BF,* 24).

What is this "different kind of nothingness" to which a vermin image for the act of writing bears witness? Can it be grasped, as many critics believe, through Kafka's impulse to view the writer in the perspective of the nonwriter, the normal *Bürger*? In Kafka's earliest works—for example, in the developed but unfinished story beginning, "'You,' I said"—the writer appears in the eyes of others as the dim figure of the bachelor, the nonentity who must drag out his days in feeble solitude, without children or possessions (*DI*, 22–29). "The Judgment," too, presents the writer in an alien and insulting perspective; the essential character of this relation is stressed through the alliance said to exist between the vindictive father and the friend, a transparent persona of the writer. The clearest formulation of this theme occurs in 1919, in Kafka's "Letter to His Father": "My writing was all about you," Kafka declared to his father. "All I did there, after all, was to bemoan what I could not bemoan upon your breast. It was an intentionally long-drawn-out leave-taking from you, yet, although it was brought about by force on your part, it did take its course in the direction determined by me" (*DF*, 177).[44] In these passages, the origin of the writer appears to be fundamentally shaped by the perspective of the father; Gregor Samsa, too, needs to have his metamorphosis confirmed by the judgment of his family.

But in fact this idea is neither predominant nor even highly significant in *The Metamorphosis.* The work frequently stresses the son's defiance of the father: Gregor comes out in the open to hear the language of music despite his father's prohibition. What is more, the truth and pathos of the story stem from the reader's occupying throughout—with the exception of the "unreadable ending"—a consciousness very nearly identical with Gregor's own [78]. The center of gravity of the work is Gregor's sense of the world: he sees himself as a vermin, we do not see him as a vermin through the eyes of the others. Significantly, the omniscient narrator of the close of the story confirms Gregor's body to be actually verminous.

The negativity of the vermin has to be seen as rooted, in an absolute sense, in the literary enterprise itself, as coming to light in the perspective that the act of writing offers of itself. Here the activity of writing appears only autonomous enough to demand the loss of happiness and the renunciation of life. But of its own accord it has no power to restitute these sacrifices in a finer key.

Over Kafka's writing stands a constant sign of negativity and incompleteness:

> When it became clear in my organism that writing was the most productive direction for my being to take, everything rushed in that direction and left empty all those abilities which were directed toward the joys of sex, eating, drinking, philosophical reflection and above all music. I atrophied in all these directions.... My development is now complete and, so far as I can see, there is nothing left to sacrifice; I need only throw my work in the office out of this complex in order to begin my real life. (*DI,* 211)

The path to Kafka's "real life" is strewn with sacrifices; and the fact that he was never able to throw off his professional work until he had become fatally ill reflects the inherent inaccessibility of his ideal.

In a letter of July 5, 1922, to Max Brod, Kafka envisions the writer as inhabiting a place outside the house of life—as a dead man, one of those "departed," of the "Reflections," who long to be flooded back to us (*DF,* 34). It cannot be otherwise; the writer "has no basis, has no substance [*ist etwas nicht Bestehendes*]"; what he produces is devilish, "the reward for service to the devil. This descent to the dark powers, this unbinding of spirits by nature bound, dubious embraces and whatever else may go on below, of which one no longer knows anything above ground, when in the sunlight one writes stories. Perhaps there is another kind of writing, I only know this one" (*Br,* 385) [83–84].[45] "Yet," as Erich Heller remarks, "it remains dubious who this 'one' is who 'writes stories in the sunshine.' Kafka himself? 'The Judgment'—and sunshine? *Metamorphosis* ... and sunshine? ... How must it have been 'in the nether parts' if 'in the higher parts' blossoms like these burst forth?" (*BF*, 22).

Kafka's art, which Kafka elsewhere calls a conjuration of spirits, brings into the light of language the experience of descent and doubt. And even this experience has to be repeated perpetually. "And so I waver, fly incessantly to the summit of the mountain, but can keep myself on top for hardly a moment. . . . [I]t is not death, alas, but the eternal torments of dying" (*DII*, 77) [79]. There is no true duration in this desperate flight; conjuring up his own death, Kafka writes: "The writer in me of course will die at once, for such a figure has no basis, has no substance, isn't even of dust; it is only a little bit possible in the maddest earthly life, it is only a construction of the craving for enjoyment [*Genußsucht*]. This is the writer" (*Br*, 385) [84–85]. The self-indulgence that defines the writer is that of the being who perpetually reflects on himself and others. The word "figure" in the passage above can be taken literally: the writer is defined by his verbal figures, conceived at a distance from life, inspired by a devilish aesthetic detachment with a craving to indulge itself; but he suffers as well the meaninglessness of the figure uprooted from the language of life—the dead figure. Kafka's spirit, then, does spend itself "zur Illuminierung meines Leichnams," in lighting up—but also in furnishing figural decorations for—his corpse (*Br*, 385; *L*, 334).

It is this dwelling outside the house of life, *Schriftstellersein*,[46] the negative condition of writing as such, that is named in *The Metamorphosis;* but it cannot name itself directly, in a language that designates things that exist or in the figures that suggest the relations between things constituting the common imagination of life. Instead, in *The Metamorphosis* Kafka utters a word for a being unacceptable to man (*ungeheuer*) and unacceptable to God (*Ungeziefer*), a word unsuited either to intimate speech or to prayer (*E*, 71). This word evokes a distortion without visual identity or self-awareness—engenders, for a hero, a pure sign. The creature of *The Metamorphosis* is not a self speaking or keeping silent but language itself (*parole*)—a word broken loose from the context of language (*langue*), fallen into a void the meaning of which it cannot signify, near others who cannot understand it.

As the story of a metamorphosed metaphor, *The Metamorphosis* is not just one among Kafka's stories but an exemplary Kafkan story; the title reflects the generative principle of Kafka's fiction—a metamorphosis of the function of language. In organizing itself around a distortion of ordinary language, *The Metamorphosis* projects into its center a sign that absorbs its own significance (as Gregor's opaque body occludes his awareness of self) and thus aims in a direction opposite to the art of the symbol; for there, in the words of Maurice Merleau-Ponty, the sign is "devoured" by its signification.[47] The outcome of this tendency of *The Metamorphosis* is its ugliness. Symbolic art, modeled on the metaphor that occults the signifier to the level of signification, strikes us as beautiful: our notion of the beautiful harmony of sign and significance is one dominated by the human signification, by the form of the person which in Schiller's classical conception of art "extirpates the material reference."[48] These expectations are disappointed by the opaque and impoverished sign in Kafka. His art devours the human meaning of itself and, indeed, must soon raise the question of a suitable nourishment. It is thus internally coherent that the vermin—the word without significance—should divine fresh nourishment and affinity in music, the language of signs without significance.[49]

But the song Gregor hears does not transform his suffering: the music breaks off; the monster finds nourishment in a cruder fantasy of anger and possession. This scene communicates the total discrepancy between the vermin's body and the cravings appropriate to it and the other sort of nourishment for which he yearns; the moment produces not symbolic harmony but the intolerable tension of irreconcilables. In Kafka's unfathomable sentence, "Was he an animal, that music could move him so?" (*M*, 49) [54], paradox echoes jarringly without end.

At the close of *The Metamorphosis* Gregor is issued a death sentence by his family which he promptly adopts as his own; he then passes into a vacant trance.

> He had pains, of course, throughout his whole body, but it seemed to him that they were gradually getting fainter and fainter and would finally go away altogether. The rotten apple in his back and the inflamed area around it, which were completely covered with fluffy dust, already hardly bothered him. He thought back on his family with deep emotion and love. His conviction that he would have to disappear was, if possible, even firmer than his sister's. He remained in this state of empty and peaceful reflection until the tower clock struck three in the morning. (*M*, 53–54) [59]

He is empty of all practical concerns; his body has dwindled to a mere dry husk, substantial enough to have become sonorous, too substantial not to have been betrayed by the promise of harmony in music. He suggests the Christ of John (19:30)—but not the Christ of Matthew (27:50) or Mark (15:37)—for Gregor's last moment is silent and painless. "He still saw that outside the window everything was beginning to grow light. Then, without his consent, his head sank down to the floor, and from his nostrils streamed his last weak breath" (*M*, 54) [59]. For a moment the dim desert of Gregor's world grows luminous; his opaque body, progressively impoverished, achieves a faint translucency. Through the destruction of the specious harmony of the metaphor and the aesthetic claims of the symbol, Kafka engenders another sort of beauty and, with this, closes a circle of reflection on his own work. For in 1910, just before his mature art originated as the distortion of the metaphor, Kafka wrote in the story fragment, "'You,' I said . . .": "Already, what protected me seemed to dissolve here in the city. I was beautiful in the early days, for this dissolution takes place as an apotheosis, in which everything that holds us to life flies away, but even in flying away illumines us for the last time with its human light" (*DI,* 28).

At the close of *The Metamorphosis*, the ongoing metamorphosis of the metaphor accomplishes itself through a consciousness empty of all practical attention and a body that preserves its opacity, but in so dwindled a form that it achieves the condition of a painless translucency, a kind of beauty. In creating in the vermin a figure for the distortion of the metaphor, the generative principle of his art, Kafka underscores the negativity of writing but at the same time enters the music of the historical world at a crucial juncture. His art reveals at its root a powerful Romantic aesthetic tradition associated with the names of Rousseau, Hölderlin, Wordsworth, and Schlegel, which criticizes symbolic form and metaphorical diction in the name of a kind of allegorical language.[50] The figures of this secular allegory do not refer doctrinally to scripture; rather, they relate to the source of the decision to constitute them. They replace the dogmatic unity of sign and significance with the temporal relation of the sign to its luminous source. This relation comes to light through the temporal difference between the allegorical sign and the sign prefiguring it; the exact meaning of the signs is less important than the temporal character of their relation. The vermin that alludes to vermin figures in Kafka's early work, and whose death amid increasing luminosity alludes casually to Christ's, is just such a figure. But to stress the temporal character of the metamorphosed metaphor of *The Metamorphosis* is to distinguish it importantly from the "extended metaphor" of Anders's and Sokel's discussion, for in this organistic conception of the figure, sign and significance coincide as forms of extension. And if Expressionism is to be defined by its further extension of metaphor, then *The Metamorphosis* cannot be accommodated in an Expressionist tradition. The matter should be put differently and more strongly: if Expressionism is the literary movement that takes a continual impetus from metamorphosis of the metaphor—from the allegory, critique, and deconstruction of metaphor—then Kafka is primordially Expressionist.

The Metamorphosis alludes to a certain tradition of Romantic allegory but does so only for a moment before abruptly departing from it. The light in which Gregor dies is said explicitly to emanate from outside the window and not from a source within the subject. The creature turned away from life, facing death—and, as such, a pure sign of the poetic consciousness—keeps for Kafka its opaque and tellurian character. It is as a distorted body that Gregor is struck by the light; and it is in this light, principally unlike the source of poetic creation, that the work of art barely comes to recognize its own truth. For, wrote Kafka, "our art is a way of being dazzled by truth; the light on the grotesquely grimacing retreating face is true, and nothing else" (*DF,* 41). Because the language of Kafka's fiction originates so knowingly from a reflection on ordinary speech, it cannot show the truth except as a solid body reflecting the light, a blank fragment of "what we call the world of the senses, [which] is the Evil in the spiritual world" (*DF,* 39).

And so the figure of the nameless vermin remains principally opaque. More fundamental than the moment of translucency, reflected in the fact that this moment is obtained only at death and without a witness, is the horror that writing can never amount to anything more than the twisted grimace on which glances a light not its own. Here Kafka's essentially linguistic imagination joins him to a disruptive modern tradition, described by Michel Foucault:

> The literature in our day, fascinated by the being of language, . . . gives prominence, in all their empirical vivacity, to the fundamental forms of finitude. From within language experienced and traversed as language, in the play of its possibilities extended to their furthest point, what emerges is that man has "come to an end," and that, by reaching the summit of all possible speech, he arrives not at the very heart of himself but at the brink of that which limits him; in that region where death prowls, where thought is extinguished, where the promise of the origin interminably recedes. . . . And as if this experiencing of the forms of finitude in language were insupportable . . . it is within madness that it manifested itself—the figure of finitude thus positing itself in language (as that which unveils itself within it), but also before it, preceding it, as that formless, mute, unsignifying region where language can find its freedom. And it is indeed in this space thus revealed that literature . . . more and more purely, with Kafka, Bataille, and Blanchot, posited itself . . . as experience of finitude.[51]

Elements of Jewish Folklore in Kafka's *Metamorphosis*

Iris Bruce

Most readers have quite rightly seen Gregor Samsa's metamorphosis as a metaphor of alienation; yet they have also tended to downplay the significance of the transformation itself as a thematic and structural narrative device.[1] To ignore Gregor's metamorphosis, however, along with the various senses of metamorphosis with which Kafka was acquainted, is to ignore an important level of textual reference in the story. Aside from Ovid's *Metamorphoses*, which Kafka read in school, and fairy-tale metamorphoses, which he must have known, Kafka was familiar with the metamorphosis motif from Jewish literature. In the following discussion of *The Metamorphosis*, I will highlight intertexts from the Jewish narrative tradition. True, the Samsa family is not specifically Jewish, but Christian, yet as such they represent the dominant German culture with which the majority of Prague Jews identified. This fact should not therefore lead scholars to ignore the many Jewish elements that Kafka employs in his story. A knowledge of the popular and mystic dimensions of this tradition is essential for an understanding of the text.

A look at Kafka's actual knowledge of Judaism before he

wrote *The Metamorphosis* (November/December 1912) testifies to Kafka's interest in the history of Judaism, as well as in texts of the religious tradition. Kafka's provable interest in Judaism began in 1911 when he was introduced to a Yiddish theater group which visited Prague from October 24, 1911, to January 21, 1912.[2] Despite his awareness of the poor quality of some of the performances, Kafka attended one play after the other and even saw some of them several times.[3] His interest in Yiddish culture became a catalyst for learning more about Judaism in general.[4] In January 1912 he read Meyer I. Pinès' Yiddish literary history: ". . . read, and indeed greedily, Pinès' *L'histoire de la littérature judéo-allemande* [The History of German-Jewish Literature], 500 pages, with such thoroughness, haste and joy as I have never yet shown in the case of similar books; . . ."[5] Pinès' study is a doctoral dissertation aimed at a European audience unfamiliar with Yiddish culture and literature and without access to any of its literary productions, since these texts were written in Hebrew characters. For this reason Pinès strives to give the reader as complete an overview as possible, providing the necessary cultural background as well as numerous plot summaries and quotations from representative works of major Yiddish writers up to the turn of the nineteenth century. Pinès devotes much space to folk and hasidic[6] tales, which are infused with kabbalistic thought and symbolism, including metamorphoses. Moreover, by the time *The Metamorphosis* was written, Kafka was also already familiar with the writings of Martin Buber, who had started collecting hasidic tales in the first decade of the twentieth century.[7]

The concept of metamorphosis is a very common motif in Jewish folklore, so common, in fact, that the eminent scholar Gershom Scholem calls it an "integral part of Jewish popular belief and Jewish folklore."[8] A more specific term for metamorphosis is *gilgul*, the Hebrew word for "metempsychosis," i.e., the belief in transmigration of the soul.[9] The origin of this belief is not specifically Jewish: the concept of metamorphosis was widespread in antiquity, as evidenced by Ovid's *Metamorphoses* (ca. A.D. 8).[10] Yet this does not contradict the fact that the notion later on came to assume a variety of forms and functions in Jewish writing. Many such narratives can be seen, according to one authority, as "Judaized versions of myths or folk-motifs that must have circulated throughout the ancient world."[11] In the Jewish narrative tradition, the concept can be traced back to the late twelfth century, where it found its "first literary expression in the *Sefer ha-Behir* [book Bahir]"—"the earliest work of kabbalistic literature" (Scholem, *Kabbalah* 345, 312). A common point of origin with metamorphosis in antiquity—in Ovid, for instance—is its connection with punishment for sexual transgressions. The same view was held by the early kabbalists: They, too, believed metempsychosis was "connected essentially with offenses against procreation and sexual transgressions" (Scholem, *Kabbalah* 346).

As the concept evolved, its function became increasingly religious: in sixteenth-century Lurianic Kabbala, for example, it involved a complex set of symbolisms and became a whole philosophy of life.[12] Its particular significance was to help provide religious consolation. The belief in the existence of a continual metamorphosis after death was reassuring to the sinful, for reincarnation gave individuals "a chance of fulfilling the commandments which it was not given to the soul to fulfil before . . ." (Scholem, *Major Trends* 282). It became part of an entire philosophy of life by offering a rational explanation for the existence of injustice and "an answer to the problem of the suffering of the righteous and the prospering of the wicked: the righteous man, for example, is punished for his sins in a previous *gilgul*" (Scholem, *Kabbalah* 345). Furthermore, within the framework of Jewish history, the experience of displacement and repeated "punishment" in the absence of a clearly identifiable crime demanded a rational or religious explanation. Hence, the concept of metamorphosis came to be increasingly charged with biblical notions of transgression, punishment, exile, and redemption, offering a specifically Jewish philosophy of life.

This world view is prominent in the hasidic tales of Rabbi Nachman of Bratslav (1772–1810). His religious folk parables present the cycle of transgression, punishment, exile, numerous trials, and the longing for redemption in various allegorical disguises which call for an interpretation within a narrowly confined cultural and religious field of references.[13] In his tales, metamorphosis is a major structural and thematic device. The particular form of animal metamorphosis is only one of its many possible manifestations. Generally the protagonists are shown to undergo several metamorphoses in their lives as they move through the kabbalistic cycle of transgression, punishment, exile, and trials in hope of deliverance and redemption.

Rabbi Nachman's treatment of metamorphosis can be illustrated through his parable "The Prince Who Thought He Was a Rooster." Here a prince believes he is a rooster, takes off all his clothes, sits under the table, and refuses to eat anything but cornseed. No one can cure him, until a wise man comes; he pretends to be a rooster himself, and so the two of them sit under the table. Step by step, the wise man convinces the prince that a rooster can wear clothes if he wants to, that he can also eat human food and still be a good rooster, and that there is no reason why a rooster should not walk about. The "moral" is: "After he began dressing like a person, eating like a person, and walking like a person, he gradually recovered his senses and began to live like a person" (*Gates* 458).

Here, the metamorphosis into a rooster does not actually

take place, but the metaphor is used to allude to a state of existence that can best be characterized as "dehumanization of the humane," a phrase which well describes the function of metamorphosis in Kafka.[14] The prince's imagined metamorphosis indicates his reduction to a less than human level, and Nachman presents the reader/listener with an idealistic moral solution to the problem. In a hasidic sense, by "descending" to the level of the victim's own delusion, the wise man is able to "raise" that person and cure him. Critics have pointed out similarities between Kafka and Nachman,[15] and Laurent Cohen cites Elie Wiesel's insightful comment that the above story "brings us close to *The Metamorphosis*,"[16] though this story was not actually included in Buber's retelling of Nachman's legends in *The Tales of Rabbi Nachman.*

In the middle and late nineteenth century, with the rise and growing popularity of the Jewish Enlightenment—the Haskalah—the originally religious function of metamorphosis changed radically. Although, in representations of metamorphoses, religious and biblical references were still employed, they lost their religious function for the most part and took on a secular meaning which was often humorous or satiric. Metamorphosis is treated in a humorously ironic fashion, for example, in the tales of the Yiddish writer I. L. Peretz (1852–1915), particularly in "Thou Shalt Not Covet."[17] At the outset, the narrator announces the religious function of reincarnation in a preaching tone that foreshadows the following ironic treatment:

> As you all know, every Jew must fulfill all the commandments of the Torah. And whatever one fails to perform in one incarnation,[18] must be made up in another. The faults of one incarnation have to be made

> good in another because the soul must return to the throne of glory perfect and without fault, pure and without blemish (*Selected Stories* 29).

A life of metamorphosis is identified here with the condition of exile in this world—and again, it is associated with religious notions of transgression, punishment, exile and (possibly) redemption, a state in which the soul will be allowed to return "to the throne of glory." Peretz develops the concept clearly for humorous ends when he suggests that, quite conceivably, this cycle could be endless, particularly if we are dealing with ordinary sinful mortals: "Great saints undergo but one incarnation, or at most two, while ordinary mortals—may you be spared such a fate!—undergo a hundred or more incarnations" (*Selected Stories* 29). In fact, Peretz shows through the trials of a great rabbi that even "saints" are only "ordinary mortals" (*Selected Stories* 29). Having lived a virtuous and strict life according to the Commandments, the rabbi has never really "lived" and enjoyed life. Now his time has come when he is to be rewarded in heaven, but the Angel of Death has to struggle to make the soul leave the body. All the individual members of the rabbi's body revolt, and his agony is so great that the rabbi wishes for an easy death. But a Jew is not allowed to "covet" anything, not even an easy death (*Selected Stories* 30). Thus a new cycle of metamorphosis begins. In his new life, the rabbi is once again very virtuous—but . . . just before he has completed his cycle, the evil spirit tempts him again. As he is standing in the cold, his attention is caught by an inn across from him. He enters and sees peasants sitting by a warm stove, "drinking liquor, wiping it down with herring and pickles, and talking obscenities" (*Selected Stories* 33). Only for a split second he "envies" them and wishes he could do the same. But this is his downfall. His trials are never-ending as a new cycle begins. Peretz humorously satirizes the strict religious laws by underlining the all too human nature of the rabbi's transgressions, which are "some trivial matter, a mere nothing" (*Selected Stories* 29) and out of proportion with the punishment he receives.

In such Haskalah representations of metamorphosis, four perspectives can be distinguished that present the notion of transformation from different though interrelated angles. The first perspective is to treat it humorously, the second to see it in terms of transgression and punishment, the third to emphasize the experience of exile, and the last to address the possibility of liberation or atonement. The interconnection of these perspectives is vivid in a passage from a nineteenth-century Yiddish story by A. B. Gotlober (1811–1899), in which a man undergoes transformations from horse to fish, donkey, leech, and dog until he is finally turned into a pig:

> When I was a horse, a fish, a donkey, a leech, even a dog, I always ended up with Jews, . . . until my soul ascended and I was reincarnated as a human being, a Jew, an awful Jew, yet still and all a Jew! But now that I had become a swine, how dreadful was my life! What suffering! No Jew would lay eyes upon me! I could only associate with Gentiles, I was miserable, . . . —how was my soul to be elevated? I did everything I possibly could to get into a Jewish home, . . . —but all my trouble was for nothing. The moment the Jew caught sight of my unkosher snout, he was thunderstruck.[19]

It is striking that the transformations are treated humorously; all are inflicted as punishment for transgressions against the Commandments; the result of each transformation is the individual's banishment from his family or community, so that his transgressions make an outcast of him and condemn him to a life in both inner and outer exile; and, finally, his existence as a pig in Exile is tainted and impure. There is, furthermore, a religious reason behind his desperate efforts to return to the Jewish community, a longing for redemption, for he asks: "How was my soul to be elevated?"

The central aspect of Kafka's relation to Judaism emerges from Kafka's belief, in the words of one observer, that "all archetypical patterns of Fall, Expulsion or Redemption happen now and forever."[20] In *The Metamorphosis* Kafka's preoccupation with notions of transgression, punishment, and redemption is apparent, and Kafka's use of the folk motif of metamorphosis further places the story within a Jewish context.[21] In terms of the religious associations of uncleanness, Gregor's metamorphosis is just as degrading as the transformation into a pig described in Gotlober's text; nonetheless, Gregor's transformation is also treated humorously. It, too, is associated with punishment for transgression; Gregor is banished from his community and condemned to lead an impure existence in both inner and outer exile; and, finally, Gregor, too, makes several attempts to return to his family. There is, moreover, a religious significance in the trials he undergoes.

In the tradition of modern Jewish literature, metamorphoses tend to be treated humorously; in Kafka studies, however, the question of humor tends to be avoided.[22] After World War II, it is understandable that scholars would not readily regard the transformation of a human being into vermin as funny. The scholar and playwright George Steiner argues that Kafka was

> possessed of a fearful premonition: he saw, to the point of exact detail, the horror gathering. . . . Gregor

> Samsa's metamorphosis . . . was to be the literal fate of millions of human beings. The very word for vermin, *Ungeziefer*, is a stroke of tragic clairvoyance; so the Nazis were to designate the gassed.[23]

By implication, however, a great deal of the humor in Yiddish literature would be lost if seen from only a post-Holocaust perspective. In Gotlober's story, for example, the protagonist is at one time transformed into a hasidic singer who, at the moment of highest religious ecstasy, is so saturated with alcohol that he provokes a spontaneous combustion: "The alcohol, which filled me like a barrel, had grown so hot that it kindled and began to burn quite cheerily . . . and I was charred to a crisp" (*Yenne Velt* 393). Asked by the Angel of the Dead about his name, he cannot remember it and replies:

> Dead drunk, burnt to a crisp—how was I supposed to remember? I didn't answer. He even wanted to get to work and whip me a bit, which is what he normally does to a corpse that can't tell him its name. But what can you whip if everything's burnt up? How could he whip a heap of cinders? The hell with it! He didn't fool around with me for long, he promptly told me my judgment . . . and—*poof*! I was a horse!! (*Yenne Velt* 394)

For anyone who has seen Claude Lanzmann's film *Shoah*, it might be very difficult to find this funny, and Gregor's metamorphosis admittedly creates a similar problem. Yet while stressing that "[i]t is unlikely that many of Kafka's readers since the war have been able to detect the playful element in any of his death scenes," Stanley Corngold, for one, detects an "element of play" in the recurring motifs of "deaths and survivals" in Kafka's work."[24] Certainly death and humor can be interrelated if the link is seen as an attempt to face the unimaginable and not succumb to despair or be driven into madness.

In *The Metamorphosis*, the mood at the outset is not one of terror, nor does Gregor view himself as a horrible monster. As long as he sees the metamorphosis as a trick played on him by his imagination,[25] he is willing momentarily to accept his new verminous shape and to play with it. When he tries to rock himself out of bed, for example, he considers ". . . the new method . . . more of a game than a struggle" (8)[9]. Having accepted the "reality" of his metamorphosis, Gregor's associative thinking can take other leaps as well. He tries to picture an encounter between himself and his family and finds the situation amusing: "In spite of all his miseries, he could not repress a smile at this thought" (8–9) [9]. As a result of his own experience he begins to see everything around him in a different light, and he can imagine a world in which supernatural events are ordinary daily occurrences. Thus he starts speculating as to whether such transformations might not happen to other people as well, wishing one on his adversary, his superior—a kind of revenge which is accompanied by *Schadenfreude* [malicious joy]: "Gregor tried to imagine whether something like what had happened to him today could one day happen even to the manager; you really had to grant the possibility" (9–10) [10].

The sort of humor that accompanies Gregor's transformation, as well as the state of mind of a person who can momentarily accept the "reality" of transformations, is part of the Jewish literary tradition. It is particularly well-described, for example, in the following parody from *The Mare* (1876), a nineteenth-century Yiddish novel by Mendele Moicher-Sforim (c. 1836–1917), which Kafka was familiar with through Pinès:

> The Hindus, who believe that human souls pass into all sorts of creatures, and the Kabbalists (if you'll excuse my mentioning them in the same breath) are right, so it seems. The entire world is nothing but transmigrations. . . . And if such is the case, the world seems altogether different, you have to look at it with different eyes and regard everything in a completely different way. That may really be a man in the doghouse, and a dog in the man's house. A pound of fresh fish may really be a pound of palpitating souls, a fine carp may contain a chatterbox, an orator, with pepper and onions, on the platter right in front of me.[26]

Of course there is an element of tragi-comedy in the uncertainty displayed by Gregor Samsa vis-à-vis himself and with regard to others. In Mendele's *The Mare*, the protagonist similarly experiences a severe identity crisis, which is, however, described in an engaging way: he becomes

> skeptical of everything, not only of other people, being perplexed as to who and what they are—but skeptical even of yours truly, my own true self. Perhaps I was not truly I. Perhaps I was in the hand of another power living within me and I was not the master of my body, doing everything according to my will and mind. Perhaps that other force controlled me and compelled me to do what he wants, to do his business and live his life as he once lived it. Perhaps I am the substance and he the spirit; I, the matter, and he, the mind. Perhaps I am merely the mule who doesn't matter and who has to mind the master, whereas he, the master, is all that matters, and it is he

> who does the minding. But no matter. And never mind. (*Yenne Velt* 565)

Gregor the vermin could indeed be seen as a *dybbuk*, an evil spirit from Jewish folklore, which enters and possesses people. The metamorphosis into vermin would then suggest a kind of alter-ego that assumes control and makes Gregor give in to his self-destructive desires, rendering him ultimately helpless and passive. In Peretz's story "The Mad Talmudist" (which Kafka also knew through Pinès), we see the effect such a *dybbuk* has on people; the following passage shows the merging of humor and despair which we also see in Gregor:

> . . . who the devil am I? A *dybbuk* must have entered me, someone else, an Other who thinks for me—while I go around thinking it's I who do the thinking. . . . How is it possible for a man in this world to understand himself? What does it mean to want to understand yourself? I want to tear myself out of my body, I want to stand apart from myself, or have the Other stand apart from me. Then "he" can look at me or I-he can look at him-I. (*Gates* 235)

In *The Metamorphosis*, the humor, too, in part derives from the fact that Gregor has split in two.[27] Gregor's rational self regards the transformation as a trick played on him by his imagination; thus, he still believes that he will eventually be able to catch the train and go to work. This confusion between reality and imagination has a humorous effect. Gregor's split personality is again in play when Gregor the human being, who has kept his reason, observes but is unable to control Gregor the vermin, who reacts instinctively. Gregor's attempt to hold back the manager starts up a chain of comic reactions that begins to suggest a Chaplinesque tragi-comedy:[28] it is both tragic and comic that he feels so sorry for his mother, and yet he cannot control his instinctive reactions. The sight of Gregor suddenly in front of her "rocking with repressed motion" (17) [19] makes the mother first jump up into the air and then sit on the table and knock over the coffee. This in turn leads Gregor to "snap his jaws several times in the air" (18) [20], which makes his mother faint. The climax is reached when the manager jumps down the stairs. The importance of gesture and sound in this situation comedy has a strong theatrical effect and quite possibly goes back to Kafka's experience of the Yiddish theater, since Chaplin's films came to Europe only in 1920.

But a transformation can be humorous only as long as it is seen as a product of the imagination. The experience of turning into vermin becomes increasingly "real" when Gregor is rejected and particularly when, at the end of Part I, he is physically attacked by his father. At this point, the humor stops altogether: ". . . now this was really no joke any more" (19) [21]. From now on, the metamorphosis must be seen as a symbol of degradation and humiliation.

Transformations in Jewish folklore are generally inflicted as punishment for transgressions. Gregor's metamorphosis, too, is related to man's first transgression, which represents the root of all evil: Original Sin. The connection with the "Fall" is clearly established at the end of Part II, when the "father" (in the paternal and the religious sense) "punishes" Gregor by bombarding him with apples.

The interpretation of Original Sin in the story accords with the Jewish tradition, which has been distinguished from the Christian as follows:

> Christian tradition reads [the Garden] story as evidence of "original sin," the irreparable flaw in human nature that can be redeemed only by God's sacrifice of his only son. In the context of the Torah, however, the man and woman leave the mythical garden to live a mundane existence in the real world. They do not "fall" from grace.[29]

At the end of *The Metamorphosis* life begins anew for the Samsa family. They literally leave the apartment, i.e., the place associated with Original Sin, and go out into the world. "New life" becomes a concrete possibility through Grete, and the parents are suddenly aware "that it would soon be time, too, to find her a good husband" (58) [64]. Thus Gregor's metamorphosis can be seen as a metaphor for the internal process of transgression and punishment that everyone in his family undergoes, the result of which is a longing for redemption. When this cycle is about to be completed, Gregor, as metaphor, ceases to be.

In an important sense Gregor and Grete exemplify together the interpretation of the Garden Story in the context of the Jewish tradition. The fact that they represent opposite poles is no argument to the contrary because there is an inherent paradox in the Garden Story itself that leads to seemingly contradictory interpretations. The dialectical ambiguity in the original text consists in the following: on the one hand, Original Sin is represented as a curse in that it puts an end to eternal life; on the other hand, however, this curse can be interpreted positively, in that it leads to procreation, "without which generational continuity and history as such are impossible."[30] One could say that Gregor as vermin metaphorically represents one side of the dialectic, i.e., the curse, while Grete personifies the positive side of Original Sin: she is capable of initiating new life and of establishing "a new link in the chain of generations" (Rosenberg 55)—a kind of modified version of the original "eternal life," though in the temporal world. Furthermore, a dialectical ambiguity is already embodied in the vermin metaphor itself: the negative attributes associated with Gregor seem to justify his expulsion from the community, and yet the equally clear process of victimization that he undergoes puts the inhuman treatment of Gregor into question. Such inherent incongruities partly account for the many contradictory interpretations of *The Metamorphosis.*

The transgression implied in Original Sin can also be interpreted as an assertion of the self towards independence: "In the Garden of Eden . . . the humans assert their difference, the independence of their will from God's by disobeying him . . ." (Greenstein 91). In this wider sense we can discern a pattern in *The Metamorphosis*, a cycle of transgression and punishment in which everyone gets caught up and which runs full circle in the "fall" and "rise" of the Samsa family.

Before the story begins, Gregor has displaced the "father" by becoming the sole provider for the family, choosing their abode, feeling responsible for the sister's education, and so forth. He is punished for his self-assertion by the "father." The manager asserts himself by humiliating Gregor and is inadvertently humiliated and driven out of the apartment by Gregor in return. The mother asserts herself twice: the first time to plead for Gregor's life—significantly she is not punished for this. But then she, too, becomes caught up in the cycle. When she takes the initiative the second time and cleans Gregor's room, she is promptly "punished" by Grete and the "father": ". . . his mother's punishment was not long in coming" (44) [48].

Grete gradually makes Gregor as well as her parents dependent on herself: the more individuality she gains, the more Gregor and his parents lose. In Part II, Grete tries to gain absolute power when she deprives Gregor of his furniture: "Into a room in which Gregor ruled the bare walls all alone, no human being beside Grete was ever likely to set foot" (34) [38]. In this scene and shortly thereafter, Grete is called by her first name twelve times, whereas she is referred to as the "sister" only four times. Her ascent to power is further underlined by her language and gestures: when Gregor tries to rebel in Part II, she threatens him and turns against him "with raised fist" (36) [40]. Her father had used a similar gesture in Part I on seeing Gregor for the first time (he "clenched his fist"—15 [16])—an attempt to demonstrate his power and superiority before he breaks down. Grete has thus achieved equal status with the "father" at this moment. But she is "punished," too. Like the rest of the family she is displaced by the roomers: she has to give up her room and sleep in the living room (55) [60]. Notably, in Part III she is addressed as "Grete" only once by the mother (42) [47]—as in Part I (13) [14]—and otherwise simply referred to as the "sister" until Gregor's death (54) [61]. With Gregor's death, though, the "wheel of transgression and punishment" finally comes full circle. The Samsa family asserts itself again and regains its earlier identity: the parents are seen as united ("The couple Mr. and Mrs. Samsa"—54 [60]) and referred to respectfully as "Mr. and Mrs. Samsa," while the sister is called "Grete" again. Now it is the roomers' and the cleaning woman's turn to be humbled and dismissed.

The interpretation of Original Sin as initiating a whole cycle of transgressions and punishments goes beyond the religious notion of punishment for a particular transgression that is associated with metamorphosis. The vermin metaphor can represent a more nearly universal state of sinfulness which is characterized as a whole cycle of transgressions and punishments that no one seems able to escape.

Thus Gregor's metamorphosis also comes to exemplify the victimized state of all the individuals who are caught up in the wheel of transgression and punishment. The mother, for example, who earlier pleaded for Gregor, cannot stand up for him any more once she is caught in the cycle. The sister passes judgment on him when the family finds itself at the lowest point on the wheel, being displaced by and dependent on the roomers who have just threatened to move out. Like everyone else in the story, Grete, at this point, has fallen victim to the particular circumstances and plays her part in the vicious circle. The "father" himself is portrayed as being implicated in the "original" transgression: not only is he the one who throws the apples, but he is also associated with the snake, "hissing like a wild man" (19) [20]. In this context the vermin metaphor does indeed represent a "curse" that does not end with Gregor's death but will continue in the chain of generations.

The concept of metamorphosis also expresses "the reality of Exile" (Scholem, *Major Trends* 281). In Mendele's novel *The Mare* a Wandering Mare states that she has been in this peculiar shape "[a]s long as the Jewish Exile!"[31] The result of the specific historical exile is a more general, personal "inner" exile, and thus transformations are also "a symbol for the exile of the soul" (Scholem, *Major Trends* 281). Furthermore, there are different *degrees* of "inner" exile, because "banishment into the prison of strange forms of existence, into wild beasts, into plants and stones, is regarded as a particularly dreadful form of exile" (Scholem, *Major Trends* 282). This description allows us to see many of the animals in Kafka's stories—ranging from vermin to apes, jackals, the martenlike creature in the synagogue, dogs and mice—as signifying different degrees of exile.

Gregor, then, represents another such "dreadful form of exile," particularly since life in Exile is connected with uncleanliness. He certainly surpasses all of the other animals in this regard and reaches the height of impurity in Part III: ". . . he too was completely covered with dust; he dragged around with him on his back and along his sides fluff and hairs and scraps of food" (48) [00]. When we see him at this moment, he is drawn to the living room by his sister playing the violin. The music is associated with the higher religious realm, with Christmas, in that it reminds Gregor of the violin lessons he had planned for his sister as a Christmas present. The contrast with the "divine" realm shows how low Gregor has sunk.

However, it is not just Gregor who becomes increasingly impure, but his room and his family as well. Again we can discern a pattern: everyone becomes associated with uncleanliness after the apple scene at the end of Part II, i.e., after the connection with the Fall is established. The father's uniform becomes and remains "dirty" (the German *fleckig* carries associations of *befleckt* [tainted]) "in spite of all the mother's and sister's care" (41) [45]. When Grete plays the violin—for the first time since Gregor's transformation—the whole family has reached its nadir, too, to the extent of needing the roomers' permission to play music in their own living room.

In this framework, then, Gregor's desire to be tolerated as "a member of the family, . . . who could not be treated as an enemy; [it being . . .] the commandment of family duty to swallow their disgust and endure him, endure him and nothing more" (40) [44] assumes a greater significance. The fact that both Gregor *and* his family lead an impure existence after the Fall stresses the need for a "humane" treatment of Gregor. In Judaism, with the experience of the Diaspora,[32] religious laws were reformulated towards humanitarian ends; and one famous midrashic[33] passage reads: "The Temple and its sacrifices do not alone expiate our sins, rather we have an equivalent way of making atonement and that is through deeds of human kindness."[34]

Finally, Jewish Exile in general is regarded "either as a punishment for Israel's sins or as a test of Israel's faith" (Scholem, *Major Trends* 284). Thus, Gregor's "exile" can also be seen as a further infliction of punishment; as for exile's serving to test faith, however, the Samsas' increasingly inhuman treatment of Gregor suggests that exile here will not prove successful. Kafka increasingly transforms the particular historical and biblical associations of metamorphosis to convey his own philosophical position.

Biblical law prescribes that "one must undergo a metamorphosis of ritual stages" in order "to reinstate oneself in the divine presence" (Greenstein 95). But the humorous treatment of metamorphosis, the secular wheel of transgression and punishment, as well as the characters' growing impurity culminating in Gregor's death without redemption, all seem to support a modernist position which is summed up by Walter Benjamin as follows: "The achievement of the Thora, to be sure, has been thwarted if we abide by Kafka's representation" (*Benjamin über Kafka* 78). From a modernist perspective, *The Metamorphosis* on the whole suggests a reversal of "[t]he sequence creation-revelation-redemption [that] forms the essential theological drama of Judaism,"[35] in that Part I depicts the creation of something impure, Part II the revelation not of the Torah but of Original Sin, and Part III profound skepticism about the possibility of redemption.

Kafka's reversal of formal religion can be shown, however, to be characteristic of the mystic position, as Scholem argues. What Benjamin sees as "breakdown of tradition," i.e., the break with the religious realm and the loss of truth, "lies in the very nature of the mystic tradition itself," according to Scholem (*Benjamin über Kafka* 87, 89–90), and is indeed the starting point in mysticism. The loss of Truth begins with Original Sin: "Only the Fall has caused God to become 'transcendent'" (Scholem, *Major Trends* 224). Consequently, mysticism is based on the notion of a gap between "the lower world, or the world of separation" and the religious realm, "the upper world, or the world of unity."[36]

In *The Metamorphosis*, the Samsas' break with the religious tradition is obvious when Gregor asks himself the question, "Certainly Christmas had come and gone?" (49) [54]. This implies not only that Gregor has lost all sense of time but that the whole family has missed Christmas, the birth of the Savior, and thus signals an increasing indifference to religion as a consequence of their impure existence after the Fall. But there are other elements in the story that can be linked with the mystic tradition more clearly. First of all, there is the complexity of the question of evil in *The Metamorphosis*, where everyone including the "father" is seen as "implicated": in the mystic tradition, evil is seen as having "its root somewhere in the mystery of God" (Scholem, *Major Trends* 238), i.e., in the "father."

Again, in Jewish mysticism any transformation is regarded as "part of the process of restoration" (Scholem, *Major Trends* 283). In fact, the sole purpose of metamorphosis is "the purification of the soul and the opportunity, in a new trial, to improve its deeds."[37] The use of the word "trial" is significant here, in that it characterizes the process (cf. Kafka's novel *Der Proceß* [*The Trial*]) of striving for redemption that is initiated by the metamorphosis. In Peretz's story "Thou Shalt Not Covet," the narrator similarly calls the rabbi's transformation "the saint's trial" (*Selected Stories* 30). This indicates a likely connection between Gregor's trial and that of Josef K. in *The Trial*, whose transgression is also related to Original Sin. To extend the notion of trial even further, in mysticism "every individual provides, by his behavior, countless occasions for ever renewed exile" (Scholem, *Major Trends* 282), and "[t]he task of all human beings is to *restore* the original harmony through ritual and moral activity" (Fine 328). For this reason there are numerous occasions for ever-renewed trials of penitents. This concept also constitutes a very common motif in hasidic folklore.

A crucial motif in hasidic tales is the mystic longing for redemption. Atonement can here be reached only by going through the ritual stages of punishment, including exile—in other words according to the principle "[d]escent for the sake of ascent."[38] In another of Peretz's stories, "Devotion Without End" (also discussed by Pinès), a youth is cursed for his transgressions: his punishment is that he forgets the Torah, and "it was further decreed that he wander in exile, clad in sackcloth" (*Selected Stories* 125). The way to redemption is through punishment and humiliation: "'But I must suffer, Rabbi, I should suffer, and the more I am shamed the sooner will my curse be lifted'" (*Selected Stories* 122). In this context, then, the two patterns we discerned in *The Metamorphosis* (transgression and punishment, and increasing impurity) can be seen as necessary stages that have to be passed through in the quest for atonement.

The concept of "turning" is crucial for redemption. Benjamin comments on its importance for Kafka: "Kafka's messianic category is that of the 'turning' [*Umkehr*] or of 'study'" (*Benjamin über Kafka* 78). In Part I we see Gregor *dancing* around the lock in order to "turn" the key (14) [16]. Then, at the height of impurity in Part III and confronted with the "divine" music, Gregor is ready for the crucial process of "turning": "Now maybe they'll let me turn around, Gregor thought, and began his labors again" (53) [58]. And a little later we hear, "When he had completed the turn, he immediately began to crawl back in a straight line" (53)

[58]. However, as in the earlier attempt where Gregor succeeds in "turning" the "key" but defiles it with brown liquid at the same time (14) [15], here, too, he successfully completes the process of "turning"—except that he is turning in the wrong direction, away from the music and back to his room. What we have here resembles the many examples of "false" turning in Buber's hasidic tales, where the very concept of "true" and "false" turning is a topos.

Furthermore, the music of the violin that Gregor and his family are drawn to is a key tragic motif associated with the longing for redemption. Both Gregor and his family have reached the height of impurity, humiliation, and displacement at this point, and, significantly, they can respond to the music while the roomers cannot: like Gregor, the family is said to be "completely absorbed by the violin-playing; the roomers, on the other hand . . . soon withdrew to the window, talking to each other in an undertone, their heads lowered . . ." (48) [53]. There is a similar relationship between personal debasement and increasing readiness for attaining the realm of the divine in Peretz's "Cabalists" (also discussed by Pinès): a Yeshivah[39] student imposes a penitence fast on himself and achieves different degrees of revelation until he finally hears "a kind of music . . . as if I had a violin within me. . . ."[40]

In both stories the clear sound of the violin symbolizes the purity of the divine in contrast to the impure environment. And Gregor, too, has been fasting. When he hears the music of the violin, he feels "as if the way to the unknown nourishment he longed for were coming to light" (49) [54]. Fasting thus becomes a means for gaining spiritual nourishment through the divine.

Gregor fails to reach redemption. But such "failure" is inherent in most trials. In Rabbi Nachman's stories redemption is out of reach but always striven for: in "The King's Son and the Maidservant's Son Who Were Switched" (1809), the protagonists are told by a wise forest man that the melody they hear is nothing compared to what he remembers: "Is *this* a marvel in your opinion? Even greater is the instrument I received from my parents who had inherited it from their forefathers . . ." (Band, *Nahman of Bratslav* 203). Even the Yeshivah student in Peretz's "Cabalists" does not find ultimate redemption. He is admitted as a singer in the heavenly host, but "the master of the yeshivah was not satisfied. 'Only a few fasts more,' he said, sighing, 'and he would have died with the Divine Kiss!' "[41] As a matter of fact, the rabbi in "Cabalists" is helpless himself: all he can do is hand on tradition with the hope that some day a student might once more gain intimate knowledge of the realm of the divine. He himself no longer knows more than "the fasts and 'combinations' required for this purpose" (*Treasury* 221); everything else is only a memory to him:

> " . . . there are numerous degrees," the master said. "One man knows a part, another knows a half, a third knows the entire melody. The rabbi, of blessed memory, knew the melody in its wholeness, with musical accompaniment, but I," he added mournfully, "I barely merit a little bit, no larger than this"—and he measured the small degree of his knowledge on his bony finger. (*Treasury* 220)

In Peretz's story "The Golem"[42] (discussed as well by Pinès) we have a similarly hopeless predicament. Here the golem is seen as a "savior" who, in the past, could be called upon in times of need. Now, however, he is no longer accessible to man, even though he has not quite disappeared, either, lying "hidden in the attic of the Prague synagogue, covered with cobwebs. . . ." In this story, too, memory remains the only tie to the past:

> The *golem*, you see, has not been forgotten. It is still here! But the Name by which it could be called to life in a day of need, the Name has disappeared. And the cobwebs grow and grow, and no one may touch them.
> What are we to do? (*Treasury* 246)

For Gregor, too, there is no new life and no redemption. But if his metamorphosis is indeed a metaphor for the cycle of transgression and punishment, including exile and the longing for redemption, he has not failed. Rather, he has completed his metaphorical purpose now and is no longer needed. Thus his death is not tragic but calm; Gregor has quite accepted his fate and agrees with it: "His conviction that he would have to disappear was, if possible, even firmer than his sister's" (54) [59]. In fact, even though he is all alone in the dark and cannot move any more, he feels "relatively comfortable" (53) [59] and ends his days "in this state of empty and peaceful reflection" (54) [59]. Moreover, just before he dies he is granted a shimmer of hope in the form of the breaking day: "He still saw that outside the window everything was beginning to grow light" (54) [59]. In Peretz's "Cabalists" the Yeshivah student suddenly sees "a great light" during his penitence fast, even though his eyes are closed (*Treasury* 222). With Gregor, the light of the breaking day is still dim; nonetheless, it intimates a possible future redemption not for him but for others. This is what allows Gregor to die in peace.

Whereas the vermin metaphor "succeeds" in that it fulfils its function in the structure of the text and can be discarded at the end, Gregor as vermin on the literal level of meaning most certainly "fails" to reach atonement. But even if we grant this, we might recall the ever-renewed trials in the hasidic tales despite the seemingly hopeless situation, and thus there is always a slight possibility of hope. In *The Metamorphosis*, too, even though the Samsas' break with the religious tradition is obvious, there is yet a very slight possibility of redemption with regard to future generations. The family experiences relief for the first time not at Gregor's death, but when a butcher's boy walks *up* the stairs, passing the roomers who are on their way *down.* The butcher is an important image in Kafka's work, being associated with ritual slaughter, sacrifice, and purification. In *The Metamorphosis* it is not the butcher himself who appears but his apprentice—a messenger who might represent a touch of hope, like the children in "A Hunger Artist," who show through "the brightness of their intent eyes that new and better times might be coming,"[43] when the message might once more be understood.

However, at the same time, the prospect for future generations looks chiefly bleak. Kurt Weinberg rightly points out "Kafka's rather dark irony,"[44] which emerges from the ironic contrast between Gregor's death and the dawn of a beautiful spring day that brings about feelings of hope and liberation for the family. In fact, this seemingly positive ending contains yet another ironic twist because the parents' final rise to power manifests itself in their sudden realization "that it would soon be time, too, to find [Grete] a good husband" (58) [64]. This resolution makes the ending appear highly ironic, since the parents are planning to re-establish the traditional patriarchal power relationship, in which yet another head of a family will be able to embark anew on the wheel of transgression and punishment.

In the context of the Jewish narrative tradition, then, *The Metamorphosis* emerges as a story about transgression and punishment, exile, and redemption. The concept of metamorphosis itself has its roots in the folk and mystic tradition, and Gregor's repeated attempts at restoration and his constant rebuffs can be said to resemble the numerous trials of the hasidic tales. The cycle of transgression, punishment, and the longing for redemption characterizes the trial that Gregor and his family undergo. The vermin metaphor makes this trial visible and thus exteriorizes the internal trial of Gregor and his family.

Obviously the use of motifs from the folk and mystic tradition should not suggest that Kafka was a mystic himself. As much as he was attracted by hasidic tales, Kafka made it very clear that he did not believe in hasidic piety: "I think that the deeper meaning is that there is none and in my opinion this is quite enough."[45] Scholars have long ago recognized Kafka's non-religious stance: Gershom Scholem, for one, regards Kafka's work as "a secular statement of the Kabbalistic world-feeling in a modern spirit. . . ."[46] There is no contradiction, then, in acknowledging the largely secular nature of Kafka's texts and arguing at the same time that Kafka, nonetheless, makes extensive use of motifs and narrative devices drawn from the sacred, folk, and mystic Jewish tradition.

KAFKA'S *METAMORPHOSIS* AND THE WRITING OF ABJECTION

Eric Santner

I

The story of Gregor Samsa is an initiation into a universe of abjection.[1] Not only is Gregor transformed into a species of repulsive vermin, not only is he fed garbage, but his family gradually turns his room into a dumping grounds for all sorts of refuse—for what is refused from the family. Gregor's desiccated body is also finally expelled as so much trash, as if he had come to embody the waste products of the very family he had previously nourished with care and dedication. Although Kafka does not offer the reader anything like a causal account of Gregor's transformation, he does suggest a number of possible systemic or structural features that help make sense of it. In other words, Gregor's fall into abjection can be approached as a *symptom* whose fascinating presence serves as a displaced condensation of larger and more diffuse disturbances within the social field marked out by the text.

The story begins with a community—the Samsa family—in disarray. A strange, even miraculous, physical transformation has made it impossible for Gregor to perform the duties that had heretofore been the lifeblood of the family. The reader first encounters the members of this microcommunity as a series of *voices* recalling Gregor to his "official" responsibilities. Among the voices imploring Gregor to do his duty, the father's voice doubtlessly distinguishes itself as the most urgent and insistent one. This quasi-operatic *mise-en-scène*,[2] whereby characters are introduced as voices with distinctive vocal registers, may be, on Kafka's part, an allusion not merely to the world of opera in general but rather to a particular work whose cultural significance would not have escaped him: Wagner's final opera, *Parsifal*.[3]

In *Parsifal*, too, we find a community—the Grail Society—in disarray; there too the communal state of emergency is called forth by a son's inability to perform his official duties because of a bodily mutation or mutilation. Amfortas, the Fisher King, is unable to officiate over the Grail miracle. Seduced by Kundry—embodiment of Woman and Wandering Jew[4]—and wounded by the evil wizard Klingsor, Amfortas now longs only for the death that would put an end to his suffering. The gaping wound in his thigh materializes his liminal state between symbolic death—he is unable to assume his symbolic identity as King of the Grail Society—and the real death he so powerfully desires.[5] Finally, as in the early pages of *Metamorphosis*, the paternal voice—here, the voice of Titurel—assumes a special status and urgency. Slavoj Žižek has noted a more general analogy between *Parsifal* and the world of Kafka's fiction:

> At first sight, Wagner and Kafka are as far apart as they can be: on one hand, we have the late-Romantic revival of a medieval legend; on the other, the description of the fate of the individual in contempo-

> rary totalitarian bureaucracy . . . but if we look closely we perceive that the fundamental problem of *Parsifal* is eminently a *bureaucratic* one: the incapacity, the incompetence of Amfortas in performing his ritual-bureaucratic duty. The terrifying voice of Amfortas's father Titurel, this superego-injunction of the living dead, addresses his impotent son in the first act with the words: "Mein Sohn Amfortas, bist du am Amt?," to which we have to give all bureaucratic weight: Are you at your post? Are you ready to officiate?[6]

In *Metamorphosis*, the paternal injunction recalling the son to his post is, however, marked by a peculiar ambiguity. In Kafka's story, we are never quite certain about the status of the father as a source of social power and authority, never sure of the degree of *imposture* informing that authority. Already in the short prose text "The Judgment," written months before *Metamorphosis*, Kafka had placed this uncertainty apropos of the father's potency in the foreground of his fictional universe. No doubt the most breathtaking scene of that story involves the father's sudden mutation from frail and childlike dependent to death-bringing tyrant. With regard to that metamorphosis, Stanley Corngold has remarked that its surreality "suggests the loss of even fictional coherence; we are entering a world of sheer hypothesis."[7] A careful reading of *Metamorphosis* suggests that the hypothesis in question refers to a change in the nature of patriarchal power and authority that infects its stability, dependability, and consistency with radical uncertainty.

The first indication of this uncertainty concerns not the father but the other paternal master in Gregor's life, his boss. Reminding himself that were it not for the family's outstanding, though curiously unspecified, debt to his boss, he would have long ago given notice, Gregor muses about this master's ultimate imposture:

> He would have fallen off the desk! It is funny, too, the way he sits on the desk and talks down from the heights to the employees, especially when they have to come right up close on account of the boss's being hard of hearing. (4) [4–5]

This curious uncertainty about the force of institutional power and authority is, as it were, transferred to Gregor's father several pages later, in a single sentence: "But their little exchange had made the rest of the family aware that, contrary to expectations, Gregor was still in the house, and already his father was knocking on one of the side doors, *feebly but with his fist*" (6; my emphasis [6]). In each instance a male figure of authority seems to reveal a double aspect: a master's force and power is shown to contain an impotent, even laughable dimension. One of the most uncanny features of Kafka's literary universe is doubtless the way in which such impotence can suddenly reverse itself into awesome power, or better, the way in which impotence reveals itself to be one of the most disturbing attributes of power.

The inconsistencies and uncertainties informing patriarchal power get played out in *Metamorphosis* above all through the apparent and otherwise inexplicable reinvigoration of the father in the wake of Gregor's transformation. For the previous five years, i.e., since the collapse of the father's business, Gregor had lived a life of sacrifice and self-denial, becoming the sole means of support for his family and even securing its present lodgings. In the course of his early morning musings made possible by the forced interruption of normal activities, Gregor makes abundantly clear just how much he has suffered under the burdens of this sacrificial existence, burdens which have been, as noted earlier, aggravated by the parents' debt:

> "Oh God," he thought, "what a grueling job I've picked! Day in, day out—on the road. . . . I've got the torture of traveling, worrying about changing trains, eating miserable food at all hours, constantly seeing new faces, no relationships that last or get more intimate. . . . If I didn't hold back for my parents' sake, I would have quit long ago. . . ." (4) [4]

This sacrificial logic is reiterated and given a turn of the screw in the direction of middle-class sentimentality in the second part of the story:

> In those days Gregor's sole concern had been to do everything in his power to make the family forget as quickly as possible the business disaster which had plunged everyone into a state of total despair. And so he had begun to work with special ardor and had risen almost overnight from stock clerk to traveling salesman. . . . (27) [29–30]

In short order it is only Grete, Gregor's sister, who seems not to take Gregor's sacrifices completely for granted:

> Only his sister had remained close to Gregor, and it was his secret plan that she, who, unlike him, loved music and could play the violin movingly, should be sent next year to the Conservatory, regardless of the great expense involved. . . . (27) [30]

After his transformation, however, Gregor quickly learns that his family's financial situation was not nearly as grave as he had previously assumed. On the very first day of his new condition, he overhears his father opening a strongbox containing monies rescued from the failed business: "He had always believed that his father had not been able to save a penny from the business, at least his father had never told him anything to the contrary, and Gregor, for his part, had never asked him any questions . . ." (27) [29]. Although Gregor seems to be pleasantly surprised by this discovery, noting that his father had even managed to stash away some of Gregor's own salary, he also realizes that his father's "unexpected foresight and thrift" has also postponed the day on which the family debt could be paid off and he, Gregor, could quit his job and be free. But now, he concludes, "things were undoubtedly better the way his father had arranged them"(28) [31].

Just as Gregor has been mistaken about the state of his family's financial health, he appears to be equally deluded about his sister's warm and seemingly nonexploitative regard for him. It is hardly possible, for example, to take at face value Gregor's assumptions about his sister's motives when she locks the door behind her after bringing Gregor an assortment of half-rotten leftovers: "And out of a sense of delicacy, since she knew that Gregor would not eat in front of her, she left hurriedly and even turned the key, just so that Gregor should know that he might make himself as comfortable as he wanted" (24) [26]. How, then, are we to make sense of Gregor's apparent confusion and ignorance as to how things really stand in the family? And how is Gregor's original "innocence" and progressive initiation into the family's secrets related to his physical transformation and the father's (and family's) renewal and regeneration upon his death and decay?

It would seem that Gregor's new knowledge about the family is related to the rupture in the sacrificial logic by which he had previously organized his life. No longer able to live the life of the long-suffering son, he is compelled to perform what might be called the *sacrifice of sacrifice.* This radical act of sacrifice, i.e., of the very sacrificial logic that had given his life its doubtlessly bleak consistency, makes possible Gregor's discovery that the necessity of his former life, its apparent fatefulness, had been an artificial construction. His life of self-abnegation had been, it now appears, a kind of social game he had actively worked to perpetuate (one will recall that Gregor never asked about the father's finances, never asked what was in the strongbox). In this light, Gregor's condition anticipates that of the man from the country in the parable from *The Trial* who, after a lifetime of waiting at the gates of the Law, learns that its entrance had been designed for him all along and that his exclusion had been staged with his own complicitous participation. Gregor's metamorphosis might thus be understood as a sign of his abjuration of just such complicity, in this case with the "plot" imposing on him a life of self-sacrifice. His abjection would indicate his new position outside that plot, i.e., outside the narrative frame that had given his life meaning and value. This reading is, it turns out, supported by the etymological resonances of the words Kafka uses—*ungeheuere(s) Ungeziefer* ("monstrous vermin")—to introduce Gregor's transformation in the famous first sentence of the story. "'*Ungeheuer*,'" as Stanley Corngold has emphasized, "connotes the creature who has no place in the family; '*Ungeziefer*,' the unclean animal unsuited for sacrifice, the creature without a place in God's order" (xix) [169].[8]

To bring these findings to a point, I am arguing that Gregor's fall into abjection be understood as a by-product of his encounter with the ultimate *uncertainty* as to his place in the community of which his father is the nominal master. Gregor's mutation into an *Ungeziefer*, a creature without a place in God's order, suggests, in other words, not Gregor's unsuitability for sacrifice due to some positive, pathological attribute but rather a disturbance *within the divine order itself.* Gregor discovers one of the central paradoxes of modern experience: uncertainty as to what, to use Lacan's term, the "big Other" of the symbolic order[9] really wants from us can be far more disturbing than subordination to an agency or structure whose demands—even for self-sacrifice—are experienced as stable and consistent. The failure to live up to such demands still guarantees a sense of place, meaning, and recognition; but the subject who is uncertain as to the very existence of an Other whose demands might or might not be placated loses the ground from under his feet.[10] The mythic order of fate where one's lot is determined behind one's back—in Kafka's story, as in ancient tragedy, the force of fate corresponds to a familial debt or guilt—is displaced by a post-mythic order in which the individual can no longer find his place in the texture of fate. This distance from the mythic force of fate, this interruption of the transference of a debt from generation to generation, introduces into the world a new and more radical kind of guilt. As Žižek has elsewhere argued,

> Therein consists the constitutive, fundamental guilt attested to by the neurotic symptoms which pertain to the very being of what we call "the modern man": the fact that, ultimately, there is no agency in the eyes of which he can be guilty weighs upon him as a redoubled guilt. The "death of God"—another name for this retreat of fate—makes our guilt absolute.[11]

In *Metamorphosis*, the interruption of those entanglements we call fate opens up a space within which monstrosities can appear. This interruption is figured in the story by means of a series of ambiguities pertaining to patriarchal power and authority.

Significantly, as in *Parsifal*, a disturbance in the domain of patriarchal authority is registered at the level of voice and staging. At the end of the first part of the story, Gregor's father chases his son back into his room, producing a strange and disturbing hissing noise: "Pitilessly his father came on, hissing like a wild man . . ." (19) [20]. Gregor struggles to comply but is distracted and unnerved by this curious vocalization: "If only his father did not keep making this intolerable hissing sound! It made Gregor lose his head completely. He had almost finished the turn when—his mind continually on this hissing—he made a mistake and even started turning back around to his original position" (19) [21]. During the final moments of this ordeal, the father's hissing achieves an intensity such that "*the voice behind Gregor did not sound like that of only a single father*, now this was really no joke anymore . . ." [(19) [21]; my emphasis]. It is as if the father's voice had assumed the quality of an uncanny chorus, signaling the dimension of an implacable and horrific paternal force exceeding that of any single individual. Our perplexity about this weird amplification and distortion of the father's voice is heightened in the third and final part of the story. At a moment when the family's rejuvenation is well underway, Kafka indicates that the father's reinvigoration may be nothing more than a pathetic imposture:

> Sometimes his father woke up, and as if he had absolutely no idea that he had been asleep, said to his mother, "Look how long you're sewing again today!"

> and went right back to sleep, while mother and sister smiled wearily at each other. (41) [45].

It is in the next sentence that the question of imposture is placed directly into the foreground:

> With a kind of perverse obstinacy his father refused to take off his official uniform even in the house; and while his robe hung uselessly on the clothes hook, his father dozed, completely dressed, in his chair, as if he were always ready for duty and were waiting even here for the voice of his superior. (41) [45]

The ambiguity of Kafka's diction makes possible the reading that the father has refused to remove his uniform not just at home but in public as well; his recent "investiture" with a kind of official status and authority, low though it might be, might, in other words, be a sham. Be that as it may, the father's clinging to the outward appearance—to the vestments—of institutional authority suggests just how precarious and uncertain this authority really is. Gregor's father achieves his new patriarchal authority, restores his damaged masculinity, by means of a kind of cross-dressing.

II

In a diary entry of September 23, 1912, Kafka registers the miraculous composition of "The Judgment" in the course of a single night's labor, one he would, the following year, characterize as a kind of *couvade*[12] in which his story emerged covered with the "filth and mucus" of birth. In the entry of September 23, he recollects various associations that passed through his head during the composition of the story and notes, "naturally, thoughts of Freud."[13] The year before the composition of "The Judgment" and *Metamorphosis*, Sigmund Freud published his only case study dealing with psychosis, his *Psychoanalytic Notes Upon an Autobiographical Account of a Case of Paranoia* (*Dementia Paranoides*).[14] Freud based his study, as the title suggests, not on a clinical encounter with a patient but rather on a text: Daniel Paul Schreber's now famous account of his own mental illness, *Denkwürdigkeiten eines Nervenkranken* (*Memoirs of My Nervous Illness*), published in 1903 and written toward the end of nine years of confinement in various private and state psychiatric institutions. In these memoirs, Schreber, who, just prior to his mental collapse in 1893, had been named *Senatspräsident* (presiding judge) of the third civil chamber of the Saxon Supreme Court, tells a remarkable story of descent into a paranoid universe where body and mind are subjected to the often cruel, often merely mischievous, manipulations of doctors, spirits of the dead, and eventually God Himself. The nervous agitation generated by all this "nerve-contact"—Schreber's technical term for these multifarious influences and manipulations—resulted in a kind of cosmic disequilibrium, an apocalyptic state of emergency in God's order or what he calls the "Order of the World." The more agitated Schreber became, the more he began to undergo his own curious process of metamorphosis, not into an insect but rather into a woman and indeed one whose considerable forces of sexual attraction not even God was able to resist, thus endangering the normal relations between sacred and profane realms. It was this delusional experience of feminization that Freud placed at the heart of his interpretation of the case, reading it as the return, at a moment of extreme mental stress, of long repressed homosexual longings.[15] There is no direct evidence that Kafka read Freud's essay on

Schreber or Schreber's own text; the parallels between Kafka's story of bodily metamorphosis and Schreber's are, however, quite stunning.[16] Indeed, the remarkable similarities of these stories allow us to turn to Schreber for illumination about Gregor Samsa.[17]

As with Gregor, Schreber's demise is correlated with a form of vocational failure: an inability to heed an official call, to assume a symbolic mandate, in this case as presiding judge in the Saxon Court of Appeals. After his mental collapse and forced withdrawal from his position in the courts, Schreber begins to suffer from what eventually becomes one of his core symptoms: the hearing of voices. These voices, which torment Schreber for most of the rest of his life, embody the excess of demands that made the administration of his office insupportable. Indeed, they seem to represent these demands purified of any instrumental value or meaning-content, a kind of pure and nonsensical "You must!" abstracted from the use value of any particular activity. At this zero-level of meaning, the voices eventually come to be heard as a steady hissing sound, i.e., the sound which for Gregor was that of a kind of wild and perverse paternal chorus: "But the slowing down has recently become still more marked and the voices . . . degenerated into an indistinct hissing."[18]

On one particular day, however, the voices that spoke to Schreber became overwhelmingly clear and distinct. On that day, Ahriman, one of the two (Zoroastrian)[19] deities that tormented him, appeared in the form of a booming, operatic voice:

> It resounded in a mighty bass as if directly in front of my bedroom window. The impression was intense, so that anybody not hardened to terrifying miraculous impressions as I was, would have been shaken to the core. Also *what* was spoken did not sound friendly by

> any means: everything seemed calculated to instil fright and terror into me and the word "wretch" [*Luder*] was frequently heard—an expression quite common in the basic language to denote a human being destined to be destroyed by God and to feel God's power and wrath. (124)

In spite of the rage and terror manifest in the *content* of this epiphany of divine power, the effects produced at the level of its enunciation turn out to be, as Schreber insists, strangely beneficial (here we are reminded of Gregor's momentary experiences of physical well-being):

> Yet everything that was spoken was *genuine*, not phrases learnt by rote as they later were, but the immediate expression of true feeling. . . . For this reason my impression was not one of alarm or fear, but largely one of admiration for the magnificent and the sublime; the effect on my nerves was therefore beneficial despite the insults contained in some of the *words*. . . . (124–25)

The most important of these words, *Luder*, has rich connotations both in the context of Schreber's torments and in *The Metamorphosis.* It can indeed mean, as Schreber's translators suggest, "wretch," in the sense of a lost and pathetic figure, but can also signify: whore, tart, or slut; and finally, the dead, rotting flesh of an animal, especially in the sense of carrion used as bait in hunting. The last two significations in particular capture Schreber's fear of being turned over to others for the purposes of sexual exploitation as well as his anxieties, which would seem to flow from such abuse, about putrefaction, being left to rot. These latter anxieties merge at times with fantasies of being sick with the plague, leprosy, or syphilis. Schreber is, in other words, like Gregor Samsa, compelled to experience the world from the locus of abjection.

At this point another dimension of Schreber's metamorphosis forces itself on our attention. Not only does he experience himself being turned into a woman whose sexuality bleeds, as it were, into putrefaction, but also into the mythic figure of the Wandering or Eternal Jew. To become a *Luder* means, in Schreber's universe, to become a *Jude* (Jew).[20] According to the cosmic laws revealed to Schreber over the course of his illness, God might decide, in periods of extreme moral decadence and nervousness, to destroy mankind. "In such an event," Schreber writes, "in order to maintain the species, one single human being was spared—perhaps the relatively most moral—called by the voices that talk to me the '*Eternal Jew*'" (73). This Eternal Jew, Schreber continues,

> had to be *unmanned* (transformed into a woman) to be able to bear children. This process of unmanning consisted in the (external) male genitals (scrotum and penis) being retracted into the body and the internal sexual organs being at the same time transformed into the corresponding female sexual organs, a process which might have been completed in a sleep lasting hundreds of years. . . . (73–74)

How might we correlate these details of Schreber's metamorphosis into a feminized Wandering Jew—i.e., into a kind of Kundry-figure—with the fate of Gregor Samsa?[21]

Amidst the wealth of striking details that have preoccupied readers of Kafka's *Metamorphosis*, the one which situates Kafka's text most firmly within fin-de-siècle[22] obsessions with gender and sexuality is the brief indication of Gregor's erotic life suggested by a bit of interior decorating he had engaged in shortly before his verminous transformation:

> Over the table . . . hung the picture which he had recently cut out of a glossy magazine and lodged in a pretty gilt frame. It showed a lady done up in a fur hat and a fur boa, sitting upright and raising up against the viewer a heavy fur muff in which her whole forearm had disappeared. (3) [3]

The importance of this peculiar detail, alluding, very likely, to Leopold von Sacher-Masoch's infamous novella, *Venus in Furs* (1870),[23] is underlined by its placement in the text: it appears in the second paragraph following immediately upon the famous inaugural sentences announcing Gregor's metamorphosis and is introduced as if in answer to the question with which the paragraph begins: "What's happened to me?" The picture, most likely part of an advertisement, figures once more, in the second part of the story, when Gregor is struggling to save some piece of his former life from the efforts of his mother and sister to clear his room:

> And so he broke out—the women were just leaning against the desk in the next room to catch their breath for a minute—changed his course four times, he really didn't know what to salvage first, then he saw hanging conspicuously on the wall, which was otherwise bare already, the picture of the lady all dressed in furs, hurriedly crawled up on it and pressed himself against the glass, which gave a good surface to

> stick to and soothed his hot belly. At least no one would take away this picture, while Gregor completely covered it up. (35) [39]

The importance of this possession is further emphasized by Gregor's willingness to attack his otherwise beloved sister rather than part with his picture: "He squatted on his picture and would not give it up. He would rather fly in Grete's face" (36) [39].

Gregor's peculiar attachment to this piece of pornographic kitsch is obviously central to the text. Indeed, the entire story seems to crystallize around it as an elaborate punishment scenario called forth by guilt-ridden sexual obsession. The indications of putrescence which proliferate in the course of the story suggest fantasies of the consequences of a young man's autoerotic activities. In this perspective, many hitherto unintelligible details take on importance. When, for example, the maid announces at the end of the story that she has removed "*das Zeug*" ("the stuff") from Gregor's room, this word connotes what would be cut short or degenerated by compulsive autoeroticism, namely the capacity for *Zeugen*, the generation of offspring. The final sentences of the story, which circle around Grete's sexual coming-of-age and prospects of imminent union with "a good husband," constitute the closure made possible by the elimination of the perverse, i.e., nonreproductive, sexuality embodied in Gregor's abject, putrescent condition.

This reading is supported by a wide array of medical treatises and popular literature concerning the dangers of masturbation circulating in fin-de-siècle Europe; it presupposes, however, that the woman in furs must be understood as an object of heterosexual desire. But if we are to take the comparison with Schreber seriously, a different, more "perverse," reading becomes possible, namely, one in which the woman in furs is not an object of desire but rather one of (unconscious) *identification.* In other words, Gregor's picture of the woman in furs represents the unconscious "truth" of the other picture described in the story, the photograph of Gregor from his "army days, in a lieutenant's uniform, his hand on his sword, a carefree smile on his lips, demanding respect for his bearing and his rank" (15) [17]. Gregor's metamorphosis now becomes legible as a kind of feminization; his verminous state suggests the mode of appearance of a femininity disavowed under the pressures of a misogynist and homophobic cultural imperative shared by Kafka's Austria-Hungary and Schreber's Germany.[24]

This reading is supported by a detail pertaining, once again, to the voice. After missing the train on the first morning of his new condition, Gregor's mother calls to him from the other side of his locked door to remind him of the time. After noting the softness of his mother's voice, he notices a new quality in his own voice:

> Gregor was shocked to hear his own voice answering, unmistakably his own voice, true, but in which, as if from below, an insistent distressed chirping [*ein nicht zu unterdrückendes, schmerzliches Piepsen*] intruded, which left the clarity of his words intact only for a moment really, before so badly garbling them as they carried that no one could be sure if he had heard right. (5) [6]

Gregor's *Piepsen* suggests the mutation of the male voice in the direction of the feminine.

The importance of this birdlike vocalization is confirmed, once more, by an important detail in Schreber's memoir. At various moments, the voices that tormented Schreber miraculously took the form of little birds—*gewunderte Vögel*—who were understood by Schreber to be made up of residues of departed human souls which had, in his delusional cosmology, previously made up the so-called "forecourts of heaven." Schreber characterizes their chirpings as a series of mechanically repeated turns of phrase. Thanks to their purely repetitive and meaningless nature—their *deadness*—Schreber associates these vocalizations with putrescence or what he calls *Leichengift*, the poison of corpses. Freud, for his part, hears them as the voices of young girls: "In a carping mood people often compare them to geese, ungallantly accuse them of having 'the brains of a bird,' declare that they can say nothing but phrases learnt by rote, and that they betray their lack of education by confusing foreign words that sound alike."[25] Schreber confirms this interpretation when he gives some of the birds girls' names. But Gregor's *Piepsen* points also in the direction indicated by Schreber's other pole of identification: that of the Wandering Jew.

The fin-de-siècle culture of Kafka and Schreber was at many levels preoccupied with the peculiarities of the Jewish physical and mental constitution.[26] Central to these preoccupations was an obsession with the Jewish voice and Jewish language production. This obsession, already important in premodern Europe, was recoded in the nineteenth century in the idiom of racial biology and was conjoined with fantasies about Jewish sexuality. Jewish men, for example, were often regarded as exhibiting feminine characteristics, an association that placed them in the domain of a larger set of "impaired masculinities" that included the newly medicalized "homosexual" and came increasingly under the surveillance of various state, medical, and church-affiliated institutions.[27] Thus Otto Weininger's infamous treatise, *Sex and Charakter* (1903), reformulates many of Wagner's earlier theses apropos of the Jewish relation to language and music by consolidating the linkage of Jewishness and femininity.[28] If Jews lack a profound relation to music, as Wagner had claimed, it was, Weininger now argued, because they, *like women,* had an impaired relation to logic, ethics, and language (the preferred term for this impairment was, of course, *hysteria*). At the end of the nineteenth century, the faulty command of discourse attributed to Jews and condensed in the term *mauscheln*, meaning to speak (German) like Moses, was, in other words, coupled with femininity and, hence, homosexuality. To return to *Metamorphosis*, we might say that the Jew's *Mauscheln* was recoded as a kind of feminized, queer *Piepsen.*[29]

Kafka's text, however, is more than a literary version of a kind of Jewish self-hatred, more than the narrative and poetic elaboration of a series of internalized anti-Semitic prejudices. For though Kafka is a writer whose work is at times burdened by negative conceptions about Jews, Judaism, and Jewishness, *Metamorphosis* is a text which indicates Kafka's profound awareness of the ideological role such conceptions played within the larger culture. In *Metamorphosis*, the cultural fantasies positioning the Jew, along with everything feminine, at the place of abjection, are led back to the deeper cultural crises and anxieties fueling them. These anxieties arise, as we have seen, from a fundamental dysfunctionality at the core of patriarchal power and authority. Kafka's story suggests, in other words, that at least in the modern period the domain of the abject and monstrous, or, to use the term that would prove so fateful and fatal during the Nazi period, the "degenerate," is linked to a chronic uncertainty haunting the institutions of power. The "redemption" of the Samsa family at the conclusion of Kafka's story thus represents the ultimate ideological fantasy, not unlike the conclusion of Wagner's *Parsifal*, where the restoration of the Grail Society is linked to Kundry's demise. With the destruction of Gregor *qua*[30] feminized Wandering Jew, the family can thrive, perhaps now for the very first time.

Kafka's story, however, offers an alternative to this Wagnerian scenario. It asks the reader to identify with Gregor's abjection as an imaginative support for the much more difficult task of staying with and working through the uncertainties that inform the subject's relation to institutional authority in the modern period. We might even say that the capacity and the will to risk such an identification is Kafka's own version of the heroism of modern life. This process of working through implies, however, an appreciation of the limits of any attempt to decipher Gregor Samsa, for interpretation is also, in the end, a form of redemption, an effort to heal the symptomatic blockages in the text. Any purely ideological reading of Kafka, whether as Jewish self-hater who has internalized the discourse of degeneration or, alternatively, as analyst of the very socio-psychological mechanisms behind such a discourse, will miss Kafka's most original contribution: the figuration of precisely that which dooms interpretation to failure, *even a correct one* (in this context, we should recall, once more, Kafka's explicit prohibition against the representation of the insect in any illustration [79]).[31] Gregor's abjection is, in other words, more than a symptom to be read and decoded, more than a condensation of social forces or contradictions, and thus more than a scapegoat figure. He remains a foreign body in the text and in any interpretation. Indeed, if there is anything that is completely foreign to Kafka's aesthetic and ethical imagination, it is the will to do away with such remainders.

This conclusion need not be taken as an argument against history or the importance of historicization. We can and should, for example, speculate as to the connections between Gregor's unreadability, i.e., the impossibility of forming a consistent and unified representation of him, and what Kafka would later characterize as an *impossibility of writing* which he in turn linked to the particular *historical* situation of German Jews at the turn of the century. In a now famous letter to his lifelong friend Max Brod, Kafka comments on Karl Kraus's critique of the *Mauscheln* he claimed to detect in the work of German-Jewish authors like Kafka's fellow Prague writer Franz Werfel. Before turning this charge against Kraus himself—"no one can *mauscheln* like Kraus"—Kafka confesses that he experiences the truth of Kraus's claims in a profoundly physical way. This physical dimension is reiterated later in this letter when Kafka retools the psychoanalytic notion of oedipal conflict to better fit the particular historical situation of Jewish families at the boundaries between traditional Eastern European and posttraditional Western European cultures. The image Kafka uses recalls Gregor's inability, upon waking to his new condition, to coordinate the movement of his legs:

> Most young Jews who began to write German wanted to leave Jewishness behind them, and their fathers approved of this, but vaguely (this vagueness was what was so outrageous to them). But with their posterior legs they were still glued to their fathers' Jewishness and with their waving anterior legs they found no new ground. The ensuing despair became their inspiration.

Kafka goes on to link this—paradoxically—inspiring state of despair and desperation—of *Verzweiflung*—to what he characterizes as a life lived amidst a series of linguistic impossibilities: "These are: the impossibility of not writing, the impossibility of writing German, the impossibility of writing differently. One might also add a fourth impossibility, the impossibility of writing. . . ."[32] These "impossibilities," as Kafka notes at the end of the letter, keep the writer in a kind of perpetual *liminality*, a borderline-state between symbolic and real death, like that of a man who has written his will but not yet hanged himself. The story of the traveling salesman Gregor Samsa unfolds, in its entirety, within just such a liminal space between two deaths: between the exit from the sacrificial order of the family and the destruction of the body made monstrous by that first, symbolic, death.

Finally, the greatest mistake a reader could make would be to imagine that by historicizing this series of impossibilities, by locating their emergence within a particular historical state of emergency—that of German Jews at the turn of the century—that one has effectively distanced oneself from them and the painful disorientations that they imply. It is, rather, the ultimate strength of Kafka's aesthetic and ethical vision that he is able to take us through and beyond that fantasy—to reveal that the emergency, to cite another of his works, "cannot be made good, not ever."[33]

"Samsa Was a Traveling Salesman": Trains, Trauma, and the Unreadable Body

John Zilcosky

Franz Kafka once claimed that all human beings were caught between two competing technological systems: one sponsoring "ghostly" absence (the postal system, telegraph, and telephone) and one encouraging "natural" presence (trains, planes, and automobiles). To humanity's woe, the ghostly side was winning: "To attain a natural intercourse, a tranquility of souls, [humanity] has invented the railway, the motor car, the aeroplane—but nothing helps anymore: These are evidently inventions devised at the moment of crashing" (*LM*, 223; *BM*, 302).[1] Kafka famously spent most of his life on the side of the ghosts, sending Felice Bauer up to three letters per day for weeks on end, yet never boarding a train that would have brought him to Berlin in a few hours. This question—Why does Kafka not get on a train?—recurs for media theoreticians, and their answer is clear: Kafka, the techno-wizard, wants to create a literary "feed-back loop" (*Endlosschleife*) rivaling those produced by films, gramophones, and parlographs.[2] But this argument fails to acknowledge the quiet irony in Kafka's claim that the "natural" technologies transport humans at decidedly unnatural speeds; they are invented precisely "at the moment of crashing."[3] If traditional critics have fatefully forgotten the medial "other" of Kafka's literature,[4] then media theorists have equally forgotten that other's other: Kafka's counter-alliance of modern transportation technologies, which allow faraway lovers to engage in "natural intercourse [*natürlichen Verkehr*]" yet unnaturally alter these lovers through mechanization and speed. Kafka's trepidation regarding such technologies extends back to his early years as a tourist and business traveler, when racing automobiles appear, as in the 1911 accident Kafka witnesses on the Parisian boulevard, the lines of cars bumping into each other in *Amerika: The Missing Person* (*Der Verschollene*, 1927), the rumbling omnibus in *The Judgment* (*Das Urteil*, 1913), and the daredevil Munich sightseeing trip in the 1911 novel fragment, *Richard and Samuel (Richard und Samuel*). Even more than automobiles, trains are for Kafka constitutionally "violen[t]," not least because they almost doubled their speeds in his lifetime alone (*D*1, 69; *Ta*, 43, entry of 29 Sept. 1911).[5] As Karl Rossmann notes in *The Missing Person*, trains ferociously "thunder" across rails and over "vibrating"—*sich schwingenden*—viaducts (*A*, 101; *V*, 151, trans. rev.). This railway turbulence transforms Kafka's protagonists into unnatural bundles of symptoms as ghostly as the letters themselves.

Kafka's interest in train-transported bodies is already in evidence in his novel fragment, *Wedding Preparations in the Country (Hochzeitsvorbereitungen auf dem Lande*, 1907), where the hero, Eduard Raban, boards a train that "beat[s] on the rails like a hammer" and even keeps "shaking" (*zitter*[*n*]) after it stops (*CS*, 64, 66; *NS*1, 31, 35). Across from Raban sits a traveling salesman who bears the marks of this turbulence: he can find no place to rest his vibrating arm, and his notebook "trembles" (*zittert; CS*, 64; *NS*1, 31). This traveler then mentions some worries about his profession and, for no clear reason, begins to shake and cry: "not ashamed of the tears in his eyes," he looks at Raban and presses his knuckles into his "quivering" lips (*seine Lippen zitterten; CS*, 65; *NS*1, 34). This shaking and sobbing man prefigures the post–First World War "war tremblers"—*Kriegszitterer*—and echoes an earlier traveler from *Wedding Preparations*: the "clothed body" that Raban had always sent on journeys in his stead; this body now appears as "sobbing," "stumbling," and "staggering" (*CS*, 55; *NS*1, 17–18).[6] Yet another early Kafkan train traveler—Samuel from *Richard and Samuel*—is likewise exposed to the initially soothing "action of the [train's] carriage springs," "friction of the wheels," "collision of the rail points," and "vibration [*Zittern*] of the whole wooden, glass, and iron structure," until the accelerations, jerks, and stops eventually startle him awake and render his body one with the train's vibration: a change in speed "transmits itself through the whole of my sleep just as through the whole body of the train." Like the traveling salesman and the "clothed body" before him, Samuel, now covered in "railway grit," ultimately finds himself inexplicably at the point of "tears" (*MP*, 293, 294, 296; *DL*, 436, 437, 438, 440).

Although these characters' symptoms are overdetermined—the traveling salesman also has work worries; the clothed body must meet with the dreaded fiancée; Samuel is sexually frustrated—the very fact that they appear repeatedly during or after turbulent train travel suggests the influence of contemporaneous medical discourse. "Railway doctors" (*Eisenbahnärzte*) specializing in "railway illnesses" (*Eisenbahnkrankheiten*) and "railway health" (*Eisenbahnhygiene*) regularly saw similar bodies that quivered, shook, and trembled without apparent cause. Beginning as early as the 1860s, British, French, and German researchers had reported that railway personnel and passengers experienced "contract[ing]" muscles throughout the entire journey and "continuous tremors [*Erzittern*] of all the joints" long after deboarding.[7] After the legal debate heated up in the 1890s about whether train-induced neuroses were physio- or psychogenic, researchers still insisted on the pathogenic importance of material vibrations; the train's shaking seemed to transfer directly to the body. Many doctors cited passengers who even continued to tremble in their sleep.[8] One German researcher argued in 1908 that railway neurosis was—like seasickness—a "kinetosis," an illness brought on by "abnormal motion" that led, in severe cases, to "traumatic shock."[9] In these birth years of modern trauma theory, Freud similarly speculated that the railway's mechanical *Erschütterung*—meaning both "shaking" and "shock"—combined with fright to produce a "traumatic neurosis."[10] The British *Book of Health* had already insisted on these neuroses' material substratum twenty years earlier: "Man, for the time being, becomes a part of the machine in which he has placed himself, being jarred by the self-same movement, and receiving impressions upon nerves of skin and muscle."[11] Whereas horse-drawn carriages put wooden wheels on dirt, trains set steel upon steel, and this rigidity—for Kafka, "the collision of the rail points"—sent a series of "small and rapid concussions" through the traveler's body.[12] The "nervous-making shaking" nestled into the passenger's nervous system and left him quivering long afterwards.[13] In Kafka's words, the turbulence transmits itself "through the whole body of the train" into the physiognomy of the traveler. To steel travelers against such damage, one German expert recommended sitting in a vibrating chair—a *Vibrationsstuhl*—before a journey; but even this could not ultimately protect passengers, who still mirrored uncannily the vehicles that had transported them.[14] In his bestselling 1892 book, *Degeneration*, Max Nordau, like many cultural commentators of his day, came to the same conclusion as the doctors: modern nervous diseases issued from civilization itself, and often from the "shaking" (*Erschütterung*) that travelers "constantly suffer in railway trains."[15]

Kafka's awareness of this popular discourse is clear in the technological diction of his early heroes—the "action of the carriage springs," the "friction of the wheels," and the "vibration of the entire wooden, glass and iron structure"—but also in his later story, *The Metamorphosis* (*Die Verwandlung*, 1915), which borrows heavily from *Wedding Preparations.* When Raban sent his "clothed body" traveling in 1907, he famously wanted to remain in bed and metamorphose into a "beetle" (*CS*, 56; *NS*1, 18). The widespread critical assumption that Raban prefigures the 1912 Gregor Samsa forgets, however, an important distinction: whereas Samsa is explicitly a traveler—*"Samsa war Reisender"* ("Samsa was a traveling salesman")—Raban unequivocally is not: "I have never traveled" *(Ich bin nie gereist; CS,* 89, 45; *DL,* 115; *NS*1, 15).[16] From this perspective, Samsa has more in common with the sobbing traveling salesman (*"Reisender"*) from *Wedding Preparations* than he does with Raban. If we imagine, as Kafka often did, that his stories conversed internally with one another,[17] it is even possible that this early "Reisender" *becomes* Samsa, playfully reconfigured by Kafka five years later. We learn in the opening paragraphs of *The Metamorphosis* that Samsa has worked as a traveling salesman for exactly five years: from precisely the time Kafka wrote most of *Wedding Preparations*, in 1907, to the year he began *The Metamorphosis* (1912; *CS*, 91; *DL*, 118). That Kafka was more than passingly interested in this traveler from *Wedding Preparations* is evident in the traveler's unusually intimate relation to Raban. This traveling salesman looks intently at Raban the entire time, never once "turn[ing] his face away from Raban," until Raban feels compelled to engage him in small talk. But then this traveler, like the clothed body before him, begins to shake and cry (*CS*, 63, 65; *NS*1, 30–31, 34). If Samsa has a cameo in *Wedding Preparations*, then, it is not as Raban's happily lounging, stay-at-home "beetle" but as this proto-hysterical traveler tossed about in a train that "beats on the rails like a hammer."

This supposition gains force when we learn that Raban—long seen as a cipher for "Kafka"[18]—cannot understand the business talk of this traveling salesman, claiming that "much preparation [*Vorbereitung*] would first be required" (*CS*, 64; *NS*1, 31). The "preparations" for *The Metamorphosis* begin precisely here, on this 1907 train, with Kafka/Raban declaring his need to gain more knowledge of professional travel, which Kafka notoriously does during his five subsequent years of "maddening" business journeys (*LF*, 64; *BF*, 125).[19] While writing *The Metamorphosis*, Kafka uses the same word that Samsa does—"agitations" *(Aufregungen)*—to describe his workaday woes, and Kafka's recurring complaints about professional travel mirror Samsa's (*LF*, 48; *BF*, 102; *CS*, 92; *DL*, 121, trans. rev.; [4]). Kafka, too, must repeatedly catch early trains—"Tomorrow I have to get up at 4:30 AM again"—and Kafka, too, suffers what Samsa calls the "trouble of constant traveling": the "irregular, bad meals," the lack of sleep, and the general loneliness (*LF*, 229; *BF*, 346; *CS*, 90; *DL*, 116, trans. rev.; [4]). Consider, for example, Kafka's departure for a business trip to Leitmeritz just two days after completing *The Metamorphosis*: "Off I march while it's still almost night, wander through the streets in the piercing cold—past the breakfast room at the 'Blaue Stern,' its lights already on but curtains still drawn" (*LF*, 97; *BF*, 170). A couple of months later, before a trip to Aussig, Kafka cannot sleep despite great weariness, because he is haunted by visions of the very trains that will transport him: "Trains came, one after another they ran over my body, outstretched on the tracks, deepening and widening the two cuts in my neck and legs." The trains of course do not actually slice him up, but they do exhaust him, to the point that he, like the "clothed body," sits soullessly at his hotel table "like a puppet" (*LF*, 230; *BF*, 347). Beside himself for days with "sleepiness, exhaustion, and anxiety [*Unruhe*]," Kafka eventually even transforms into an animal, like Samsa: "What I bore on my body was no longer a human head" (*LF*, 229, 230; *BF*, 346, 347).

Business travel repeatedly gives Kafka this same anxiety (Unruhe). Consider again his trip to Leitmeritz, when he feels "all the time uneasy, all the time uneasy [*unruhig*]," and his journey to Kratzau, in the midst of writing *The Metamorphosis:* "There wasn't a single moment on the trip when I didn't feel at least a tiny bit unhappy," most notably during the train ride itself, when "[I] felt restless [*unruhig*]" from very beginning of the journey (*LF*, 97, 67; *BF*, 171, 130). Worrying "that the trip may have harmed my story," Kafka concludes bluntly to Bauer: "One shouldn't ever go away," should not ever travel (*wegfahren*; 67; 130). Yet he soon finds himself "threatened" again by an impending journey.[20] It is however precisely these journeys that "prepare" Kafka—as Samsa later insists, *am eigenen Leibe*—for *The Metamorphosis* (*CS*, 101; *DL*, 136–37; [18]). Kafka awakens one morning five years after writing *Wedding Preparations*, in misery, dreading another "beastly" professional journey, only to invent a new story (*LF*, 47, 66; *BF*, 102, 127). The "incubation period" typical for traumatic neuroses had begun five years earlier, in 1907, and ends now, with a young traveler waking from "uneasy dreams" *(unruhigen Träumen)* to find himself pathologically transformed (*CS*, 89; *DL*, 115; [3]).[21]

The Metamorphosis begins precisely with the assumption that Gregor is "ill" from the same beastly rigors of professional travel that afflicted his author. Mrs. Samsa says, "Gregor is ill"; Grete asks, "Aren't you well?"; and Gregor himself concludes that he has contracted a "standing ailment of traveling salesmen"

(*Berufskrankheit der Reisenden*; *CS*, 98, 92; *DL*, 131, 120, 121; [14, 6, 7]). Gregor's symptoms tally with the findings of train-illness research from the earliest years onward, which claimed that five years of regular train travel would be dangerous to anyone—especially to traveling salesmen, who were more susceptible to everything from "overexcitement" to premature aging.[22] Gregor's symptoms echo the railway doctors' descriptions, which included the same melancholia, anxiety, and involuntary muscle movements present in travelers in *Wedding Preparations*. Gregor, anxious and dejected, can suddenly "not control" his limbs, which wave "wildly in a high degree of unpleasant agitation" (*Aufregung*; 92; 121). Researchers furthermore cited chronic fatigue as a symptom of railway illness, and Gregor, like his author, complains repeatedly of "exhausti[on]," "drowsiness," and "general fatigue" (*allgemeiner Müdigkeit*; *CS*, 89, 91, 101, 111, 123; *DL*, 116, 119, 136, 153, 173, trans. rev.; [4, 6, 18, 30, 45]).[23] Doctors also discovered that victims of railway crashes and those simply afraid of crashes had "distressing and horrible" dreams; they woke up "suddenly with a vague sense of alarm" and were "unusually talkative" and "excited."[24] Such premonitions of modern trauma theory apply to Gregor, who suffers first from *unruhigen Träumen* and then, after remaining silent at first, explodes in nervous "twittering squeak[s]" that tumble out of him "pell-mell" (*CS*, 91, 98; *DL*, 119, 130; [6, 13]).

Another regularly-reported symptom of train travelers was failing vision caused by eye fatigue and blurring landscapes. Observers claimed that the human eye, accustomed to the leisurely pace of horse carriages—eight kilometers per hour—could not focus at the subsequent fifty (1840), sixty-five (1860), and 100 kilometers per hour (1910) of trains.[25] The "incessant shifting of the adaptive apparatus by which [objects] are focused upon the retina" was particularly harmful to traveling salesmen who "in the course of one day have to cast their eyes upon the panoramas of several hundreds of places."[26] Nordau made similar claims in 1892: "Every image that we perceive from the compartment-window of an express train sets our sensory nerves and brain centers in action."[27] When Raban looks out of his "racing" train window in 1907, he likewise sees only "lights flitting past," villages "com[ing] toward us and flash[ing] past," and bridges that appear to be moving: "torn apart and pressed together," or so "it seemed" (*CS,* 64, 65; *NSI,* 31, 33). These high-speed apparitions tire Raban's eyes and those of his fellow travelers. When Raban gets off the train, the others see him blurrily from the train window, "as though the train were [still] in motion" (67; 36). The 1912 professional traveler, Gregor Samsa, similarly discovers his vision abruptly weakened: "Day by day things that were even a little way off were growing dimmer to his sight." Even the hospital across the street, which might have been the ill traveler's only hope, is now "beyond his range of vision." If Gregor hadn't known that he lived on a city street, he would have thought he was still looking out of a train window onto a blur, where "gray sky and gray land blended indistinguishably into each other" (*CS,* 112–13; *DL,* 155–56; [32]).

Like Gregor's failing eyesight, his "worrying about train connections" jibes with medical claims that the railway's ruthless punctuality caused debilitating psychological stress, especially because of travelers' lingering confusions about standardized time (*CS,* 90; *DL,* 116; [4]). Before the railway, every town had a slightly different time: Reading, for example, was four minutes later than London, but ten minutes ahead of Bridgewater. Because these differences did not allow for interregional timetabling and often caused crashes, railway companies eventually introduced "railway time"—*Bahnzeit*—which at first meant only that each company kept its own time, enforced by the originating conductor passing his watch to a new conductor at the next station. Not surprisingly, mix-ups between "railway" and "local" time persisted long after the introduction of international standard time (in 1893 in Germany and Austria-Hungary). Arthur Schnitzler's 1900 protagonist of *Lieutenant Gustl*, for example, comically can't decide whether he should commit suicide at 7 AM "Vienna time" or "railway time."[28] More seriously, researchers from the mid-nineteenth through to the early-twentieth century claimed that many railway illnesses issued not primarily from industrial mechanics but rather from time's mechanization: from the "excitement, anxiety, and nervous shock" caused by the "fearfully punctual train."[29] This anxiety about missing trains runs through Kafka's fiction from *Wedding Preparations* all the way to the 1922 parable, "Give It Up!" (*Ein Kommentar*, 1922, sometimes translated as "A Comment"): "I was on my way to the station. As I compared the tower clock with my watch I realized it was much later than I had thought and that I had to hurry; the shock [*Schrekken* (*sic*)] of this discovery made me feel uncertain of the way" (*CS*, 456; *NS*2, 530). Raban had already experienced this same time-*Schrekken* during his 1907 walk to the station: a clock suddenly strikes a quarter to five, which should give him "plenty of time," but he is nonetheless certain he'll "miss the train"; a friend tells Raban that it's now a quarter to six, but the station clock only strikes this time later, when Raban arrives. When the porter finally rushes Raban onto the train, Raban experiences the same excitement and heart "palpitations" *(Herzklopfen)* that in 1908 railway doctors still attributed to punctuality fears, as already detailed by Dr. Alfred Haviland in his 1868 medical monograph about the railway, *Hurried to Death* (*CS*, 55, 59, 60, 61, 62; *NS*1, 17, 23, 25, 26, 28).

Gregor suffers likewise from anxieties about missing trains, to the point that he spends his evenings obsessively perusing railway timetables (*CS*, 96; *DL*, 126). He recalls here his author, who speaks to Felice Bauer of "train hours" *(Eisenbahnstunden)* and of his debilitating personal timetabling *(sonderbare Zeiteinteilung)*: "I have to leave at 6 tomorrow evening; I get to Reichenberg at 10, and go on to Kratzau at 7 the next morning"; "[I can write] until 5 in the morning; no later, because my train leaves at 5:45"; and "before my trip to Aussig, I did not get to bed until 11:30 . . . ; I still heard 1 o'clock strike, and yet had to be up again [to catch a train] at 4:30" (*LF*, 62, 95, 230; *BF*, 122, 168, 347). On the morning of his transformation, Gregor Samsa similarly thinks comically only about the railway's pitiless punctuality, not about his physical state: "I'd better get up, since my train goes at five" (*CS*, 90; *DL*, 118; [5]). Railway time oppresses Gregor partially because it moves irrationally fast, as it did for Raban. After realizing that he has overslept and that it is already half-past six, Samsa watches as the clock hands move on uncannily quickly, continuing "past the half-hour," with Gregor now watching as the hands move, before his eyes, toward a quarter to seven (*CS*, 90; *DL*, 118). Like the clock in Fritz Lang's *Metropolis*, these accelerated hands parody global modern mechanized time. Gregor's clock continues to torment him for the next forty-five minutes, the entire duration of the first third of the story. To cite just a few examples: "the alarm clock had just struck a quarter to seven"; "'Seven o'clock already,' [Gregor] said to himself when the alarm clock chimed again"; and "before it strikes a quarter past seven I must be quite out of this bed" (*CS*, 91, 93; *DL*, 119, 123; [6, 8–9]). Gregor attributes this unforgiving timekeeping to the punctuality of trains: "The next train went at seven o'clock; to catch that he would need to hurry like mad," and "even if he did catch the train he wouldn't avoid a row with the boss, since the firm's porter would have been waiting for the five o'clock train" (*CS*, 91; *DL*, 118; trans. rev.; [5]). Gregor's family, too, is obsessed with railway time: "Gregor, it's a quarter to seven," Mrs. Samsa asks, "Hadn't you a train to catch?"; Mr. Samsa yells, "Gregor, the chief clerk has come and wants to know why you didn't catch the early train"; and Mrs. Samsa adds, "[Gregor's] not well, sir, believe me. What else would make him miss a train!" (*CS*, 91, 95; *DL*, 119, 126; [6, 11]). Time slips by with each missed departure, and, as if Gregor didn't already know it, the chief clerk reminds him that time is money: "You are wasting my time" (*CS*, 97; *DL*, 129; [13]). Out of joint with time, Kafka's always-prompt traveler loses his bearings: tormented by conscience for "wast[ing] only an hour or so of the firm's time," Gregor is "driven out of his mind" and becomes "actually incapable of leaving his bed" (*CS*, 94–95; *DL*, 125; [10]). When Gregor finally dies at the end of the story, he does even this according to the timepiece: "In this state of vacant and peaceful meditation he remained until the tower clock struck three in the morning" (*CS*, 135; *DL*, 193; [59]).

Driven mad by railway time, Gregor is, as critics have noted, an alienated worker: a subject transformed into a Marxian object.[30] But it is vital to add that Gregor's objectification is amplified because of his job as a professional traveler. As Marx insists, transportation is the only industry where production and consumption occur "simultaneously"; that is, where the product—change of place—is consumed at the same time it is produced, resulting in a commingling of labor and consumption.[31] Even though the traveler—unlike the conductors, stokers, and personnel—is not explicitly working, the machinery works on him. The train's vibrations and noise give the modern bourgeois his only direct experience of industry: in Samsa's words, "on his own body" *(am eigenen Leibe)*.[32] It is as if consumers of industrial goods were to consume them *inside* the factory. This comparison cannot ultimately be nullified by the upholstered train compartments of the first and second classes, and certainly not by the third-class wooden benches on which Kafka and probably Gregor Samsa traveled.[33] With production and consumption so unusually intertwined, the transport industry unmasked any last delusions about a bourgeois subject that could remain autonomous and non-commodified. As Marx writes, "humans and commodities" travel with the same "means of transport"; more explicitly than in other industries, consumers become here "living appendages" to machinery.[34] Early train travelers from all political stripes agreed: unlike the passenger in a horse carriage, who could see the natural sources of horse power and of the bumps and jerks, the industrial passenger knew neither how his vehicle functioned nor why it shook and clattered. The traveler was alienated and unaware, ultimately nothing more than a "package," a "bale of commodities," or, in the words of Joseph Maria von Radowitz, a "piece of freight."[35] Gregor Samsa becomes precisely such a commodity, a body transported from place to place for the profit of both his firm and his family.[36]

Given Gregor's symptoms—fatigue, twitching muscles, uneasy dreams, nervous volubility, blurred vision, and psychological stress from timetables and alienation—it is not surprising that he minces no words about his diagnosis: "traveling about day in, day out," "the trouble of constant traveling," and "worrying about train connections" have caused these traumatic agitations (*Aufregungen; CS,* 89–90; *DL,* 116; [4]). Gregor does not have "the least possible doubt" that he is suffering from this common "standing ailment of traveling salesmen" (*CS,* 92; *DL,* 121; [7]).[37] But as with so many other possible interpretations of *The Metamorphosis,* this one is challenged by Kafka, from as early as the pre-story—*Wedding Preparations*—when Raban explicitly denies that his clothed body is diagnosable in any way. According to Raban, his body's first symptom ("staggering") "indicate[s] not fear but its nothingness." Raban does not simply refute the reading, "My 'clothed body' is pathologically scarred by train travel"; he refutes *any* such direct relation of a signifier ("staggering") to a signified ("fear"). The body points only to "nothingness." Its "stumbling," Raban continues, is furthermore *not* "a sign of agitation [Aufregung]." Like Gregor's hermeneutically resistant shell, Raban's "clothed body" is vehemently *not* a "sign"; it *"zeigt . . . nicht"* (*CS*, 55; *NS*1, 17–18). Indeed, as critics have pointed out, Kafka's bodies resist metaphorical—and diagnostic—readings, because Kafka's human tenors and material vehicles are labile: the metaphor is always in motion.[38] Samsa's transformation is unfinished—Is he an animal or is he our son?—and all readings remain unstable. Because Samsa's body, like the clothed body, cannot function reliably as a "sign," the reader is at an interpretative impasse: Why does the traveler stagger and stumble? Why does he cry? Why, in its most extreme form, does he metamorphose? Kafka's bodies deny our answers before we can formulate them.

But precisely this problem of the opaque sign lies at the heart of fin de siècle trauma discourse, especially its legal branch. For Gregor, the confusion about his bodily symptoms leads him to fear the "health-insurance doctor" *(Kassenarzt)*, whose job resembles that of the deconstructivist critic: he must prove that the body is *not* a functioning sign, that it points to *nothing.* According to the feared *Kassenarzt*, nothing at all is causing Gregor's symptoms; he simply doesn't want to go to work, is "work-shy" (*arbeitsscheu; CS*, 91; *DL*, 119; [6]).[39] Gregor's dread of the *Kassenarzt* lends a legal-technological context to the long-standing literary problem of Gregor's apparently unreadable body. As Kafka certainly knew, severe railway turbulence and crashes had already created many people who presented no physical injuries but nonetheless suffered breakdowns and were, like Gregor, unable to work *(unfähig zu arbeiten)* (*CS*, 101; *DL*, 135; [17]). Because the German railways became legally liable for injuries after 1871—almost single-handedly creating Kafka's profession of accident insurance in 1884 (1887 in Austria-Hungary)—the legal-medical debate about traumatic neuroses exploded by the fin de siècle.[40] Doctors now had to distinguish between the truly injured and what Samsa's *Kassenarzt* calls the "perfectly healthy" simulators (*CS*, 91; *DL*, 119; [6]).

The debate had begun after railways became liable in England in 1864, with medico-legal doctrine generally following John Erichsen's 1866 claim that victims of crashes or of severe shaking in trains were anatomically damaged: they had received lesions on their spinal column, known as "railway spine."[41] From the early 1880s, often after autopsies of spines proved negative, researchers argued that there was no spinal damage. They shifted the focus to the brain—"railway brain"—and to what Hermann Oppenheim in 1889 influentially termed a "traumatic neurosis" of the cerebral cortex. This move from spine to brain simultaneously replaced Erichsen's theory of pathological anatomy with chemistry: "molecular displacements" or "functional disturbances" in the cerebral cortex affected "the psyche as well as the centers for motility, sensitiveness, and sensate functions."[42] Oppenheim's book led to immediate changes in German insurance law: the Imperial Insurance Office now rendered "traumatic neuroses" eligible for compensation.[43] But because Oppenheim's "molecular" or "functional" damage remained submicroscopic, doctors had difficulty distinguishing between the work-shy simulators and the truly ill, leading to an explosion of the already simmering battle around simulation: the *Simulationsstreit*, which culminated in the 1890 Medical Congress in Berlin.[44] Opponents of Oppenheim argued that neuroses could be too easily simulated, claiming that more than twenty-five percent of all "traumatic neuroses" were faked.[45] Oppenheim argued that most of his opponents were *Kassenärzte* who, just as Samsa had feared, were in the pockets of the insurance industry and "saw simulation everywhere they looked [*erblickte*[*n*] *überall Simulation*]."[46]

Enough doubt was shed here on Oppenheim's "molecular" argument that the 1880s psychogenic theories of Herbert Page, Jean Martin Charcot, Pierre Janet, and Paul Julius Möbius gained new momentum.[47] Although all of these still held, more or less, to the likelihood of accompanying somatic traumas, they argued that Oppenheim's "traumatic neuroses"—which Charcot had termed "traumatic hysterias" as early as 1876—could also be caused by ideas, suggestions, or fantasies.[48] Even before Freud deemphasized his seduction theory in 1897, he stressed the etiological importance of psychic predisposition: each patient's life story determined whether they could endure shock—psychic or mechanical—without suffering the profound disruption of the "sexual mechanism" that caused hysteria (*SE*, 7:201–2; *GW*, 5:103).[49] Despite Freud's hope of improving his patients' lives, his insistence on psychogenesis did not help the victims of the railway or of the First World War financially, leaving Freud with strange bed partners: the nationalist simulator-hunters *("Simulantenjäger")* used psychoanalysis during the war to buffer their theory that traumatic neuroses were all in the soldiers' heads.[50] And the legal principle remained that only primarily physical injuries could be compensated, with European tort law not altering this position until after the Second World War.[51]

During this period after the theorization of psychogenic trauma but before its legal acceptance, Kafka, a legal clerk at Prague's Imperial Accident Insurance Institute, created a damaged body that had to submit itself to a *Kassenarzt* for interpretation. This *Kassenarzt*, even if he were benevolently inclined, could never find the somatic source necessary for legal compensation. Samsa has the typically hysterical body of his day; symptomatic but with an "undetectable pathological-anatomical substrate." This "submicroscopic" cause of his suffering is at once also the missing origin; molecular damage could not be proven. In this way, the "ultramodern" medical language of hermeneutic undetectability mirrors the "postmodern" assertion of Samsa's "unreadability."[52] But this interpretative language now develops significance beyond literary criticism's games of semiotic self-reference; opaqueness points instead toward the traumatized body itself. Like the slanderous rumors swirling around about traveling salesmen, Samsa's symptoms are only felt subjectively, on his own body—*am eigenen Leibe*—and can therefore never be "trace[d] back to their original causes [*auf ihre Ursachen hin*]" (*CS*, 101; *DL*, 136; [20]). His injured body is left only to make mute or garbled entreaties that are not even understood (*CS*, 103; *DL*, 140; [20]). By the end of Gregor's story, the three boarders threaten to use his body as legal proof in a suit against the Samsa family, but the tragedy is that this same body cannot be used to supply evidence for itself: it cannot help doctors to uncover an "original cause" and therefore, perhaps, a cure (*CS*, 132; *DL*, 188; [55]). Even Gregor admits, despite his telltale symptoms, that his job-related diagnosis will not convince the authorities: the *Kassenarzt* would not be so wrong in assuming that he is simulating (*CS*, 91; *DL*, 119; [6]). Gregor's statement here prefigures Freud's of 1920, "All neurotics are malingerers; they simulate without knowing it, and this is their sickness."[53] To rephrase this in terms of my reading: we can not know whether Gregor is suffering from a train-induced trauma, but we do know that he suffers from that same illness of suspected simulation that haunted traveling bodies at the fin de siècle.

Even if railway trauma inheres precisely in diagnostic doubt, one could still object to my reading on the basis of Gregor's radical transformation, which parodies any imaginable case history of traumatic neurosis. Gregor does not simply quiver, blather, and sleep badly; he becomes a giant insect. But if we look at Kafka's story in the context of his general interest in mechanized bodies from 1907 through 1914, we see a steady progression toward hyperbole that could explain such an overstatement. On the heels of the lightly damaged travelers from *Wedding Preparations* and *Richard and Samuel*, Kafka now creates a traveling salesman who explodes medical orthodoxy: travel "agitations" lead not only to uneasy dreams, fatigue, twitching muscles, and blurred vision but to a complete metamorphosis. The way is now clear for Kafka's exaggerated victim-bodies, as foreshadowed in the above-mentioned 1913 dream, where "trains came, one after another they ran over my body, . . . deepening and widening the two cuts in my neck and legs" (*LF*, 230; *BF*, 347). The 1914 "In the Penal Colony" ("In der Strafkolonie," 1914) creates such a body by reconfiguring the steam locomotives from *Wedding Preparations* and *Richard and Samuel.* The new machine has "screeching" [*kreischende*] "wheels" that cause a thoroughgoing trembling (Zittern): "It quivers [*zittert*] in minute, very rapid vibrations, both from side to side and up and down" (*CS*, 143; *DL*, 209). As in contemporary medical discourse, this vibrating machinery reproduces itself on the vibrating [*zitternd*] body, which, in Kafka's hyperbole, now becomes either wholly "transfigur[ed]" or "murder[ed]" (*CS*, 147, 165, 154, 165; *DL*, 215, 244, 226, 245).

Kafka's 1914 penal apparatus is not simply a train in disguise, but neither is it, as scholars have asserted, a planing machine, a phonograph, or even a new weapon from the First World War.[54] As a symbol of mechanized violence, however, the machine's screeching wheels and vibrating frame connect it to an overdetermined atmosphere of technological brutality that culminated in the Great War—also known as the "war by timetable."[55] In the prewar years the German General Staff concentrated more on improving railway effectiveness than on developing new weapons systems, and officers gained prestige for saving minutes off timetables.[56] By the time tensions boiled over in July 1914, a sense of railway inevitability had set in. The German military scheduled the nine railway directorates nearest the French and Russian borders to receive 530 locomotives and 8,650 freight cars in just four days, and envisaged sending 650 trains to France through the city of Cologne alone.[57] Because it would take weeks for each side to transport their soldiers and weaponry to the fronts, mobilization took on the severity of a declaration of war, thus explaining Tsar Nicholas II's comical signing, then revoking, then re-signing of a general mobilization in the space of one day.[58] His final mobilization did mean counter-mobilization and war, as illustrated by Kafka, who generally ignored the saber rattling of summer 1914, yet remarked on July 31st: "General mobilization. K[arl] and P[epa] [Kafka's brothers in law] called up." Kafka understood firsthand that the war was a massive transportation effort when he walked the next day "to the train to see K[arl] off." The eventual declaration of war was comparably anticlimactic, a *fait accompli* that earned only Kafka's apathy: "Germany has declared war on Russia—Swimming lessons in the afternoon" (*D2*, 75; *Ta*, 543). Although military historians debate whether the intricate prewar timetabling really made war inevitable, it is clear that decades of railway-planning created a material logic that overwhelmed even the General Staff.[59] Consider when Wilhelm II, encouraged by illusory hopes of British and French neutrality, told Chief of Staff von Moltke that Germany could now concentrate its full fighting force on Russia and so stop train movements to the West. Instead of feeling relief, Moltke insisted that structural mayhem would ensue, and he suffered a nervous breakdown.[60] Timetables rendered Moltke mad just as they had Samsa two years earlier. Both Moltke and

Samsa—likewise a military officer—know that changed plans never mean just "wasting an hour or so"; rather, they catalyze a series of missed connections and possible crashes. The thought of this drives Moltke, too, "out of his mind," leaving him, like Samsa, "actually incapable of leaving his bed" (*CS*, 101, 94–95; *DL*, 135, 125; [17, 10]).

War timetabling also provoked unheard-of rail traffic and exponentially more crashes, including the most lethal in British and French history,[61] encouraging Freud to cite the railway again in his 1920 revision of his traumatic-neurosis theory.[62] Because of "railway disasters" and "the terrible war that has just ended," Freud sees bodies that refuse to signify anything beyond themselves (*SE*, 18:12; *GW*, 13:9). They repeatedly dream of their original traumas, thereby troubling Freud's belief in the pleasure principle and also causing him to modify his claim that neuroses always spring from sexual sources.[63] Unable to uncover an origin, Freud argues that these dreams might refer back to a submicroscopic physical injury of the "cerebral cortex" or the "organ of the mind," a speculation that, he realizes, embarrassingly resembles that long-discredited, somaticist "old, naïve theory of shock" championed by the 1880s American "railway brain" theorists and by Oppenheim (*SE*, 18:24, 31; *GW*, 13:23, 31). But Freud ventures beyond Oppenheim, toward Georg Simmel's cultural criticism, when arguing that the cerebral cortex develops a "protective shield" against nervous stimulation; trauma results only when this shield is unexpectedly breached, causing "fright" and "shock."[64] As questionable as Freud's cerebral cartography is, Walter Benjamin was right to view the "protective shield" as a powerful material metaphor for modernity.[65] The shocks of modern technology increase, as does the thickness of our "shields." Like Samsa, we develop "armor," but, in so doing, become dialectically intertwined with the technology we had wanted to ward off. Samsa is "armor-like" (panzerartig), redolent of the body of the medieval knight but also of the armored trains and tanks that first appeared on battlefields in 1916, as well as of Kafka's own body: "For a moment I felt myself clad in steel [umpanzert]" (*CS*, 89; *DL*, 115; *D*, 39; *Ta*, 31, trans. rev.). Because Samsa is a frequent train traveler, his "armor" has been hardening long before his ultimate metamorphosis, but no armor is solid enough; it can always be ruptured. Although Freud insists that psychic causes for trauma remain primary, he admits that, in the cases of the railway and war, these can become less relevant: where the "strength of a trauma exceeds a certain limit," the patient's psychological preparedness "will no doubt cease to carry weight." When there is "no doubt" of biology's primacy, Freud's patients end up not so much beyond the pleasure principle as beyond analysis (*SE*, 18:32; *GW*, 13:32). Perhaps for this reason, Freud loses interest in the traumatic neuroses after 1920, only returning to them at the end of his life. As he admits in his final work, *Outline of Psychoanalysis*, traumatic neuroses caused by "railway collisions and war" seem to repudiate the general rule of analysis: "their relations to determinants in childhood have hitherto eluded investigation" (*SE*, 23:184; *GW*, 17:111).

After Kafka finished "In the Penal Colony" and another chapter of *The Trial* (*Der Proceß*, 1925), he wrote almost no fiction for two years; after recommencing in 1916, he stopped writing about mechanized bodies.[66] Trains and machines rarely appear, and Kafka turns almost exclusively to rural technologies. To name just a few examples relating to travel: the horses in "A Country Doctor"; the ancient "bark" of the hunter Gracchus; and Klamm's sleigh in *The Castle* (*Das Schloß*, 1926). It is as if, in his later years, Kafka returns to the rural traffic of Raban's home neighborhood, safely distanced from the train station.[67] Why? Perhaps because Kafka's literary premonitions have come true. The streets of

Prague, Vienna, and Berlin are now shot through with bodies that twitch nervously, as depicted in the work of Otto Dix and others.[68] With the mechanically damaged body now in public view, it no longer belongs to Kafka's nighttime fiction but rather to the daylight of political action. Just ten days before Kafka read "In the Penal Colony" aloud in war-torn Munich, he completed a newspaper appeal calling attention to the injured soldiers who now "twitch and jump with nerves in the streets of our cities." Like Raban's staggering "clothed body," these men signify only their own damage, simulated or not, and they require scientific—not literary—help. Kafka continues that the Great War is primarily a "war on the nervous system" and demands that German Bohemia construct its first hospital for the treatment of nervous diseases. Kafka, like Freud, views these victims as successors to the "peacetime neurasthenics" who suffered from the "intensive industrialization of the past decades." With these prewar victims in mind, Kafka asks for donations from the likely culprits: the railroad management as well as the entire accident industry that springs from it, specifically private insurance companies and social insurance institutes like the one that employed him (*LF*, 580; *BF*, 764–65).

Even though Kafka's mechanically damaged bodies eventually disappeared from his fiction, he did not lose interest in them, at least not as a warning to himself. Six years after completing this call to action, Kafka contracted a mysterious anxiety before a twelve-hour train trip to visit Oskar Baum in Georgental. Vehemently denying that he had the widespread pathology known as "travel phobia"—*Reiseangst*—Kafka insisted instead that his fear was existential and spiritual or psychic (geistig): a fear of change, a fear of not writing, even a fear of death (*L*, 336, 333–35; *Br*, 388, 384–86). His sister Ottla disagreed, claiming that his fear's source was physical; Kafka resisted her but had to sense, despite his protests, that his psychic source was ultimately as elusive as Ottla's physical one (336; 388). As researchers on train and war traumas—including Freud—discovered, there are symptomatic bodies that have *neither* a detectable physical injury nor a hidden psychic one: molecular damage cannot be proved and psychic explanations "cease to carry weight." Just as Samsa's mechanized body becomes a pure sign—lacking either a clear physical injury or a psychic source from his childhood—Kafka's body might also end up referring only to itself: "twitching and jumping" on the streets of Prague. A hospital for nervous diseases could symbolize hope, but this hope is as blurry as the hospital outside Gregor's window: neurology and psychiatry, too, have failed to discover an "original cause," only a *mise en abyme* of submicroscopic substrata and pathological simulations. Kafka fears precisely this undiagnosability, this etiology vaguer than tissue damage, childhood trauma, or even the "fear of death": an unnameable injury whose only source, as with Nordau's "degeneration," is modernity itself, and whose victims are primarily "feminine" men.[69] Kafka knows that what happened to Samsa could happen to anyone, especially to a weakened company proxy *(Prokurist)* such as Franz Kafka, who, like Samsa, has been stuck riding the rails for years: "What had happened to [Samsa] today might someday happen to the company proxy [*Prokurist*]; one really could not deny that it was possible" (*CS*, 95; *DL*, 125–26, trans. rev.; [10]).[70]

This fear of an undiagnosable injury brought on by the mysteries of modernity puts a fine point on my argument. To be clear: I am not claiming that Samsa's transformation is a direct result of train trauma. Such trauma cannot cause a man to turn into a giant bug. Nor am I arguing that Samsa is a malingerer, at least not in the sense suspected by the *Kassenarzt.* Rather, I see Samsa as embodying the modern technological anxiety of indeterminacy, in which even the victims do not know whether they are ill and in which simulation itself becomes the illness. Samsa's body is modernity's prototypical broken sign: a conglomeration of symptoms that does not refer to a physical cause. Vital here is Kafka's decision to transform Samsa into an *Ungeziefer*, a creature "not suited for sacrifice": an un-animal existing somewhere between beast and man.[71] This uncategorizability marries Kafka's interest in medico-legal trauma to his famous "*Schriftstellersein*" (being-as-a-writer). For Kafka would never have been interested in trains and trauma on their own; he was not a Zolaesque realist, even on this more sophisticated level of presenting modern bodies' tragic undiagnosability. Rather, Kafka sees in trauma's semiotic dubiousness the social-political verification of his poetics. As critics have demonstrated for decades, Kafka's writing sprang out of his "despair" regarding metaphor and metaphoric language: vehicles did not refer back to tenors just as signifiers did not point to signifieds (*D*, 398; *T*, 875).[72] Like language itself, Samsa's body emphasizes this unreadability: it is an accumulation of symptoms without causes and, as such, *the* cipher for Kafka's original combining of literary and medico-legal discourses. Kafka's figuration of the fin-de-siècle "language crisis" *(Sprachkrise)* does not ring hollow, as it does with some of his peers, because he places this linguistic trauma within its analogous social one, creating an aesthetic that truly investigates the suffering of indeterminacy.

In a letter written ten days after his debate about diagnosability with Ottla, Kafka tells Oskar Baum, too, of his travel phobia, now suggesting that he, like Freud, might be suffering from the more specific "railway phobia" *(Eisenbahnangst)*. He playfully tells Baum that he will travel to Georgental only if he doesn't have to take the train: "[I] try to wheedle out of you the most favorable railroad connections in the secret hope that if I only ask often enough it will turn out that Georgental can be reached only by streetcar *(nur mit der Elektrischen)*" (*L*, 342; *Br*, 395, trans. rev.). Kafka wants a long-distance streetcar, something slower and more placid than the "rumbling and rattling," "jolting and jouncing" train denounced by Gerhart Hauptmann in "In the Night Train" (*Im Nachtzug,* 1888). And Kafka had already reported his joy at jumping on and off Prague's streetcars as a grown man, even though he prohibited this same pleasure to Felice Bauer (*LF*, 36, 31; *BF*, 87, 80). Consider a story Kafka wrote in the same year as *Wedding Preparations*, "The Passenger" ("Der Fahrgast," 1908), where a streetcar transforms an unsure, depressive protagonist into a virile voyeur: staring at a woman next to him in the tram, he confidently remarks that "she is as distinct to me as if I had run my hands over her" (*CS*, 388–89; *DL*, 27). Fourteen years later, in a letter to Milena Jesenská, Kafka praises the streetcar as a catalyst for gregariousness and desire. He would like to become a streetcar conductor, because such men thrive in social traffic, and, moreover, Milena is attracted to them: "You [Milena] also like conductors, don't you?" (*LM*, 174).[73]

Kafka's enduring love of the streetcar brings us back to the ending of *The Metamorphosis*, which is often interpreted as an ironic opposition between authentic death and cheapened life, between artistic suffering and dull-witted sexuality. While Gregor's decrepit corpse is taken out with the garbage, his petit bourgeois family heads to the flourishing countryside, naively feeling reborn and radiant. But what readers have failed to notice is the story's technological frame: after opening with an infirm protagonist complaining about excessive train travel, *The Metamorphosis* closes with his family coming to life in a streetcar. Trains make Gregor ill, at least in his opinion, and the streetcar awakens his family's sexual awareness.[74] After Grete and Mrs. Samsa caress the victorious father, the three of them leave the apartment together, which they had not done for months, and go "by tram into the open countryside [*ins Freie*]." Once inside the streetcar, the parents notice their daughter's pretty face and "voluptuous" (*üppig*) figure. She stretches her young body before them, and they realize that it is high time to find her a man (*CS*, 139; *DL*, 199–200, trans. rev.; [64]).

Given this image of health and sexuality, we are reminded of Kafka's fantasy of a "natural traffic/intercourse" (natürlichen Verkehr)—and see here a relation of travel and epistolarity directly opposed to the one governing most of Kafka's career. Kafka generally views letters as "ghostly" defenses against physical presence and travel technologies as paradoxically unnatural sponsors of natural traffic/intercourse. But here letters and trains together encourage a "natural intercourse" without apparent side effects. The streetcar brings Grete's body to the site of freedom and sexuality, now with the *assistance* of letters. Grete and her parents use missives to stave off undesired presence, writing to their employers and thereby gaining what Gregor could attain only by becoming an *Ungeziefer*: a day off work.[75] But the Samsas, unlike Kafka with Felice Bauer, ultimately use this epistolary distance to get closer to their intimates and even to plan a procreative "natural" intercourse for their daughter. Critics have pointed to the irony in this ending and viewed it almost unanimously as a parodic stab at philistinism.[76] But this finale also speaks to a more serious utopian possibility. Kafka changed the Samsas' destination from a "city park" to "ins Freie" in his manuscript, meaning "into the countryside" but hinting also at "freedom," suggesting that Kafka wants this streetcar to continue on past Georgental, past Berlin, as a streetcar named desire that will, as Freud argues for slow-moving vehicles, produce pleasurable sensations and even "an exquisite sexual symbolism" (*SE*, 7:201; *GW*, 5:103). For Kafka, this symbolism appears full-bore when Bauer writes a letter to him from a streetcar in 1912, just five days after he had completed the conclusion to *The Metamorphosis:* "Your letter from the tram makes me feel almost insanely close to you *(bringt mich in eine fast irrsinnige Nähe zu Dir).* How do you manage to write in a tram? With the paper on your knees, your head bent that far down while writing?" (*LF*, 101; *BF*, 176). Whereas Samsa's job on trains drives him "out of his mind" with anxiety, Bauer's writing from trams makes Kafka insane with desire (*CS*, 94–95; *DL*, 125; [10]). Writing cooperates with transportation machinery here to create a contradictory techno-natural intercourse, as in *The Metamorphosis:* letters bring people together erotically, the streetcar stimulates bodies, and these bodies remain uninjured, unmarked, and unsymptomatic.[77] They resemble Kafka's own body in his 1920 fantasy with Milena Jesenská, where he promises to crawl into every parcel he sends to her "just in order to travel inside [them] to Vienna." "Please," he continues, "give me as many opportunities to travel as possible" (*LM*, 141; *BM*, 189).[78] But Kafka also warned against such postal utopias—later calling them the "most dangerous" fantasies of all—and his Samsas are right at the edge of this, boarding a technology that promises them a "natural," insane closeness beyond the realm of the ghosts (*LM*, 224; *BM*, 303).

Recommended Further Reading

Adorno, Theodore W. "Notes on Kafka." *Prisms.* Trans. Samuel and Shierry Weber. London: Spearman, 1967. 245–72.

Alter, Robert. *Necessary Angels: Tradition and Modernity in Kafka, Benjamin, and Scholem.* Cambridge: Harvard UP, 2001.

Anders, Günther. *Franz Kafka.* Trans. A. Steer and A. K. Thorlby. London: Bowes & Bowes, 1960.

Anderson, Mark. "Kafka and Sacher-Masoch." *Journal of the Kafka Society of America* 7, 2 (1983): 4–19.

——. *Kafka's Clothes: Ornament and Aestheticism in the Hapsburg Fin de Siècle.* Oxford: Oxford UP, 1996.

Auden, W. H. "The Wandering Jew." *W. H. Auden: Prose, Volume II, 1939–1948.* Ed. Edward Mendelson. London: Faber and Faber, 2002. 110–13.

Beck, Evelyn Torton. *Kafka and the Yiddish Theater: Its Impact on His Work.* Madison: U of Wisconsin P, 1971.

Beicken, Peter. "Transformation of Criticism: The Impact of Kafka's *Metamorphosis.*" *The Dove and the Mole: Kafka's Journey into Darkness and Creativity.* Eds. Moshe Lazar and Ronald Gottesman. Malibu, CA: Undena, 1987. 13–34.

Beissner, Friedrich. "Kafka the Artist." Trans. Ronald Gray. *Kafka: A Collection of Critical Essays.* Ed. Ronald Gray. Englewood Cliffs, NJ: Prentice Hall, 1962. 15–31.

Benjamin, Walter. "Franz Kafka. On the Tenth Anniversary of His Death." *Illuminations.* Ed. Hannah Arendt, trans. Harry Zohn. New York: Harcourt Brace, 1968. 111–40.

Bennett, E. K. *A History of the German Novelle.* Revised and continued by H. M. Waidson. Cambridge: Cambridge UP, 1961. 267–68.

Bermejo-Rubio, Fernando. "Convergent Literary Echoes in Kafka's *Die Verwandlung.* What Intertextuality Tells Us About Gregor Samsa." *Interlitteraria* 16, 1 (2011): 348–64.

——. "Grete Samsa's Inconsistent Speech. Victimary Lies and Distortions in Kafka's *Die Verwandlung.*" *Revista de Filología Alemana* 20 (2012): 47–65.

——. "Truth and Lies about Gregor Samsa. The Logic Underlying the Two Conflicting Versions in Kafka's *Verwandlung.*" *Deutsche Vierteljahrsschrift* 86, 3 (2012): 419–79.

——. "Does Gregor Samsa Crawl over the Ceiling and Walls? Intranarrative Fiction in Kafka's *Die Verwandlung.*" *Monatshefte,* forthcoming.

Bernheimer, Charles. *Flaubert and Kafka: Studies in Psychopoetic Structure.* New Haven: Yale UP, 1982.

Binder, Hartmut. *The Metamorphosis: The Long Journey into Print. The Metamorphosis by Franz Kafka.* Ed. and trans. Stanley Corngold. New York: W. W. Norton, 1996. 172–94.

Binion, Rudolf. "What the Metamorphosis Means." *Symposium* 15 (1961): 214–20.

Blanchot, Maurice. "The Diaries: The Exigency of the Work of Art." Trans. Lyall H. Powers. *Franz Kafka Today.* Eds. Angel Flores and Homer Swander. Madison: U of Wisconsin P, 1964. 195–220.

Bloom, Harold. Ed. *Franz Kafka's The Metamorphosis.* New York: Chelsea House, 1988.

Boa, Elizabeth. *Kafka: Gender, Class, and Race in the Letters and Fictions.* Oxford: Oxford UP, 1986.

Booth, Wayne C. *The Rhetoric of Fiction.* Chicago: U of Chicago P, 1961. 281–82.

Brod, Max. *Franz Kafka—A Biography.* Trans. G. Humphreys Roberts and Richard Winston. New York: Schocken Books, 1960.

Bruce, Iris. *Kafka and Cultural Zionism. Dates in Palestine.* Madison: U of Wisconsin P, 2007.

——. "The Cultural and Historical Context of Kafka's *Metamorphosis:* Anti-Semitism, Zionism, and the Yiddish Plays." Ed. James Whitlark. *Critical Insights. The Metamorphosis.* Pasadena, CA/Hackensack, NJ: Salem P, 2012.

Camus, Albert. "Hope and Absurdity." Trans. William Barrett. *The Kafka Problem.* Ed. Angel Flores. New York: New Directions, 1946. 251–61.

Corngold, Stanley. Ed. and trans. *The Metamorphosis by Franz Kafka.* New York: Bantam, 1972.

——. *The Commentators' Despair: The Interpretation of Kafka's "Metamorphosis."* London/Port Washington, NY: Kennikat, 1973.

——. *Franz Kafka. The Necessity of Form.* Ithaca: Cornell UP, 1988.

——. Ed. and trans. *The Metamorphosis by Franz Kafka.* A Norton Critical Edition. New York: W. W. Norton, 1996.

——. *Lambent Traces. Franz Kafka.* Princeton: Princeton UP, 2004.

——. Ed. and trans. *Kafka's Selected Stories. A Norton Critical Edition.* New York: W. W. Norton, 2007.

——. Ed. (with Benno Wagner and Jack Greenberg). *Franz Kafka. The Office Writings.* Princeton: Princeton UP, 2009.

——. (with Benno Wagner). *Franz Kafka. The Ghosts in the Machine.* Evanston, IL: Northwestern UP, 2011.

Deleuze, Gilles and Félix Guattari. *Kafka—Toward a Minor Literature.* Trans. Dana Polan. Minneapolis: U of Minnesota P, 1986.

Duttlinger, Carolin. *Kafka and Photography.* Oxford: Oxford UP, 2007.

Eggenschwiler, David. "*Die Verwandlung*, Freud, and the Chains of Odysseus." *Modern Language Quarterly* 39 (1978): 363–85.

Empson, William. "A Family Monster" [a review of *The Metamorphosis*]. *The Nation* 162 (1946): 652–53.

Emrich, Wilhelm. *Franz Kafka: A Critical Study of His Writings.* Trans. Sheema Z. Buehne. New York: Ungar, 1968. 132–34.

Flores, Angel. Ed. *The Kafka Problem.* New York: New Directions, 1946.

——. *Franz Kafka Today.* Ed. (with Homer Swander). New York: Gordian, 1977.

Gallagher, David. *Metamorphosis: Transformations of the Body and the Influence of Ovid's Metamorphoses on Germanic Literature of the Nineteenth and Twentieth Centuries.* Amsterdam/New York: Rodopi, 2009.

Gilman, Sander L. "A View of Kafka's Treatment of Actuality in *Die Verwandlung*." *Germanic Notes* 2, 4 (1971): 26–30.

——. *Franz Kafka. The Jewish Patient.* New York: Routledge, 1995.

——. *Franz Kafka. Critical Lives.* London: Reaktion, 2005.

Goldstein, Bluma. "The Wound in Stories by Kafka." *Germanic Review* 41 (1966): 206–14.

——. "Bachelors and Work. Social and Economic Conditions of 'The Judgment,' 'The Metamorphosis,' and 'The Trial.'" *The Kafka Debate: New Perspectives for Our Time.* Ed. Angel Flores. New York: Gordian, 1977. 147–75.

Gray, Richard T., Ruth V. Gross, Rolf J. Goebel, and Clayton Koelb. Eds. *A Franz Kafka Encyclopedia.* Westport, CT: Greenwood, 2005.

Greenberg, Martin. "Gregor Samsa and Modern Spirituality." *The Terror of Art: Kafka and Modern Literature.* New York: Basic Books, 1968. 69–91.

Gross, Ruth V. *Critical Essays on Franz Kafka.* Boston: G. K. Hall, 1990.

Heller, Erich. *Franz Kafka.* New York: Viking, 1974.

Honig, Edwin. *Dark Conceit: The Making of Allegory.* New York: Oxford UP, 1966. 63–68.

Janouch, Gustav. *Conversations with Kafka: Notes and Reminiscence.* Trans. Goronwy Rees. New York: New Directions, 1969.

Kafka, Franz. *The Metamorphosis.* Ed. and trans. Stanley Corngold. New York: Bantam, 1972.

Karl, Frederick R. *Franz Kafka: Representative Man.* New York: Ticknor and Fields, 1991.

Koelb, Clayton. *Kafka's Rhetoric: The Passion of Reading.* Ithaca: Cornell UP, 1989.

Lawson, Richard H. "*Ungeheures Ungeziefer* in Kafka's *Die Verwandlung.*" *German Quarterly* 33 (1960): 216–19.

Levine, Michael G. "The Sense of an *Unding:* Kafka, Ovid, and the Misfits of Metamorphosis." *Writing Through Repression.* Baltimore: The Johns Hopkins UP, 1994. 149–77.

Liska, Vivian. *When Kafka Says "We": Uncommon Communities in German-Jewish Literature.* Bloomington: Indiana UP, 2009.

Lukács, György. *The Meaning of Contemporary Realism.* Trans. John and Necke Mander. London: Merlin P, 1969.

Luke, F. D. "The Metamorphosis." *Franz Kafka Today.* Ed. Angel Flores and Homer Swander. Madison: U of Wisconsin P, 1964. 25–43.

Murray, Nicholas. *Franz Kafka.* New Haven: Yale UP, 2004.

Nabokov, Vladimir. "Franz Kafka (1883–1924): 'The Metamorphosis' (1915)." *Lectures on Literature.* Ed. Fredson Bowers. New York: Harcourt Brace Jovanovich, 1980. 251–83.

O'Neill, Patrick J. "Kafka's Metamorphoses: Texts and Textualities." Ed. James Whitlark. *Critical Insights. The Metamorphosis.* Pasadena/Hackensack: Salem P, 2012.

Pascal, Roy. *Kafka's Narrators: A Study of His Stories and Sketches.* Cambridge: Cambridge UP, 1982. 32–59.

Pawel, Ernst. *The Nightmare of Reason: A Life of Franz Kafka.* New York: Farrar, Straus, and Giroux, 1992.

Politzer, Heinz. *Franz Kafka: Parable and Paradox.* Ithaca: Cornell UP, 1962. 65–84.

Preece, Julian. Ed. *The Cambridge Companion to Kafka.* Cambridge: Cambridge UP, 2002.

Robertson, Ritchie. *Kafka: Judaism, Politics, and Literature.* Oxford: Clarendon P, 1985.

——. *Kafka: A Very Short Introduction.* Oxford: Oxford UP, 2005.

Rolleston, James. *Kafka's Narrative Theater.* U Park: Pennsylvania State UP, 1974.

——. Ed. *A Companion to the Works of Franz Kafka.* Rochester: Camden House, 2002.

Ryan, Michael P. "Samsa and Saṃsāra: Suffering, Death, and Rebirth in 'The Metamorphosis,'" *German Quarterly* 72, 2 (Spring 1999): 133–52.

Ryan, Simon C. "Franz Kafka's *Die Verwandlung:* Transformation, Metaphor, and the Perils of Assimilation." *Seminar: A Journal of Germanic Studies* 43, 1 (2007): 3–20.

——. "A Selective Survey of the Reception of *The Metamorphosis.*" *Critical Insights. The Metamorphosis.* Ed. James Whitlark. Pasadena/Hackensack: Salem P, 2012.

Simka, Margit M. "Kafka's 'The Metamorphosis' and the Search for Meaning in Twentieth-Century German Literature." *Approaches to Teaching Kafka's Short Fiction.* Ed. Richard T. Gray. New York: The Modern Language Association of America, 1995. 105–113.

Sokel, Walter H. "Kafka's 'Metamorphosis': Rebellion and Punishment." *Monatshefte* 48 (1956): 203–14.

——. *The Writer in Extremis: Expressionism in Twentieth-Century Literature.* Stanford, CA: Stanford UP, 1959. 45–48.

——. *Franz Kafka. Columbia Essays on Modern Writers.* New York and London: Columbia UP, 1966.

——. "From Marx to Myth: The Structure and Function of Self-Alienation in Kafka's Metamorphosis." *The Dove and the Mole: Kafka's Journey into Darkness and Creativity.* Eds. Ronald Gottesman and Moshe Lazar. Malibu, CA: Undena, 1987.

——. *The Myth of Power and the Self.* Detroit: Wayne State UP, 1987.

Sparks, Kimberly. "Kafka's *Metamorphosis:* On Banishing the Lodgers." *Journal of European Studies* 3 (1973): 230–40.

Spilka, Mark. "Kafka's Sources for *The Metamorphosis.*" *Comparative Literature* 11 (1959): 289–307.

——. *Dickens and Kafka: A Mutual Interpretation.* Bloomington: Indiana UP, 1963. 77–79, 252–54.

Stach, Reiner. *Kafka: The Decisive Years.* New York: Harcourt, 2005.

Straus, Nina Pelikan. "Transforming Franz Kafka's *Metamorphosis.* Ed. James Whitlark. *Critical Insights. The Metamorphosis.* Pasadena/Hackensack: Salem P, 2012.

Sweeney, Kevin W. "Competing Theories of Identity in Kafka's *Metamorphosis.*" *The Metamorphosis by Franz Kafka.* Ed. and trans. Stanley Corngold. New York: W. W. Norton, 1996. 140–53.

Thiher, Allen. *Franz Kafka: A Study of the Short Fiction.* Boston: Twayne, 1990.

Tiefenbrun, Ruth. *Moment of Torment: An Interpretation of Franz Kafka's Short Stories.* Carbondale, London, Amsterdam: Southern Illinois UP, 1973.

Udoff, Alan. Ed. *Kafka and the Contemporary Critical Performance. Centenary Readings.* Bloomington: Indiana UP, 1987.

Urzidil, Johannes. "Meetings with Franz Kafka." *Menorah Journal* 40 (1952): 112–16.

——. "In the Prague of Expressionism," "Brand." *There Goes Kafka.* Trans. Harold A. Basilius. Detroit: Wayne State UP, 1968. 18–19, 82–96.

Wagenbach, Klaus. *Kafka.* Cambridge: Harvard UP, 2003.

Webster, Peter Dow. "Franz Kafka's 'Metamorphosis' as Death and Resurrection Fantasy." *American Imago* 16 (1959): 349–65.

Wexelblatt, Robert. "The Higher Parody: Ivan Ilych's Metamorphosis and the Death of Gregor Samsa." *Massachusetts Review: A Quarterly of Literature, the Arts, and Public Affairs* 21, 3 (1980): 601–28.

Whitlark, James. *Critical Insights. The Metamorphosis.* Pasadena, CA/Hackensack, NJ: Salem P, 2012.

Wood, Michael G. *Franz Kafka.* London: Tavistock, 2004.

Zilcosky, John. *Kafka's Travels: Exoticism, Colonialism, and The traffic of Writing.* New York: Palgrave Macmillan, 2003.

Notes

Preface

Originally, "Preface," *The Metamorphosis by Franz Kafka*, A Norton Critical Edition, trans. and ed. Stanley Corngold (New York: W. W. Norton, 1996). Revised 2013.

Introduction

Parts of this introduction originally appeared in *Kafka for the Twenty-First Century*, ed. Stanley Corngold and Ruth V. Gross (Rochester, NY: Camden House, 2011), 1–9; and in "Kafka's Law in a Universe of Risk," *The American Reader*, 1:3 (January 2013): 110–19. Reprinted by permission of the publishers. Revised in 2013, with a comparable number of new pages added.

Abbreviations of Works by Kafka

BM *Briefe an Milena*. Ed. Jürgen Born and Michael Müller. Frankfurt a. M.: S. Fischer, 1983.

C *The Castle.* Trans. Mark Harman. New York: Schocken, 1998.

D1 *The Diaries of Franz Kafka, 1910–1913.* Trans. Joseph Kresh. New York: Schocken, 1948.

D2 *The Diaries of Franz Kafka, 1914–1923.* Trans. Martin Greenberg (with the assistance of Hannah Arendt). New York: Schocken, 1949.

DF *Dearest Father.* Trans. Ernest Kaiser and Eithne Wilkins. New York: Schocken, 1954.

GW *The Great Wall of China.* Trans. Willa and Edwin Muir. New York: Schocken, 1946.

KSS *Kafka's Selected Stories. A Norton Critical Edition.* Ed. and trans. Stanley Corngold. New York: W. W. Norton, 2007.

LF *Letters to Felice.* Trans. James Stern and Elizabeth Duckworth. New York: Schocken, 1973.

OW *The Office Writings.* Ed. Stanley Corngold, Jack Greenberg, and Benno Wagner. Princeton: Princeton UP, 2009.

T *The Trial.* Trans. Breon Mitchell. New York: Schocken, 1998.

Ta *Tagebücher in der Fassung der Handschrift.* Ed. Michael Müller. Frankfurt, a.M.: Eischer, 1983.

Abbreviations of Secondary Works

GM Stanley Corngold and Benno Wagner. *Franz Kafka. The Ghosts in the Machine.* Evanston, IL: Northwestern UP, 2011.

PN Nietzsche, Friedrich. *The Portable Nietzsche.* Ed. and trans. Walter Kaufmann. New York: Viking, 1954.

1. Reiner Stach, *Kafka: Die Jahre der Erkenntnis* (Frankfurt a.M.: Fischer, 2008), 244.
2. Amanda Torres, "Kafka and the Common Law: The Roots of the 'Kafkaesque' in The Trial," an unpublished seminar paper for "Kafka and the Law," Columbia University School of Law (May 7, 2007): 10–11.
3. This sentence was contributed by Ritchie Robertson to the "Proposal" for the Princeton-Oxford-Humboldt Kafka Consortium. http://www.princeton.edu/international/doc/GCRF-KAFKA-network.pdf.
4. "Die besondere Art meiner Inspiration in der ich Glücklichster und Unglücklichster jetzt um 2 Uhr nachts schlafen gehe [sie wird vielleicht, wenn ich nur den Gedanken daran ertrage, bleiben, denn sie ist höher als alle früheren], ~~[und zweifellos bin ich jetzt im Geistigen der Mittelpunkt von Prag]~~ ist die, daß ich alles kann, nicht nur auf eine bestimmte Arbeit hin. Wenn ich wahllos einen Satz hinschreibe z.B. Er schaute aus dem Fenster so ist er schon vollkommen" (*Ta,* 30), cf. also: *Kritische Kafka-Ausgabe: Tagebücher.* Apparatband (1990), 169.
5. Kafka admired a few other rival field marshals—Alexander the Great and Napoleon—but from a considerable height. Both generals, according to expert opinion, were five feet six inches; Kafka was six feet tall.
6. J. C. Nyíri, "Einleitung," Thomas G. Masaryk, *Der Selbstmord als sociale Massenerscheinung der modernen Civilisation* (Munich/Vienna: Philosophia Verlag, 1982), 7.
7. Mann's story was composed in 1905 and due for publication that year in the *Neue Rundschau.* It was already typeset when Mann suddenly withdrew it, realizing that its anti-Semitic tenor would give grievous offense to his wife and her Jewish family. He finally published it privately in 1921. How, then, can Kafka have known of it? In 1906, Mann had sent copies of the

story to Arthur Schnitzler and Jakob Wassermann, among others. The story then circulated in samizdat, and news of the scandal was bruited about in Vienna and thereafter, it might well be supposed, in Prague. Kafka was a devoted reader of the *Neue Rundschau* and of the works of Schnitzler and Wassermann and would have perked up at any mention of writings coming from their desk. (Wassermann was one of the several authors whom Kafka declares he was "thinking of" apropos of "The Judgment.")

8. Walter Pater, *The Renaissance: Studies in Art and Poetry*, ed. Adam Phillips (Oxford: Oxford UP, 1986), 152.
9. This is the view of Kafka's foremost biographer, Reiner Stach. In an interview published in the *Jerusalem Post*, Stach declares, "I suspect that [in October 1918] Kafka had already recovered from tuberculosis, and for him the Spanish flu presented the real threat." Kafka was very ill from the flu for weeks after he was infected but recovered while millions of other patients died. http://jewishnews.at/jewish-news-from-austria-21/the-impossibility-of-being-kafka.html. Further details are found in Stach, *Kafka: Die Jahre der Erkenntis.*
10. ". . . (real hell is there in the office, no other can hold any terror for me)" (*LF*, 238).
11. In a book review of *OW*, the Kafka expert Louis Begley wrote, "We are told [by the editors] that 'during the war years [Kafka] was [the Institute's] virtual CEO [ix].' A virtual CEO, indeed: he was on the verge of a nervous breakdown most of 1915, and, after the hemorrhage he suffered in August 1917." *The New Republic*, "Books: Before the Law," May 6, 2009. This is the reviewer's sarcastic way of disputing the claim, but the objection is unfounded. Until his breakdown in August 1917, Kafka worked constantly and on overtime for the Institute. His efforts are evident from a number of documents, especially those concerning his work for the care of wounded veterans. In fact, he was meant to be awarded an imperial Orden for his special engagement in this field in 1918, an honor that he managed to escape thanks only to the collapse of the empire. Furthermore, in light of the documents newly presented in *OW*, Kafka's visit to the Frankenstein psychiatric hospital in 1915 almost certainly had to do with the Institute's search for a site for shell-shocked veterans, a campaign that he organized (all this notwithstanding, of course, his own personal fate as a nervous patient). This clarification is contained in a letter from Benno Wagner, a co-editor of both the German and the American editions of Kafka's office writings.
12. The latter sentences are adapted from *OW*.
13. Kafka's letter to Milena is dated Saturday evening, July 31, 1920.
14. Paul North, in an unpublished review of *GM*.
15. This matter is discussed at length in *OW*, 77–79.
16. W. H. Auden, *Prose, 1939–1948*, in *The Complete Works of W. H. Auden*, ed. Edward Mendelson (Princeton, NJ: Princeton UP, 1986), 2:110.

17. http://nietzsche.holtof.com/reader/friedrich-nietzsche/daybreak/aphorism-119-quote_655cf8d0c.html.
18. Theodor W. Adorno, "Notes on Kafka," in *Prisms*, trans. Samuel Weber and Shierry Weber (London: Spearman, 1967), 246.
19. There is an explicit mention of the "sixth hour"—and the ritual hand washing—in another of Kafka's stories, "In the Penal Colony."
20. Kurt Weinberg, *Kafkas Dichtungen: Die Travestien des Myt*hos (Berne: Francke, 1963).
21. See Michael P. Ryan, "Samsa and Saṃsāra: Suffering, Death, and Rebirth in 'The Metamorphosis,'" *German Quarterly* 72, no. 2 (Spring 1999): 133–52.
22. Sigmund Freud, *Die Traumdeutung* (*The Interpretation of Dreams*), Studienausgabe (Frankfurt a. M.: S. Fischer, 1972), 2:227.
23. Benno Wagner and I develop this point in similar language in our *GM*, x.
24. Gustav Janouch, *Conversations with Kafka*, trans. Goronwy Rees (New York: New Directions, 1971), 31.
25. Vladimir Nabokov, "An Interview with Vladimir Nabokov," Alfred Appel, Jr. In *Nabokov: The Man and His Work, Wisconsin Studies in Contemporary Literature*, ed. L. S. Dembo (Madison: U of Wisconsin P, 1967), 8:42–43.
26. "Perhaps the most famous religious dispute of the latter half of the sixteenth century was that between Walter Haddon (1516–1572), the distinguished English Latinist, and Jerome Osorio de Fonseca (1506–1580), the Portuguese bishop and eminent Ciceronian. . . . Though neither participant was primarily a theologian, the affair attracted a great deal of attention in its time because of the commanding reputations of both men as Latin stylists. Haddon was regarded by his fellow Englishmen as the best Latin orator, poet, and epistolist of his generation; and on the Continent Osorio was widely admired not only for his skill in Scriptural studies but also for his excellent Ciceronianism.

    "The result was Contra Hieron. Osorium . . . Responsio Apologetica (1577), dedicated to Sebastian, King of Portugal. . . . In the prefatory epistle, Haddon expresses regret at having to re-enter the controversy in such sharp language as Osorio had forced him to employ." Lawrence V. Ryan, "The Haddon-Osirio Controversy (1563–1583)," *Church History* 22, no. 2 (June 1953): 142.
27. J. M. Coetzee, *Diary of a Bad Year* (New York: Viking Adult, 2007), 23.
28. "The fact that such common locutions as 'my leg,' 'my eye,' 'my brain,' and even 'my body' exist suggests that we believe there is some non-material, perhaps fictive, entity that stands in the relation of possessor to possessed to the body's 'parts' and even to the whole body." Coetzee, ibid., 59.

The Metamorphosis

The theme of metamorphosis is found in classical literature, most famously in the *Metamorphoses* of Ovid (43 B.C.–A.D. 17 or 18), which traces through mythology the development of the human race to its culmination in the Roman order.

See below, pp. 197–98. Kafka's word for "metamorphosis"—*Verwandlung*—also means a scene change in a stage play. The English word "metamorphosis" is slightly more elevated in tone than the German, which could also arguably be translated as "The Transformation."

1. The name "Gregor Samsa" appears to derive partly from literary works Kafka had read. The hero of *The Story of Young Renate Fuchs*, by the German-Jewish novelist Jakob Wassermann (1873–1934), is a certain Gregor Samassa. The Viennese author Leopold von Sacher-Masoch (1836–95), whose sexual imagination gave rise to the idea of masochism, is also an influence. Sacher-Masoch (note the letters Sa-Mas) wrote *Venus in Furs* (1870), a novel whose hero is named Gregor. A "Venus in furs" literally recurs in *The Metamorphosis* in the picture that Gregor Samsa has hung on his bedroom wall. See below, n. 4. The name Samsa also resembles Kafka in its play of vowels and consonants. See below, "Introduction," p. xxxiii.
2. Kafka uses the words *unruhige Träumen* (literally, "restless dreams"), an odd expression combining the more usual phrases "restless sleep" and "bad dreams." For a discussion of "monstrous vermin," see below, pp. 170–71.
3. "An unusual expression, roughly analogous to 'children's room.' Gregor's nearest surroundings (in the story Gregor is doing the observing and reflecting) appear to him as something matter-of-fact and humanly normal, while this expression itself implies *his* unnaturalness as a metamorphosed animal" (Peter Beicken, *Erläuterungen und Dokumente. Franz Kafka: Die Verwandlung* [Clarifications and documents. Franz Kafka: *The Metamorphosis*], [Stuttgart: Reclam, 1983], 8).
4. An ornamental scarf, typically of fur or feathers, draped *snakelike* around a woman's neck. It could evoke an image of Eve before the Fall. For further discussion of this image, see below, pp. 237–38.
5. In Kafka's German literally "Heavenly Father," indicating that the Samsa family is Christian and almost certainly Catholic. See below, p. 28 n. 13, and p. 60 n. 17.
6. Kafka literally writes "It [*Es*]" was a "tool," using for "tool" the German word *Kreatur* (creature). Both German words introduce an atmosphere of animality—of displaced animality, for it is Gregor, after all, who is the animal.
7. See below, p. 197.
8. A saw with a long, narrow, fine-toothed blade used for cutting thin wooden boards into patterns.
9. Anna is presumably the name of the maid who also does the cooking; hence she is later referred to as "the previous cook." See below, p. 35, n. 12.
10. A belief found among Jewish mystics, as well as in many older European cultures, holds that the doors or windows of a house in which there has been a recent death must be left open to facilitate the exit of the Angel of Death.
11. Literally, "the door."

12. Presumably a new maid, a girl of sixteen; the former maid, Anna, left on the very first day of Gregor's metamorphosis. See below, pp. 28–29.
13. Further evidence of the Samsas' probable Catholicism.
14. Presumably the new maid, who replaced Anna, the maid of all work who also did the cooking—here called "the previous cook."
15. In the version of *The Metamorphosis* which Kafka oversaw and published in his lifetime, he punctuated the sentence so that it would have to be translated differently—indeed, in two different ways. One way of reading says, "With a kind of perverse obstinacy, his father refused also to take off his official uniform in the house." This would make the point that among the various forms of obstinate behavior the father displays at home, refusing to take off his uniform is one of them. But the sentence can also be translated as follows: "With a kind of perverse obstinacy, his father refused to take off his official uniform in the house as well." About this interpretation of the sentence, critic Eric Santner comments: "The ambiguity of Kafka's diction makes possible the reading that the father has refused to remove his uniform not just at home but in public as well." Santner then develops this point by speculating that Mr. Samsa's "recent 'investiture' with a kind of official status and authority, low though it might be, might, in other words, be a sham." This observation contributes importantly to Santner's reading of *The Metamorphosis* as the representation of a crisis in the constitution of authority. See below, pp. 223–44, esp. 235.

    Interestingly enough, despite the claim to authenticity made by the so-called Manuscript Version of Kafka's complete works, recently published in Germany, the crucial sentence is printed in the normalized way: the editors place the comma in a position to produce the more "sensible" reading that the translation, above, reflects.
16. Presumably the new maid, the girl of sixteen.
17. Final evidence of the Samsas' probable Catholicism.

BACKGROUNDS

FROM WEDDING PREPARATIONS IN THE COUNTRY

Franz Kafka, "Hochzeitsvorbereitungen auf dem Lande," in *Hochzeitsvorbereitungen auf dem Lande und andere Prosa aus dem Nachlaß*, ed. Max Brod (Frankfurt a.M.: Fischer, 1953), 11–12 (translated by the editor of this Modern Library edition). This is an unfinished novel, fragments of which survive; Kafka began writing it in 1907, at the age of twenty-four. Words in brackets appear in the text of "Hochzeitsvorbereitungen auf dem Lande," "Fassung [version] A," in Franz Kafka, *Beschreibung eines Kampfes und andere Schriften aus dem Nachlaß*, nach der Kritischen Ausgabe, ed. Hans-Gerd Koch (Frankfurt a.M.: Fischer Taschenbuch Verlag, 1994), 18.

Letters and Diaries

1. Franz Kafka, *Briefe, 1902–1924*, ed. Max Brod (Frankfurt a.M.: Fischer, 1958), 107–9 (translated by the editor of this Modern Library edition). Max Brod (1884–1968) was Kafka's close friend and literary executor and himself a prolific writer.
2. "Happy absentmindedness" is Kafka's phrase to describe Gregor Samsa hanging from the ceiling of his room [35].
3. Grete's abandonment of Gregor at the close of *The Metamorphosis* provokes his death.
4. This is the novel that Kafka called *Der Verschollene* [The Missing Person], more familiar under the title that Max Brod gave to it: *Amerika.* It was never finished. It appeared in English as *Amerika: A Novel*, trans. Edwin Muir and Willa Muir (New York: Schocken, 1962).
5. Note by Max Brod (translated by the editor): "Without my friend's knowledge, I brought a copy of his letter (without the N.B.) to the attention of his mother, as I was seriously afraid for Franz's life. His mother's reply, as well as further facts important for a judgment of the situation which supplement the *Letter to His Father*, are found on page 113 of my biography." See Max Brod, *Franz Kafka—A Biography*, trans. G. Humphreys Roberts (New York: Schocken, 1947), 91–93. Julie Kafka's reply was full of concern.
6. Franz Kafka, *Briefe an Felice*, ed. Erich Heller and Jürgen Born (Frankfurt a.M.: Fischer, 1967), 101–2. (All extracts from this volume of letters have been translated by the editor of this Modern Library edition, who has consulted *Letters to Felice*, trans. James Stern and Elizabeth Duckworth [New York: Schocken, 1973]). Felice Bauer (1887–1960) was Kafka's fiancée in the year 1914 (the engagement was dissolved) and then again in 1917 (the engagement was again dissolved). During this time, she lived in Berlin and worked as executive secretary of a manufacturer of dictating machines; she was also active in social work. Kafka described her once as a "happy, healthy, self-confident girl." After their relationship ended, Felice married and had two children. She lived with her family in Switzerland and then in the United States until her death.
7. *The Missing Person.*
8. This is the first mention of *The Metamorphosis.*
9. *Briefe an Felice,* 102.
10. Ibid., 105.
11. Ibid., 116.
12. Ibid., 117.
13. Ibid., 122.
14. Ibid., 125.
15. Ibid., 130.
16. Ibid., 135.
17. Ibid., 145.
18. Ibid., 147.

19. Ibid., 153.
20. Kafka was going to read aloud his story "The Judgment" at an evening event devoted to Prague writers.
21. *Briefe an Felice,* 155.
22. Ibid., 160.
23. Presumably his reading "The Judgment" aloud at the Prague authors' evening.
24. *The Missing Person.*
25. *Briefe an Felice,* 163.
26. Ibid., 320.
27. Franz Kafka, *Tagebücher,* ed. Max Brod (Frankfurt a.M.: Fischer, 1951), 323 (translated by the editor of this Modern Library edition). The reader may consult *The Diaries of Franz Kafka, 1910–1913,* trans. Joseph Kresh (New York: Schocken, 1948), and *The Diaries of Franz Kafka, 1914–1923,* trans. Martin Greenberg (New York: Schocken, 1949).
28. Ibid., 351.
29. *Briefe an Felice,* 561. Grete Bloch (1892–1943?) was a Berlin friend of Felice Bauer; Kafka got to know her in Prague in 1913, when she came to act as an intermediary in their troubled relationship. She was probably murdered in a Nazi concentration camp.
30. The first chapter of Kafka's unfinished, "unfortunate" novel *The Missing Person,* published separately to critical acclaim.
31. *Tagebücher,* 420.
32. *Briefe,* 135–36 (translated by the editor of this Modern Library edition).
33. *Briefe an Felice,* 719–20.
34. The *Neue Rundschau* was an influential literary journal, a weekly edited in Vienna by the novelist Robert Musil (1880–1939). *Ur* is a prefix meaning "originally" or "primordially."
35. *Briefe an Felice,* 744.
36. Rainer Maria Rilke (1875–1926), perhaps the greatest German lyric poet of the twentieth century and author of the modernist novel *The Notebooks of Malte Laurids Brigge* (1910). He was born in Prague but wrote mostly in Germany, France, and Switzerland. He was an admirer of Kafka's work. Cf. *Letters to Felice,* 577. An acquaintance of Rilke, Lou Albert-Lasard (1891–1969), an eminent portrait painter, declared that Rilke had read *The Metamorphosis* aloud to her (*Wege mit Rilke* [Frankfurt a.M.: Fischer, 1952], 43). Cf. *Briefe an Felice,* 744.
37. "Brief an den Vater," in *Hochzeitsvorbereitungen auf dem Lande,* 221–22 (translated by the editor of this Modern Library edition).
38. *Briefe,* 344–45 (translated by the editor of this Modern Library edition). Elli (Gabriele) Hermann (b. 1889) was Kafka's oldest sister. In October 1941, together with her husband and children, she was deported by the Nazis to the Lodz ghetto, where she subsequently perished.
39. Jonathan Swift, *Gulliver's Travels* ("A Voyage to Lilliput," Part I, Chap. 6)

(London: Methuen, 1960), 48. Swift (1667–1745) was a great Anglo-Irish satirical writer.

40. *Briefe*, 383–86.

Critical Essays

Kafka's *The Metamorphosis*: Metamorphosis of the Metaphor

Adapted from *Franz Kafka. The Necessity of Form* (Ithaca: Cornell UP, 1988), 47–80 (1970, rev. 1986). Used by permission of the publisher, Cornell University Press. Modern Library edition page numbers appear in brackets.

Abbreviations

The following abbreviations are used throughout Corngold's text and notes, followed by the appropriate page numbers.

A *Amerika: A Novel*, trans. Edwin and Willa Muir. New York: Schocken, 1962. See *R*.

B *Beschreibung eines Kampfes*, ed. Max Brod. Frankfurt am Main: Fischer, 1954. See *DS* and *GW*.

BF *Briefe an Felice*, ed. Erich Heller and Jürgen Born. Frankfurt am Main: Fischer, 1967. See *LF*.

Br *Briefe, 1902–1924*, ed. Max Brod. Frankfurt am Main: Fischer, 1958. See *L*.

C *The Castle*, trans. Willa and Edwin Muir. Harmondsworth, Middlesex: Penguin, 1966.

DI *The Diaries of Franz Kafka, 1910–1913*, trans. Joseph Kresh. New York: Schocken, 1948. See *Ta*.

DII *The Diaries of Franz Kafka, 1914–1923*, trans. Martin Greenberg. New York: Schocken, 1949. See *Ta*.

DF *Dearest Father*, trans. Ernst Kaiser and Eithne Wilkins. New York: Schocken, 1954. See *H*.

DS *Description of a Struggle*, trans. Tania and James Stern. New York: Schocken, 1958. See *B*.

E *Erzählungen*, ed. Max Brod. Frankfurt am Main: Fischer, 1946. See *S*.

GW *The Great Wall of China*, trans. Willa and Edwin Muir. New York: Schocken, 1960.

H *Hochzeitsvorbereitungen auf dem Lande und andere Prosa aus dem Nachlaß*, ed. Max Brod. Frankfurt am Main: Fischer, 1953. See *DF*.

J Gustav Janouch, *Conversations with Kafka*, trans. Goronwy Rees. New York: New Directions, 1971.

L *Letters to Friends, Family, and Editors*, trans. Richard and Clara Winston. New York: Schocken, 1977. See *Br.*

LF *Letters to Felice*, trans. James Stern and Elizabeth Duckworth. New York: Schocken, 1973. See *BF.*

LM *Letters to Milena*, ed. Willi Haas, trans. Tania and James Stern. New York: Schocken, 1953.

M *The Metamorphosis*, ed. and trans. Stanley Corngold. New York: Bantam Books, 1972. See *E.*

S *The Complete Stories*, ed. Nahum Glatzer. New York: Schocken, 1971. See *E.*

Ta *Tagebücher*, ed. Max Brod. Frankfurt am Main: Fischer, 1951. See *DI, DII.*

1. Elias Canetti wrote: "In *The Metamorphosis* Kafka reached the height of his mastery: he wrote something which he could never surpass, because there is nothing which *The Metamorphosis* could be surpassed by—one of the few great, perfect poetic works of this century" (*Der andere Prozeß: Kafkas Briefe an Felice* [Munich: Hanser, 1969], pp. 22–23).
2. Dieter Hasselblatt, *Zauber und Logik: Eine Kafka Studie* (Cologne: Verlag Wissenschaft und Politik), 61.
3. Edward Said, "Beginnings," *Salmagundi*, Fall 1968, 49.
4. Günther Anders, *Kafka—Pro und Contra* (Munich: Beck, 1951), 40–41, 20, 41. For an English version (not a literal translation), see Günther Anders, *Franz Kafka*, trans. A. Steer and A. K. Thorlby (London: Bowes & Bowes, 1960). The translations here are mine.
5. Walter H. Sokel, "Kafka's 'Metamorphosis': Rebellion and Punishment," *Monatshefte* 48 (April–May 1956): 203.
6. Walter H. Sokel, *The Writer in Extremis: Expressionism in Twentieth-Century Literature* (Stanford, CA: Stanford UP, 1959), 47, 46.
7. Walter H. Sokel, *Franz Kafka: Tragik und Ironie, Zur Struktur seiner Kunst* (Frankfurt am Main: Fischer Taschenbuch, 1983), 110.
8. Walter H. Sokel, *Franz Kafka Columbia Essays on Modern Writers* (New York: Columbia UP, 1966), 5.
9. Walter H. Sokel, "Kafka's 'Metamorphosis,'" 205. John [*sic*] Urzidil, "Recollections," in *The Kafka Problem*, ed. Angel Flores (New York: Octagon, 1963), 22.
10. Anders, *Kafka*, 42.
11. Jacques Derrida, "Violence et Métaphysique," *Lécriture et la différence* (Paris: Seuil, 1967), 137; Martin Heidegger, "Den Bedeutungen wachsen Worte zu," in *Sein und Zeit* (Tübingen: Klostermann, 1963), 161.
12. This suspicious critique of metaphor is proto-Expressionist. It will be taken up again and again by Expressionist writers—e.g., Carl Einstein, writing retrospectively: "Metaphor and metaphoricity refer to more than an isolated literary process; they characterize a general mood and attitude. In the metaphor one avoids repeating facts and weakens contact with real-

ity. Metaphoricity is justified by the illusion of arbitrarily creating something new at every moment The literati lost a sense of factual events and trusted in the empty power of their words" (*Die Fabrikationen der Fiktionen*, ed. Sibylle Penkert [Hamburg: Rowohlt, 1973], 283).

13. Maurice Blanchot, "The Diaries: The Exigency of the Work of Art," trans. Lyall H. Powers, in *Franz Kafka Today*, ed. Angel Flores and Homer Swander (Madison: U of Wisconsin P, 1964), 207.
14. In other words, the tenor of a metaphor is the thing or person it means; the vehicle is its immediate, literal content. See I. A. Richards, *The Philosophy of Rhetoric* (New York: Oxford UP, 1936), 96.
15. Hasselblatt, *Zauber und Logik*, 195, 200. This is consistent with the Expressionist desideratum par excellence: "For we are here to re-create every created thing: in language. To bring to life for the first time through ourselves: in language. *Sine verecundia* [without shame (Latin)]. Many have tried out the criticism of language. . . . More urgent than criticism is the creation of language" (Alfred Kerr, "Sexueller Ursprung der Sprache," *Pan* 3, nos. 16–17 [1913–1914]: 280).
16. Theodor W. Adorno, "Notes on Kafka,"*Prisms*, trans. Samuel and Shierry Weber (London: Spearman, 1967), 271.
17. Kafka studied medieval German literature at the University of Prague in 1902. Cf. Klaus Wagenbach, *Franz Kafka: Eine Biographie seiner Jugend (1883–1912)* (Bern: Francke, 1958), 100. He assiduously consulted Grimm's etymological dictionary. Cf. Max Brod, *Über Franz Kafka* (Frankfurt am Main: Fischer, 1966), 110, 213. The citation from Grimm is discussed in depth by Kurt Weinberg, *Kafkas Dichtungen: Die Travestien des Mythos* (Bern: Francke, 1963), 316–17.
18. Weinberg, *Kafkas Dichtungen*, 317.
19. Kimberly Sparks, "Drei schwarze Kaninchen: Zu einer Deutung der Zimmerherren in Kafkas 'Die Verwandlung,'" *Zeitschrift für deutsche Philologie* 84 (1965): 78–79.
20. See above, p. 285.
21. William Empson, "A Family Monster" (review of *The Metamorphosis*), *The Nation* 138 (December 7, 1946): 653. Empson's surmise—"Maybe [Kafka] could never bear to read over the manuscript"—is incorrect; Kafka speaks of proofreading *The Metamorphosis* (*DII*, 13). For the scrupulousness with which he edited his stories, see Ludwig Dietz, "Franz Kafka, Drucke zu seinen Lebzeiten: Eine textkritisch-bibliographische Studie," *Jahrbuch der deutschen Schillergesellschaft* 7 (1963), 416–57.
22. Brod, *Über Franz Kafka*, 89.
23. Klaus Wagenbach, *Franz Kafka in Selbstzeugnissen und Bilddokumenten* (Hamburg: Rowohlt, 1964), 41–56.
24. Hermann Pongs, "Franz Kafka—'Die Verwandlung': Zwischen West und Ost," *Dichtung im gespaltenen Deutschland* (Stuttgart: Union, 1966), 276.
25. Wagenbach, *Franz Kafka in Selbstzeugnissen*, 56.

26. Martin Greenberg, *The Terror of Art: Kafka and Modern Literature* (New York: Basic Books, 1968), 26–27.
27. Martin Walser, *Beschreibung einer Form* (Munich: Hanser, 1961), 11.
28. Tzvetan Todorov, *Littérature et signification* (Paris: Larousse, 1967), 115–17.
29. Autobiographical critics frequently attempt to force the identification of Kafka and Gregor Samsa by citing the passage (*DF*, 195) in which Kafka has his father compare him to a stinging, bloodsucking vermin. This is done despite Kafka's explicit warning that "Samsa is not altogether Kafka" (J, 55).
30. Helmut Richter, *Franz Kafka: Werk und Entwurf* (Berlin: Ruetten & Loening), 112–19; Sokel, "Kafka's 'Metamorphosis,'" 213; Hellmuth Kaiser, "Franz Kafkas Inferno: Eine psychologische Deutung seiner Strafphantasie," *Imago* 17, no. 1 (1931): 41–104; Wilfredo Dalmau Castañón, "El caso clinico de Kafka en 'La Metamorfosis,'" *Cuadernos Hispanoamericanos* (Madrid) 27 (March 1952): 385–88.
31. "The highest degree" (Latin).
32. Giuliano Baioni, *Kafka: Romanzo e parabola* (Milan: Feltrinelli, 1962), 81–100.
33. In Stanley Corngold, *The Commentators' Despair: The Interpretation of Kafka's "Metamorphosis"* (Port Washington, NY: Kennikat P, 1973).
34. This text mistakenly reads the word *Leid* ("sorrow") as *Lied* ("song"); I have made the correction.
35. Jürg Schubiger, *Franz Kafka: Die Verwandlung, Eine Interpretation* (Zurich: Atlantis, 1969), 55–57.
36. Jacques Lacan, "The Insistence of the Letter in the Unconscious," *Yale French Studies* 36/37 (October 1966): 125.
37. Anders, *Kafka—Pro und Contra*, 40; Hasselblatt, *Zauber und Logik*, 203.
38. Failed artist (French).
39. Sokel, "Kafka's 'Metamorphosis,'" 81.
40. "For writing to be possible, it must be born out of the death of what it speaks about; but this death makes writing itself impossible, for there is no longer anything to write" (Tzvetan Todorov, discussing Blanchot's Kafka, in *The Fantastic: A Structural Approach to a Literary Genre*, trans. Richard Howard [Cleveland, OH: Case Western Reserve UP, 1973], 175).
41. Greenberg, *The Terror of Art*, 48.
42. *The Metamorphosis* distorts a metaphor alluding to an earlier act of writing; as such it prefigures Kafka's next published work, "In the Penal Colony." The main action of this story, the operation of a terrible machine that kills a criminal by inscribing immediately into his flesh the commandment he had disobeyed, follows from the distortion of a metaphor about writing or engraving, of the experience that engraves itself on a person's memory. The vehicle here, an act of writing, is without even a residual sense of Kafka's empirical personality. Kafka himself noted: "But for me, who believe that I shall be able to lie contentedly on my deathbed, such scenes are

secretly a game" (*DII,* 102). The more comprehensive meaning of this vehicle is supplied by Kafka's sense that in writing he was engraving his own tombstone.

43. An episode from the life of Kierkegaard parallels remarkably this sentiment and the incident from *Metamorphosis:* "Well," the cleaning woman answered, "you don't have to worry about getting rid of the stuff next door. It's already been taken care of" (M, 57) [63]. Walter Lowrie, writing in his *Short Life of Kierkegaard* (Princeton, NJ: Princeton UP, 1971), 41, of the spinal trouble that eventually caused Kierkegaard's death, reports: "We have several accounts of similar attacks which were not permanent. For example, at a social gathering he once fell from the sofa and lay impotent upon the floor—beseeching his friends not to pick 'it' up but to 'leave it there till the maid comes in the morning to sweep.'" Theodore Ziolkowski noted this parallel with the Danish philosopher and religious thinker (1813–55). For a study of the relation between Kafka and Kierkegaard, see Fritz Billeter, *Das Dichterische bei Kafka und Kierkegaard* (Winterthur: Keller, 1965).
44. I have modified this translation. The German text concludes, of Kafka's writing as a leave-taking, "daß er zwar von Dir erzwungen war, aber in der von mir bestimmten Richtung verlief" (*H,* 203). Kaiser and Wilkins translate these clauses, "although it was brought about by force on your part, it did not [*sic*] take its course in the direction determined by me" (*DF,* 177).
45. I have modified the Winstons' translation.
46. The state of being a writer (German).
47. Maurice Merleau-Ponty, *Phénoménologie de la perception* (Paris: Gallimard, 1945), 213.
48. "Darin also besteht das eigentliche Kunstgeheimnis des Meisters, daß er den Stoff durch die Form vertilgt" ("The real artistic secret of the master consists in his erasing the substance [or matter] by means of form") (Friedrich Schiller, "Zweiundzwanzigster Brief," *Über die ästhetische Erziehung des Menschen in einer Reihe von Briefen, Sämtliche Werke* [Munich: Carl Hanser, 1967], 5:639).
49. "[Music] speaks by means of mere sensations without concepts and so does not, like poetry, leave behind it any food for reflection" (Immanuel Kant, *The Critique of Judgement,* trans. James Creed Meredith [Oxford: Clarendon, 1928], 193).
50. This observation and those in the three sentences that follow it are taken from Paul de Man's "The Rhetoric of Temporality," *Blindness and Insight: Essays in the Rhetoric of Contemporary Criticism,* rev. 2d ed. (Minneapolis: U of Minnesota, 1983), 207. [Jean-Jacques Rousseau (1712–78), French philosopher, novelist, and social thinker; Friedrich Hölderlin (1770–1843), German poet; William Wordsworth (1770–1850), English poet; Friedrich von Schlegel (1772–1829), German critic, philosopher, and poet.]
51. Michel Foucault, *The Order of Things: An Archaeology of the Human Sciences* (a translation of *Les mots et les choses*) (New York: Pantheon, 1970), 383–84.

Elements of Jewish Folklore in Kafka's *Metamorphosis*

Originally "Kafka's *Metamorphosis*: Folklore, Hasidism and the Jewish Tradition," *Journal of the Kafka Society of America* 11.1/2 (June/December 1987), 9–27. Revised 1994. Reprinted by permission of the *Journal of the Kafka Society of America*. Copyright © Kafka Society of America. Unless otherwise indicated, all translations are by Iris Bruce. Many thanks to Stanley Corngold for his generous and invaluable criticism.

1. Marthe Robert, for example, in her psychological biography on Kafka, believes that even Gregor's metamorphosis can be ignored: "If we disregard the metamorphosis itself," she writes, "which is quite possible without disrupting the logic of the events, we observe that the story describes the characteristic development of a schizophrenic state with remarkable accuracy" (Marthe Robert, *As Lonely as Franz Kafka*, trans. Ralph Manheim [*Seul, comme Franz Kafka* (1979)] [New York: Schocken, 1986], 240 n. 32).
2. Hugo Bergmann rightly sees the encounter with the Yiddish theater group from Oct. 1911 to Feb. 1912 as a "turning point in Franz's life" ("Erinnerungen an Franz Kafka," *Universitas: Zeitschrift für Wissenschaft, Kunst und Literatur* 27.7 [1972]: 746). For a description of the Yiddish theater and the kind of group Kafka encountered, see, further, Evelyn Torton Beck, *Kafka and the Yiddish Theater: Its Impact on His Work* (Madison: U of Wisconsin P, 1971) and Guido Massimo, *Franz Kafka, Jizchak und das jiddische Theater*, trans. Norbert Bickert (Frankfurt a.M.: Stroemfeld [Nexus, 2007]).
3. After attending his first play, Kafka wrote, "Would like to see a large Yiddish theater as the production may after all suffer because of the small cast and inadequate rehearsal" (*The Diaries of Franz Kafka, 1910–1913*, ed. Max Brod, trans. Joseph Kresh [New York: Schocken, 1948], 87).
4. In November 1911, for example, Kafka began reading Heinrich Graetz's *Geschichte des Judentums* [History of Jewry], a standard work on Jewish history, and in January 1912 Jakob Fromer's *Organismus des Judentums* [The Organism of Jewry] (*Diaries, 1910–1913*, 125, 223).
5. Ibid., 223.
6. "Hasidie" tales are legends and anecdotes about miracles performed by Israel Baal Schem Tov (1699–1761) and his followers. Baal Schem is the founder of hasidism, a revivalist religious and social movement in Eastern Europe in the eighteenth and nineteenth centuries. "Kabbalistic" refers to *Kabbalah*, lit. "tradition," a Hebrew term for (1) the texts of medieval Jewish mysticism, in which (for example) every letter, word, or number contains mysteries to be interpreted; or (2) the complex structure of Kabbalah symbolism.
7. Martin Buber (1878–1965), German-Jewish man of letters, philosopher, and theologian, translated and commented on legends and tales from the

religious culture of Eastern European Jewry [*Editor*]. In his correspondence with Felice Bauer, Kafka refers to Buber's "books of legends" (i.e., *The Tales of Rabbi Nachman* and *The Legend of the Baal Shem*) (Franz Kafka, *Letters to Felice*, ed. Erich Heller and Jürgen Born, trans. James Stern and Elisabeth Duckworth [1963; New York: Schocken, 1973], 164).

8. Gershom G. Scholem, *Major Trends in Jewish Mysticism* (New York: Schocken, 1961), 283.
9. For an overview of the history of *gilgul*, see Scholem, "Gilgul," *Kabbalah* (Jerusalem: Keter Publishing House, 1974), 344–50, and *Major Trends*, 280–84.
10. See introductory note to *The Metamorphosis*, p. 285, above.
11. David Stern, "Aggadah," *Contemporary Jewish Religious Thought*, ed. A. A. Cohen and P. Mendes-Flohr (New York: Charles Scribner's, 1987), 8.
12. "The Kabbalah of Isaac Luria (1534–72) may be described as a mystical interpretation of Exile and Redemption. . . . This new doctrine of God and the universe corresponds to the new moral idea of humanity which it propagates: the ideal of the ascetic whose aim is . . . the extinction of the world's blemish, the restitution of all things in God . . ." (Scholem, *Major Trends*, 286).
13. See Arnold Band for a discussion of the allegorical nature of the Bratslav Tales: "Introduction," *Nahman of Bratslav. The Tales*, ed./trans. A. Band (New York: Paulist Press, 1978), 37–38. For further animal motifs in Nachman which bear religious allegorical meaning, see "The Spider and the Fly," *Gates to the New City: A Treasury of Modern Jewish Tales*, ed. H. Schwartz (New York: Avon, 1983), 199–203.
14. Karl-Heinz Fingerhut, *Die Funktion der Tierfiguren im Werke Franz Kafkas* (Bonn: H. Bouvier & Co. Verlag, 1969), 97.
15. Jack Riemer, "Franz Kafka and Rabbi Nachman," *Jewish Frontier* (April 1961): 16–20. Howard Schwartz, "Introduction," *Gates*, 43–44.
16. Laurent Cohen, *Variations autour de K. Pour une lecture juive de Franz Kafka* (Paris: Intertextes, 1991), 68.
17. I. L. Peretz, "Thou Shalt Not Covet," *Selected Stories*, ed. Irving Howe and Eliezer Greenberg (New York: Schocken, 1975). This text is included in Peretz's *Volkstümliche Erzählungen* (Berlin: Jüdischer Verlag, 1913), a book which Kafka sent to his fiancée Felice Bauer in 1916 as suitable reading material for the refugee children in the Jewish *Volksheim* in Berlin.
18. *Torah* refers to (1) the Five Books of Moses—i.e., to written law, or (2) to both written and oral dimensions of the law (i.e., the Bible and the sum total of everything that has been said by scholars and sages in explanation of this written corpus).
19. A. B. Gotlober, "The Gilgul or The Transmigration," *Yenne Velt: The Great Works of Jewish Fantasy and Occult*, ed./trans. Joachim Neugroschel (New York: Pocket Books, 1976), 432.
20. Leslie A. Fiedler, "Kafka and the Myth of the Jew" (*No! In Thunder: Essays on Myth and Literature* [Boston: Beacon Press, 1960], 99–100).

21. The first scholar, to my knowledge, to have pointed out the relationship of Gregor's metamorphosis to the Jewish folk and mystic tradition is Maurice Blanchot, who writes: "That the theme of 'The Metamorphosis' (as well as the obsessing fictions of animality) is a reminiscence, an allusion to the cabalistic metempsychosis, can well be imagined . . ." ("The Diaries: The Exigency of the Work of Art," trans. Lyall H. Powers, in *Franz Kafka Today*, ed. Angel Flores and Homer Swander [Madison: U of Wisconsin P, 1964], 218, n. 5). Blanchot also refers to the concept of metamorphosis as having developed out of the experience of the Jewish exile.
22. In 1939 Walter Benjamin pointed out the importance of humor in Kafka: "It seems to me more and more that the most essential point about Kafka is his humor. . . . I believe someone who tried to see *the humorous side of Jewish theology* would have the key to Kafka" (*Benjamin über Kafka. Texte, Briefzeugnisse, Aufzeichnungen*, ed. Hermann Schweppenhäuser [Frankfurt: Suhrkamp, 1981], 90–91). Benjamin's argument has never really been critically pursued. However, a serious attempt to study the humorous dimension in Kafka has been made by Michel Dentan in his *Humour et création littéraire dans l'oeuvre de Kafka* (Geneva and Paris: Droz and Minard, 1961); see pp. 11–16 on *The Metamorphosis.* This is as it should be. Malcolm Pasley rightly takes issue with the general reluctance among Kafka scholars to acknowledge the presence of humor in Kafka's texts: "Kafka's covert jokes and puns are as much disputed as his riddling devices to which they are related. It is often thought derogatory and impudent even to suggest their presence in such 'serious writing.' And yet if we ignore the playful spirit which informs many of his stories, we miss their special flavor. . . . This playfulness is not only compatible with the highest seriousness, but it is actually inseparable from it" ("Semi-Private Games," *The Kafka Debate*, ed. Angel Flores [New York: Gordian Press, 1977], 189).
23. George Steiner, *Language and Silence* (New York: Atheneum, 1970), 121.
24. Stanley Corngold, "Introduction," *The Metamorphosis by Franz Kafka*, trans./ed. S. Corngold (New York: Bantam, 1972), xxi. All subsequent quotations from *Metamorphosis* are cited parenthetically in the text. Modern Library edition page numbers appear in brackets.
25. His rational self tells him that his imagination is playing a trick on him because he is over-worked: ". . . he was eager to see how today's fantasy would gradually fade away" (6)[7]. He also talks about "a dizzy spell" [*Schwindelanfall*] (12) [13], the double meaning of *Schwindel* in German—fainting and trick—again suggesting that he sees it as a kind of bad joke.
26. Mendele Moicher-Sforim, *The Mare* (1876) (*Yenne Velt,* 565). Meyer Isser Pinès, in his Yiddish literary history, which Kafka read, devotes seventy pages to a discussion of Mendele's work; twenty pages are on *The Mare* alone. *L'Histoire de la littérature judéo-allemande* (Paris: Jouve, 1911).
27. For a detailed analysis of narrative distance in this respect, which would

allow for humor, see Stanley Corngold, "The Author Survives on the Margin of His Breaks: Kafka's Narrative Perspective," *The Fate of the Self* (Durham, NC: Duke UP, 1994), 161–79.

28. See Evelyn T. Beck, who also points out the presence of humor in this scene, *Kafka and the Yiddish Theater,* 141, as well as Meno Spann, *Franz Kafka* (Boston: Twayne, 1976), 73.
29. Edward L. Greenstein, "Biblical Law," *Back to the Sources: Reading the Classic Jewish Texts*, ed. Barry W. Holtz (New York: Summit Books, 1984), 88.
30. Joel Rosenberg, "Biblical Narrative," *Back to the Sources,* 55.
31. *Yenne Velt,* 557. *The Mare* is discussed in Pinès' Yiddish literary history, especially in its relation to the experience of exile [*Editor*].
32. The dispersion of the Jews outside Palestine following the Babylonian exile. [*Editor*].
33. From the word *Midrash*, meaning "to search out." It is not a single book but the act and process of interpreting the Jewish Bible. *Midrash* fills in the gaps and details that the Bible leaves out in the realms of biblical law (*Halakha*) and biblical legends (*Aggadah*).
34. Cited in Barry W. Holtz, "Midrash," *Back to the Sources,* 181.
35. Alan Mintz, "Prayer and the Prayerbook," *Back to the Sources,* 410.
36. Lawrence Fine, "Kabbalistic Texts," *Back to the Sources,* 325.
37. In *Encyclopaedia Judaica*, vol. 7 (Jerusalem: Keter Publishing House, 1971), 575.
38. Arthur Green, "Teachings of the Hasidic Masters," *Back to the Sources,* 392.
39. A Talmudic academy or rabbinical seminary [*Editor*].
40. *A Treasury of Yiddish Stories*, ed. Irving Howe and Eliezer Greenberg (New York: Schocken, 1973), 222.
41. Kafka noted down the reference to the Divine Kiss from Pinès' discussion of "Cabalists": "Mitat neshika, death by a kiss: reserved only for the most pious" (*Diaries, 1910–1913,* 226). Kafka takes up the image of the kiss at the end of "A Hunger Artist." Cf. also Jean Jofen, *The Jewish Mystic in Kafka* (New York: Peter Lang, 1987), 94.
42. Lit. "shapeless mass," a creature in human form created by magical means and endowed with life in order to help and protect the Jews. The best-known legends are associated with the golem created by Rabbi Judah Loew of Prague: the remains of the golem are supposedly still in the Old-New Synagogue in Prague.
43. Franz Kafka, *The Complete Stories*, ed. N. Glatzer (1946; New York: Schocken, 1983), 275.
44. Kurt Weinberg, *Kafkas Dichtungen: Die Travestien eines Mythos* (Bern/München: Francke Verlag, 1963), 241.
45. *Letters to Friends, Family, and Editors*, ed. B. Colman, N. Glatzer, C. Kuppig, W. Sauerlander, trans. Richard Winston and Clara Winston (New York: Schocken, 1977), 122.
46. David Biale, *Gershom Scholem: Kabbalah and Counter-History* (Cambridge:

Harvard UP, 1982), 31. George Steiner also sees Kafka as a "modern Kabbalist" (*After Babel* [Oxford: Oxford UP, 1975], 67); and for Ernst Pawel, too, Kafka is "the worldly talmudist, the rational cabbalist" ("Franz Kafkas Judentum," in *Kafka und das Judentum*, ed. Karl Erich Grözinger, Stéphane Mosès, Hans Dieter Zimmermann [Frankfurt a. M.: Athenäum, 1987], 257).

Kafka's *Metamorphosis* and the Writing of Abjection

1. Among the definitions of "abjection" offered by the *Oxford English Dictionary* are: the condition or estate of one cast down; abasement, humiliation, degradation; rejection; that which is cast off or away; refuse, scum, dregs.
2. Staging [*Editor*].
3. Richard Wagner completed *Parsifal* in 1882, a year before his death [*Editor*].
4. A figure in the legends of many countries who urged Jesus to hasten on the road to Golgotha and was thus doomed to know no rest himself [*Editor*].
5. We should recall that Gregor, too, becomes the bearer of a wound that refuses to heal, the product of an apple thrown by his father.
6. Slavoj Žižek, *The Sublime Object of Ideology* (London: Verso, 1989), 76–77.
7. Stanley Corngold, "Introduction," *The Metamorphosis by Franz Kafka*, trans. and ed. Stanley Corngold (New York: Bantam, 1986), xv. All subsequent quotations from *Metamorphosis* are cited parenthetically in the text. Modern Library edition page numbers appear in brackets.
8. I am arguing, in effect, that we may observe two orders of abjection at work in Kafka's story. Abjection of the first order refers to Gregor's history prior to his metamorphosis, i.e., to his status as a sacrificial object *within* the family structure, and is thus linked to the introjection of the family debt or guilt. Abjection of the second order, a turn of the screw of the first, is the state of the metamorphosis: it signals precisely a radical separation from that family structure and the assumption of a position outside the texture of fate. From the perspective of this new position, what was concealed by the life of self-sacrifice, i.e., by the first order of abjection, becomes visible: the lack of a consistent and dependable Other from whom one could expect a determination of one's identity, whose gaze could guarantee one's recognition, even as *an object worthy of sacrifice*. From a structural point of view, Gregor's verminousness *is* the becoming-visible of this very lack, and that is why he provokes attempts not so much to sacrifice him as to *destroy* him. What must be destroyed is the object in which the inconsistency of the Other—and so of the sacrificial order itself—has become visible. The inconsistency of Gregor's own physical attributes, which makes it impossible to form a coherent image of the insect, is no doubt a crucial aspect of

his monstrousness, i.e., what makes it possible for him to embody the dysfunction of the Other. Kafka converted this impossibility into a prohibition when he stipulated to his publisher, Kurt Wolff, that no illustration of the insect adorn the title page of the 1916 edition of the story.

9. According to the French psychoanalyst Jacques Lacan (1901–81), the symbolic order is the field of language and culture—a system of symbols into which human beings are inserted and which becomes a law to them [*Editor*].
10. Thus the office manager's negative evaluation of Gregor's performance as a salesman represents the lure of a consistent Other whose demands one can still struggle to satisfy. The failure to meet those demands does not yet produce the extreme form of abjection which marks Gregor's new condition.
11. Slavoj Žižek, *Enjoy Your Symptom! Jacques Lacan in Hollywood and Out* (New York: Routledge, 1992), 167. Žižek summarizes these two levels of guilt and sacrifice in terms that elucidate the experience of Gregor Samsa: "The first level is the symbolic pact: the subject identifies the kernel of his being with a symbolic feature to which he is prepared to subordinate his entire life, for the sake of which he is prepared to sacrifice everything—in short, alienation in the symbolic mandate. The second level consists in sacrificing this sacrifice itself: in a most radical sense, we 'break the word,' we renounce the symbolic alliance which defines the very kernel of our being—the abyss, the void in which we find ourselves thereby, is what we call 'modern-age subjectivity' " (167).
12. A custom among many peoples, in which a father acts as though he had experienced the pains of giving birth to his newborn child [*Editor*].
13. Franz Kafka, *Tagebücher, 1910–1923* (Frankfurt a.M.: Fischer, 1990), 217; 215.
14. Sigmund Freud, "Psychoanalytic Notes Upon an Autobiographical Account of a Case of Paranoia (Dementia Paranoides)," *The Standard Edition of the Complete Psychological Works of Sigmund Freud*, ed. James Strachey, vol. 12 (London: The Hogarth Press, 1958), 9–79.
15. Freud's emphasis on Schreber's ostensible homosexuality has been challenged by subsequent readers of the case material. It is clear from Freud's study, however, that he did perceive what I would call the modern or postmythic nature of the disorder. The persecutory figure who pulls the strings behind the scenes and calls forth Schreber's metamorphosis is *not* an agency of fate in the usual sense. He is, rather, a figure who emerges precisely in the tear of the texture of fate.
16. A possible source of knowledge about Schreber on Kafka's part was an essay by Otto Gross, "Über Bewu*ß*tseinszerfall" ("On the Disintegration of Consciousness"), published in 1904 (*Monatsschrift für Psychiatrie und Neurologie* 15/1: 45–51; I am grateful to Dr. Zvi Lothane for drawing this essay to my attention, which very likely represents the first mention of Schreber

in the psychiatric literature). Kafka met Gross for the first time only in 1917, but he very likely had some familiarity with his work prior to that. Kafka had studied criminology with Gross's father, Hanns Gross, at the University of Prague, and the latter's tyrannical treatment of his son was well known in intellectual circles in Central Europe.

17. Schreber's delusional universe, constituting a fantasy space that one could call his "own private Germany," might even be read as the secret mediator between the aesthetic projects of Wagner and Kafka. Schreber's memoir contains a number of references and allusions to Wagner's works. Schreber may be seen as providing us with a view of Kafka's mad universe as seen from the perspective of the *judge* rather than that of a supplicant to the Law.
18. Daniel Paul Schreber, *Memoirs of My Nervous Illness*, trans. Ida Macalpine and Richard A. Hunter (Cambridge: Harvard UP, 1988), 226. Further references will be made in the text.
19. Cf. Zoroastrianism, the religion of the Persians before their conversion to Islam, founded in Persia in the sixth century B.C. by Zoroaster, who was, according to Nietzsche, "the first moralist." Zoroaster (in Persian, "Zarathustra") asserts the ongoing struggle of the universal spirit of good (Ormazd) with the spirit of evil (Ahriman) [*Editor*].
20. Schreber remarks that the lower God Ahriman, who, of course, represents the evil principle in Zoroastrian theology, "seems to have felt attracted to nations of originally brunette race (the Semites) and the upper God [Ormuzd] to nations of originally blonde race (the Aryan peoples)" (53).
21. Schreber's feminization indicates that he shifts symbolic positions from that of Amfortas, the one unable to officiate as presiding judge of the Grail Society, to that of Kundry, the figure who, as composite of Woman and Wandering Jew, embodies in Wagner's ideological universe the blockage in the otherwise harmonious functioning of the community.
22. End of the nineteenth century [*Editor*].
23. One will recall that in Sacher-Masoch's story, the protagonist, Severin, receives a new name once he enters into his contract with his dominatrix Wanda: *Gregor* (the term "masochism" derives from the author's name).
24. Note that Gregor expresses his envy vis-à-vis his colleagues at work by noting that they get to live like "harem women" (4) [4]. For a discussion of the complex and wide-ranging political ramifications of the cultural anxieties about femininity and homosexuality in fin-de-siècle Europe, see George L. Mosse, *Nationalism and Sexuality: Middle-Class Morality and Sexual Norms in Modern Europe* (Madison: U of Wisconsin P, 1985), and John C. Fout, "Sexual Politics in Wilhelmine Germany: The Male Gender Crisis, Moral Purity, and Homophobia," *Journal of the History of Sexuality* 2/3: 388–421.
25. Freud, "Psychoanalytic Notes," 36–37.
26. Sander Gilman's work has been crucial in revealing the intensity of these preoccupations. See, for example, Gilman, *Jewish Self-Hatred: Anti-Semitism*

and the Hidden Language of the Jews (Baltimore: The Johns Hopkins UP, 1986), as well as more recently, *Freud, Race, and Gender* (Princeton: Princeton UP, 1993).

27. For a literary historical reading of fin-de-siècle German and Austrian literature under the sign of a generalized crisis of masculinity, see Jacques Le Rider, *Modernity and Crises of Identity. Culture and Society in Fin-de-siècle Vienna*, trans. Rosemary Morris (New York: Continuum, 1993).
28. Wagner first published these views in his essay "Judaism in Music" in 1850. For a rich, though polemical, discussion of the essay and Wagner's anti-Semitism more generally, see Paul Lawrence Rose, *Wagner: Race and Revolution* (New Haven: Yale UP, 1992).
29. On the cultural association of the male Jew and homosexual through the mediation of the queer voice, see Gilman, *Freud*, 164. For a compelling reading of Kafka's last story, "Josephine the Singer, or the Mouse Folk," through the prism of these cultural associations, see Mark Anderson's *Kafka's Clothes: Ornament and Aestheticism in the Habsburg Fin de Siècle* (Oxford: Clarendon Press, 1992) 194–215.
30. In his capacity as (Latin) [*Editor*]. The "redemptive" closure of story and family around the death and removal of Gregor is given a Christological coloration when the Samsas are first brought by the cleaning woman to Gregor's corpse: "'Well,' said Mr. Samsa, 'now we can thank God!' He crossed himself, and the three women followed his example" (55) [60]. This passage reads as a conversion scenario, as if with Gregor's self-nullification the Samsas can enter into a new covenant free of the obligations of the old. Here we should recall the final lines of Wagner's essay "Judaism in Music," a chilling exhortation directed to all Jews: "But remember, that only one thing can bring about the redemption of the curse weighing down on you: the redemption of Ahasver,—destruction [*Untergang*]."
31. I am arguing, in other words, that the two orders of abjection we have discovered in the story correspond to two different orders of error to which any interpretation of the story is prone. The first order of error might be deemed "empirical" and refers to the reader's (always contingent) failure to interpret the details of the story in a way consistent with textual evidence or with an organizing thesis. This sort of error is always the reader's "fault" and is by definition correctable through harder and more careful work, i.e., through an act of self-sacrifice on the part of the reader. The second order of error might be deemed "ontological" and refers to the fact that the assumption of fictional coherence, of consistency on the part of the text, *has no guarantee.* As with the two orders of abjection, this second order of error has meaning only if it is encountered as a turn of the screw of the first, as the first order of error *in extremis.* These two orders or kinds of error pertain, in principle, to any text. What makes Kafka's text different is that he has, in the abject body of Gregor Samsa, figured the second order

of error *within his own text.* Gregor's abjection is, in other words, the locus of a paradoxical knowledge of the chronic uncertainty of the hermeneutic enterprise. (This view is, of course, very close to Paul de Man's notion of an allegory of reading, i.e., of the way a text allegorizes the limits of its own readability: cf. *Allegories of Reading: Figural Language in Rousseau, Nietzsche, Rilke, and Proust* [New Haven: Yale UP, 1979].) By reading *The Metamorphosis* with Schreber's *Memoirs,* we have learned not only that such knowledge defines the position of the psychotic, but also that in the nineteenth century this position was coded as feminine, queer, and Jewish.

32. Franz Kafka, *Letters to Friends, Family, and Editors*, trans. Richard Winston and Clara Winston (New York: Schocken, 1977), 288–89.
33. Franz Kafka, "A Country Doctor," trans. Willa Muir and Edwin Muir, *Franz Kafka: The Complete Stories*, ed. Nahum N. Glatzer (New York: Schocken, 1971), 225.

"Samsa Was a Traveling Salesman": Trains, Trauma, and the Unreadable Body

Abbreviations for Kafka Citations

A *Amerika: The Missing Person.* Translated by Mark Harman. New York: Schocken, 2008.

AS *Amtliche Schriften.* Edited by Klaus Hermsderf and Benno Wagner. Frankfurt am Main: S. Fischer, 2004.

BF *Briefe an Felice.* Edited by Erich Heller and Jürgen Born. Frankfurt am Main: S. Fischer, 1967.

BM *Briefe an Milena.* Edited by Jürgen Born and Michael Müller. Frankfurt am Main: S. Fischer, 1983.

BR *Briefe, 1902–1924.* Edited by Max Brod. Frankfurt am Main: S. Fischer, 1958.

CS *The Complete Stories.* Edited by Nahum Glatzer. New York: Schocken, 1971.

D *The Diaries of Franz Kafka, 1910–1923.* Edited by Max Brod. New York: Schocken Books, 1975.

D1 *The Diaries of Franz Kafka, 1910–1913.* Translated by Joseph Kresh. New York: Schocken, 1948.

D2 *The Diaries of Franz Kafka, 1914–1923.* Translated by Martin Greenberg (with the assistance of Hannah Arendt). New York: Schocken, 1949.

DL *Drucke zu Lebzeiten.* Edited by Wolf Kittler, Hans-Gerd Koch, and Gerhard Neumann. Frankfurt am Main: S. Fischer, 1994.

L *Letters to Friends, Family, and Editors.* Translated by Richard Winston and Clara Winston. New York: Schocken, 1977.

LF *Letters to Felice.* Translated by James Stern and Elizabeth Duckworth. New York: Schocken, 1973.

LM *Letters to Milena.* Translated by Philip Boehm. New York: Schocken, 1990.

MP *The Metamorphosis, In the Penal Colony, and other Stories.* Translated by Willa Muir and Edwin Muir. New York: Schocken, 1975.

NS1 *Nachgelassene Schriften und Fragmente I.* Edited by Malcolm Pasley. Frankfurt am Main: S. Fischer, 1990.

NS2 *Nachgelassene Schriften und Fragmente II.* Edited by Jost Schillemeit. Frankfurt am Main: S. Fischer, 1992.

P *Der Proceß.* Edited by Malcolm Pasley. Frankfurt am Main: S. Fischer, 1990.

T *The Trial.* Translated by Breon Mitchell. New York: Schocken, 1998.

Ta *Tagebücher in der Fassung der Handschrift.* Edited by Michael Müller. Frankfurt am Main: S. Fischer, 1990.

1. When necessary, I have emended the standard English translations of Kafka, marking them as "trans. rev."; the original German page numbers for Kafka's texts are always supplied. For the other German texts, the translations are my own, unless specified otherwise. I thank Lara Pehar for her bibliographic assistance.
2. Friedrich Kittler, *Grammophon, Film, Typewriter* (Berlin: Brinkmann & Bose, 1986), 327. Bernhard Siegert builds on Kittler's *Endlosschleife* argument (227–46), claiming that the "ghostly" media have transported us, via Kafka, into an interminable loop of post-humanism and post-hermeneutics (247–64), in *Relays: Literature as an Epoch of the Postal System*, trans. Kevin Repp (Stanford, CA: Stanford UP, 1999).
3. Michel Cournot notes with astonishment that Kafka writes Bauer up to three letters per day for twenty-four weeks yet "doesn't get on a train that would have brought him to Berlin in a few hours," in "Toi qui as de si grande dentes. . . . ," *Le Nouvel Observateur*, 17 April 1972, 59–61; F. Kittler cites Cournot, noting that "time and again," Kafka "avoided traveling to Berlin"—not because of the dangers of "natural" travel but because of his desire to create a "feedback loop" that could compete with modern media (*Grammophon, Film, Typewriter*, 323, 327); Gilles Deleuze and Félix Guattari miss Kafka's irony completely, referring to travel technologies as his "nice series of beneficial innovations," in *Kafka: Towards a Minor Literature* (Minneapolis: U of Minnesota P, 1986), 94–95n5; Klaus Theweleit argues that Kafka eventually leaves the medial alliance to join the benevolent "counter-alliance" that "transports bodies instead of ghosts," in *Buch der könige*, vol. 1, 976–1055 (Basel: Stroemfeld, 1988), 1026.
4. Siegert, *Relays*, 246 (see also 231).
5. Fritz Voigt, *Die Entwicklung des Verkehrssystems*, vol. 2 of *Verkehr* (Berlin: Duncker & Humblot, 1965), 598, and *Die Theorie der Verkehrswirtschaft*, vol. 1 of *Verkehr* (Berlin: Duncker & Humblot, 1973), 865. See also Joachim Radkau, *Das Zeitalter der Nervosität: Deutschland zwischen Bismarck und Hitler* (Munich: Carl Hanser, 1998), 193, and Wolfgang Kaschuba, *Die Überwind-*

ung der Distanz: Zeit und Raum in der europäischen Moderne (Frankfurt am Main: Fischer, 2004), 174.

6. For more on shaking as the paradigmatic symptom of traumatic neuroses, see Esther Fischer-Homberger, *Die traumatische Neurose: Vom somatischen zum sozialen Leiden* (Bern: Verlag Hans Huber, 1975), 86–87, and Paul Lerner, *Hysterical Men: War, Psychiatry, and the Politics of Trauma in Germany, 1890–1930* (Ithaca, NY: Cornell UP, 2003), 61–62, 167, 226–28.
7. *The Influence of Railway Travelling on Public Health* (published by the leading British medical journal, *The Lancet*, London, 1862), 40; Max Maria von Weber, "Die Abnutzung des physischen Organismus beim Fahrpersonal der Eisenbahnen," *Wieck Deutsche Illustrirte Gewerbezeitung* 25 (1860): 228. For an overview of the early research on the debilitating effects of the railway's shaking and its essential inelasticity, see Wolfgang Schivelbusch, *Geschichte der Eisenbahnreise: Zur Industrialisierung von Raum und Zeit im 19. Jahrhundert* (Munich: Hanser, 1977), 106–13.
8. Rudolf Wagner, "Simulation im Bahnbetriebe mit besonderer Berücksichtigung der sogenannten 'traumatischen Neurose,'" *Aerztliche Sachverständigen Zeitung* 6 (1900): 52.
9. Max Hirsch, "Reisekrankheiten," *Therapeutische Rundschau* (Halle), 2nd series 19 (10 May 1908): 302. Hirsch attributes the roughness of the train ride to the "poor track-construction for the rails" (schlechtem Oberbau der Schienen), especially when the "rails form severe curves," and notes that, as with extreme seasickness, railway "shaking" (zitter[n]) often culminates in severe anxieties, even the "fear of death" (301).
10. Sigmund Freud, "Three Essays on the Theory of Sexuality [1905]," in *The Standard Edition of the Complete Psychological Works*, trans. James Strachey, ed. Anna Freud (London: Hogarth & the Institute of Psycho-analysis, 1953–74), 7:201–2; "Drei Abhandlungen zur Sexualtheorie," in *Gesammelte Werke*, ed. Anna Freud (London: Imago, 1940–52), 5:103. Subsequent references to Freud's corpus are cited hereafter as *SE* and *GW* respectively.
11. J. Russell Reynolds, "Travelling: Its Influence on Health," in *The Book of Health*, ed. Malcolm Morris (London: Castle, 1884), 581.
12. *The Influence of Railway Travelling on Public Health*, 41.
13. Otto Gotthilf, "Wie schützt man sich beim Eisenbahnfahren gegen Gesundheitsschädigungen," *Deutsche Alpenzeitung*, vol 9, 1901/2, 17. Gotthilf claims that one can travel healthily in trains if one takes the right precautions. "Nervously predisposed" people, for example, should never sit in the last, "especially swaying" car of an express train (18).
14. See Hirsch, who cites Ernst Peters's *Vibrationsstuhl* as one of several possible cures for the two main kinetoses of his day: seasickness and railway neuroses ("Reisekrankheiten," 303).
15. Max Nordau, *Entartung* (Berlin: Duncker, 1892), 1:66. Other late-nineteenth- and early-twentieth-century commentators similarly viewed neuroses as *Zivilisations-krankheiten* caused by, among other factors, railway

travel. See George Beard's *American Nervousness: Its Causes and Consequences* (New York: G. P. Putnam's Sons, 1881), 112–13, and Sir Clifford Allbutt's "Nervous Disease and Modern Life," *Contemporary Review* 67 (1895): 214–15; for a summary of the early railway's effect on nervous diseases, see Schivelbusch, *Geschichte der Eisenbahnreise*, 51–66 and 106–51, and George Frederick Drinka, *The Birth of Neurosis: Myth, Malady, and the Victorians* (New York: Simon & Schuster, 1984), 108–22. Contemporaneous German texts that broadly diagnosed the fin de siècle as the "age of nervousness" were Karl Lamprecht's *Zur jüngsten deutschen Vergangenheit* (1902), Willy Hellpach's *Nervosität und Kultur* (1902), Georg Simmel's "Die Großstädte und das Geistesleben" (1903), and Johannes Marcinowski's *Nervosität und Weltanschauung* (1910). For overviews, see Andreas Steiner, *Das nervöse Zeitalter: Der Begriff der Nervosität bei Laien und Ärzten in Deutschland und Österreich um 1900* (Zurich: Juris-Verlag, 1964); Radkau, *Das Zeitalter der Nervosität* (1998); Andreas Killen, *Berlin Electropolis: Shocks, Nerves, and German Modernity* (Berkeley: U of California P, 2005); and Michael Cowan, *Cult of the Will: Nervousness and German Modernity* (University Park: Pennsylvania State UP, 2008).

16. The importance of this assertion ("—Samsa war Reisender—") is emphasized by its ostentatious typographical position, between long curved dashes, in the middle of the first page of the first edition of *Die Verwandlung*. I thank Thorsten Bothe for calling my attention to this.
17. For example, Kafka once imagined that one story could "mediate" between two other stories: without *The Metamorphosis*, "The Judgment" and "In the Penal Colony" would be "foreign heads [fremde Köpfe] banging violently against each other" (*L*, 126; *Br*, 149). For more on the internal dialogues between specific Kafka texts, see Stanley Corngold, *Franz Kafka: The Necessity of Form* (Ithaca, NY: Cornell UP, 1988), 228–49, and Mark M. Anderson, *Kafka's Clothes: Ornament and Aestheticism in the Habsburg Fin de Siècle* (Oxford: Clarendon, 1992), 185–86. On Kafka's general intra-oeuvre communications, see Malcolm Pasley, "Kafka's Semi-Private Games," *Oxford German Studies* 6 (1971/72): 112–32.
18. Wilhelm Emrich, *Franz Kafka* (Bonn: Athenäum, 1958), 127; Hartmut Binder, *Kafka-Kommentar zu sämtlichen Erzählungen* (Munich: Winkler, 1975), 64.
19. Most of Kafka's business journeys (primarily to northern Bohemia) occur from 1908, when he was still working on *Wedding Preparations*, through to 1916. See *AS*, 981–90.
20. "Gott, mir droht schon wieder eine Reise" (*LF*, 89; *BF*, 160).
21. In line with mainstream medical thought about traumatic neuroses and traumatic hysterias, Charcot and Freud insisted that railway-induced symptoms appeared only after a period of incubation (Inkubationszeit), albeit a shorter one than Samsa's. See John Eric Erichsen, *On Railway and other Injuries of the Nervous System* (1866; repr., Philadelphia: Henry C. Lea,

1867), 74–75; Jean-Martin Charcot, *Poliklinische Vorträge* (*Leçons du mardi*), vol. 1, trans. Sigmund Freud (Leipzig: Deutike, 1892), 99–100; and Sigmund Freud, *SE*, 1:52–53; *GW*, Nachtragsband, 85, *SE*, 23:67; *GW*, 16:171. For more on incubation time, see Schivelbusch, *Geschichte der Eisenbahnreise*, 123–26; Fischer-Homberger, *Die traumatische Neurose*, 110–11; Cathy Caruth, *Trauma: Explorations in Memory* (Baltimore: Johns Hopkins UP), 7; and Ruth Leys, *Trauma: A Genealogy* (Chicago: U of Chicago P, 2000), 19–20, 277–78.

22. Gustave Claudin, *Paris* (Paris: Faurc, 1867), 73. A doctor studying travelers who rode frequently from London to Brighton claims never to have "seen any set of men so rapidly aged as these [professional travelers]" (Claudin, *The Influence of Railway Travel on Public Health*, 53). Cf. Schivelbusch, *Geschichte der Eisenbahnreise*, 57, 110.
23. *The Influence of Railway Travel on Public Health*, 40, 41, 53. On the general topic of "fatigue" in railway travelers, see Schivelbush, *Geschichte der Eisenbahnreise*, 109–10 and 113–16.
24. Erichsen, *On Railway and other Injuries of the Nervous System*, 76, 74. Not only crash victims but also people who simply "catch sight of a locomotive" or continually think of "the possibility of collision" can develop railway neuroses. F. K. A. Schulze, *Die ersten deutschen Eisenbahnen*, 2nd ed. (Leipzig: Voigtländer, 1917), 24; *The Influence of Railway Travel on Public Health*, 43. Cf. Fischer-Homberger, *Die traumatische Neurose*, 40, and Schivelbusch, *Geschichte der Eisenbahnreise*, 198n1.
25. Voigt, *Die Theorie der Verkehrswirtschaft*, 865, and *Die Entwicklung des Verkehrssystems*, 857.
26. *The Influence of Railway Travel on Public Health*, 44; Cludin, *Paris*, 72. Many doctors in Kafka's day built on the influential 1889 theory of Hermann Oppenheim, which claimed that severe railway vibrations or crashes caused a shrinking of the field of vision (Wagner, "Simulation im Bahnbetriebe," 70). For more on the effects of railway travel upon vision, see Schivelbusch, *Geschichte der Eisenbahnreise*, 54–57.
27. Nordau, *Entartung*, 1:63.
28. Arthur Schnitzler, *Gesammelte Werke* (Frankfurt am Main: Fischer, 1961), 1:228.
29. Winn, J. M., "Railway Traveling, and Its Effects on Health," *The Journal of Public Health* 4 (Dec. 1855): 425. The fear that the railway's punctuality caused pathologies did not disappear in the decades following this British study. A German doctor reported in 1901 that many people rush to the station distressed and sweating, leading to "tooth or even facial pain, throat and lung catarrh"; another warned in 1908 that eating "in haste," combined with the "rush and excitement before departure" can lead to "revolution-motions in the stomach" (Gotthilf, "Wie schützt man sich beim Eisenbahnfahren gegen Gesundheitsschädigungen," 17–18; Hirsch, "Reisekrankheiten," 302). For an overview of the railway's effects on the

perception of time in the second half of the nineteenth century, see Ralph Harrington, "Trains, Technology and Time-Travellers: How the Victorians Re-invented Time" (2003), http://harringtonmiscellany.wordpress.com/essays/time-travellers/ (retrieved 24 Oct. 2010).

30. Peter Beicken summarizes early socio-critical interpretations of *The Metamorphosis* in *Franz Kafka: Eine kritische Einführung in die Forschung* (Frankfurt am Main: Athenaion, 1974), 265–66. See also Eduard Goldstücker, ed., *Franz Kafka aus Prager Sicht* (Berlin: Voltaire Verlag, 1966), and Kenneth Hughes, ed., *Franz Kafka: An Anthology of Marxist Criticism* (Hanover, NH: UP of New England, 1981).
31. Karl Marx, *Das Kapital* (vol. 2), in *Marx Engels Werke* (Berlin: Dietz, 1956–90), 24:60; hereafter cited as *MEW*. My argument for the remainder of this paragraph concerning Marx's comments on the transportation industry follows Schivelbusch's (Schivelbusch, *Geschichte der Eisenbahnyeise*, 110–12).
32. *CS*, 101; *DL*, 136–37. Although Schivelbusch does not mention Kafka, he uses Samsa's phrase—*am eigenen Leibe*—to describe the powerful effect of train travel on the human body (Schivelbusch, *Geschichte der Eisenbahnreise*, 112).
33. In a letter to Bauer, Kafka reports that he only travels "third class" (*LF*, 530; *BF*, 736; cf. *LF*, 186; *BF*, 290); cf. also Max Brod and Franz Kafka, *Eine Freundschaft*, vol. 1 (Reiseaufzeichnungen), ed. Malcolm Pasley (Frankfurt am Main: Fischer, 1987), 191. See also Rainer Stach, *Kafka: die Jahre der Erkenntnis* (Frankfurt am Main: Fischer, 2008), 110. Although we don't get a description of Samsa's actual train journeys, we can assume that he, like his fellow traveler from *Wedding Preparations*, travels in a third-class carriage crowded with other traveling salesmen. On the attempt to increase corporeal "elasticity" through upholstery, see Shivelbusch, *Geschichte der Eisenbahnreise*, 112.
34. Marx, *MEW*, 24:60; 23:445.
35. Cited in Schivelbusch, *Geschichte der Eisenbahnreise*, 187n8.
36. Gregor's father has secretly been keeping part of Gregor's wages instead of using this to pay off his debts, thereby increasing the time that Gregor must spend at his onerous job (*CS*, 112; *DL*, 154).
37. Scholars have generally ignored Gregor's claim that he is suffering from a "standing ailment of civilization" *(Zivilisationskrankheit)*, instead viewing Samsa's transformation as an externalization of an internal conflict: his desire to punish himself (for having usurped his father's dominant role), his masochistic "self-hatred," or his latent "death drive." This "externalization" reading extends even to contemporary post-structuralist readings, which interpret Gregor's transformation as a "becoming-visible" of the "lack" of a "consistent and dependable Other" (Eric Santner, "Kafka's *Metamorphosis* and the Writing of Abjection," in *M*, 199n8 [299]). For an overview of the early criticism of *The Metamorphosis*, see Beicken, *Franz Kafka*, 261–72, and Stanley Corngold, *The Commentators' Despair: The Inter-*

pretation of Kafka's "Metamorphosis" (Port Washington, NY: Kennikat, 1973). Sander Gilman emphasizes the diagnosis of "illness," but he never relates this to the railway or Gregor's claim of *"Berufskrankheit" (Franz Kafka: The Jewish Patient*, 65, 80–81).

38. In his seminal 1970 essay, "Metamorphosis of the Metaphor" (revised and republished in 1988 and 1996), Stanley Corngold argues that "the indeterminate, fluid crossing of a human tenor and a material vehicle is itself unsettling"; Gregor is an "opaque sign," a "mutilated metaphor, uprooted from familiar language" (*M*, 86, 87, 89 [169, 169, 172]). Although arguing (contra Corngold) for the creative aspect of this opaqueness, Clayton Koelb makes a similar point in 1989: the text's "indeterminacy" results from the possibility that "signifiers"—such as "*Ungeziefer*"—"might detach themselves from their immediate contextual limits" and become "free-floating." Koelb, *Kafka's Rhetoric: The Passion of Reading* (Ithaca: Cornell UP, 1989), 15, 16.
39. Psychiatrists and neurologists devoted to unmasking simulators (Simulantenjäger) often used this term, "work-shy" (arbeitsscheu or arbeitsunlustig), to describe apparent malingerers. See Max Nonne's report on Walter Cimbal's 1915 lecture, "Die seelischen und nervösen Erkrankungen seit der Mobilmachung," in "Ärztlicher Verein in Hamburg: Sitzung vom 23. Februar 1915," *Neurologisches Zentralblatt* 34 (1915): 414. For an overview of the debates about simulation and malingering, see Lerner, *Hysterical Men*, 62–67, 137–39, 202–4, and Fischer Homberger, *Die traumatische Neurose*, 56–73.
40. For the German and Austro-Hungarian context, see Wolfgang Schäffner, "Event, Series, Trauma: The Probabilistic Revolution of the Mind in the Late Nineteenth and Early Twentieth Centuries," in *Traumatic Pasts: History, Psychiatry, and Trauma in the Modern Age, 1870–1930*, ed. Mark S. Micale and Paul Lerner (Cambridge: Cambridge UP, 2001), 81; Greg A. Eghigian, "The German Welfare State as a Discourse of Trauma," in Micale and Lerner, *Traumatic Pasts*, 99; and Lerner, *Hysterical Men*, 32–33. For the European-wide context of trauma and accident insurance legislation, see Mark S. Micale, *Hysterical Men: The Hidden History of Male Nervous Illness* (Cambridge, MA: Harvard UP, 2008), 140, 317n67.
41. Erichsen tried to distance himself from this specific term, calling it "absurd," but it stuck to him nonetheless (Erichsen, *On Railway and Other Injuries of the Nervous System*, 23). See Fischer-Homberger's *Die traumatische Neurose*, 16–17, and her "Railway Spine und traumatische Neurose—Seele und Rückenmark," *Gesnerus* 27 (1970): 96–111.
42. Hermann Oppenheim, *Die traumatischen Neurosen nach den in der Nervenklinik der Charité in den letzten 5 Jahren gesammelten Beobachtungen* (Berlin: Hirschwald, 1889), 125, 127. See Fischer-Homberger, *Die traumatische Neurose*, 32–34, and Schivelbusch, *Geschichte der Eisenbahn*, 130–31.
43. See Lerner, *Hysterical Men*, 32–33.

44. See Fischer-Homberger, *Die traumatische Neurose*, 56–73, and Lerner, *Hysterical Men*, 32–36.
45. Fischer-Homberger, *Die traumatische Neurose*, 71.
46. Hermann Oppenheim, "Der Krieg und die traumatischen Neurosen," *Berliner klinische Wochenschrift* 52 (15 Mar. 1915): 257. See Lerner, *Hysterical Men*, 35–36.
47. Möbius argued that he would rather have relatively reliable and testable psychological theories than Oppenheim's "labile molecules," for which there were no "demonstrable data." Cited in Fischer-Homberger, *Die traumatische Neurosen*, 116.
48. See Fischer-Homberger, *Die traumatische Neurose*, 73–83, 30.
49. Freud insists on the importance of psychic predisposition throughout his work, beginning as early as 1895 in his "Reply to Criticisms of My Paper on Anxiety Neurosis" and carrying through to the 1905 *Three Essays on the Theory of Sexuality*, the 1917 *Introductory Lectures on Psychoanalysis*, and the 1920 *Beyond the Pleasure Principle* (*SE*, 3:130–31; *GW*, 1:366, *SE*, 16:362; *GW*, 11:376, *SE*, 7:201; *GW*, 5:103, *SE*, 18:31–32, *GW*, 13:31–32).
50. Psychoanalysis enjoyed unusual acceptance by established medicine toward the end of the First World War. Freud was proud that the wartime governments now employed some of his terms ("flight into illness," "gain from illness") and were even prepared to build "psychoanalytic centers" behind the front lines (*SE*, 17:209; *GW*, 12: 321–22).
51. See Eghighian, "The German Welfare State as a Discourse of Trauma" (on West German legal changes in 1962), 110, and Schivelbusch, *Geschichte der Eisenbahnreise* (on British legal changes in 1963), 132.
52. Fischer-Homberger, *Die traumatische Neurose*, 73, 23, 24.
53. Cited in K. R. Eissler, *Freud as Expert Witness: The Discussion of War Neuroses between Freud and Wagner-Jauregg*, trans. Christine Trollope (Madison, CT: International UP, 1986), 62. With this statement, we see how Freud distanced himself after the war from *Simulantenjäger* like Wagner-Jauregg, as well as from Freud's own wartime enthusiasm for working together with the "highest quarters of the Central European Powers" (*SE*, 17:209; *GW*, 12:321).
54. For planing machines, new weaponry, and other possible mechanical sources, see Klaus Wagenbach, ed., *In der Strafkolonie: Eine Geschichte aus dem Jahre 1914*, expanded edition (Berlin: Wagenbach, 1995), 77–79, 113–15. For the phonograph, see Wolf Kittler's discussion in "Schreibmaschinen, Sprechmaschinen: Effekte technischer Medien im Werk Franz Kafkas," in *Franz Kafka: Schriftverkehr*, ed. Wolf Kittler and Gerhard Neumann (Freiburg: Rombach, 1990), 116–41.
55. A. J. P. Taylor, *War by Timetable: How the First World War Began* (London: MacDonald, 1969). Cf. John Westwood, *Railways at War* (San Diego, CA: Howell-North, 1980), 129, and Dennis E. Showalter, "Railroads, the Prussian Army, and the German Way of War in the Nineteenth Century," in

Railways and International Politics: Paths of Empire, 1848–1945, ed. T. G. Otte and Keith Neilson (New York: Routledge, 2006), 40.

56. Showalter, "Railroads, the Prussian Army, and the German Way of War," 21, 40.
57. Westwood, *Railways at War*, 122, 125.
58. Ibid., 129.
59. On August 1st, before hostilities began, Chief of Staff von Moltke claimed that "the deployment in the West could no longer be stopped." Annika Mombauer, *Helmuth von Moltke and the Origins of the First World War* (Cambridge UP, 2001), 219. See also Showalter, "Railroads, the Prussian Army, and the German Way of War," 40, and Westwood, *Railways at War*, 131.
60. After Moltke's meeting with the Kaiser, Moltke's wife found his pulse "hardly countable" and claimed that he had suffered a "light stroke." Although Moltke's final collapse did not occur until 22 October, after the Battle of the Marne, he never regained his health after this first breakdown on 1 August: his wife asked as early as 9 August if she could accompany him to the front because of his health (Mombauer, *Helmuth von Moltke*, 222, 234).
61. On 22 May 1915 a British troop train collided with a stationary passenger train, leaving at least 200 dead. On 12 December 1917 a French military train derailed, and 543 soldiers were killed. Nicholas Faith, *Derail: Why Trains Crash* (London: Macmillan, 2000), 78–79.
62. The railway is, for Freud, the primary non-military cause of the traumatic neuroses throughout his career, especially at three points in time: the late 1880s and early 1890s, while he was reworking Charcot's theories of traumatic hysteria and developing his own; in 1919–20, when he was comparing the railways to the war; and at the very end of his life, in *Moses and Monotheism* and *Outline of Psychoanalysis*. *SE*, 1:12 (1886); *GW*, Nachtragsband, 42–44, *SE*, 1:51–52 (1888); *GW*, Nachtragsband, 84, *SE*, 1:152 (1892); *GW*, 17:10–11, *SE*, 7:201–2 (1905); *GW*, 5:103, *SE*, 16:274–76 (1917); *GW*, 11:283, *SE*, 17:211 (1920); *GW*, Nachtragsband, 706, *SE*, 20:127–28 (1925); *GW*, 14:157–58, *SE*, 23:67 (1934–38); *GW*, 16:171, *SE*, 23:184 (1938); *GW*, 17:111.
63. As late as his introduction to the volume on war neuroses from the 1918 Psychoanalytic Conference, Freud still insisted on the "sexual etiology" of all neuroses. Freud's colleague, Karl Abraham, did so even more vehemently, linking shell shock to latent homosexuality (*SE*, 17:209; *GW*, 12:323) See also Karl Abraham, "Erstes Korreferat," in *Zur Psychoanalyse der Kriegsneurosen* (Leipzig: Internationaler Psychoanalytischer Verlag, 1919), 31–41.
64. Freud, *SE*, 18:27, 31; *GW*, 13:26, 31. Especially the first part of Freud's biosociological theory is remarkably similar to Simmel's, who claims that that modern man "develops an organ protecting him against the threatening currents and discrepancies of his external environment": against "nervous

stimulation." For Simmel, however, this organ is "the intellect" itself, which he sees as relatively resistant to shock; the tragedy for Simmel is not that this organ is eventually penetrated but rather that it dominates modern man, leading him always to "react with his head instead of his heart." Georg Simmel, "The Metropolis and Mental Life" (1903), in *The Sociology of Georg Simmel*, ed. Kurt H. Wolff (London: Free Press of Glencoe, 1950), 410.

65. Walter Benjamin, *Charles Baudelaire: Ein Lyrikerim Zeitalter des Hochkapitalismus* (Frankfurt am Main: Surhkamp, 1955).
66. On 7 December 1916 Kafka speaks of "2 years of not writing" (*LF*, 536; *BF*, 744). The meager post-December 1914 exceptions prove the rule: the "Blumfeld" fragment; a couple of pages on "The Village Schoolmaster" and "The Assistant District Attorney"; and seven lines of *Der Verschollene* (*NS*1, 447–48). See also Binder, *Kafka-Kommentar zu sämtlichen Erzählungen*, 186–92; and Bezzel, *Kafka Chronik zusammengestellt von Chris Bezzel* (Munich: Hanser, 1975), 103–21.
67. Again, the exception proves the rule. After 1914, only the 1922 short stories "First Sorrow" and "Give It Up!" describe modern traffic. Not surprisingly, these travelers, like their predecessors, experience destroyed nerves and shock (*CS*, 447, 456; *DL*, 319; *NS*2, 530). For the horse-drawn carts of Raban's home neighborhood—before the gets to the illuminated square filled with street cars—see *CS*, 52–56; *NS*1, 12–18.
68. The wartime shakers (Kriegszitterer) were followed in 1919 by the uniformed panhandling *Zitterer*, many of whom had not even been in the war but discovered that borrowed uniforms increased their income (Lerner, *Hysterical Men*, 226–27).
69. Because of the stereotype of hysteria as a "feminine" disorder, Charcot insisted that his male hysterics were unquestionably virile, including one "manly artisan, solid, unemotional, a railway engineer." Charcot, "A propos de six cas d'hystère chez l'homme," in *J. M. Charcot: L'Hystérie*, ed. E. Trillat (Toulouse: Privat, 1971), 157–58. See also Elaine Showalter, "Hysteria, Feminism, Gender," in Sander Gilman et al., *Hysteria Beyond Freud* (Berkeley: U of California P, 1993), 308–9. This fear of being labeled "feminine" may explain why Kafka insisted that he was suffering neither from the hysteric disorder of fear of travel (Reiseangst) nor from "weakness of the will" (Willenschwäche; *L*, 333; *Br*, 384). For the male tendency to deny *Reiseangst*, see Fischer-Homberger, *Die traumatische Neurose*, 41–42; for the relation of *Willenschwäche* to hysteria and femininity, see Cowan, *Cult of the Will*, 10–15, 104–10, 269n61. Sander Gilman argues that Jewish men were seen to be especially predisposed to hysteria—including railway hysteria—especially because they were stigmatized as "feminized" (Gilman, "The Image of the Hysteric," in *Hysteria Beyond Freud*, 416–18, 405–6).
70. By the time Kafka wrote *The Metamorphosis*, his official title was "Konzipist" (project manager) not "Prokurist," but he did hold the important institu-

tional "Prokura" (proxy power), granted to him on 10 February 1911. Kafka would never have officially been called "Prokurist," simply because governmental or partly governmental institutions like Kafka's did not use this term, even for someone who, like Kafka, had "Prokura" powers (*AS*, 984). I thank Benno Wagner for the reference to *AS*.

71. On the etymology of "Ungeziefer," see Corngold, "Metamorphosis of the Metaphor," *M*, 87 [169].
72. See Corngold, "Metamorphosis of the Metaphor," in *M*, 84–85 [165–66].
73. "Du [Milena] hast auch Kondukteure gern, nicht wahr?" (*BM*, 236).
74. If, as Nina Pelikan Straus claims, Kafka transforms "Gregor" into "Grete," then this happens only with the help of the streetcar, which encourages Grete to metamorphose Gregor's "trouble with travel" (Plage des Reisens) into an ultimately positive "sorrow" (Plage), out of which she can rejuvenate herself (*CS*, 90, 139; *DL*, 116, 200). See Straus, "Transforming Franz Kafka's *Metamorphosis*," in *M*, 129.
75. Cf. W. Kittler, "Schreibmaschinen, Sprechmaschinen," 100.
76. For Herbert Kraft, the "exaggeration of the parody" is precisely what caused Kafka to label the ending of *The Metamorphosis* "unreadable"; Kraft, *Kafka: Wirklichkeit und Perspektive* (Bebenhausen: Lothar Rotsch, 1972), 49. Peter Beicken concurs, claiming that this parodic "sentimental, petty bourgeois" ending leads too easily to "moralistic partiality." Beicken, *Franz Kafka*, 271–72. Carsten Schlingmann reads the "banal ending," with its "depressing bourgeois-ness," as "undoubtedly cynical." Schlingmann, "Die Verwandlung," in *Interpretationen zu Franz Kafka: Das Urteil, Die Verwandlung, Ein Landartzt, Kleine Prosastücke* (Munich: Oldenbourg, 1968), 89, 88. For more recent interpretations, see Straus ("In the finale of *Metamorphosis* a return to normal sex roles is parodically celebrated"; Straus, "Transforming Franz Kafka's *Metamorphosis*," 139); Corngold (Kafka changes a phrase because the original was "too kitschy," "even" for the Samsa family; *M*, 56); and Kevin W. Sweeney (the "smug" family produces a "false sense of closure"; Sweeney, "Competing Theories of Identity in Kafka's *The Metamorphosis*," in *M*, 152).
77. Given the futurists' antagonism toward "nature," Kafka's ending represents an unusually naturalist futurism, but it nonetheless has futurist tendencies, thereby connecting Kafka to the techno-vitalist avant-garde. Kafka's inclusion in this modernist stream—against the "unconscious"-oriented "surrealist" stream—troubles Michael Cowan's attempt to ally futurism/vitalism with proto-fascism (Cowan, *Cult of the Will*, 257–64, and 315n29).
78. See John Zilcosky, *Kafka's Travels: Exoticism, Colonialism, and the Traffic of Writing* (New York: Palgrave, 2003), 171. Kafka had a version of this same fantasy as early as 1903, when he imagined mailing to Oskar Pollak "a piece of my heart," packed "neatly in a few sheets of inscribed paper" (*L*, 9; *Br*, 19). I thank Mark Harman for the reference to Pollak.

About the Translator

Stanley Corngold is Professor Emeritus of German and Comparative Literature at Princeton University, where he taught for more than forty years. He is the author of many books on German literature, including *Franz Kafka: The Ghosts in the Machine*; *Lambent Traces: Franz Kafka*; *Complex Pleasure: Forms of Feeling in German Literature*; and *The Fate of the Self: German Writers and French Theory*. He has also edited and translated J. W. Goethe's novel *The Sufferings of Young Werther* and *Kafka's Selected Stories*. He is a Fellow of the American Academy of Arts and Sciences.

A Note on the Type

The principal text of this Modern Library edition was set in a digitized version of Janson, a typeface that dates from about 1690 and was cut by Nicholas Kis (1650–1702), a Hungarian working in Amsterdam. The original matrices have survived and are held by the Stempel foundry in Germany. Hermann Zapf (b. 1918) redesigned some of the weights and sizes for Stempel, basing his revisions on the original design.